TO CAGE A GOD

TO CAGE A GOD

ELIZABETH MAY

Daphne Press

First published in the UK in 2024 by Daphne Press

www.daphnepress.com

A CIP catalogue record for this book is available from the British Library.

Hardback ISBN: 978-1-83784-018-2
eBook ISBN: 978-1-83784-020-5
Paperback ISBN: 978-1-83784-019-9
Waterstones Exclusive ISBN: 978-1-83784-092-2

The authorised representative in the EEA is Authorised Rep Compliance Ltd
71 Baggot Street Lower, Dublin, D02 P593, Ireland.
Email: info@arccompliance.com

Printed and bound by CPI Group (UK) Ltd, Croydon CR0 4YY

1

MIX
Paper | Supporting responsible forestry
FSC® C171272
FSC
www.fsc.org

For the weary warriors,
and the battle-scarred,
marked by war but not broken.

PROLOGUE

The empress blazed against the twilight sky. Fire licked at her fingertips as flames spread across the meadow at the top of the hill—a portent of what was to come.

Hers was a power that had conquered empires.

A girl in the village below lifted her head from a spray of wildflowers, their blooms dancing in the smoke-tainted breeze. "Momma, look! There's a lady up there!"

Her mother's face drained of color. "Come here, my love," she ordered, her voice sharp and urgent. "*Now.*"

Flowers slipped from the girl's grasp, the petals scattering on the ground like falling ash.

The mother seized her child and dragged her to their cottage as the firestorm surged over the crest of the hill. It reached the hamlet, consuming all it touched in an instant.

The girl's mother shoved her into the cellar. "Get as low as you can and curl up tight. Don't come out, understand? I'll be right behind you." The girl heard nothing else but the roar of the inferno outside, followed by one last thing—a whisper from her mother amidst the chaos: "I love you, *vmekhva.*"

She sealed the girl in the darkness and didn't come back.

The girl would never forget the screams. She would always remember the overwhelming heat, the thick smoke that threatened to choke her. How the fire brushed against her skin and left marks that no time would heal.

And she remembered—

Silence.

A stillness that echoed through the dark as days passed. Then, finally, hushed voices reached her. Residents from a neighboring village arrived to mourn and found only a wasteland—no bodies to bury, no survivors. Except for one.

A girl who rose from the ashes.

I

SERA

Twenty years later

The god caged in Sera's body hated her.

She paced outside her forest cottage in irritation, frost crunching beneath her boots. The extended winter had taken a toll on the iatric plants in her garden, leaving a pitiful sight of withered foliage under a fresh layer of snow. A fever had swept through the outskirts of Dolsk—her medicines were in short supply.

And her deity was a fickle bastard that demanded a sacrifice in exchange for power.

An audience of blackbirds perched atop a nearby stone wall, their feathers ruffling in the morning breeze while they chirped in an irritating chorus that did little to improve Sera's foul temper.

"Shut up, all of you," she snapped at the avian gathering.

A foolhardy bird dared to trill in dissent.

Sera rounded on the creature and fixed it with her iciest glare. "One more chirp, and I'll pluck you from that wall and eat you."

The bird wisely held its beak still.

Sera kneeled beside the wilted plants, running her hands over the cold soil. She appealed to her god. "Give me your godpower."

Scales shifted beneath Sera's skin. Trapped wings fluttered. Talons flexed and scraped across her bones as it tested the limits of its enclosure. For over two decades, the zmeya, her caged god, had writhed and slashed within her—first with violence and desperation, and now with a quiet loathing.

The deity did not listen to her. If it yielded its abilities, it spoke with the deep, menacing rumble of a furious hostage. The Exalted Tongue was its language of resentment.

Every use of its power came with a message: *Fuck you, hope you suffer.*

Sera couldn't blame the beast; they were shackled together in this wretched arrangement. A cursed pair: an imprisoned dragon and a woman who never asked for her body to be offered to such a vindictive god.

Sera gritted her teeth as the god's claws sent another fissure of discomfort through her. A deliberate provocation; its rage seeped into her veins, burning embers beneath her skin.

"Give me your godpower," she hissed again. When the zmeya didn't listen, Sera yanked the blade from her belt. "Fine. If this is the only language you know—"

"*Polina Ivanovna!*"

Sera turned to see a scrawny lad hastening up the path toward her cottage, waving a broadsheet. Sera's heart lurched with anticipation. Anna, one of two spies Sera still communicated with back home, only sent missives when it was urgent.

"Polina Ivanovna, I have a message for you!"

Polina Ivanovna was the alias she'd taken up in Dolsk, a nondescript town deep in the territory of Kseniyevsky. For the past four years, Sera's identity had been adopted and discarded with regularity: Marina, Svetlana, Aleksandra, and Feodora—but Polina stuck the longest. *Serafima Mikhailovna* had vanished the same day the empress executed her mother for sedition.

Residing within a region contested by two monarchs was a gamble, but the locals were used to foreigners coming and going. They didn't ask questions.

Best of all, they minded their damn business—for a couple of fugitives, it was ideal.

Sera clicked her tongue at the boy. "Slow down before you hurt yourself."

This was why she kept her distance from the village children: their fidgeting, their antics, their general lack of coordination. But she needed to remain in their good graces, or they wouldn't bring her newspapers with coded messages, so she paid the little bandits far too much silver to do her bidding.

Viktor halted before he reached her. "Polina Ivanovna, what are you doing with that knife?"

"Never mind that. Give it here." She wasn't about to explain herself to someone barely out of swaddling clothes. She slid the weapon back into her belt and dropped a coin into his small, gloved hand. "Don't spend it all on sweets or your mother will ban you from running errands for me," she warned, taking the paper from him.

Viktor grinned, displaying his milk-teeth-gapped smile, which she hoped resulted from childhood rather than the surfeit of confections he'd likely purchased with her money.

Sera carefully unfolded the broadsheet, and her breath caught as the headline blared from the page: *EMPEROR YURI NIKOLAEVICH DURNOV DEAD IN CARRIAGE ACCIDENT. No foul play suspected.*

As she scanned the article, the lack of details regarding the Tumanny monarch's death hinted at censorship. She knew better than to trust the *Blackshore Courier*—every sentence, word, and exclamation point was meticulously edited to present the royal court's version of events. Anna must have sent the newspaper knowing it contained a heavily altered report.

"A letter came for you, too." Viktor handed her the envelope.

Sera tucked it into her pocket, her gaze still glued to the article. She'd read Anna's coded message later.

"What are they saying about this in Dolsk?" she asked the boy.

He scratched his head, dislodging a few snowflakes from his woolen hat, and toed a rock on the snow-covered ground. "Not much," he said. "But my mama seemed worried." He looked up at her, concern casting a shadow on his young face. "Should I be scared?"

Sera toyed with a lie—an act of maternal deceit, easily within her capacity.

But, with a sigh and a long pause, she chose honesty. "I'm not sure."

The alurea took malicious glee in exploiting their rivals' weaknesses. Those nobles ruled across the continent of Sundyr—all bonded to deities unwillingly caged in their bodies and granted godpower that obliterated empires. Just a few hundred years ago, sixty-eight small nations comprised Sundyr, now absorbed into the holdings of more powerful monarchs. Battles had raged to seize control, leaving behind destruction and ruined lives.

Commoners had no choice but to obey the laws set down by their cruel rulers or face retribution, and every sennight they paid tribute to their oppressors at local temples.

No matter how fiercely people rebelled, uprisings always failed.

Sera gave Viktor an affectionate pat on the shoulder. "Go home, Vitenka. Comfort your mama." What else did one say to frightened children? "Erm. Be brave."

It was perhaps for the best that she was not a mother.

"Am I gonna see you at the temple in two days?"

"No. I'm busy," Sera said. She left out the possibility that it might be her last two days in town.

After she saw Viktor off, Sera took Anna's cryptogram out of her pocket and opened it. Their code was complex, but after four years of running, Sera had learned the cipher by heart. The message was concise and concisely dreadful:

Intel indicates an explosive device. The palace has cracked down on the gossip, but Vitaly Sergeyevich has claimed responsibility. He's not hiding anymore. Thought you should know. — Anna

Sera crumpled the paper in her fist. "Godsdamn it," she hissed under her breath. "What are you doing, Vitalik?"

Vitaly Sergeyevich Rysakov—her mother Irina's ruthless and younger second-in-command—had returned to the Blackshore and assassinated the emperor.

Sera tried to ignore the warning bells going off in her head. She remembered the executions they had witnessed together, bodies writhing in agony as they burned in the empress's godfire.

Vitaly's brother had been on that execution platform beside Irina, along with every other faithless member in the secret press room raided by the palace sentries. Printing and distributing seditious pamphlets against the alurea was a crime punishable by death—and there was no leniency for the pathetic piece of shit in the rebellion who betrayed his fellow faithless, either. Treason was always paid for in blood. That traitor had named Sera and Vitaly, forcing them to flee the Blackshore.

Now the emperor was dead, and when rulers fell, war followed.

Vitaly was going to get himself killed.

Sera shoved the paper back into her pocket, shaking her head. Revolution was a game of strategy, patience, and intelligence—waiting for the right moment to light the match. She'd watched too many uprisings end with carelessness and stupidity.

That was why Sera's mother kept secrets from the faithless even into her death: she'd learned how to cage gods in the bodies of commoners—and she'd succeeded. Then she trained an orphaned girl she'd chosen to breach the royal palace and seize the throne.

A girl who was the sole survivor of her village's destruction, a symbol of the empress's cruelty.

A girl who understood the motivations of vengeance from a tender age.

Her mind made, Sera unsheathed a blade, lifted her coat's sleeve, and dragged it along her pale arm. She watched her blood drip onto the snow and seep into the soil. She closed her eyes and gritted her teeth as she reached for the dragon that lived in her skin.

"Give me your godpower."

This time, the god listened—she had spoken in the violent language it required.

A surge of energy coursed through her, and the deity whispered from Sera's mouth in the Exalted Tongue. Green spread beneath the layers of frost—but it wasn't enough. The bastard demanded more. Her injury would heal too quickly, knit back together and mend without scars, a power her zmeya imparted against its will.

It wanted her to suffer.

The dragon stretched within her bones and sank its claws into Sera's wound, opening the gash wide. It never granted power without consequence, would not allow her to heal unless it extracted its price from her flesh. It was a monster, and it did not aid by nature.

Sera's god loved to make her bleed.

2

GALINA

Galina ignored the knock on her door.

Answering meant getting out of bed (*and you're incapable of getting out of bed. You've been here for days*). She was comfortable in the shadows, watching the dust motes dance in the broad beam of light that shone through the cracked curtains. Recently, her only marker of passing days was the rise and fall of the sun.

When night fell anew, maybe she'd find the motivation to leave her nest of worn quilts (*that's unlikely, be realistic*).

The knock came again, more insistent. "*Za tasht stru,*" Galina said in Zverti, her voice muffled by her pillow. Another knock. "Ugh, go away."

She reached for the floor beside her bed, fingers searching for a bottle amongst the clutter of empties. Her fingertips met the smooth edge of the glass, and it rolled across the hardwood with a sharp clink.

Galina heard the faint and unmistakable metallic scrape of someone picking her locks. The door opened with a low creak and shut with a click. A dull thud of boots crossed the apartment to her bedroom.

"What happened in here?"

Sera. Of course it was Sera. She was the only one determined and irritating enough to break into Galina's flat.

Galina ignored her foster sister and continued fumbling for the liquid-filled bottle she recalled was somewhere near her bed a few days ago. Was it three days or five? She couldn't remember.

"Had guests," she mumbled.

Sera came into view, irradiated by a ray of sunlight that set her plaited blonde locks ablaze like a halo of fire. Her complexion was pale, her cheeks rosy from the bitter kiss of the wind outside. Snowflakes melted across the shoulders of her dark green coat, the droplets shimmering like diamonds.

Her green eyes flickered over the room before settling on Galina's face. "The troupe of fiddlers in the pub, or have you invited all those big men building Olga Pavlovna's cottage into your flat?"

Galina took a cigarette from her nightstand and lit it. She gave Sera a reproachful look before inhaling deeply. "Why would I invite those men," she said, blowing out the smoke with a laugh, "when their wives kiss so much better?"

Sera chuckled and shook her head. "You're going to get yourself thrown out of Dolsk for fucking all their wives and end up as a hermit witch banished to some dismal forest." She paused. "In other words, you'll end up just like me."

Galina rolled her eyes. "Don't be so dramatic. You could live in the village if you weren't such a recluse." She exhaled a slow stream of smoke and reached under her bed, giving Sera a wry look. "Besides, I only have a problem if the husbands find out. As far as they know, I'm a woman with many *very* good friends."

Her fingers wrapped around the cold neck of the bottle just in time; the god's voice echoed in her mind, a desperate call that she had grown accustomed to ignoring. Galina pulled out the cork with her teeth and spat it onto the floor before taking a swig. The growl inside her body quieted to an angry rumble that sent a chill across Galina's skin.

For the god, her silence had become a weapon of defiance.

For her, it was salvation (*because you're too weak for your memories*). And in a little while, maybe she'd get out of bed (*you're pathetic*).

Sera's leather boot nudged one of the empty jugs Galina had discarded. "Galya." Her voice dripped with concern.

"Here it comes," Galina muttered.

Her lip curled in self-disgust, all too aware of her pitiful state. She knew precisely what she looked like—the mirror had been tormenting her for days. Long, pale blonde hair matted and tangled like a rodent's nest. Skin too pale, frame too thin, collarbones jutting up from the rough-hewn wool she wore. Her blue eyes were dulled—the consequence of excessive liquor and guilt from isolating the dragon caged in her bones. Everyone, even the village wives, couldn't resist trying to feed her.

And now her god's voice had been replaced with painful thoughts and unwanted memories. All those ghostly whispers reminded her of every secret and sin she had tried so hard to bury.

(*You allowed yourself to be manipulated and used, and that's why you'll never forget.*)

Sera raised an eyebrow. "Here what comes?"

"That tone you get right before you lecture me. You sound like Irina."

She took another drag from her cigarette and then lifted the bottle. The pungent smell of alcohol filled the air as she brought it to her lips. She drank a long swig and tipped her head as the fiery liquid burned her throat. Cheap liquor did not go down smoothly, and Galina liked it that way. The potent drink was a reminder of the interloper in her body, of the things she'd seen and done—an insignificant punishment before complete oblivion.

And she found peace in oblivion.

Sera's jaw went tight. "My mother wouldn't let you lie there drinking and smoking and debauching all day. But this? *This* is something Irina would do." With a huff, she strode over to the curtains and gave them a savage wrench, tearing them wide open.

Galina flinched from the onslaught of light. "*Shut it.*"

"No."

Galina put out her cigarette in the ashtray and glared at Sera. "*Sa zlu,*" she spat in Zverti, swinging her legs over the side of the bed. "Go away. I have things to do."

"Things to do?" Sera smirked. "Seducing unsatisfied village wives?"

"*Sleeping.*"

"Yes, I can see you've been doing a great deal of"—she kicked an empty bottle across the room—"sleeping." At Galina's obstinate silence, Sera sighed and sat on the window seat. "You know you can't quiet it forever with that."

Galina set her liquor on the nightstand. "One hour," she said bitterly. "And by then, the god will finish burning off all the alcohol, and I'll shut it up again. Repeat."

"Maybe you should let it talk," Sera suggested.

Galina arched an eyebrow. "And this is coming from the woman who calls hers a bastard?"

"*My* zmeya is a vindictive little shit that extracts a blood price for paltry godpower. Yours used to listen to you."

Galina let out a humorless laugh. "Listen to me? It helped me do things that still keep me up at night. And for what?"

For nothing.

Her memories dredged up all the violence she'd inflicted for Irina's cause. But nothing had come from it—no victory or revenge. Her family was dead.

Her home was gone.

Nothing changed.

She rubbed her fingers over her robe-clad thigh, feeling the bumps of her scars—a topography of pain forged by the empress's destructive godfire. The heat had peeled flesh and burned her skin black. Now, twenty years later, her right side was as rough as the sandbanks of the Lyutoga Sea. And the reminders were etched into her soul, like the marks on her body.

Sera's attention fell on Galina's hand, and she winced, pulling her gaze away. "What Irina made you do wasn't right," she said in a low, steely voice. "If I'd known she'd use your zmeya for her own vendettas, I would never have—"

"Let her summon it? You were ten." Galina had been eight—mere children manipulated by a woman who promised a better world and lied.

"I would never have *left*," Sera corrected gently. "When she trusted me on smuggling missions, I was adult enough to notice you changed every time I returned, and I was too much of a coward to ask why."

Galina didn't respond. She drank until her throat was raw. The god was muted now, and when Sera departed, Galina would begin putting the shards of her jagged soul back together.

Because that was what she did: woke up and repaired the tattered pieces of herself (*they'll never fit right. The cracks will always show*).

Galina rose from the bed and stood beside Sera at the window, taking in the cold evening air. The town of Dolsk was bustling with life. People filled the cobblestone streets, talking and laughing in carefree abandon. Many of them had never left the safety of their humble village, never seen the horrors of the outside world. Nor had they encountered an alurea beyond the temple icons—the privilege of living in hamlets beneath the notice of nobles, where war had yet to touch.

None of them were afraid of their entire lives burning to the ground.

"Irina called it a means to an end," Galina said bitterly.

Her skin prickled with the barely contained energy of

the godfire, courtesy of the rare zmeya she was bonded to. Only she and Empress Isidora had that skill in the last nine hundred years—and hers was all thanks to Irina.

"I don't care what she called it. She promised justice against the empress and never let you take it."

Galina loosed a breath. "I don't think your mother put this god inside me for justice, *vitsvi*. She made promises to gullible children."

Sera's jaw clenched. "And we're not gullible children anymore."

She snatched a newspaper from her inner coat pocket and showed it to Galina, who stilled upon seeing the headline blaring the emperor's tragic death.

"Not an accident, then?"

Sera's mouth thinned into a grim line. "Vitaly Sergeyevich Rysakov."

Galina chuckled. "Nicely done." When Sera failed to return the humor, she shrugged. "What?"

"It would've been *funny* if the faithless planted a bomb while His Imperial Majesty was in the middle of shitting on a golden commode. This is sloppy. There need to be plans in place before the resulting power void—"

"*Now* you sound like Irina."

Sera straightened in irritation. "Irina and I disagreed on tactics, and that's why she was executed for sedition and I'm still alive. Bombs are a tool, not a solution."

"Then let Vitaly Sergeyevich worry about the consequences. Unless you care about what happens to him."

"Of course I care," Sera said. "That isn't the point."

Galina cleared away some jugs from the carpet. "No, the point is you're judging strategy for a rebellion you're no longer a part of."

Sera fell silent, her focus on some distant place out the window. Then she quietly asked, "What if we were part of it again?"

Galina froze. "No." An automatic response. "I'm not going back to the Blackshore."

Her sister let out a breath. "Listen. Another kingdom will exploit Tumanny's vulnerability. News of the assassination would have spread to the ruling families long before us. If the Sopolese forces invade, this is one of the first places in Kseniyevsky they'll occupy. It won't be safe here."

"It's not safe in the Blackshore, either."

"Doesn't matter." Her stare was intent. "We need to leave."

Galina shook her head in refusal. She enjoyed the peaceful life she had built in Dolsk, the little apartment that was her sanctuary from the chaos outside. "King Maksim is powerful, but Empress Isidora's godfire will annihilate any army he sends. He won't challenge her."

"He would if he rallies enough allies," Sera said. "Soldiers *will* come to Dolsk, and people are going to die. Have you forgotten Olensk?"

(Yes, you did. You buried Olensk in a grave and drowned yourself in alcohol to forget.)

Galina forcefully shook off the intrusive thought. "*Get out.*"

Sera winced, guilt flashing across her features, before she nodded and crossed the room to leave. She hesitated at the door and tipped her head back with a long exhale. "Two days, *vitsvi*," she said wearily. "Pack one bag and leave everything else—just like before." Her shoulders bent. "I'm sorry."

Galina closed her eyes as the door clicked shut behind Sera. Then she returned to her bed and settled under the blankets.

The dark helped her forget.

3

GALINA

Galina lay in bed for endless hours, watching the shadows on the wall as the light shifted with the passing clouds, and another day turned to night.

Finally, she pushed back her blankets and began packing her bag with essentials. She reached under her desk to retrieve a stack of silver coins she had pilfered from a wealthy merchant in Starapolė. She closed her eyes, trying not to think. Thoughts were dangerous, slippery things—especially when they became memories. Memories of a life she'd known. A life she'd loved and lost.

And now she'd have to start over again.

A chill wind blew through the room, tinged with the scent of wood smoke. Galina shivered, listening to the lively melody of fiddles from the tavern below and the distant laughter and conversation—a tapestry of sound that had become a comfort since she and Sera had first come to Dolsk. Outside, the cobblestone streets were slick with rain and dotted with puddles, reflecting the amber twinkle of candlelit windows. Galina shifted closer to the window, taking it all in: the crispness of the air, the gentle hum of activity, a stark contrast to her memories of Olensk and the Blackshore.

Dolsk had no reminders of the horrors she had endured. No screams of her parents rang in her ears as their house blazed around them. No faces of Kiyskoye neighbors pulling her from the wreckage.

No reminders of what Irina had forced her to do.

Galina was like a vase glued back together, each line and crack of her past still visible underneath. She would always be brittle; the slightest pressure would shatter her into something fragmented beyond repair (*you already are*).

No one in Dolsk asked anything of her. The villagers made no demands. They did not look at her with pity or ask Sera's pointed questions.

They didn't try to fix her.

The god stirred, pushing through Galina's quiet moment to make its presence known. Lurking within the depths of her consciousness and screaming for acknowledgment. She reached for the liquor bottle with trembling hands and slammed the drink down, wincing as it burned her throat.

Shame wrapped its fingers around her heart, and Galina tried to shake it away. The zmeya hadn't asked for this. She could feel its wings, once free to soar the skies of Smokova, the realm of the gods, before it was snatched from its home and jammed into her body against its will. And she was too damaged to listen to it.

They were both suffocating in the cage of her mind.

Galina shook her head, sending pale strands of hair across her damp forehead. She had to avoid the thoughts that threatened to consume her. (*You're broken, shattered beyond repair—losing your grasp on reality. You might as well be drowning.*) She'd lose control. The godfire would burn beneath her skin. She'd scream until someone held her down like a feral animal.

The way Irina used to.

But she had been stable in Dolsk—and now she had to rebuild her life again from nothing.

Her heart in her throat, Galina resumed packing as the sounds of the village overwhelmed her: hushed conversations and laughter, cheerful music, the occasional horse's whinny or bird's cry echoing in the streets. She took another drink, and her desolate god faded into the background haze of intoxication.

Galina closed her eyes and let her body sway with the fiddle's melody as its sweet notes curled around her. She felt the ache in her chest for Dolsk and all the people who had warmly welcomed her. For all the things she had to leave behind and may never find again.

Then a muted rumble, like the growl of a waking beast, sounded in the distance. It was akin to thunder reverberating off the mountainside—but it seemed too close, too loud for an oncoming storm.

Galina held her breath as the music faltered and laughter ceased. A tense silence, heavy and suffocating, descended upon the village.

Then a *CLAP!* ripped through the air like a lightning bolt.

A deafening flood of memories crashed over her, the smash of exploding glass, crumbled stone, and broken wood assaulting her senses, of shouts in the night and an endless roaring of flames above her. Galina stepped back from the window, her legs trembling, and dropped the bottle. She tried to swallow, but her throat was parched, as if the blaze from her memories had scorched her from within.

"No," she whispered, her voice shaking. "Please, no."

CLAP!

A different town. Another day with no warning.

She watched the buildings in Dolsk fall.

4

SERA

Sera trudged through the temple in exhaustion.

The priestess had finally succumbed to the inevitable. Sera had sat by the woman's side through the long, feverish struggle, with memories of Irina's terse commands and expert knowledge of medicine guiding her as she attempted to keep the woman alive.

Despite Sera's best efforts, the night ended with a pair of vitreous eyes gazing into nothingness.

She had seen so much death—one more corpse should have been just another tally in her ledger. But every failure stripped away small pieces of her until there was little left but emptiness and the bitter taste of defeat. She felt like the lowest form of shit.

Her shoulders slumped as she slung her bag across her chest. The temple was shrouded in silence, save for a lone prayer murmured in some dark corner and the soft dripping of distant water. She passed by a mosaic of votive paintings depicting the rulers of Tumanny and Sopol over the centuries. Sera gritted her teeth, refusing to let her gaze linger on the images.

Only royals were memorialized in votives, worshipped as vessels to old gods unwillingly bound to noble hosts at birth, forced conscripts in the alurean game of power.

The zmei were little more than weapons to be wielded by the powerful, trapped in mortal shells of flesh and bone. It was a brutal clash of death and conquest, played out across the blood-soaked fields of Sundyr, where only the most ruthless could claim the prize.

Above the temple archway loomed a carving of a zmei, its form majestic and beautiful as it soared through the clouds of its native Smokova, a realm separated from humans by a veil of godpower. Its scales shimmered in the sunlight, its wings beating freely.

It was a cruel irony, this shrine to the gods' imprisonment. A place of worship dedicated to the theft of the zmei from their homes and forced to serve their captors in a never-ending cycle of cruelty and domination.

Sera wrenched open the temple door, bracing herself against a punishing gust of frigid mountain wind—an icy slap across her face. She shivered, pulling her coat tightly around herself as she stepped outside. The sky was clear, with stars shimmering like a million diamonds on black velvet. She started toward her cottage, eager to escape the chill.

A roaring *clap* split the air and ricocheted off the wall of trees.

Sera froze.

The silence that followed was deafening, broken only by the rustle of leaves in the breeze.

A second *clap* sounded, even louder than the first. The earth shook beneath her feet. A jolt of dread shot down her spine as a cacophony of screams came from the direction of Dolsk.

"Oh gods," she breathed.

She took off in a frenzied sprint.

The clamor of destruction blared with each step, and claws of fear raked through her as she tried to sort through the tumult of crashing stone, thunderous rumbling, and panicked wails of villagers. Every noise reverberated through Sera's body, pushing her further and further to the edge of panic.

As Sera crested the hill and looked down toward Dolsk, an apocalyptic sight unfolded.

The charming wooden cottages lay in ruins, smashed beyond recognition. Further into town, lightning struck tenements and houses, leaving nothing but ash and rubble. Acrid black smoke filled Sera's lungs and stung her eyes. She coughed and gagged, struggling to draw in a breath.

"*Galya,*" she gasped.

Desperate people ran in all directions. Screams of terror saturated the air. She skidded past a woman cradling a crying child, shouting for them to seek shelter, but the mother didn't respond. The wind whipped through the street, tearing down homes and sending debris flying.

Sera went motionless when she spotted the uniformed troops advancing through Dolsk—the weather mavens of the Sopol army. Their gleaming gold buttons were unmistakable.

Sera knew this was coming. She *knew* Emperor Yuri's death would embolden King Maksim, giving him the excuse to seize control of the contested territory by force.

She had to find Galina.

The mavens' tempests shook the earth and sundered buildings, shattering windows and stone. Other soldiers butchered the fleeing villagers with ruthless abandon. No one was spared—old and young, man, woman, or child—all fell beneath the wrath of Sopol's merciless troops. Sera's fingers clenched and unclenched, her body enveloped in the choking haze and searing flames of war.

She reached for the dragon in her bones. "Give me your godpower."

But the zmeya remained silent—it didn't care if the storm pummeled and crushed her. It seemed to relish the idea of her violent demise, even if it meant suffering alongside her. "*Please.*"

You wretched bastard.

But her zmeya did not acknowledge begging, either.

It demanded blood—and it would not be satisfied until it had its fill.

With an exasperated snarl, she unsheathed a dagger from her belt and yanked up her sleeve. In one swift, resolute motion, Sera slashed her forearm. Her blood dripped onto the ground, crimson droplets mingling with snow and ash.

The god stirred from its indifference. The Exalted Tongue spilled from her lips, and power surged through her veins. Her body thrummed with energy and heat as godpower formed around her, protecting her from the destructive maelstrom that threatened to consume Dolsk.

Sera's feet pounded over shattered cobblestones as she pushed through the pandemonium and slaughter, dodging falling detritus and violent wind gusts. Beads of sweat streamed down her face as she fought for survival.

For Galina's survival.

Find Galina, save Galina, get her out of Dolsk.

Everywhere she looked, she saw residents she'd healed, people she'd chatted with on quiet nights—dead.

But she had to stay focused. Her fingers curled into fists as she ran faster, determined to save at least one life tonight.

The air punched from her lungs when she finally reached Galina's street, only to be greeted by a desolate landscape of ruin.

"Galya!" she choked out.

She hurled herself at the heap of broken bricks, glass, and scattered mortar. She cleared stones frantically, searching for any sign of movement. A woman's face emerged from the rubble, but it was motionless—one of Galina's neighbors.

Sera's chest tightened, tears gathering in her eyes. She returned to the wreckage, calling desperately for her sister.

She dug as rain soaked her hair and clothes, plastering them to her skin. The wind tore at the buildings and ripped them apart in a surge of flying debris. Splinters of wood and bits of stone left her fingers marred and bleeding, but she felt none of it.

Her voice rose over the din, throat raw with desperation.

"Galya!" She was screaming now. She didn't care who found her. "*Galya!*"

A muted whimper reached Sera's ears, barely audible over the roaring storm.

Sera surged to her feet. "Galya, if that's you, please, *please* say something. I'll find you."

Then she heard it, a plea that almost had her collapsing with relief: "*Sera.*"

Sera's heart pounded as she scrambled over the rubble, scanning the wreckage for any sign of her sister. And then, finally, she saw Galina wedged between the remnants of two walls that were once part of a larger structure.

Galina's eyes were tightly shut, her arms wrapped protectively around her knees. Blood and soot covered her face and clothes. Sera rushed to her sister's side, enfolding her in a tight embrace that was returned with equal fervor. Her shield expanded, a luminous halo of protection for them both.

"Godsblood," Sera hissed, gasping for breath. "I was so worried, I thought I'd piss myself."

Galina managed a weak smile, her voice barely above a whisper. "Love you too," she rasped.

But before they could share another word, a nearby building crumbled under the relentless bombardment of the Sopolese army. The ground quaked beneath their feet, and Sera knew they had to move.

"Are you hurt anywhere?" she asked urgently.

Galina shook her head, looking dazed. "I don't think so. I ran for the street when the storm started." She was no stranger to tragedy, having endured worse.

Sera withdrew a handkerchief from her pocket to dab at the scratch on Galina's cheek. "We can try to reach the forest, but if the soldiers make it that far, even your godfire won't be enough to protect us," she said. "Can you open a door?"

It was a rare skill among alurea, achievable only by a god of immense strength. Irina hoped to use Galina's gift to gather intelligence in Zolotiye Palace, but opening doors required an exact mental image of the desired location—something Empress Isidora would never permit.

Galina went still. "Where?"

Sera's lungs constricted as the outdoor temperature abruptly plunged. If anyone survived the destruction of Dolsk, the weather mavens would make damn sure they didn't survive the cold.

"The Blackshore tunnels."

A harsh noise left Galina. "*I can't.*"

Sera cupped Galina's face. "I know we said we'd never go back there, but it's just you and me. Irina's dead." She paused to let her words sink in. "I'd never use you like she did."

Her sister's chest rose and fell rapidly. "But I haven't listened to my god in four years."

"I need you to listen to it now. Or we won't leave here alive. *Lo tve sekh za?*"

Sera spoke Zverti deliberately to break through Galina's fear. The only comfort she could offer in this catastrophe.

"Yes, I understand," her sister whispered.

After a beat of uncertainty, Galina closed her eyes, exhaling slowly. Determination lined her delicate features.

Sera watched her sister silently, knowing she was communicating with the god in her body.

"Can you hear it?" she asked.

Galina grimaced. "It's furious with me."

Her face drew tight with effort, every muscle tense. Waves of energy shimmered through the sky, and a blistering chill stung Sera's skin—a wild tempest of raw power that charged the atmosphere with electricity.

Even Sera's zmeya seemed to hold its breath—a rare quiet moment for the stubborn dragon.

Galina shuddered as sweat pearled on her forehead. The god spoke through her lips, a command in the Exalted Tongue that shook the ground beneath them. The surrounding ruins hummed and crackled with godpower, and a portal ripped through the fabric of reality like a knife through silk. The scene of the ruined village was cleaved in two, revealing a gaping black fissure that beckoned like a maw waiting to swallow them whole.

Sera yanked Galina upright and through the god's gateway. Everything twisted and warped around them, colors bleeding together in a dizzying whirlwind that threatened to overwhelm Sera's senses. The dense and oppressive air weighed down her lungs.

Galina shook and shuddered in her grip as the deity's raw power surged. Sera gritted her teeth and clung on tight, terrified her sister might black out before they made it to the other side. But then, with a suddenness that left Sera gasping, they emerged into the inky shadows of the Blackshore tunnels.

An oppressive hush crashed over the two women, as if the world had stopped spinning. A smothering darkness pushed from all sides, and the atmosphere seemed to bottle their every breath. Sera's shaky exhales were punctuated by the thunderous clatter of horse-drawn carriages on cobblestone streets above, by dust that fell from the ceiling.

Corridors stretched before them, choked with the miasma of mold and decay. The reek of it threatened to unhinge Sera's resolve.

She swallowed hard, grasping the bag from her shoulder to rummage blindly for a candle and flint. The spark struck, and the flame blazed to life.

Galina's face was pale and waxy as she inhaled sharply. Then she gagged, bent over, and vomited on the stone floor.

Sera gently swept her sister's hair aside. "*Vitsví*," she crooned in Zverti. "Sister."

As she ran a soothing palm down Galina's back, she stared down the long, winding corridors of their secret childhood home. Dark and unchanged, the tunnels expanded before her, illuminated by the candle's glow. Later, she would light sconces her mother had left behind, find her old rooms and nurse her injuries.

But for now...

Her hand found Galina's.

They had returned to the place that gave them the gods they despised.

5

GALINA

The tunnels beneath the old university were as immense as Galina remembered.

The darkness writhed and twisted along the walls as if the shadows had teeth. The air was stale, damp, and thick with the scent of rot, a reminder of the years since the last footsteps had echoed through this place.

Galina ran her fingertips over the rough-hewn surface as she proceeded deeper into the abandoned annex. She could almost hear students' chants from sixty years before, echoing through its corridors—a memory rooted within the foundations of long-forgotten rallies rebelling against alurean reign.

According to Irina, the imperial family's response then was swift and savage: a purge that slaughtered thousands, blood staining the execution platform at the palace.

The university was forever sealed shut by decree of the ruling family.

Now the only way in or out was through a hidden door in the nameless cemetery, a secret so closely guarded that even Irina's most devout faithless were unaware of its existence. Her trust only went so far.

Galina paused at the smudged message in charcoal on the wall, a relic of the student uprising: *na itsi pris om vmonkt stvu zde mazvo fsta mazvo.*

You can only bend the alder tree little by little.

Zverti, the old common language, was the forbidden tongue of uprisings. It was illegal, spoken only in hushed tones between families and villages across Sundyr. Written into dirt or snow and erased with swift boots.

Irina spoke to Galina in Zverti to gain her confidence. She'd taught her the letters as a girl, how to read and write—more tools of manipulation. Give someone the vocabulary of retribution and they'll stop at nothing for vengeance.

(*Poor, stupid, easily controlled Galechka. You listened because you wanted to believe in lies.*)

Galina flinched, tamping down the intrusive thought as she hesitantly stepped closer to the door of Irina's study.

Memories of being strapped to the leather chair in the center of the room flooded her thoughts. Irina's brusque fingers pressed against her skin as she injected her with elixirs that changed Galina's body right down to the shape of her bones. Etching every inch of her skeleton with the summoning symbols for a deity Irina hoped to use as a weapon against the imperial family.

Galina endured months of torture with promises of revenge—for Olensk, her village, the loss of her home, and the bone-white ash of bodies she could never bury.

Irina had weaponized her grief; she had forged a little girl into a tool of destruction.

Footsteps echoed behind Galina, slow and deliberate.

When she turned, Sera studied her with a searching gaze. "Did you sleep?"

The previous night, Galina had staggered into her bedroom—untouched for four years. Her god's whispers had cut through her mind like a dagger, punishing her for neglect. She'd ached for the comforting numbness of liquor, but she settled beneath the covers and let exhaustion drag her into a fitful slumber.

Her nightmares filled with the pungent stench of the interrogation room down the hall, the stonework scorched black with her sins. Screams echoed through her thoughts like ghosts.

(*So many people killed by poor, poor stupid Galechka.*)

"Not really," Galina said, very quietly.

Sera's expression softened. "Neither did I." She surveyed the long hallway, her eyes lingering on the faded walls and scuffed floors. "Irina's plans are still scattered across her desk. I spent the night reading some."

"I didn't crawl out of the rubble in Dolsk just to throw my life away for the faithless," Galina told her sister sharply. "I already did that once."

Sera released a heavy sigh. "What if—"

"No," Galina interrupted. "I want to be clear: I will *not* sacrifice myself."

Hadn't she given up enough?

Her childhood (*your innocence*).

Her body (*your mind*).

Years of her life (*years you'll never get back*).

Sera slid past Galina and pushed open the door to the study. "*Vitsvi*," she said, voice like a blade skimming the surface of a lake. "I would never let you do something as absurd as martyr yourself. If you don't like what I say—" She shrugged, a gesture both accepting and resolute. "Then tell me to fuck off."

A brief, reluctant smile broke across Galina's face. After a moment of hesitation, she followed Sera inside.

Irina's research materials were strewn everywhere, haphazardly stacked on shelves and crammed into drawers. The sisters' boots scuffed against the stone floor as they made their way to the desk cluttered with yellowing notebooks and scrawled annotations.

Sera rummaged through the papers. "I found a bunch of Irina's old notes hidden in a compartment," she said, producing a red leather-bound tome with a gilded clasp. "The journal's encoded, but luckily I'm fluent in my mother's deranged ramblings."

Galina sighed.

She couldn't believe Irina was still manipulating her life from beyond the grave.

"*Vítsvi*," she said tiredly.

"Don't tell me to go piss in a river yet." Sera shifted more journals. "Irina would have had you launch a suicidal attack on the palace, but after what she made you do in that interrogation room, we're ignoring her plans. I have a better idea."

Galina remained silent, shaking with a violent surge of emotions: anger, frustration, shame. Her body tensed as she remembered the dark chamber at the end of the hall where she had lost her innocence. The too-recent events in Dolsk, another victim to the alurea and their war.

But she owed it to Dolsk to listen. She owed it to Olensk, to the childhood that was burned to dust and swept into the Lyutoga Sea.

She owed it to herself.

"What's *your* plan, then?" Galina demanded through gritted teeth.

Sera met her glare head-on. "We'll play this smart. No storming Zolotiye Palace by force. You'll walk right through the front gates, pretending to be a lost alurea searching for your home. You already know what it's like to be an orphan. Claim you were raised by commoners."

Galina's memories came flooding back. The steps of the hospital weeks after Olensk, the snow settling on her shoulders. How Irina had wrapped a scarf around her. That act of tenderness seemed so significant—after all the pitying looks and brusque touches from healers, Galina had been so starved for kindness. So greedy for affection.

Irina offered it.

All of it lies.

(Oh, poor, trusting Galechka.)

Galina quashed those unsettling thoughts, her voice carefully composed. "What makes you think the empress will even let me live?"

"She's been the only one bonded to a zmeya with the godfire in nine hundred years, and she has an army marching on her borders. She'll be salivating at the chance to exploit your abilities. You'll leverage your upbringing as a commoner to win the support of the Blackshore, and people will be more inclined to accept you when you take the throne. Afterward, we'll set up a provisional government of citizen leaders and initiate a transition. Want me to fuck off, or keep going? Because I have more."

Galina gaped at her sister. Sera's idea was far from what she'd envisaged, but she had to admit it held a specter of hope. Something she hadn't felt in so long.

Her mind worked, seizing on Sera's strategy. "But if Sopol is marching on Tumanny's borders, a coup is a temporary solution. We need to plan for war."

Sera pushed a notebook over to Galina and tapped the page. "Irina's tactics for the palace are useless, but she references a supplement to the serums she created to summon our gods."

Galina's eyes fell onto the journal she couldn't decipher. "Supplement?"

Sera nodded. "Designed to deepen the bond with your zmeya so you have the strength to use its lustrate godpower."

The lustrate was rare, commanded only by the most powerful and dominant zmei—a godpower that forcibly broke bonds between humans and gods. It could free deities caged in human bones and render alurea as helpless and vulnerable as commoners.

According to Irina, Galina's god had been bonded to Empress Maria Romanovna Koltovskaya five thousand years ago. Irina claimed she used the lustrate like a surgeon's scalpel—effortlessly tearing apart the oppressive magic that bound zmei to humans. Of course, it was only a matter of time before a group of nobles staged an uprising and assassinated Maria.

Galina shook her head with finality. An alurea's powers were immutable once they were bonded to a god. "My zmeya wasn't the one bonded to Empress Maria," she said. "It was another mistake, like yours."

Sera flinched as if struck. She looked away, emotions flickering across her features. Irina never let Sera forget she was a failed experiment.

Natural-born alurea had no control over the zmei caged in their bodies. The summoning marks were inscribed into their bones before birth—as unique and individual as fingerprints. Those carvings were magic that dragged the dragons from Smokova against their will, trapping them within human hosts.

Irina had studied the centuries-old records and details of alurean markings at the university and used them to decide which dragon to summon.

But no matter how much knowledge one had, conjuring gods was never an exact science—Irina had been wrong before. Her first attempt to call forth Empress Maria's god failed, leaving Sera with an unknown, violent zmeya that wouldn't be identified until after she died and someone compared her marks to those in the records.

Sera cleared her throat. Her voice was soft, yet firm, as she spoke. "The volumes in the university library detailed every element used to trap the original gods, right down to the additives applied in their serums," she said slowly. "The alurea destroyed each component—most of these plants are almost extinct. It took Irina decades to find them, and she barely had enough for both of us. She was careful with your markings after mine. She couldn't afford another failure."

Galina's brows drew together. "But I can't break bonds between humans and zmei. I already tried, remember?"

Sera's features tightened at the reminder of Galina's futile attempts to sever her godbond years ago. "Irina thinks she made a mistake with the proportions she injected to summon your zmeya. Your body wasn't primed enough. So you have the godfire but not Empress Maria's secondary ability."

"Or maybe she couldn't admit she messed up twice," countered Galina.

"Irina's skill was better than her judgment," Sera said firmly. "No one else has summoned a god from Smokova and bound it to a human born without the bone marks for thousands of years." She paused as if gathering courage, turning away from Galina to face the shelves of elixirs with renewed resolve. "We have enough of her mixtures for a panacea. If you trust me to try."

"Sera..."

Failure meant death—for her and her sister.

"You spoke about war earlier," Sera said quietly. "That would make us no better than the alurea, and Vitalik's bombs can't fight a Sopolese invasion. You infiltrate the palace while I translate Irina's notes and prepare the panacea, and when I'm done, we'll take the lustrate to Sundyr and expel every god we find. No pointless deaths. No futile martyrdoms."

Sera laid a hand atop hers, and Galina felt a spark of hope.

"No pointless deaths," she agreed. "No futile martyrdoms." Galina studied her. "But what about Vitaly Sergeyevich? If he assassinated the emperor, he'll attack again. Unless you think we should tell him your plan?"

Sera's features hardened, and her words stabbed like a rapier. "Under no circumstance, *in no conceivable universe,* is he to know about this. He has the morals of an infant with access to knives."

Galina raised an eyebrow, her tone incredulous. "Aren't you both—you fought alongside him for a decade. Hasn't he saved your life?"

She clenched her jaw, her fingernails cutting into the mahogany surface of the desk. "I was an exception to Vitalik's lack of morality—but he would throw me to a pack of wolves if he knew I was an alurea. We can't trust a man with bombs in his pockets."

"You designed the bombs, Serafima," Galina said with a snort.

Her sister glared like a cornered animal. "Let's not dwell on that now." Sera scowled at the documents. "I'll locate Vitalik's explosives stash while you're in the palace. The last thing we need is you getting blown up because he has the tactical acumen of a bucket of turnips."

Galina knew a bit about Sera's association with Irina's former second-in-command, but she'd kept so much of that part of her life secret. Sera and Vitaly had traveled to Sundyr on multiple expeditions for espionage and smuggling, often for months at a time.

And while Galina and Sera were on the run, she'd sometimes catch her sister peering out the window of some safe house—in Starapolė, in Mysovaya, in Dolsk—with a distant longing that spoke of regret.

Galina studied her briefly before speaking again, her voice low and even. "You miss him. Don't you?" At Sera's silence, she asked, "And if you figure out how to activate my lustrate ability?"

Sera sighed in exasperation. "For gods' sake, Galya. Ask your real question. Is this about saving Vitalik's sorry ass or ridding myself of the god?" She gritted her teeth. "It's both. He'd hate me if he found out, and that makes me sick to my stomach. And as for my dragon, if I could cut it out with a rusty blade, I would. If the panacea works, send the thing back to Smokova where it belongs. All right?"

Galina flinched at her sister's confession. The room was silent, the air heavy with unspoken words. A void that could not be filled. Galina thought she knew her sister better than anyone else, but it was as if she were looking at a stranger. Sera had a heart full of secrets; that was where she kept Vitaly.

She exhaled slowly. "We won't involve the faithless then."

"Only Anna," Sera said. "She never liked Irina. When you're in the palace, don't trust anyone there but Katya. It's just us four."

Galina's expression twisted with surprise. "You mean to tell them...everything? About our gods?"

Sera's fingers tapped against the desk as she pondered the question. "*Everything*. I don't know how I'll squeeze it into a message small enough to fit in a counterfeit coin for Katya, but I'll figure it out. We need her on our side."

Ekaterina Isidorakh, Empress Isidora's handmaiden, had been Sera's secret informant in Zolotiye for nearly half a decade, providing critical intelligence to the rebellion that had saved countless lives. Ekaterina's knowledge of court secrets had placed her in a precarious position—one misstep could cost her life. But she'd risked herself four years ago to warn Sera that Irina's faithless were compromised, and the sisters were still alive because of her.

Galina held Sera's gaze. "So how am I getting into the palace?"

Sera's lip curled into a smirk. "I have an idea."

6

GALINA

For weeks, Galina and her god warily circled one another like two wolves in a clearing—a tense meeting of minds.

The deity had saved their lives in Dolsk, but years of abandonment had left an indelible mark. Its rage radiated through her veins, each forgotten night of loneliness a blade between Galina's ribs. Its carapace shifted beneath her ribcage—edges like razors, bones keen and sharp. Teeth that bit in reprimands.

It demanded penance, punishments for her neglect.

(*Punishments you deserve.*)

She steeled against the zmeya's scorn and forced herself not to look for Irina's liquor stash. Forced herself to endure the scorching nights with gritted teeth, knowing her dragon could spare her the pain of alcohol withdrawal and was choosing not to. Agony was her constant companion in those first days. Her skull throbbed, pulsating like a drumbeat. Her skin crawled with an insatiable itch, a maddening sensation no clawing would ease, while her mouth tasted of tarnished copper.

Sleep evaded her—as did any solace or pleasure. Each moment was stretched out like a vast desert, an unending expanse of sand with no relief in sight.

But Galina waited, the weight of time pressing down on her shoulders.

For her body to mend.

For the god to forgive her.

Finally, a fortnight after Dolsk, the zmeya's fury cooled. Her physical torments faded. Her intrusive thoughts became fewer, no longer shoving through the fog of her intoxicated mind to taunt her. It was time.

Sera squeezed Galina's hand in comfort as they climbed the tunnel stairs to the tomb that led to the cemetery. The air hung heavy and still, with only the distant toll of temple bells and drums punctuating the silence.

Sera spoke in a hushed tone at the door. "We can turn back. Take a ship to Kulsk. You can spend the rest of your days seducing bored village wives while I pursue the art of goat husbandry."

Galina mustered a faint smile. "You don't know anything about goats."

"I'm sure I could learn."

(Yes, go back to debauchery and drinking. It's worked out so well for you!)

A spark of conviction surged in Galina's veins as she pushed that thought down beneath the rubble of Dolsk to bury it. "No. We're doing this. It's time."

The snow gleamed like a million shards of glass as they exited the vault, throwing off harsh glints in all directions. The graveyard's trees resembled ancient sentinels watching over the dead, with twisted limbs reaching out like skeletal fingers, casting ominous shadows over pathways.

Beyond the necropolis, the towers of the Blackshore dominated the sky. Banners and florid mosaics adorned every building, gleaming in the bright sunshine—a kaleidoscope of colors and patterns.

Thousands of people walked in the palace's direction for *obryad*, the day of worship.

Frost crackled beneath Galina's fur-lined boots as they exited the boneyard. A chill cut through her dress, the vibrant floral pattern of the ceremonial sarafan and rubakha a reminder of home. The stunning shades of blue and green mirrored the leaves of the *pana ae*, a native wildflower found near the Lyutoga Sea.

Galina wanted to have a part of Olensk with her when she went into enemy territory.

Her heart pounded as she and Sera proceeded up the cobbled road, weaving through the throng of worshippers. Zolotiye Palace sat like a jagged crown atop the hill, its spires and domes a beacon of wealth and power. Intricate patterns of gold shimmered in the sunlight as the edifice stretched toward the heavens.

Obryad brought a cacophony of voices, laughter, music, and clanging bells to the bustling metropolis. Citizens sang hymns, their songs rising in supplication to their gods, enveloping the capital in a chorus of devotion.

"We're about to meet the crowd on the thoroughfare," Sera yelled into Galina's ear. "Don't let them push you away from me."

Galina tightened her grip on Sera's hand as the throng buffeted her from side to side. She focused on the sarafans ahead of them, embroidered violet and crimson flowers blooming against a sea of people.

The sisters scaled the hill, flanked by a canvas of colors. Windows showcased ornate patterns, sculpted crenellations, and gilded onion domes—all kissed by the morning sunlight.

Wild peals of royal temple bells reverberated through the city as the hour of worship neared. The thundering crash threatened to overwhelm Galina's senses until Sera's cool fingers intertwined with hers—a comfort in the chaos.

A reminder of their mission.

Focus and resolve flooded her veins, steeling her against the onslaught of sound.

The duo forged forward among the devout. Ahead, Zolotiye Palace's golden shards and cupolas gleamed in the iridescent sky. The walls were festooned with ornate carvings, tales of epic battles, and legendary rulers. Ivory turrets, capped with sparkling golden domes, rose into the heavens.

Guards cloaked in full ceremonial armor stood stoic and watchful along the ramparts, their breastplates and shields emblazoned with prominent imperial crests of Tumanny. Meanwhile, the temple balconies fluttered with glittering gowns and gleaming uniforms of alurean nobles as they sat in a position of prominence above the commoners.

"We'll wait for the empress to make her appearance. Stay close to me," Sera said, her grip tightening.

The temple chimes pealed, halting the chatter and bustle of the crowd.

"Ready, *vitsvi*?" Sera murmured, her breath crystallizing in the crisp morning air. Around them, the faithful unrolled prayer blankets across the snow-covered road. "The empress is coming."

Galina closed her eyes, inhaling until her muscles tensed with determination.

She had to be ready.

The faithful rose in a frenzy, cheering at the empress's arrival, some raising the infamous icons of the monarch alight with her godfire, an ever-burning symbol of her power.

Isidora appeared upon the balcony railing, the silvered hues of her embroidered vestment glimmering as she held out her arms. The air vibrated with power as the sovereign swept her piercing gaze across her court—

Young Galina picked wildflowers in the meadow, her eyes wide as she spotted the silhouette shrouded in flames on the hill. Fire devoured the fields on the outskirts of Olensk.

"Momma," she called out. "Look! There's a lady up there!"

Galina's mother glanced up—and paled. "Come here, my love. Now!"

The wildflowers slipped from Galina's hand.

The last thing she ever heard from her mother was screams.

The memory vanished as the crowd's chanting swelled, their voices melding together in a song that echoed through the streets—honoring the ancient rulers of Tumanny who conquered and unified the country.

When the hymn finally faded, an expectant hush settled over the city. Every eye was upon their sovereign as Empress Isidora surveyed the gathered masses.

Then, with a flourish, the empress lifted her arms higher—and petals of flame erupted from her palms.

Ice replaced Galina's blood as she watched the monarch bathed in godfire—the same fire that had razed entire villages, leaving nothing but smoke and screams.

The same fire that had stolen everything from her.

Galina inhaled sharply, the oppressive heat of that fateful morning long ago pressing against her skin. The faces surrounding her morphed into ghosts—haunting mementos of the dead and guilt-ridden reminders that she alone had survived.

She shook off the memories, refocusing her thoughts on the present. The empress's godfire had robbed her of Olensk, but this was not a time for grief.

This was the time for anger.

For years, Galina had buried her rage beneath an addiction that had become a grave, where it withered and decayed like a corpse under six feet of dirt.

But now that wrath blazed within her, brighter than ever—a wildfire rekindled in her soul.

This was a time for revenge.

Galina met her sister's gaze, and a faint smile graced Sera's lips. "Goat husbandry? Village wives?" she teased.

(*Back to hiding. Being useless and afraid.*)

Galina shook her head. "For Olensk," she said with determination. "For Dolsk."

"*For us,*" Sera added, squeezing Galina's hand before releasing it.

A surge of power coursed through Galina's body, like a vast tide crashing against the shore, as her god awakened within its cage.

The Exalted Tongue tore from her throat.

Building foundations trembled. Lightning split the sky, illuminating the terrified faces of citizens. Sparks of electricity danced and twisted in the charged atmosphere. Godfire was her zmeya's element, but it controlled the wind and air surrounding her, a fierce ability that could conjure storms.

Galina spread her arms wide, summoning the elements to her will. The scent of ozone thickened as the god's power roared to life.

Hundreds of thousands of eyes followed Galina as she soared above them. She felt the zmeya's lungs expand, its imprisoned wings thrumming with memories of flight. She surrendered to it, let the dragon gaze through her at the sprawling city and its people below. She reveled in the breeze rushing through her hair, her sarafan billowing like a defiant, vibrant banner. A garment that no noble would deign to wear—the clothes of a commoner, her embroidered flowers a testament to her humble upbringing. A declaration she wore with pride.

Just as Sera intended.

Gasps sang through the streets, rippling to the gates of Zolotiye Palace. The empress stood on her balcony, focused on Galina with searing intensity. Wrath and iron-hard purpose thickened the air, a taste like bile on Galina's tongue.

She clenched her fists as thoughts solidified in her mind.

Let my face be the last you ever see.

I will burn myself into your memory.

7

SERA

Sera watched in awe as Galina lifted into the air, her pale hair shining as it danced in the breeze.

Energy pulsed in the atmosphere, sparks of electricity crackling as the god spoke through Galina in the Exalted Tongue. Every syllable ricocheted off the buildings, shaking the cobblestones beneath the feet of the gathered masses.

With a grand flourish, Galina swept her arms wide, and her sarafan billowed like a curtain rising on a stage. The assembled crowd gasped, speaking in hushed murmurs.

Thousands of eyes followed Galina as she glided toward the gilded portcullis.

Sera hovered on the fringes of the mob, eavesdropping on their whispers of bewilderment at the sight of an alurea dressed in the humble garments of a commoner. A stark contrast to the nobles, who perched on their balconies like preening peacocks, each thread of their opulent fabric serving as a reminder of their lofty station.

She watched as Galina began her descent to the palace

gates. The crowd stilled, whispers swirling like smoke. Even the alurean sentries standing watch on the palace's ramparts seemed mesmerized.

Be careful, vitsvi, Sera thought as Galina touched down, her sarafan fluttering around her.

The throng of onlookers hushed as Galina strode toward the gates, her steps steady and sure. Some dared to reach out and brush her shoulder as she passed, their fingertips lingering on her dress.

The ear-splitting screech of metal filled the air as the portcullis yawned open, and guards swooped in, shoving aside the commoners like they were worth less than the shit on their boots.

As they grabbed Galina by the arms, discontent rippled through the crowd, an undercurrent of resistance. Some shouted objections. The sentries used their violent godpower to subdue the rabble, knocking them to the ground with a wave of invisible force. Sera winced at the anguished cries that echoed through the air—guards weren't bonded to powerful zmei, but their godpower often left commoners writhing in the dirt with shattered bones and blood frothing from their mouths.

The gates shut tight with a shuddering clang of iron.

The masses erupted in a cacophony of rage. Some spat vulgarities at the guards, while others hammered their fists against the gates with such ferocity that Sera feared the metal might buckle under the assault. She had never witnessed such a frenzy before, but this was no ordinary transgression—today was different.

Today, the sentries arrested an alurea dressed as a commoner.

Courtiers atop the lesser balcony attempted to appease the mob's ire by showering them with sweets, a traditional *obryad* custom. But those gathered below just threw them back, rejecting the offering. They were in no mood for sugary bribes, and the collective fury only built. The sea of people surged forward and rocked the gates, the tranquil song of prayer replaced by bewildered and outraged cries of supplicants.

Fear gripped Sera as she watched the scene unfold, her thoughts conjuring every disastrous possibility for her sister's fate should the empress decide to make an example of her for this.

Through her panic, something snagged her notice—a man standing in the crowd, not watching the spectacle.

Looking directly at Sera.

Sera froze, gaze touching on his familiar face. His visage was etched into her mind so deeply she could draw it from memory. The line of a jaw that her fingers had skimmed in the darkness. High cheekbones cut with the same precision as a blade's edge. Features some might consider too pretty were it not for those eyes—the color of ashen winter frost. Like a flawless weapon, they were all too sharp.

Vitaly Sergeyevich Rysakov. Her mother's second-in-command.

The distance between them grew stifling and hot. Was Vitaly real or a figment of Sera's imagination? Or was it just a foolish desire to see him again?

But he looked different. His hair was longer. His frame still held the lithe grace of a thief, yet his muscled body spoke of hard labor and countless skirmishes. He didn't occupy a space so much as conquer every inch in the way of a marauder smashing her walls. Walls she had built to keep him out.

She should have known she couldn't escape a thief.

Sera watched Vitaly's lips carve out the syllables of her name, and the sound seemed to freeze her in place.

Serafima.

The crowd roared and surged like a breaking wave, shattering the moment. Sera stumbled as the sea of bodies narrowed in around her. She clawed at the air, searching for Vitaly amidst the turbulent throng. But he was gone, swallowed up by the tumultuous tide.

The chaos of the street was a blinding array of flags, fabric, and voices—a harsh reminder that this was no time for lingering. She had to get home and plan her next steps.

Galina's fate depended on it.

Sera steeled herself and pushed forward, weaving between people with a skill born of experience. The press of bodies was dense, a wall of humanity that stretched into the horizon. The city's architecture seemed to shrink in comparison—the ornate gilded domes and intricate spires appeared almost insignificant against the expanse.

Sera's gaze swept across the skyline. A haze of smoky prayer herbs hung in the air, sweet and pungent, descending from thousands of braziers with incense in the snow.

Worshipers spoke urgently, their concern palpable as they asked what had happened to the alurea dressed as a commoner. *"What happened? Did you see...? Why did they arrest her?"*

But Sera had no desire to stay and savor her and Galina's first victory—not when her sister was in the palace, in danger.

She slipped from the mass and disappeared into the labyrinthine alleys and lanes, her boots squelching through slushy puddles. Gradually, the deafening clamor of the street dissipated, replaced by an unsettling hush that enveloped her in its eerie embrace. Her feet crunched over the frost-covered ground as she made her way home.

And then she turned a corner and stopped in her tracks.

Vitaly was leaning against the wall of a derelict tenement. He shifted, taking in Sera's presence. She heard a slow, ragged breath leave him as he approached her.

Sera's skin prickled at his proximity—as if an invisible knife had been thrust into her chest.

The walls seemed to contract around them, the silence a vastness that stretched and expanded until it filled the entire alleyway. A thousand unspoken confessions stifled the air.

Sera gathered herself. "I thought I might have imagined you by the palace gates."

Vitaly's gaze drifted over her face as though cataloging every feature. "I wondered the same." He lingered on her hair, a faint smile tugging at his lips. "I've always liked it dark, but you make a beautiful blonde."

Sera felt her resolve waver, teetering on the precipice of surrender at the softness of Vitaly's words. Even her god seemed to still, lulled into a soothing slumber by the sweet sound of his voice. It had been this way for years; he had been making her zmeya weak-kneed since it first heard him speak.

Leave it to a pretty man to calm the bastard dragon in her bones.

But she stood resolute; she couldn't afford to be vulnerable. She had to be as unyielding as stone, with her heart frozen solid, adrift in the coldest sea. Her survival depended on it.

Galina's survival depended on it.

"I have things to do," Sera said, her words echoing off the alley walls.

As she tried to walk past him, Vitaly gently gripped her arm, his fingers digging into the soft fabric of her fur-lined coat. "That's it? You couldn't be bothered to send so much as a fucking note for four years, and now you saunter back into my city—"

"*Your* city?" Sera arched a brow. "And who appointed you lord and master?"

His eyes narrowed. "Someone had to replace Irina. It took me years to regain people's trust in the faithless again after they saw the empress burn your mother alive. I may not have a throne, a crown, or a god, Serafima Mikhailovna, but this is *my* fucking city."

"And you assassinated the emperor."

His expression hardened, and he jerked away as if she'd scalded him. "You've been in contact with the Blackshore."

She couldn't deny it. "A few people."

"But not me."

No taunting or sarcastic rejoinders came to her lips. Not when she had secrets to keep—lines in the sand. Plans she'd made. Things she could never tell him.

"No. Not you," Sera echoed, staring down the empty street lined with snowdrifts. She might as well have stuck a dagger through him.

A muscle twitched in his jaw. "Why did you come back, Sera?"

The angry tumult of voices in the distance could have been mistaken for the pounding of her own heart. She had spent too many days poring over Anna's letters when they named Vitaly and wondering if he thought of her. If he dreamed of her. If concern over her plagued him on sleepless nights.

If he missed her.

"I was worried about the Blackshore." *I was worried about you.* "And I was tired of running."

As if he'd read her thoughts, Vitaly seemed to soften. "I keep rooms above the Old Smoke Tavern. Stay with me. It'll be safe for you there."

Stay with me.

She savored those words like a shot of fine liquor, but Sera had downed enough of it to know that this wasn't a good idea. Four years ago, when they had fled the Blackshore, he had uttered those exact words. Now, as then, it was too perilous.

She shook her head, her throat tight. "Sentries are too busy hunting you to bother with a stale sedition charge. It's not every day someone has the temerity to blow up an emperor."

"Temerity, Serafima Mikhailovna?" he asked, flashing a fierce grin. Such was his nature, like a beast of the wild. She once delighted in the dance of back and forth with him. "A compliment? I'm flattered."

To him, this was just a pastime, a silly gamble of pain and consequence. He was a wolf, all sharp teeth and dangerous whims, instincts impossible to tame.

"It was foolish, Vitalik," she said, clenching her jaw. "Erratic and reckless to the point of self-destruction."

Vitaly's eyes glittered like diamond shards. "I love it when you say sweet things."

"*Irresponsible.* You're going to get yourself killed."

"What's life without a little danger?" Vitaly drawled. "Besides, every time I indulge in some stupidity, I can't help but think of you."

Gods above, he was *insufferable.*

Serafima scowled. "It's not funny. Now Sopol is marching on Tumanny."

His head tilted to the side. "Ah, so that's what's been troubling you." When she remained silent, a smile crept onto his lips. "Call it reckless or foolhardy, but at least he's no longer breathing. We used your design for the explosive and set it beneath the carriage. The bastard lost both legs to the blast." His eyes glinted with a feral intensity, burning bright like a raging fire. "And when he tried to use his godpower, I broke his neck—a mercy he didn't deserve."

Sera exhaled sharply. The winter wind whipped snowflakes across the cobblestone street, the cold pressing down on her.

This wasn't the same boy she first met on the beach all those years ago—both of them children just trying to survive. Nor was it the man she stood beside in Ardatovo, risking their lives to overthrow tyrants.

They'd been apart for too long.

Sera kept her composure even as her stomach lurched. "I don't think you did any of that for mercy."

His smile faded, and his jaw clenched. "No. I did it because I wanted to." He stepped closer and lowered his voice. "Help me refine the tactics and secure the explosives, and we can do the same to the empress and the Sopolese soldiers."

Sera's teeth ground together. Vitaly never failed to concoct an incendiary scheme that included bombs, blades, and lunatic daring—a volatile mix with a hundred ways to blow up in her face.

The faithless were always at odds over violence, but their survival hinged on factions working in unison. Sera and Vitaly used to supply weapons and munitions to uprisings all over Sundyr, and their covert missions stoked the fires of revolution from Tumanny to Sgor.

But weapons weren't enough anymore—they needed a better strategy. The rebellion couldn't continue the way it had been.

"No," Sera shook her head. "I won't get involved. I'm done with the faithless."

Her new plan was in motion. It was too late to back down now.

Vitaly raised an eyebrow. "And done with me, I suppose?"

"Don't," she warned, low and threatening. "You won't like my answer."

He would turn away in disgust if he knew her secret. Yet her god had always been calm in his presence. Hushed. It went entirely still, as if straining to catch the sound of his voice.

Whenever he was gone, the stillness in her mind shattered like glass.

Vitaly's eyes glinted with barely contained rage, and his lips were a tight line—no trace of the charming smile remained.

"You aiming to join the ranks of the faithful?" He gestured toward the worshippers hurrying down the street. Their sarafan skirts fanned in the wind beneath fitted crimson dushegreyas, the rich embroidery on the jackets catching in the sunlight as they bustled past. "Drop to your knees in the snow and grovel to those tyrants who let their people starve while they gloat in luxury? What about the villages they've destroyed? Or maybe you'll thank them for not counting you among the corpses?" He whispered in a low hiss. Speaking like that could get one burned alive in Blackshore. No citizen with an ounce of self-preservation voiced an opinion against the alurea. "I don't know who that woman at *obryad* was or why she wore our clothing, but she's not one of us. There's a god inside her, which makes her one of *them*."

And me? Sera wanted to ask. *What does that make me?*

Sera lifted her chin. When she spoke, her words were as hard as iron. "I'm not explaining myself. When I left four years ago, I left *you*." She could lie with such skill.

A thousand emotions blazed across his features. "Is that so?"

Sera stepped back, huddling into her coat as a frigid chill snaked through her. "Thank you for offering me shelter, but I've never been safe. I don't want anything from you. Not anymore."

A stone settled in her chest, accompanying the others, each weighed down by broken promises and deceit. Thousands she had learned to carry over the years.

It's worth it. This is for Galina. This is for you. Your heart grew too brittle, and he was going to break it. Your god is the one thing he'll never accept.

She turned and walked away.

And her dragon raked its claws through her bones as punishment.

8

GALINA

Galina flinched as the guards' hands clamped down on her arms, their fingers digging into her heavy wool coat.

Past the gates, the crowd of commoners surged forward, their protests filling the crisp winter air. They shook the gilded portcullis as they clamored for Galina's release, shouting as the sentries dragged her through the palace entrance.

Sunlight illuminated the stained-glass windows of the interior hall, refracting vibrant hues across the polished marble floor. Galina's gaze trailed over the mural that stretched over the walls, depicting a serene blue sky scattered with billowing clouds and an eternal summer day. It was the kind of opulence that made her skin crawl.

Her boots slipped as the brutes yanked her into an alcove that curved like a hungry mouth. Beyond it lay the throne room, vast and cavernous. The crystal-dripped chandeliers lit up the chamber, painting fractured starlight across the space. The marble columns towered toward the high ceiling, their intricately carved murals depicting scenes of violence and conquest. At the far end of the room, Empress Isidora reclined on an ornate dais with a handmaiden by her side.

Isidora's pale face was a mask of cold beauty, blue eyes sharp as she watched the sentries drag Galina into the chamber. She flicked back a long strand of black hair from her shoulder, the motion betraying her irritation. As the guards dropped Galina at the empress's feet, Isidora's composure shifted and fury flickered in her features.

Galina averted her gaze, her submission masking a smoldering core of rage and hatred. The echoes of her mother's screams, the stench of burning wood and thatch all seared her mind like a wildfire she couldn't extinguish.

Bile rose in her throat, yet she kept her facade of calm, guarding her secrets with rigid determination.

You will perform, she told herself. *Be docile and eager to do what she wants.*

And when the time comes, she'll pay for Olensk.

Empress Isidora descended from her dais, the rustle of silk and the glint of gemstones trailing in her wake. She studied Galina in her humbled state, as if scrutinizing an insect on her boot.

Galina's face remained stoic, betraying nothing but a carefully crafted illusion of contrition and deference. She battled the urge to meet that searing gaze, her knuckles turning white with the effort to maintain her composure.

The unyielding marble floor beneath her knees was a harsh reminder of her place.

"If you were a commoner, I would have executed you in the square," Isidora finally said, her voice like a dagger slipping between Galina's ribs. Her regal gown swished softly as she shifted her weight, the gold and silver embroidery catching the light. "I'm still considering a fitting punishment."

"Yes, Your Holiness," Galina murmured. Her entire demeanor radiated obedience, as if she were nothing more than a puppet at the empress's mercy. The cold air in the chamber seemed to settle over her skin like a shroud.

"The ceremony is over." The empress's voice dripped with disdain. "Address me accordingly."

Galina swallowed hard, her jaw clenched tight. One day, the roles would be reversed—and she would show no compassion.

"Yes, Your Imperial Majesty."

Isidora circled her with the precision of a predator stalking its prey, the sharp clack of her heels echoing through the vast room.

Galina struggled to keep her eyes downcast but couldn't resist the urge to glance at the woman beside the throne—the empress's handmaiden, and Sera's court spy. Ekaterina was dressed in a lavish gown adorned with flowers. Delicate chains of bells lined her neck, wrists, and ankles, chiming with every movement.

She was a bondmaid, subject to the whims of her mistress and the court's entertainment. If the empress condemned Galina to death, their plan would crumble, and Ekaterina's chance of freedom would vanish with it.

Isidora scrutinized Galina with an intensity that seemed to weigh her down. "You're not from Sopol. Even my cousin wouldn't be so foolish as to send an army of one to the palace—not when he's broken our stalemate in Kseniyevsky."

Galina held back a flinch at the memory of Dolsk, determined to keep her emotions in check, her breathing steady. She would show the monarch no weakness, her spine as rigid as the towering marble columns flanking her.

"No, Your Imperial Majesty."

Empress Isidora trailed her finger over Galina's sarafan, her nail catching on the sleeve of the rubakha worn beneath. "I've never met an alurea who would lower herself to don the garments of a supplicant," she sneered. "This is the attire of someone who grovels in the mud."

"Yes, Your Imperial Majesty."

Galina pressed her teeth together as she stared at the golden veins on the marble floor. In trying to bury memories of Olensk, she'd forgotten her anger. She would not let her emotions be a liability; she would fashion them into a sharp-edged weapon.

She'd never forget again.

Empress Isidora seized Galina's chin, but Galina fought the urge to recoil. Her god bristled at the contact, straining against the chains of her control. Like a smoldering ember in a bed of ash, waiting to burst into flame. She commanded her body to remain still and unyielding.

Not yet, she told her god.

Not. Yet.

The empress's icy blue gaze raked over her. "If you're not from Sopol, then who are you? And why are you wearing a commoner's clothes?"

Galina's muscles tensed, her heart pounding in her ears. The story she had concocted with Sera now seemed utterly preposterous. But there was no going back.

"My name is Galina Feodorovna Kolenkina," she said, her birth name escaping her lips easier than any other. They did not keep records in Olensk. "A commoner outside the Blackshore raised me. When she passed on this winter, I—" She let her eyes fill, a mix of despair and helplessness. "I came here. I didn't know what else to do."

The empress was watching her, weighing her words like an executioner. One slip, one wrong inflection, and that was it.

But she couldn't think about that. She had to focus on the pain of her loss, on the ache in her heart that begged for home.

Dolsk.

Olensk.

Her grief was real.

Empress Isidora's face was a mask of indifference. If she had any suspicions, they remained buried beneath composure.

"Raised by a supplicant," the empress repeated, her voice flat. "You expect me to believe that?"

Galina kept her expression even. "It's the truth, Your Imperial Majesty."

She didn't look convinced. "Then what about your parents? Where were they? Was your father named Feodor?"

"I was an infant foundling," Galina said softly, making the lie sound like a personal failure. "My foster mother gave me the name Feodorovna after her father."

Father, forgive me.

"A *foundling*?"

Galina heard a few sentries gasp in shock. She knew all too well the alurean fixation on bloodlines, their rigid requirements for breeding and marriage that demanded pairings of equal power. Her performance at *obryad* indicated she was the result of two alurea with considerable strength—and a child like that wouldn't easily be forgotten by the royal court.

An alurean child brought up outside the nobility would be seen as an intolerable offense to their kind. A desecration. An insult to their divine heritage.

To the nobles, commoners were filth, scarcely worthy of consideration.

"Yes, Your Imperial Majesty," she replied. She feigned shame and disappointment—as though her upbringing were a stain she couldn't remove. "I was too young to remember what country I came from."

"Then tell me who took you from your own," the empress hissed. "Was it the commoner who raised you? If it was, I'll find her grave and burn her corpse until there's nothing left."

Galina couldn't help the bitterness that swirled inside her. *Her own* had been taken from her, ripped away in a single morning of blood and fire.

"I don't know," she answered, the words ringing through the chamber. "I lived with my foster mother in a cottage in the wetlands. It was isolated."

Isidora watched her with eyes like a serpent. "You didn't attend temple services?"

"Yes, Your Imperial Majesty." She spoke the lie so smoothly. "Every sennight in Rontsy."

She gave the nearest remote settlement she could recall outside the Blackshore, where she and Sera had stopped four years ago on their flight from the city.

But as Ekaterina's expression tightened, Galina sensed she had erred. And when the empress's lip curled into a scowl, she understood how much.

"Arrest the priest and priestess in Rontsy," Empress Isidora commanded her guards. "Bring them to me for judgment."

Galina knew what their sentence would be: death.

The marble floor dug into Galina's knees. "Your Imperial Majesty, I beg for your mercy."

(You're a stupid fool. Now look what you've done.)

Galina tried shaking away that intrusive thought, but it gripped her with claws. Here was a woman who had destroyed entire villages and left only ruin in her wake. To her, the murder of a priest and priestess was nothing.

"*Mercy?*" Isidora repeated, her voice dripping with disdain. "You expect me to show kindness to those who *you* claimed overlooked an alurea in their temple while she suffered the indignity of being raised as a supplicant? If it's true, that's unforgivable."

Galina lowered her gaze as a smoldering rage threatened to consume her.

Not here, she thought. *Not yet.*

Not. Yet.

Isidora's fingers dug into Galina's chin. "I recommend you save your pleas and consider yourself lucky that your elevated status will reduce your sentence."

Galina contemplated her next words. She had already recklessly sent two people to their deaths. The guilt stole her breath.

"I accept the punishment Your Imperial Majesty commands," she whispered. "I deserve to bear the consequences of my actions."

From the dais, Ekaterina gave an imperceptible nod, as if to say she'd made the right choice.

Isidora smiled, though it was a calculating thing, full of judgment. "Then you'll wear the mark of my godfire. So the country sees proof of my benevolence."

As the empress tore away the collar of Galina's rubakha to bare her throat, her body tensed. The empress's palm pressed against her neck, the heat of her touch seeping into her bones.

The Exalted Tongue spilled from Empress Isidora's lips, and her godfire surged. Galina's deity erupted before she could stop it, the power of both zmei clashing in a brilliant flash of intensity.

Isidora stumbled back. "You have godfire." Her voice was a whisper of accusation.

The empress's power guttered, receding until Galina's skin grew cold. Her own god withdrew, restless and uneasy, lingering with a smoldering warmth in her veins. Ready to protect her if she needed.

"Yes, Your Imperial Majesty."

"And yet you said nothing when you entered my throne room."

The monarch was a weapon, poised to strike in an instant. The air seemed to crackle with electric tension and foreboding as Galina desperately racked her brain for a viable response.

Salvation came, unexpected and welcome.

"Your Imperial Majesty," said Ekaterina from the dais, serene in the eye of the maelstrom. "After her transgressions at *obryad*, perhaps Galina Feodorovna couldn't decide which moment was best."

Isidora's jaw twitched. "You're too trusting, Katenka."

The handmaiden lowered her head, unflinching in the face of the empress's ire. "My apologies. You're right. I'm too concerned with Sopol to think clearly."

A flare of admiration went through Galina—Ekaterina had dredged up the dark specter of war. Empress Isidora was a ruler in dire need of a show of strength to keep her kingdom intact.

Isidora's expression hardened from wrath to ruthless calculation. "I'll consider the problem, Katenka." She turned to the guards at the entrance. "Take Galina Feodorovna to the Royal Wing and lock her in the white suite until I decide on a different punishment."

9

KATYA

Katya's fate was a crystal chandelier suspended from a single fraying strand. Just a slight *tug*—

Everything shatters.

Her days existed at the whims of a monarch—a harsh word away from being unceremoniously demoted from a prized companion to a footstool for the empress's weary feet.

From friend to furniture—one moment revered, and the next reviled.

No privacy, no autonomy.

The only respite came in the ephemeral moments between slumber and awareness.

Such was the *honor* bestowed upon Isidora's favorite.

No one spoke of the many favorites preceding Katya. Or how navigating and surviving the empress's moods was like wading through an ocean tempest: your head was only above water until you grew too fatigued. The servants in Zolotiye knew that a single misstep in the ebb and flow of the monarch's favor or displeasure was all it took to drown.

Isidora had slaughtered every handmaiden she ever had.

For days, Katya had thought of Galina languishing in the halls of the Royal Wing, her fate in the hands of the capricious empress.

And Katya's freedom depended on Galina.

"You're moody today, Katenka," the empress said as they traversed Zolotiye's snowy gardens. "Is it my new prisoner?"

Katya swallowed hard, already feeling herself slipping beneath the waves.

"I'm sorry, *suvya*," Katya said, using the term of endearment to mollify her mistress. The empress liked familiarity when in an indulgent mood. Katya grasped for an excuse she believed would gratify the monarch: "I'm concerned for your safety."

Isidora wasn't as pleased as Katya had expected. "Do you think I'm weak without my husband?"

Rumors circulated that Sopol had begun amassing allies, exploiting the Tumanny emperor's death to rally strength and push further into the regions under Isidora's rule.

No matter how much the empress controlled the press, the wind still blew whispers that Emperor Yuri's funeral had not been open casket. His body had been too ravaged by explosives to display publicly—no amount of propaganda could cloak that grim truth.

The weight of the impending conflict pressed upon Katya's shoulders, threatening to smother the fire in her heart. She yearned for freedom, a chance at life beyond Isidora's dominating grasp. She wanted to visit the sands of distant shores.

Katya bowed her head and offered a careful reply. "A sovereign bonded to a zmeya with godfire could never be weak."

Empress Isidora's face remained unreadable. "I hold a prisoner with the same bond. Should I reconsider my words this morning?"

Maybe I should execute her, knesi, the empress had said. *Another alurea with godfire is a risk.*

Katya stayed silent.

The empress quietly regarded her as they strolled between the ice-flecked trees, each step crunching through the thin layer of snow. The gardens loomed ahead, where she could make out the silhouettes of courtiers and their dark mourning garments. With the slightest gesture from the empress, her nobles fell back into a gaggle of whispers and laughter.

"You want me to spare her," Isidora said.

Katya watched those aristocrats chatter, so blissfully carefree. They didn't have to worry about one wrong word. Her life had a single trajectory unless she saved Galina.

Companion. Pet. Footstool.

Dead.

"I believe she could be a powerful ally. Enough to rally support away from Sopol."

The empress considered her words for a moment. "Come with me. I want to visit my husband."

Katya trudged behind Isidora as they navigated the winding path that led to Emperor Yuri's final resting place. The air was crisp, tinged with the scent of winter's bite. The scenery unfolded before them—a tapestry of frenzied, colorful blooms sprouting from the crystalline snow, a stark contrast to the barren winter backdrop. The earth mavens had used their godpower to create a trail of petals, lush and deep, joining those already wilted and leaden with frost.

It struck Katya as an odd sight, these fragile flowers serving as markers for the burial site of Yuri the Butcher. A man so cruel, not even his wife was spared his viciousness. His deeds had stained Tumanny's history with blood.

As they approached the towering obsidian monument erected after Yuri's demise, the empress halted. The monolith, hewn from a single block of stone, stood as a testament to his memory. At its apex, a large bust had been crafted, capturing the merciless visage of the late emperor with chilling precision.

Isidora stared at it, her expression unreadable, as her coat flapped in the harsh gusts of ice-cold wind.

"I never knew relief or joy until the day he died," the empress said flatly.

Katya held her tongue. She'd learned the trick of listening when spoken to and talking only when required. The monarch had no tolerance for unwelcome interruptions.

Snowflakes settled on Isidora's black tresses as she stroked the statue of her late husband, fingertips grazing over the marble cheekbone. "I thought him so handsome once, Katenka." Her voice was soft, distant. "When he first visited to establish the alliance with my uncle, I was so taken with him." She looked over at Katya as something occurred to her. "I've told you very little about my childhood in Liesgau."

The monarch fell into memory, a visceral yearning planting itself upon her features. It was easy to forget that citizens considered Isidora a foreigner despite her decades-long reign over Tumanny. She was born and bred near the Vast Sea, in the kingdom of Liesgau.

Emperor Yuri had sealed his rule with their union, a powerful storm maven and an empress armed with the godfire. It had worked; for thirty years, Tumanny swelled its borders and became an unbreachable stronghold.

But now Emperor Yuri was dead, and some whispers questioned the legitimacy of his foreign widow on the throne.

Meanwhile, Princess Vasilisa—Yuri's only child—had not been seen since her father's funeral.

Darker rumors suggested Vasilisa had been slain by her mother to secure authority. Katya knew such talk was nonsense—but she often wondered why the princess had confined herself to the Glasshouse Wing of Zolotiye Palace, refusing even the cleaning staff.

"Yes, *suvya*," Katya said. "You mentioned you longed for the Vast Sea."

The empress let out a low hum. "To open a door that far would take more power than my god and I possess. Fortunately, I miss nothing else." She returned her focus to her husband's sculpture. "Such a simple thing, to lure a girl away from her home if she's desperate enough. Sgor threatened Liesgau with invasion, and I had a handsome foreign emperor offering our rescue in exchange for marriage. And I loved him—until I came to this country, its people hated me, and my husband made me feel so small that I wanted to die."

Her face contorted with rage, and she seized the bust in both hands, strangling it with sudden force. A burst of energy pulsed from her, and Isidora shattered her husband's face, scattering the pieces across his grave. She raised her boot and smashed an obsidian shard into the snow.

"Why do you want me to let that girl live, Ekaterina Isidorakh?" Her eyes blazed with divine wrath, flames behind azure irises. "Why should I show her kindness when no one in this country has shown it to *me*?"

Katya gave her next words the same consideration as a master strategist in combat. The empress had used her full name for a reason—the request was far above her station.

And Galina's life depended on the answer.

"*Because* no one has shown you kindness, Your Imperial Majesty," Katya finally said.

And maybe you were worthy of it once. But that was a long time ago, when you were a scared girl from Liesgau and not a monarch who destroyed lives in an instant.

You show me no kindness when you cage me like a bird and make me sing for you. When you force conditions on my freedom and give me no autonomy.

You showed my sister no kindness when you murdered her.

Empress Isidora's scrutiny had weight to it, an invisible balance of life or death. She made no judgments without that scale in her mind, gauging the value of an existence she deemed insignificant.

"I'll grant you this, Katenka. But my mercy doesn't come without a price. Not anymore." She signaled to the guard standing on the path and issued a command. "Take Galina Feodorovna and our two prisoners from Rontsy to the throne room. I will be there directly."

Katya clamped down on her panic as she trailed the empress into the palace.

Empress Isidora handed her coat to a sentry and took her place on the dais. She motioned for Katya to occupy the diminutive seat at her side. But it was not an invitation. It was an order.

"You honor me, *suvya*," Katya whispered, bowing low before taking her place and passing her own coat to a maid who gave Katya's shoulder a brief, sympathetic squeeze.

Every servant knew handmaidens bore the full brunt of Isidora's wrath. Today, Katya perched on a small chair at the edge of the lofty dais. But tomorrow, she could be kneeling before the throne, with the monarch's boots grinding into her spine.

The chamber hummed with the hushed whispers of alurean courtiers as they hurried in, each draped in heavy mourning garments for the emperor. They resembled a flock of crows there to squawk and caw about the latest gossip.

The noblemen—high-ranking soldiers and members of the royal court—dressed in uniforms of subdued elegance that befitted their noble status. The weather mavens donned identifying threads: earth manipulators wore copper hues, wind masters were cloaked in shimmering silver, and water doyens in brilliant blue.

Courtiers formed a hierarchy determined by the strength of their gods. The powerful held esteemed positions of respect within the aristocracy, while those bonded to lesser zmei were conscripted as peacekeepers and sentries, entrusted with carrying out the empress's bidding.

As the grand doors to the throne room creaked open, the courtiers' murmurs faded to silence. In marched three sentries, their polished armor gleaming under the chandeliers.

They escorted Galina, her wrists unbound and her face pale, and the elderly priest and priestess, whose robes were stained and torn from their time in Zolotiye's dungeons.

Katya's stomach churned when she saw the prisoners. She, too, had once made a mistake that resulted in someone paying the ultimate price.

The trio knelt on the marble floor, heads bowed in deference. Isidora clicked her tongue in disapproval and gestured at Galina to rise.

Their first meeting notwithstanding, alurea did not fall to their knees like commoners.

Empress Isidora addressed Galina. "My handmaiden, Ekaterina Isidorakh, has convinced me to spare you."

Katya gritted her teeth at her formal name. It was a reminder of her servitude, of the shackles that bound her to the empress.

With a grateful glance to Katya, Galina lowered her head. "Your Imperial Majesty has blessed me."

"The price for your life comes at the cost of two supplicants," Isidora said, her voice as sharp as a blade. "Now execute them for their crimes against you."

Galina's face drained of all color, her breath catching. "I beg Your Imperial Majesty for—"

"Mercy?" The empress's lip curled. "I gave it: you in exchange for them." She gestured toward the priest and priestess. "Ekaterina Isidorakh defended you, and you're rejecting her gift?"

The courtiers present hissed low in disapproval, heads shaking in disdain. No noble in the room considered a mere priest and priestess deserving of protection, nor worth risking the monarch's rage.

"No, Your Imperial Majesty," Galina whispered.

"Then do as I command." A wild conflagration burned in her gaze. "Use your godpower and show everyone in this room who these two let live as a commoner. They watched you prostrate yourself in their temple as if you were nothing. I can't permit that crime stand."

Katya tightened her fists, fingernails biting into the chair's upholstery. *Nothing* was how the nobles treated supplicants—maids, flower sellers, bakers, blacksmiths, and priestesses alike—all viewed as inferior, powerless, only there to serve. Utterly worthless.

"Please, Your Imperial Majesty," the priest begged, his voice trembling. "We don't—"

Isidora flicked her wrist, and a burst of power stole the breath from the priest's lungs. The priest choked and clutched at his throat, bloodshot eyes bulging in terror and desperation. The empress then shifted her attention to Galina.

"Punish them, or I'll break my promise to my handmaiden and tie your verdict to theirs."

Galina was silent, but Katya could feel the rage radiating off her.

Katya held Galina's gaze, sending an unspoken warning: *Don't say please or show your anger. She'll only use it against you.*

Galina seemed to understand, her features hardening imperceptibly.

Her only choice was to obey the empress's cruel command.

Isidora released her grip on the priest, who crumpled to the ground with a gasp. The priestess was motionless, face turned downward in deference—humiliating proof that a lifetime of service and devotion to her monarch had earned her nothing, not even compassion.

Galina straightened her shoulders. Katya thought she saw her lips move, as if uttering an apology.

The air crackled with electricity as Galina summoned her zmeya. Flames ignited across her body, illuminating the shocked faces of the surrounding courtiers. Her godpower filled the throne room and pushed against Katya until the breath squeezed from her lungs. The energy scraped along her shoulder blades and down her spine, electrifying every nerve ending in its path.

It was like standing at the edge of an abyss, the unrelenting grip of gravity yanking her closer to the void.

But Galina stood firm, channeling the immense power of her dragon with grim determination. Flames licked at her fingertips as she lifted her hand. The blast struck the priest and priestess, their bodies consumed by godfire.

The air in the throne room was suffocating, the stench of charred skin and the intense heat making each breath a battle. Sweat glistened on Katya's forehead as she fought for each gasping inhalation.

Isidora leaned forward, her expression unreadable as she watched.

The prisoners wailed, their agonized screams piercing Katya's skull with the precision of a surgeon's scalpel. She noticed the pain etched on Galina's face, the lines of anguish deepening with every passing moment.

Their cries ceased.

As quickly as it had come, Galina's godpower subsided and the flames disappeared into nothingness. An oppressive stillness settled over the chamber. Even Katya's heartbeat seemed deafening in the aftermath of Galina's terrifying display of power.

All that remained of the priest and priestess were two blackened husks twisted in grotesque agony.

The empress descended from the dais, her skirts whispering against the marble floor until she stood over the charred remains of her faithful servants.

"Wielding the godfire has been a solitary existence," the monarch said, voice weighed with solemnity. "No one else has been bonded to a god with it in nine hundred years, and archives are scattered between kingdoms. Tell me something.

Can your zmeya revive someone when you feel their hearts give their last beats in your flames? Mend them in their moments before death?"

Katya watched as Galina's expression constricted, but she swiftly regained composure. "I expect it's like yours, Your Imperial Majesty."

"An effective interrogation method." Empress Isidora's lips curled into a tight smile. "Burning someone to a final heartbeat and reviving them. Watching them scream and beg to die. Our pairing is a blessing, Galina Feodorovna."

She lifted a boot from beneath her voluminous silk skirts, and gently touched a toe to the thing that had been the priestess.

It collapsed into a heap of ash on the floor.

Katya watched Galina step back sharply as the empress did the same to the priest.

"How we'll frighten Tumanny's enemies," Isidora said, turning to stare at her courtiers in defiance, knowing how many of them had whispered of a weakened monarch after Yuri's death. "March into their lands, turn their armies to dust. Have you ever been in a battle?"

Galina mutely shook her head.

"No?" the empress murmured, a soft sound like a snake's hiss. "I'll have to train you, then. There's no other purpose for the godfire except destruction and conquest. You and I will be unstoppable." A vicious grin flashed as she extended her hand, palm down, brilliant rings glittering in the light. "Now, thank me."

Galina stared at the sovereign's hand, and for a moment, Katya feared the other woman would reject it.

In the end, Galina kissed the signet ring on the monarch's finger. "Thank you, Your Imperial Majesty, for your offer and mercy. You've reminded me why I'm here."

Only Katya knew the secret behind Galina's dagger-edged smile.

10

SERA

One month later

Sera scanned the crowd as she and Anna approached Zolotiye Palace.

The streets were a jumbled mass of bodies and hues, with people from all over the empire converging in one place for *obryad*. The palace loomed ahead, its gold-tipped spires obscured by the thick clouds.

"More than last time," she murmured to Anna. "I see colors from Karovny."

Anna, Sera's friend and informant in the Blackshore, kept pace with her, expression sharp and focused. A single strand of dark hair had escaped from its tight plait and rested on her high cheekbone, a contrast against her brown skin. "How do you know they're from Karovny?"

"Went there once. Had a man put his knife to my throat," Sera replied without hesitation.

Anna's nod offered no suggestion that this was in any way unusual. "Ah, yes. Nothing quite like the fond memory of a close call." She paused for a beat. "But have you ever considered fucking someone who doesn't have knives on him?"

Sera let out a low chuckle, her eyes still fixed on the colorful chaos unfolding before them. "Where's the challenge in that?"

They pushed through the throng, jostling against shoulders and hips as they neared the palace. Among the crush of bodies, the air was saturated with the scent of smoke and spiced wine, adding to the festive atmosphere.

The crowd filled the streets with a glorious riot of hues. Teals from Tikhmenevsky to the south, crimson and orange wildflowers of Gorodetsk worn by mountain folk, and flags of Karovny at the far north of Tumanny were all present, evidence that the faithful had arrived from all corners of the empire to pay their respects.

A man in gray Blackshore colors recognized Anna and waved. The other woman instantly shifted to the cheerful facade she used at her confectionery: bright-eyed and dimpled smiles, deferential to every visitor in her shop.

Anna's pleasant performance had a purpose: it encouraged people to confide in her—and that amiable nature made her a valuable asset for intelligence-gathering.

She waved back in response, and the man grinned before darting ahead between the other worshippers.

Once he disappeared from view, Anna's smile faded like a dying ember. "He held an icon for the emperor," she muttered. "I'm going to spit in his bread tomorrow."

"And stand over him with a grin as he chokes on it?"

"Of course." Anna's look was wicked. "And may the crows peck at him on his way out of my shop. May his tongue shrivel and rot in his mouth, and may his cock—"

"*Anya*," Sera interrupted with a laugh. "I thought you were exaggerating when you said you had an affinity for nursing grudges."

"I don't nurse them. I coddle them like prized children," she corrected. "I whisper sweet nothings to them at night, and they always respond with a promise of revenge."

Sera raised an eyebrow. "Sounds... healthy."

Anna's attention flickered elsewhere, and she snorted. "Look, another icon for the emperor. These stupid people.

My one regret is not seeing the Butcher's corpse when Vitaly Sergeyevich killed him." As Sera's enthusiasm plummeted, Anna winced. "I mean, godsblood, that was an idiotic move. Imbecilic. Catastrophic beyond reckoning. What was he thinking, exploding a whole emperor?"

Sera lifted a shoulder as they turned onto the bend in the road that led to the palace. "You don't have to hold back your feelings, Anya," she said. Her voice dropped below the range of any eavesdropper. "The emperor deserved his death."

Anna tugged at Sera's arm as the crowd surged. "*Sera*," she said urgently.

Sera stopped, heedless of the people pushing past her. Anna looked behind them at the throng of faithful gathering at the temple gates. Sera followed her gaze and saw what had caught Anna's attention: the new icons of Galina.

The artist had taken liberties with Galina's appearance, but the bright crimson of her sarafan was unmistakable. In the painting, Galina hovered above the masses, her golden curls cascading around her face. Her simple dress rippled in the storm she had conjured with the power of her god.

Sera had never seen a votive like it, nor had she witnessed so many worshippers carrying an image of someone other than their ruler. There had always been an excess of votive paintings—generations of rulers to choose from.

But that day, thousands of people chose Galina.

"They never stop talking about her at the confectionery," Anna said in awe. "I'd noticed that icon plastered in the city. But this..."

"Careful about your enthusiasm," Sera cautioned, a thrill of her own bubbling just below the surface. "It's easy to fall from the height of an altar."

She was all too aware that citizens were fickle, especially in times of crisis.

Shipments from Sundyr had all but come to a standstill, and the winter in Tumanny continued to ravage the country.

Those cargoes that reached the port had to traverse mountains, valleys, and rivers to avoid the Sopolese forces. And yet lavish feasts were still hosted at the palace while so many starved.

No wonder people doubted their empress's judgment and looked to Galina for hope. Empress Isidora had made it clear—to question her was to invoke her wrath.

"For gods' sake," Anna muttered under her breath. "Savor the victory for once."

"Savor it for me," Sera suggested.

She shook her head. "Then I'll meet you back at the confectionery. I want to get a closer look." Anna darted between the worshippers and dissolved within the sea of bodies.

Sera scanned the royal balconies where the nobles gathered. The princess, Vasilisa, was absent—perhaps still grieving the loss of her father. But the lower terraces were teeming with alurean courtiers, their mourning coats standing out against the palace's marble columns. Sera searched the groups for a familiar face, but Galina was nowhere to be seen. She hoped that meant her sister had secured the coveted spot beside the empress.

If she was alive.

Sera had not heard from Katya in weeks, and the silence gnawed at her. But she knew better than to expect reassurances—the stakes were too high for anything other than critical messages.

And so Sera stood in the frigid weather with the other supplicants, waiting and trying to steady her racing heart.

She was so preoccupied that she didn't notice the person next to her until he spoke. "Come to pay your respects?"

Sera pressed her fingernails into her palm. "Vitaly," she murmured.

Her gaze snagged on his face—those gorgeous, austere features and pale eyes. Proof that predators often came in lovely packages.

Then she noticed his coat. The fabric screamed highborn elegance, so out of place on a man from the Black. "You thieve that?" she asked, sharp and sudden.

A smirk toyed at his lips, and the inky hair that fell across his forehead caught the sunlight like a promise. She fought the urge to brush it back. "You give a shit?"

Sera felt her composure fraying like an old rope. "No."

Leaning in, he exuded a presence that seemed to swallow the air whole. "Then why bother asking when you know damn well the answer's always yes?"

He threatened to destabilize her focus, and Sera couldn't make him leave, not when he savored both her ire and her kindness. He was more unpredictable than a sack full of badgers.

Sera sighed in exasperation. "I'd forgotten you've never come by a single thing honestly."

"That's not true. I once won your sweet affection with nothing but a lethal blend of charm and well-sharpened blades."

"I suppose you have a certain deranged appeal."

A slow smile crept across Vitaly's face. "Is there any other kind?"

"How did you even find me?" she asked with a glare. "A million people in the streets, yet you keep slithering up beside the only person who wants to avoid you."

His soft laughter fractured her further—resonant, surrounding her like smoke. "You should know by now that I can spot you in any crowd, whether it's one hundred, one thousand, or one million." He stepped closer, until his breath feathered over her cheek, and he murmured, "Hasn't it always been that way?"

Sera pressed her teeth together. She refused to entertain the memories she had of him, the ones that crept into her mind in the dead of night when the world was quiet, and her thoughts were loud. Anna's reports had failed to quench her curiosity. She longed to know if he still dreamed of her, if he thought of her. Did he whisper her name in his sleep, as she whispered his in hers?

"I'm not sure I believe your pretty words, Vitaly Sergeyevich."

His smile slipped a fraction. "Even the little girl on the beach called me Vitalik," he murmured.

Her fists clenched at her sides. He was baiting her, bringing up the boy who had once gifted her an iridescent shell from the depths of the Dark Sea. A boy who had been her childhood companion, her mother's second-in-command, and eventually—

Stop.

If he wanted to play games, then she would play them better. She would use that youthful memory to her advantage, remind herself why she was there.

The thundering voice of the god that loathed her. The struggle to contain its wrath. And the boy, the only one who could soothe the zmeya's fury. He was the cure for the thing he despised.

Sera gritted her teeth. "The little girl on the beach needed a friend," Sera said. "I don't."

His expression shuttered as he shifted his attention to the palace, with its brilliant banners and flags draped across balconies. "At least you're admitting to being that girl. But I seem to recall she hated *obryad.* How strange to find you at two in a row."

Sera paid him no mind as the jarring chimes signaled the imminent arrival of the empress.

The crowd's din built to a deafening crescendo. Shouts erupted from every direction. Sera strained to make out the words, and when she did, her heart skipped a beat. All around her, countless voices rose in Zverti. Each voice was a solitary defiance, but together, they became an outcry.

Vmonkt pror va. The common god.

They were calling for Galina.

Worshippers set their rugs in the snow and fell to their knees.

Vmonkt pror va. They lifted their arms in the air as they chanted. *Vmonkt pror va!*

"Godsdamned idiots," Vitaly muttered.

"Let them celebrate their new courtier, Vitalik," Sera said. "She's done nothing yet to earn your anger."

If her use of his diminutive name touched Vitaly in the slightest, he gave no sign of it. Instead, some dark emotion seemed to shadow his features. "I hear she's got the godfire. That makes her worse than the other monsters. They'll see it soon enough."

His words struck Sera like a punch to the gut. She suddenly remembered that Vitaly, too, skipped *obryad*—and he'd been at two in a row. It was not for her company that he came.

Sera latched onto his wrist. "If you're scheming, by the gods, I'll slice you into pieces and feed you to the crows."

Vitaly's eyes flashed like a blade drawn from its sheath. "I'm always scheming. I'll confess my plans if you tell me why you came to *obryad*."

She pretended not to hear him. "Don't do anything stupid," she said. "We had an agreement. You keep me grounded when I overthink, and I'll call out your deplorable lack of a moral compass."

Shards of ice comprised his foundations, and he wielded them without mercy. "You walked away, remember? We're not in this together."

Before Sera could respond, the bells on the balcony chimed. The roar that it stirred was deafening.

Vmonkt pror va! Vmonkt pror va!

The drums pounded faster, reverberating down the hill and across the city.

The veiled curtains parted, and Empress Isidora emerged as the Head of Worship in all her resplendent glory. The crowd fell mostly silent, but a low murmur permeated through the throng.

Where is the Common God? Where is she? Where is she?

Though respectful in their prostrations for their sovereign, they raised the votive paintings of Galina as they bowed.

A knot of anxiety twisted in Sera's gut. From the worried whispers of the other supplicants, she wasn't the only one fretting over Galina. If her sister was absent, she was either rotting in a cell or discreetly murdered.

Empress Isidora lifted a hand to quiet the crowd and began her hymn.

The song rippled through the worshippers and calmed the fretful murmurs over the absent courtier. They swayed and clutched their icons to their chests.

If anyone else sang the aria, Sera might have been taken in by the music. It might have moved her to silence. But she wasn't some gullible dupe to be dazzled.

Fuck the hymn.

Fury burned in Sera's heart. *Where is my fucking sister?*

11

GALINA

Galina's lavish room at Zolotiye was a prison.

The suite was a display of wealth and opulence, yet it left her cold. The glittering baubles and gilded decor held no interest. Shelves lined the walls, stacked with books and writing materials that were untouched and forgotten, gathering a fine layer of dust. It seemed she had been the room's only prisoner for some time.

Each day was a monotonous routine of waiting for the empress to summon her. Execute her. Use her.

But she never did.

(*You're just a weapon. It's the only thing you're good for.*)

Galina paced the chamber, her heels clicking on the polished hardwood. Her gaze lingered on the gold-leaf inlaid furniture, the intricate granite moldings, and the heavy velvet curtains that draped down the walls like a mourning blanket. No distraction quelled her agitation.

Her god prowled within her like a hungry wolf, and her thirst for liquor was a howling answer. Galina's body no longer shook with physical withdrawals—her zmeya saw to it—but the deity's caged restlessness overwhelmed her.

She fought against the seductive call of oblivion, resolute in her purpose.

She would not fail her sister.

Galina traced her fingers over the elaborate carvings on the mahogany writing desk, trying to calm her mind. But she couldn't shake the image of Sera from her thoughts, worried about her sister's safety and wellbeing. She passed the window in agitation and—

Noise. A distant hum beyond her view.

She pressed her ear to the windowpane, straining to listen. The muffled cry of voices grew louder, coalescing into a roar.

Obryad. It must have been *obryad.* The empress had locked Galina up for so long that she'd lost track of time.

She jumped at the scrape of a key turning in the door's lock.

To Galina's relief, Ekaterina swept through the doorway, flanked by two attendants who struggled beneath the weight of a bulky trunk. Without a word, Ekaterina gestured for the maids to place it near the red settee.

Galina's heart raced as a litany of questions threatened to spill from her. Ekaterina silenced her with a slender finger pressed against her lips, then shut the door behind the departing servants with a soft click.

"Her Imperial Majesty asked me to ready you. She sent along a dress." Ekaterina kneeled next to the trunk and beckoned Galina over. When Galina sank beside her, the handmaiden whispered, "Be mindful of the guards. They eavesdrop at doors, so let's speak low."

Galina nodded. "Any word from Sopol in the last month?"

"Their army is holding in Kseniyevsky," Ekaterina began, flicking the latch on the trunk and shoving it open. "Waiting on reinforcements from their allies. Empress Isidora spread the news through Sundyr that she's sheltering an unclaimed alurea with godfire. That halted King Maksim's aid for now.

Your power combined with hers could sway some rulers to Tumanny's side."

Galina's breath caught in her throat. "What about Sera?" she asked, her voice tight. "She's safe?"

Ekaterina hesitated. "I hope so," she said, causing Galina's stomach to plummet.

"You *hope* so?"

"I haven't been able to gain information," Ekaterina said bitterly. "My request to spare your life didn't come without a price."

Galina's gut twisted as Ekaterina's grim words hung in the air. She couldn't help but feel responsible for the other woman's burden, and the debt Galina owed her could never be repaid.

As if sensing Galina's distress, Ekaterina cleared her throat and drew the gown from the trunk.

The midnight blue silk was the night sky made tangible, embellished with tiny sapphires that shimmered like stars. The lacework was so delicate that it looked as if it had been woven from stardust, and the silver filigree that adorned every fold and seam glimmered in the flickering candlelight like moonlight on water.

But each detail was a painful reminder of the stark divide between the alurean royalty and the commoners—a blatant display of wealth and power. An order from the Empress that Galina couldn't refuse.

(You're her weapon. You're a thing to be used.)

Galina loathed that dress and everything it represented.

"Compliment it loudly," Katya said with a glance at the door. "In case the guards are listening."

"It's beautiful," Galina said in her usual tone, although she wanted nothing more than to tear the fabric apart and set it on fire. "Please convey my gratitude to Her Imperial Majesty." But then, because she couldn't restrain herself, she whispered, "And tell her to go fuck herself while you're at it."

A barely perceptible smile flitted across Ekaterina's face, as if she were trying to hide it.

She gestured for Galina to turn, and with practiced efficiency, the handmaiden began unfastening Galina's modest day dress to reveal her chemise. As the silk fell away, Galina heard a sharp intake of breath from Ekaterina at the smattering of scars that marred her side. Although the handmaiden regained her composure and hurried to retrieve new undergarments from the dressing room, Galina had seen the woman flinch.

All the maids had flinched. Some had avoided looking at Galina.

The raised scars along her thigh were undoubtedly a shock and a curiosity to them. For weeks, she had feared they would whisper of it to their empress, who would force her to endure an interrogation. But to her immense relief, no such inquiry had ever occurred.

Ekaterina returned to help Galina into a new chemise. As she covered Galina's scars with layers of clothing, she asked in a low voice, "May I ask what happened?"

"The empress," she replied, her throat tight at the memory. "Before I met Sera and Irina. I wasn't bonded to a god then."

A beat of silence followed her words. Then the other woman resumed her brisk progress of tying the gown's fastenings in place. "I've never heard of anyone surviving godfire."

"I was the only one," Galina whispered.

Ekaterina finished fastening the dress and urged Galina into the chair before the dressing table. "Where?" she asked, brushing Galina's hair in long strokes.

"Olensk." Galina watched Ekaterina's hands in the mirror as they worked through her hair. "In the north. During Sgor's invasion through the mountain pass, Empress Isidora burned the village rather than allow it to be used for shelter and supplies by invading forces. Mourners arrived from a neighboring town and took me to the Blackshore municipal hospital. I'd been in the rubble for five days."

Ekaterina's nimble fingers wove several small plaits as the silence stretched taut as a bowstring, thick with unspoken words.

Finally, she spoke, her voice soft as falling snow. "I'm sorry," she said.

Galina gave a wry twist of her lips—a reflex whenever someone apologized for her grief. "Sera never told me how you met her. You were born into your position at Zolotiye?"

Ekaterina stilled, a momentary lapse, before she deftly gathered another strand of hair. "My mother was a maid, my father a footman. Both were transferred to the palace in Arzalavat when I was three. I was raised with my sister Sofia at Zolotiye; she was Empress Isidora's handmaiden before me."

Galina's breath hitched. Ekaterina produced a handful of glittering gems from her pocket and began adorning Galina's tresses. "Before you?"

Ekaterina's face hardened, and she worked with an almost angry precision. "Her Imperial Majesty killed fourteen handmaidens before Sofia," she said with her jaw clenched. "The staff alternated the unenviable task of cleaning up after the godfire or disposing of corpses. Sofia lasted six years. A visiting diplomat got the empress in a temper, and she broke Sofia's neck. A regrettable accident, she called it." Her restless fingers fidgeted as she placed the jewels in intricate patterns on Galina's forehead. "And how was I *rewarded* for my sister's murder? By being elevated to her former station and taken on a diplomatic expedition to Liesgau, where Sera was conducting some unsavory dealings. She tried bribing me for information, but money was hardly necessary. I want to see the empress destroyed, and I want my freedom."

Ekaterina stepped back, her task complete.

Galina rose from the chair. "And how long have you been in your position?"

"Six years, as of yesterday." Ekaterina slid the little case into her dress pocket. "So I'm counting on you, Galina Feodorovna. My time is running out."

Galina let out a breath. "Call me Galya in private. If we're going to be working together."

Ekaterina's lips curved into a genuine smile. "Then I'm Katya."

A spark of warmth kindled in Galina's chest. "Katya and Galya it is."

As they strode through the opulent corridors of the palace, sentries flanked them on either side, their armor clanking with each step. Attendants rushed past, hurrying to their places in the servants' colonnade. *Obryad* brought the country to a standstill; even the lowliest palace servants stopped their chores to watch the ceremony.

The air was thick with the pungent scent of incense, the din of voices echoing through the halls. Galina's skirts brushed against the marble floor as she descended the ornate staircase from the Royal Wing. The gilt-adorned walls and portraits of alurean royals loomed over her, their unblinking eyes following her every move.

Hemmed in by sentries, Galina struggled to suppress her unease as she neared the gauzy curtain veiling the empress's balcony. The dense smoke invaded her lungs, while the chanting coiled around her in eerie song.

Then a thunderous roar shook the walls. Galina instinctively gripped Katya's arm for support, and the handmaiden nudged her forward, reminding her of the task at hand.

Galina hardly recalled the final ascent when Empress Isidora appeared before her.

The monarch's white gown draped like a regal mantle, heavy with diamonds that sparkled with the brilliance of distant stars. Delicate threads of gold snaked across the fabric like liquid fire, shimmering and dancing in the flickering torchlight. Seed pearls adorned the garment and headdress, their iridescence reminiscent of morning dew on freshly bloomed flowers.

She was a vision of winter personified, with an aura that chilled the surrounding air.

"She's late, Ekaterina Isidorakh." The monarch's piercing gaze flickered over Galina with a scrutiny that made her skin crawl. "She was supposed to be here five minutes ago."

Katya lowered her head in submission, but Galina squared her shoulders and stepped forward. Six years, Katya had said—the longest of any handmaiden since her sister. And one minor error was all it took to end up with a snapped neck.

I am not a girl cowering in the darkness.

Not anymore.

"My apologies, Your Holiness," Galina said, her voice steady and firm. "I take full responsibility for the delay. I'm not accustomed to such splendor."

The empress's expression remained inscrutable. "Hmm." She gestured for Katya to sit by the gauze drapes. Then, addressing Galina again, she said, "Wait here until I've finished the hymn. You'll appear and use a light demonstration of godpower. Nothing more."

"Yes, Your Holiness."

She watched as the empress disappeared behind the curtains, the audience beyond erupting into frenzied applause as Isidora began to sing.

Galina's god stirred, sensing a nearby rival zmeya of equal power. It pulsed with energy, godpower brewing just beneath her skin. Galina closed her eyes, calming the dragon until it settled back within her.

Katya's soft hand on her arm jolted her out of her trance.

The hymn had ended, and it was time for Galina to appear before the crowd.

Katya swept aside the curtain, revealing the sprawling vista of the royal balcony, and gently nudged Galina forward.

The crowd's roar nearly pushed her off her feet. The thunderous applause jarred deep into her bones, leaving her numb as she gazed at the thousands of people below. They were calling for—calling for—

Vmonkt pror va. The common god.

Galina's fingers tightened around the balustrade as the weight of that simple phrase bore down on her shoulders. She had never considered what sharing her god with the world would mean. To stop hiding.

She had concealed herself for so long that she didn't know what it meant to exist in the light.

Sera. Are you out there? Are you seeing this?

Empress Isidora's hand gripped the back of her dress, sinking her fingernails in. The monarch's voice was bitter as she spoke. "Listen to them clamoring for you. Never forget that these supplicants are capricious creatures. You're like a glass bauble tossed into the street; they'd shatter you without remorse. It's our purpose to break them first and remind them they live only to serve us. Remember this: you're not one of them."

12

SERA

Sera's heart leaped as Galina emerged onto the balcony, the crowd's cheers drowning out the beat of her pulse.

Bathed in the early morning light, her gown shimmered like a million stars against the dark sky, a dazzling display that stole Sera's breath. Galina seemed a creature born of shadow and starlight, celestial and out of reach.

That dress was a message from the empress to the masses: *she does not belong to you.*

She is not one of you.

Sera couldn't give two shits about the damn gown. It was a fancy mask, a false front. All that mattered was keeping her sister safe. Had the empress hurt her? Had she kept Galina rotting away in some dingy dungeon for a month, tormented by sentries?

Sera's mind raced with endless questions, like a nervous wreck of a parent. It didn't matter that Galina was a survivor in her own right; they had been through too much together, saved each other's lives countless times.

And Sera missed her sister.

She appraised Galina with a critical eye, noting the pinched look on her face and the deathly pallor of her skin. Her gaze lingered on the white-knuckled grip on the balustrade. Each observation was an infraction of her care, a tally Sera would keep for revenge.

The mob shouted, their voices blending into a cacophonous din as they clamored for a display of power from their Common God. Sera watched as Empress Isidora touched Galina's back.

Galina went rigid.

The gesture may have appeared benevolent to an outsider, but Sera was no novice to such subtleties. That touch was a warning.

Sera's thoughts were a fierce snarl that could have put a wild beast to shame: *Get away from my sister.*

She stepped forward, disregarding the crowd's demands and chants, all those bodies surrounding her. Her focus was on Galina.

But then her senses ignited as Vitaly's breath caressed her ear, the soft timbre of his words like a tendril of smoke. "I know you're imagining murder, Sera."

Sera didn't correct him. "So are you."

"I'm always thinking of killing them," Vitaly whispered, barely audible above the tumult. "Every last one. I won't spare their Common God, either."

The cold of the Blackshore could never compare to his voice. It was as if the bleak winds had blown straight through him and into her. She knew the darkness within him, a bottomless well of anger and hatred.

He was a ticking bomb, a danger to Galina and anyone who stood in his way.

With a sharp turn of her head, Sera averted her gaze. "Keep those thoughts to yourself," she murmured. "Do you want the empress to burn you alive?"

Vitaly bared his teeth in a feral smile. "Killing me won't stop the next uprising, *vorovka*. Martyrs breed more revolutionaries than criminals," he said, his old endearment slipping from his lips without permission. It made her think of nights with him spent in hot, tangled sheets.

Her face hardened. "Don't call me that."

Vitaly's smile vanished, his silver irises like blades newly sharpened. "Disown me, claim you're not mine, and want nothing to do with me—but I'll never forget my vows. They're true from the moment I met you to the day I rot in the ground, *vorovka pro fse ku*."

Vorovka pro fse ku. Thief of my heart.

Her breath caught in her throat. But before Sera could answer, a solitary figure shouted from the throng: "*Murderers! Tyrants! Kill the empress!*"

A man advanced through the gathering crowds, his cry echoing through the square and gaining more force. The crowd responded with a rising swell of stunned murmurs.

"*Murderers! Tyrants! Kill the empress!*"

Sera craned her neck to glimpse the agitator, but he remained shrouded in the throng. All she could hear were his words, cutting through the chaos like a knife.

Vitaly's fingers curled around her arm. "We should go."

But Sera was motionless, focused on the scene unfolding before her. The empress's guards closed in on the rebel.

Vitaly tightened his grip. "*Serafima*."

"He's one of yours," Sera said urgently, as Vitaly steered her through the masses. "Isn't he?"

Vitaly disregarded her question. "Come with me *now*."

But Sera resisted, watching the alurean guard use a blast of godpower that stole all breath from the traitor's lungs. He gasped and crumpled to the ground in anguish.

The man convulsed, eyes bulging from their sockets as the zmeya's power choked him. Veins stood out in stark relief along his neck, his skin taking on a sickly shade of blue. His hand clawed at his throat to pry the invisible fingers of death from his windpipe.

Martyrs breed more revolutionaries than criminals.

Sera spun to face Vitaly with a snarl. "You are *unbelievable.*"

Galina rushed down the balcony stairs with a shout that mirrored Sera's thoughts: *Stop!*

Sera's blood roared in her ears as she watched the dissenter yank a metal object from his coat. Too far away for worshippers to see, but Sera identified it instantly.

And she knew exactly who the bomb was meant for.

Galina.

Vitaly pulled Sera into a crushing embrace a split second before the explosive detonated.

She braced herself for the worst, but the blast was muffled. Sera's eyes snapped open to witness Galina standing with her arms spread wide. Power crackled at her fingertips, casting a jagged incandescent light over the would-be assassin. The atmosphere hummed with charged energy, like a storm on the verge of breaking.

Galina's shield held fast, but the energy sizzled and surged, threatening to erupt from its invisible confines. Sera watched, transfixed, as the illumination cast Galina's face in stark relief.

And then, with a last burst of spectral light, the air settled, leaving the stunned crowd in its wake. A guard steadied Galina as she released the barrier and swayed on her feet.

Sera cursed under her breath. "Let me go," she snarled, wrenching free from Vitaly's embrace.

A moment later, worshippers rushed forward, shouting for the Common God again. They beat at the palace gates as sentries ushered Galina away, and votives were held aloft in the hazy sky. The assassin had failed in his task.

When Sera looked back, Vitaly had vanished.

13

GALINA

A sentry caught Galina before she could fall.

His fingers dug into her arm as he yanked her away from the commotion. She was barely aware of being dragged through the palace and into her room in the Royal Wing. The door shut behind the guard with a click that reverberated through her bones.

Galina collapsed to the floor, breath coming in ragged gasps.

Too loud.

Too fast.

Her god clawed through her mind. Whispers slithered through her thoughts, invading every corner of her consciousness. A hard scrape of scales beneath her flesh reminded her that her body was not hers.

Galina yearned for the silence that enveloped her in Dolsk, the emptiness that had been her refuge. Her fingers twitched with phantom need, searching for the cool comfort of a bottle.

(You'll be nothing again. A coward trembling in dark sheets, hiding from the world.)

She knocked her head against the wall. "Stop it," she whispered, trying to put those thoughts back into the ruins of her old homes where they belonged. "*Stop it.*"

The words echoed through her mind, taunting and pushing her further into the darkness. Galina clenched her fists, biting back a sob as the memories of Dolsk and Olensk washed over her. Ruined buildings and blood on the streets.

The zmeya scratched again, scales and wings grinding under her flesh.

She bit her tongue and slammed her head into the wall once more. Tasted copper. Repeated it.

Galina welcomed the ache, the clarity of it. In the absence of liquor, she would take the numbness of torment. It was the path she would follow to sink into an abyss. Where it was quiet and pitch-dark, and—

"You shouldn't be here," a harsh voice said, jolting Galina back to awareness.

Her eyes flew open to see a woman she didn't recognize. A dim lantern illuminated the woman's face, her delicate features framed by wavy black hair. Her irises were pale like a winter sea and her expression burned with disapproval.

Galina's senses were on high alert as she took in the unfamiliar surroundings. Darkness veiled the chamber, with only a solitary lamp casting its ghostly brightness. The air was heavy with the cloying scent of an unknown fragrance.

"Where am I?" Galina asked.

The woman slowly sat back on her heels with a dubious look. "You don't know?"

Galina bristled at the condescension in the woman's tone, but she couldn't deny the unease that had settled in her chest. "I was in my room a moment ago. I shut my eyes and—"

"Opened a door into my bedchamber?" The woman scanned her harshly. "A rare gift, that. The only other alurea at Zolotiye with that godpower is the empress and *me*."

Galina's nerves were as taut as a bowstring; she knew all too well that drawing suspicion could mean a death sentence. She'd never open a portal without good reason—*never* risk her and Sera's mission unless she had to. But there she was, with no recollection of her god using its godpower to lead her here.

She quickly tried to come up with an excuse. "I couldn't have," she said. "I have to picture the place in my mind, and I've never even been here."

"Mm." The woman leaned in closer in interest. "What did you see when you closed your eyes?"

Galina shook her head. She wasn't about to divulge her innermost thoughts to a stranger. How much she missed the taste of liquor, the deafening stillness of her apartment in Dolsk, the darkness that swaddled her in its embrace. All these were the things she'd clung to in her mind, using pain as a makeshift anchor in a world that threatened to drag her under.

She replied with a curt, "I don't remember."

The other woman clearly didn't believe her, but her attention fell on Galina's gown with amusement. "If you were planning on sneaking around my private wing, you could have dressed for the occasion."

My private wing.

Galina's breath caught as she studied the woman's face. The dark hair, the fragile beauty that concealed a deep reservoir of power, the sharp glint in her eyes—all too familiar. Features this woman shared with the monarch she hated.

"Your Imperial Highness," she murmured, using the distinct form of address for the empress's only daughter. Dread was a heavy stone in her chest. "I'm sorry I didn't recognize you."

I didn't ask for that godpower, she snapped to her dragon. *And now you might have killed us both.*

The god seethed in silence over the direction of her previous thoughts—her craving for the alcohol that had silenced it for years.

I'm sorry, she wanted to tell it. *I'm sorry for all those years. I wish they didn't tempt me back. I couldn't handle the things we did.*

(*You mean you're too weak to handle the things you did.*)

Vasilisa lifted an eyebrow, and a devious smirk spread across her lips. "Tell the truth," she said. "Did you really stumble here by chance, or were you hoping to catch a glimpse of the mysterious, cloistered princess?"

Galina swallowed. Princess Vasilisa had eyes as sharp as a rapier, even when she smiled.

"By chance, Your Imperial Highness," Galina answered.

A chill passed over the princess's features, her amusement vanishing. "I don't need fancy titles and flattery. Why do you think I choose to live as a recluse?"

She pushed to her feet—swaying slightly—and reached for the knob on the wall.

Lamps hissed to life, and Galina blinked hard against the sudden brightness. Her gaze shifted from the dazzling lights to the surroundings of the chamber. It was not as grandiose as the rest of Zolotiye, but it was opulent in its own way, with a ceiling swathed in an intricate floral tapestry and walls cocooned in lush, emerald velvet drapes. The air was still and heavy, with a sense of serenity that seemed to seclude the room from the world. Galina's god had brought her here for a reason, and it was clear that Princess Vasilisa shared the same desire for isolation and solitude.

Princess Vasilisa's gaze brushed over Galina, her regard as frigid as the remote wing of the palace. "You're Galina Feodorovna. My mother's new guest." Something must have shown in Galina's expression because the princess's lips lifted in amusement. "Ah. Prisoner, then. Well, you wouldn't be the first."

She forced her body to remain still. "Her Imperial Majesty has been very kind."

The princess's lips flattened. "I'll have to reconsider my impression of you. I thought you might have given the truth about coming here by accident. But that lie was so convincing, I almost believed it."

She snapped her mouth shut, realizing how perceptive the empress's daughter was. It was probably for the best that she was ensconced in the distant corner of Zolotiye, far from Galina and her deceit.

She rose to her feet, the ceremonial dress suddenly so heavy that it bent her bones. "I—I don't—"

I don't know how to speak to you. And that terrifies me.

"Wait," Vasilisa said, letting out a breath. "I'm sorry. It's been a while since I've had guests." She offered a faint smile. "Would you like tea?"

"Tea?" Galina echoed in confusion.

"I seem to recall it's customary to offer someone a drink. I won't kill you if you decline." When Galina hesitated, Vasilisa sighed. "Just say *'decline.'*"

Her body remained rigid, but she replied with caution, "Decline."

Galina scanned the room, trying to make sense of the princess's brash informality. A tottering stack of leather-bound volumes sat near an outsized armchair that shouted comfort over pomp. Each was titled in Grand Imperial or some regional dialect from Sundyr—a few even in languages she knew from her life as a fugitive.

When Princess Vasilisa caught her studying the tomes in interest, Galina quickly said, "I'm sorry for the loss of your father." The lie came so easily.

Vasilisa pried open a jar and spoke with a hint of bitterness. "Do they still think I'm shut away here wallowing in grief, incapable of donning a dress and performing for them like a pet on a lead?"

Galina became motionless. "I—yes, they do."

She was so taken aback by the princess's answer that she couldn't speak. She was familiar with the delicate act of submission to the empress, but the princess was an enigma—a missing piece in the grand tapestry of brutal alurean royalty she'd grown accustomed to in the palace.

Galina didn't trust it. Alurean words were as honeyed as a toxin, smiles as warm as winter frost. Every courtier was a skilled liar.

The princess filled a teapot with the jar's contents. "The entire country mourned the loss of their emperor," she said, "but you can't convince me a single person grieved the man." She lifted her gaze. "Are you sure you don't want any tea? I didn't put any poison in it. I only reserve my deadly mixtures for special occasions and extremely irritating people."

Galina was unable to craft an intelligible response. Her world had shifted onto its side. If Vasilisa hadn't withdrawn from the public to grieve her father, why was she still sequestered within these walls? Why did she remain hidden away like some sort of secret? Rumors claimed she had explored Sundyr as a youth—yet here she remained.

Galina's knuckles whitened. "I should return to my room before—"

"Yes, you need to go back to your nicely furnished prison cell before someone realizes you can escape," the woman said. "I won't tell anyone, I promise."

"Thank you for the offer of tea," Galina replied with forced civility. She was already bracing for the empress's punishment, not trusting this woman to keep her word for a moment.

Princess Vasilisa set down the pot and picked a dainty teacup from her collection. "If our paths cross again, you don't have to speak to me like a servant. If I cared about etiquette, I wouldn't be here brewing my own damn tea."

Galina's muscles tensed as she summoned every ounce of strength to bend the godpower to her will and create the door. When the slash of a portal cleaved the room from floor to ceiling, she sighed with relief. Usually, the power drained her, but she was eager to be rid of the princess's company; the woman had shaken her composure. It was like teetering on the brink of a precipice: every muscle tense, every nerve on edge.

One false step from plummeting into the abyss.

But as she was about to walk through the passage, Vasilisa's voice rang out behind her.

"Galina Feodorovna?" Galina stopped in her tracks, the princess's voice like a saber slicing through the air. "If you ever set foot in my chamber again without an invitation, I have over a hundred ways to poison you." Her lips curled into a sly smile. "Have a wonderful evening."

14

SERA

Sera looked up in relief as Anna stormed into the study.

Finding her friend in the chaotic aftermath of the bombing had been a hopeless task. So Sera returned to the tunnels, fueled by a fresh wave of anger at Vitaly's fucking audacity.

She clenched her teeth as she thought of her sister being killed and their carefully laid plans destroyed. Galina's godpower had given them a brief reprieve, but it was only a matter of time before Vitaly struck again. He was a cunning and ruthless opponent, constantly devising new strategies. So Sera gathered Irina's supplies and began laying the groundwork for their next move.

Anna's boots echoed against the stone floor, her eyes flashing with rage as she approached Sera's desk.

"I swear to the gods," Anna growled, fists clenched tight. "If that bastard at *obryad* was one of Vitaly Sergeyevich's men, I'll track him down and shove my fist into his face. Innocent people could have been blown to bits."

Sera didn't flinch at the thunder in her friend's voice. "It was," she replied, setting down her pen. "I could barely keep myself from taking a dagger to this writing paper."

Anna paced around in frustration. "What was that lunatic *thinking?*"

"Thinking? He doesn't do that." Sera set her jaw. "He wanted Galina out of the way. People seem to like her, and that makes her a threat to his plans."

"You have abysmal taste in men, Serafima Mikhailovna," Anna huffed. "Aren't there any strapping blacksmiths in this city? Ones with arms thicker than tree trunks who can break boulders with their bare hands? You had to choose the murderous cutthroat?"

Sera slouched in her chair, her face a mask of self-disgust. "I was a young, horny idiot who couldn't resist the temptation of a gorgeous, bloodthirsty assassin who let me climb his body like a mountain every night."

Anna blinked several times. "Wait. Did you say *every night?*"

"Every single night," Sera said bitterly. "And some mornings too."

Anna gave a low whistle. "Well, damn me. All right then. Fair enough."

Sera straightened with determination. "But things are different now. I need to know where he's manufacturing explosives. Have your contacts in the Black locate his supply route—we'll make sure they're unusable."

"I'll ask Emil, but he won't have it for a few days."

"Days?" They didn't have that kind of time.

"Emil is in direct contact with Vitaly Sergeyevich's second-in-command," Anna said. "So he's already putting himself at risk by agreeing to help us. But if you're desperate, you could always climb your assassin like a tree or a mountain or whatever other structure strikes your fancy," Anna added with a smirk.

Sera scowled at that idea. "Vitalik is suspicious after seeing me at *obryad* twice." She let out a breath. "We'll wait for Emil—tell him I owe him."

"No," Anna replied firmly. "He's only doing this because he trusts me, and I promised him your plan would result in fewer dead bodies. Don't make a liar out of me."

"The day I make a liar out of you is the day I die," Sera said. "If my plan fails, I'll be on the execution platform like every failed rebel."

Anna said nothing as she scanned Sera's desk. The surface was littered with vials containing over a hundred substances and components she'd acquired from Irina's stash—all necessary to summon the alurean gods.

"Any success with Irina's notes?"

Sera stared down at the crumpled pages and her notations in ink. "I cracked them—her cipher kept changing, and she used a unique encryption for each step of the process, but I put something together that might work."

"*Might?*"

Sera rubbed her weary eyes, trying to block out the memories flooding her mind. She glanced at her desk, where a collection of vessels lay scattered. "Irina never recorded the quantities," she said with a sigh. "She didn't get the chance to experiment before she died."

Anna lifted a glass tube with an encrypted label Sera had transcribed, reading: *Extract From Praepeurbu Scilot.*

"Your mother used these to summon the god?"

Sera nodded, remembering the agony of needles punching into her skin and the screaming torment of the dragon ripping her apart piece by piece.

She'd barely survived the summoning that had dragged her zmeya from Smokova and bound it to her body.

A god who loathed her—and a mistake.

All that pain, and for what? A mother who couldn't look at her daughter without seeing a failure. Cursed to a life bound to a monster that tormented her.

She picked up a vial from the table. "This is *spunc peurbu.* Injected in lethal doses, it'll make your bones as fragile as glass.

When paired with *praepeurbu scilot*, those shattered bones are slowly reconstructed, creating the perfect cage to trap the god. Alurea are born with bodies designed to hold their zmei. Summoning a god into an unprepared vessel kills the host within minutes."

Anna's eyes widened. "It *what?*"

Sera shuffled her notes, hiding her past behind a dispassionate expression. "Irina told me the archives at the old university were filled with accounts of failed early alurean trials. Thousands of years ago, some nobles planned to imprison zmei in human bodies and use their godpower to overthrow the king. The first alurea were just commoners rounded up for the experiments. Most didn't make it, but those who did murdered their oppressors, and now their descendants are the current ruling assholes."

Calm anger descended over her friend's features. "And your mother risked killing two kids?"

"Children have a better chance of surviving," Sera said bitterly. "Since they're still growing."

Anna's blue eyes iced over. "I don't give a damn. If that woman was still alive, I'd drag her sorry ass to the Dark Sea, throw her in, and watch the beasts tear her apart."

Sera forced a smirk. "You and your grudges. Never a dull moment."

"If she weren't dead, my grudges would be put to better use," Anna said. "But I'll give her ashes an urn so that I can spit on them. Now, tell me everything else she did."

Sera had kept her anger for too long; it became as permanent as the marks on her bones.

She cleared the sudden thickness in her throat, reaching for a vial. "*Coe pau*," she breathed. "Irina carved deep incisions into our bones and injected ink-like metal to recreate the natural summoning marks alurea are born with. It's what they originally used to call the zmei from Smokova, trap them and force the bond. Irina copied ancient alurean markings to summon a specific deity, but messed up my etchings. My god was a mistake."

Her zmeya rumbled inside her, a sound that could have been agreement or dissent or even a straightforward "go fuck yourself"—impossible to tell.

Anna held the vial of *praepeurbu scilot* in her hands and muttered a soft curse under her breath. "How long did it take?"

"Months," Sera softly replied. "Three for Galina, but it felt like an eternity for me."

The brutal process had battered Sera and Galina until they were teetering on the brink of death. And yet, Irina was always there, ready to plunge another treatment deep into their flesh to keep the torment alive.

Irina could be just as monstrous as the alurea she'd sought to destroy.

"I didn't know," Anna said, shaking her head. "When I worked for your mother, gathering information—"

"No one knew. She kept it that way." Then, with a heavy sigh, Sera shoved aside her mother's notes. "I need to test this serum on myself before I give it to Galina. Will you inject it for me?"

Sera slid the syringe across the desk, its contents concealed beneath its hood. She leaned back, saying nothing. Galina's life hung in the balance.

Anna's eyes flew open. "You can't be serious. You want me to jab you with a possibly fatal draught? No."

"If you don't, I'm shoving this needle in myself. I think you'll be gentler." Sera handed Anna the medical supply kit.

Anna's glare could have burned the walls black. But she took the kit and withdrew the disinfectant with grim acceptance. "Shouldn't you at least attempt to figure out how much you need before you make me do this?"

"There's no other way to test it." Sera spoke with a hard edge, born of a thousand trials. This wouldn't do anything to her she hadn't already endured.

Anna began disinfecting Sera's arm. "If this kills you..."

Sera inclined her head. "You can have my entire fortune. I'm sure my collection of seashells and spare buttons will fetch a fine price."

"Serafima Mikhailovna, you're not funny." Anna rolled her eyes. "Tell me what this is *supposed* to do."

"On me? Very little. My mother designed it for Galina to receive the power increase necessary to manage the lustrate." She watched as Anna prepped the syringe. "I might get a slight benefit in my abilities."

Anna hesitated, the needle hovering near Sera's skin. "And if it doesn't go according to plan?"

"Well," Sera said, her gaze on the ceiling, "I may or may not suffer a horrible, excruciating death."

"*Sera.*"

Sera smiled at her friend. "Inject the panacea, Anya. I'm not planning on dying today."

15

GALINA

A maid rushed into Galina's room, clutching a pristine white box. "A gift for you, Your Radiance," she panted, dropping into a curtsy.

Galina winced at the title. No matter how often she reminded the palace staff to drop the honorific when alone, they persisted in addressing her like an alurean courtier. She was a damn prisoner, for gods' sake.

"From Her Imperial Majesty?" Galina asked, taking the box from the maid.

For days, she'd braced for the guards to kick down the door and drag her away for creating a doorway into Princess Vasilisa's private chambers. But nothing had happened. Were the empress and her daughter toying with her, waiting for her to let her guard down before striking? Offering up gifts with deadly snakes or something equally vicious hidden inside?

"Don't believe so, Your Radiance," the maid replied.

Galina frowned. It couldn't be from Sera. The guards scrutinized any packages entering the palace from outside. Katya was the only one who could smuggle anything in or out.

She put the box on the table and lifted the lid, revealing a silver tea set engraved with dainty rosebuds. Accompanying the collection was a jar filled with leaves, herbs, and petals.

Holding her breath, Galina slid open the envelope with the tiny note, her heart racing with anticipation.

Since you didn't stay for tea, I made you a poison-free blend from my glasshouse as a token of apology for my earlier threat. In hindsight, joking about killing you was maybe in poor taste. If you can't boil water in your prison cell, ask your zmeya to use its godpower. Sometimes, it even listens. —Vasilisa

Galina bit back a snort of laughter. Princess Vasilisa had sent her tea.

Princess Vasilisa *made* her tea.

"Thank you for bringing this," Galina said, returning the items to the package.

She'd have to get rid of the note—it was a liability.

But the thought of tossing it out was as unthinkable as keeping it.

Another knock interrupted her deliberation, and Katya entered the room, all pleasantries and smiles. "Please see to your other duties," she said to the maid. Katya glanced at the gift. "Anything of interest?"

Galina covered it up before Katya could study it further, pocketing the missive. "Just from the empress," she lied, keeping the details of her chance encounter with Princess Vasilisa to herself. She couldn't make sense of the feelings the princess had stirred in her. "How's the empress responding to the bomb during *obryad?*"

Katya's expression darkened as she retrieved something from her pocket. "She's increasing Blackshore guards to arrest anyone suspected of being involved with the faithless." She passed Galina a delicate, crumpled piece of paper. "This is from Sera."

Galina took the note, which was small enough to fit into one of the counterfeit coins they used for communication.

First panacea finished. Have Galya open a door.

Galina tried not to let the flicker of hope inside her chest turn into a raging bonfire. The panacea might not even work, and then she'd be right back where she started.

With a flick of her wrist, she set the note ablaze, unwilling to take chances with such sensitive information. The letter from the princess still burned a hole in her pocket.

"Make sure the staff and guards are busy," Galina said. "I'll only be gone a few hours."

She used her godpower to open the door to the tunnels. Galina's intimate knowledge of the annex meant that every inch was ingrained in her memory—the stone walls, the freezing floor that made her teeth chatter regardless of the temperature outside, and the Zverti graffiti etched on the walls.

She navigated toward Irina's study, where her sister occupied the desk, surrounded by books, scattered notes, and a disorderly array of vials and jars. Her frown of concentration disappeared when she looked up.

"Galya." Sera swiftly rose from her chair and rushed over.

Galina collapsed into her sister's embrace, inhaling the familiar aroma of smoke and chemicals that clung to her. It was only a moment of solace, but Galina treasured every second.

Sera pulled back, scrutinizing Galina's face. "You're all right?"

"As well as can be expected," she replied softly.

Sera's piercing gaze swept over Galina. "The empress hasn't touched you, has she? Because I'll crash through her palace gates and murder her in her sleep. Just ask."

A grin tugged at Galina's lips. "What then?"

"We escape into the night like a couple of idiots?"

Galina permitted herself a snort of amusement. "The empress hasn't hurt me. But *someone* tried to blow me up," she said, lifting her eyebrow.

"I'm well aware of that," Sera grumbled.

"Oh, good. Because I couldn't help but notice that the bomb was one of yours."

Sera let out a heavy sigh. "I'm still trying to locate Vitaly's arsenal of explosives. But in the meantime..." She strode over to the desk and snatched up Irina's journal. "Irina's ciphers have been a pain in my ass, but I've finally cracked them all."

Galina leaned over the surface, surveying the chaotic sprawl of ink, paper fragments, and rejected ideas scattered around. "Your message said you had a dose of the panacea?" Sera nodded, but Galina caught her hesitation. "What's the matter?"

Her sister's expression smoothed over. "Nothing. I might have had more to work with if Irina had survived longer. As it is, I've scavenged enough ingredients from her old stash, but I'll be honest. I have no idea what I'm doing."

Galina groaned and rubbed the back of her neck. "Oh," she muttered. "So how confident are you this won't kill me?"

Sera shrugged. "I tested it on myself a few days ago, and I'm not lying here in a pool of my own piss and blood, so that's a point in my favor."

Sera kept her tone light, but Galina recoiled all the same. The risk her sister had taken for her was staggering—what would have happened if the remedy had failed? How could Galina mourn from within Zolotiye's halls, with the empress watching her every move?

"Don't give me that face," Sera chided softly, with a touch of affection seeping through her words. "It had to be done. It was practical. You can't be the only one taking risks."

Galina shook her head, trying to contain her fury. "You injecting yourself and risking your life for me isn't practical. It's *reckless*! What if it killed you?"

"Do I look dead to you?" Sera challenged. At Galina's withering glare, Sera relented. "Fine, it was reckless. So what will it be? Do you want the panacea or not?"

The question hung in the air like a blade poised to strike. She couldn't decide whether to hug her sister or throttle her. Sera met Galina's gaze with an unflinching stare, but the silence was brittle, a sense of vulnerability lurking under the surface.

Galina loosed a ragged breath, the sound like a prayer whispered into the void. "Fine," she said reluctantly. She wouldn't let Sera take chances for no reason. "Let's get this over with."

Sera guided her to the center of the room, where a leather chair loomed like a vengeful throne. But Galina's steps faltered, fear rising like bile in her throat. A chasm of terror opened beneath her feet, threatening to swallow her whole. She wrenched her arm from Sera's grasp and fought for control.

"We have to use the chair," Sera murmured, her voice sympathetic. "There's nowhere to secure you if your zmeya has a bad reaction."

Sera knew the torment of Irina's chair all too well, its straps squeezing tight around flesh as different serums brought fresh waves of agony. If Sera felt it was necessary, then so did she.

Still, a tremor rippled through Galina's body as she settled into the seat, memories of endless suffering flooding back. She had endured months of pain shackled to that chair, her wrists and ankles bruised and raw.

Anywhere else, she wanted to say. *Anywhere else.*

The stench of leather and metal filled her nostrils. She closed her eyes and took a deep breath, trying to steady herself. It wasn't Irina this time. It was just Sera and Galina.

And this time, she was not weak.

"Galya?" Sera said gently into the haze of terror.

Galina looked up at Sera, determination painted across her face like battle scars. "I'm ready," she said, no trace of shake or quiver in her tone.

Sera's fingers worked deftly, fastening the straps around Galina's wrists. The bindings were snug, holding her firmly in place. Galina could feel her heart racing, a drumbeat of panic building in her chest. She pressed her head back into the chair, trying to calm herself.

Her sister's touch was a balm to her frayed nerves, gentle where Irina's had been harsh and unforgiving. She had never asked for permission, only demanded obedience.

As Sera pushed up the sleeve of Galina's dress and disinfected her skin, Galina's voice shook. "What's in your panacea?"

"The same base ingredients Irina used to summon our deities," Sera said, prepping the injection. "It imitates and augments the power surge alurea experience during childhood. When your god was bonded to Empress Maria, lustration came to her in maturity."

Galina nodded in understanding. As alurea grew older, the bond between zmei and their hosts intensified, and they became more adept at withstanding the immense force of godpower. Most alurea had one primary ability, but some commanded multiple gifts, with godpower so potent it remained latent until their bodies could handle it.

She watched Sera tug the needle from her vial, its tip glistening with a drop of crimson-hued liquid. "And if this doesn't work?"

Her sister chose her words carefully. "It might increase your existing abilities. Your godfire may become more powerful than Empress Isidora's at half her age." She hesitated. "Last chance to change your mind."

Galina let out a bitter chuckle that seemed to echo off the dingy walls. "Are you already regretting our plan? You're not still thinking about taking up goat husbandry, are you?"

"Goat husbandry is out of the question. Anna told me they're escape artists and reasoned I'd probably eat them all in spite."

"And here I had such grand ambitions for you."

"Galya." Sera's voice grew quiet, the joviality of the moment evaporating into the damp air.

Galina sighed, the weight of their mission heavy on her shoulders. "No turning back now," she said, nodding toward her arm, silently granting permission for the injection.

As Sera gingerly took hold of Galina, their eyes locked in a shared understanding. "For Dolsk," Sera whispered.

Galina steeled herself for the agony to come. "For Olensk."

Their voices merged: "For us."

Sera pushed the needle into Galina's skin.

Galina's mastery over pain was honed by the scars left in Olensk. It was her sword and shield against anyone who dared to break her. The battlefield was set, the ultimate test of her willpower versus her ailing body. But she refused to surrender. Her anger became her fuel, a conflagration that devoured everything.

"Galya?" A voice pierced through the haze, beckoning her to the present. "*Galya!*"

Galina took hold of her sister's hand, squeezing it tightly to convey the moment's urgency.

Wait. Let me take care of this.

She embraced the wrath, channeling her rage until it overpowered her fear. Memories of Olensk and Dolsk ignited within her. Every time Irina turned her into a weapon. But not now. Not anymore. The zmeya's influence flowed through her, a molten force filling her heart and expanding her chest until her bones ached.

Endure.

Survive.

Galina's senses exploded to life as she gasped for breath, finding herself submerged in a tub of ice-cold water. Iron hands clamped down on her shoulders, holding her in place.

"No, stay in there," Sera said sharply. "You scared me shitless."

Galina's mind was still foggy from her sudden awakening, but her body was anything but. Naked and marbled with the chill of the water, she could feel her god's restlessness, the raw energy seeping through every inch of her skin. Was it in pain? Its scales scratched beneath her flesh, wings stretching, searching for room where there was none.

"I don't feel any different," she whispered, raising her gaze to meet Sera's. "But my god is restless, and I think it's hurt. I'm not sure it worked."

"Damn it," Sera muttered, slumping down beside the tub. "I should have—"

"No," Galina cut her off, firm with conviction. She shook her head fiercely, water droplets cascading off her hair. "Don't you dare doubt yourself now. What time is it?"

"After sundown," Sera replied, her voice heavy with worry.

Swearing, Galina rose from the freezing tub, shivering as cold air lapped against her naked skin. The underground annex's water closet was constructed of drafty stone and offered no warmth or sanctuary.

"I have to get back to Zolotiye," she said, blotting herself dry with a towel Sera had provided. "I've been gone too long."

As Galina pulled on her undergarments, Sera spoke up again. "I can't predict how this serum will affect you over the next few days. You may need a reversal agent."

"Your time is better spent creating a fresh panacea."

"Screw a new panacea," Sera snarled, eyes narrowing. "What do you think matters more to me? This stupid mission, or you?"

Galina went still, struck by the sincerity in her sister's words. Irina had never given them that kind of reassurance; the plan always came first. But it had forged an unbreakable bond between Galina and Sera, built on a foundation of whispered secrets and midnight promises.

"I know," she replied. "But Katya will send word if anything happens."

Sera softened at Galina's response. "I was thinking earlier that I miss us living in Dolsk. The quiet, the routine..."

Galina let out a chuckle. "You just miss being a recluse in the woods, tending to your little garden."

"Well, yes," Sera said. "But I wouldn't mind having some boredom in my life again. I'm always here working to keep you safe from being assassinated by my ex-lover and trying not to get us *both* killed with my own stupidity."

Galina tightened her grip on Sera's hand as warmth surged through her body. "*Zdo vitsvi to,*" she whispered tenderly. "I love you too."

16

SERA

Sera barricaded herself in the study for two straight days, her eyes glued to her mother's notes as she worked to concoct a reversal agent for the botched panacea. The failed serum hadn't hit her as hard as Galina, but she still felt like a steaming pile of gut-rot. Anna finally convinced Sera to take a break and shot her up with the antidote, but not before fussing over her like a grandmother.

The next day, Anna barged in, waving a newspaper. "Your gorgeous, bloodthirsty assassin is on the front page."

Sera grunted without looking up. "He's not mine in any way, shape, or fucking form."

Anna gave her a pointed stare and flung the broadsheet at her. Sera caught it one-handed, her other hand cramping from hours of scribbling possible ingredient combinations on scraps of paper. Then she looked and immediately wished she hadn't.

FAITHLESS GROUP CLAIMS ATTACK ON ALUREAN COURTIER. The Blackshore Courier received a message today from an anonymous faithless leader claiming responsibility for the attempted assassination of a new alurean courtier.

The palace is working to increase security measures in response. The public is urged to stay vigilant and report any suspicious activity to the alurean authorities.

Sera's rage grew with every word she read. She slammed it down on the table, her knuckles turning white as she clenched her fists.

"That daft bastard," she spat. She got up, grabbing her coat from the back of the chair and shrugging it on.

"He's going to get himself executed," Anna said. "The palace doubled the number of guards patrolling the city, and they've already arrested people for using Zverti in public."

Sera wrapped a thick scarf around her neck. "Get in touch with Emil again," she ordered, referring to Anna's informant. "If he has any information on where Vitaly's making his bombs, I want to know about it."

Anna nodded. "And you? What are you going to do?"

"See if I can talk some sense into him."

Sera stormed through the crowded streets, her breath visible in the frigid air. The buildings in the ancient parts of the Blackshore were as old as alurean rule itself, each district built and rebuilt over time. Testaments to bygone eras of war or peace. As she drew closer to Vitaly's stronghold, the Black, the structures sagged like broken willows and the alleys bent into crooked shadows.

This was Vitaly's domain, his kingdom over the slums of the Blackshore. The tenements were thrown up haphazardly, crammed one on top of the other like a pile of rotten teeth in some twisted maw. Sera noticed the sway of a rickety building as she passed, and she quickened her pace, not wanting to become entombed in the rubble.

Sera felt the residents' watchful eyes on her. It had been

four long years since she last set foot there. Back then, her mother was the one who knew everyone's name and had a smile for them. But now, with Sera's dark hair replaced by blonde, she wasn't recognized. She was an outsider here.

The streets coiled like a serpent through the heart of the city, and the buildings leaned precariously, as if trying to escape the black coal fires. Factories bellowed out the stench of coal, dyes, and tobacco—but the real killer was the soot that lingered in the air, a constant reminder of the people's struggle to stay warm in the frigid Tumanny temperatures.

Sera's mother used to say: *we're born in ice, we live in ice, and we die in ice.*

The biting cold brought more than just discomfort; hunger and deprivation followed. Even the stockpiled provisions in storehouses were devoured, and shipments from Sundyr were stymied by conflict and inclement weather on the roads and rail routes. The demand for rations outstripped the ability of the supply lines to keep up, and as the relentless black winter dragged on, people began to die from exposure and starvation, their bodies left to rot in the very streets that they once called home.

Unsurprisingly, faithless groups rose in the face of such adversity, especially when they learned that those in power were hoarding what food remained for themselves.

Sera slunk past a line of soldiers, the clanking of their heavy armor reverberating through the alleyway. She felt their stares on her like a noose tightening around her neck. A guard stopped her with a sneer, his godpower crackling in the air like electricity.

"Where do you think you're going?" he spat.

Sera resisted the urge to roll her eyes. These alurean grunts were all the same—bored, petulant, and eager to make someone else's life miserable. "Just out for a loaf of bread, Your Magnificence," she replied, gritting her teeth. She knew that any hint of defiance could spell disaster.

The guard's brow furrowed. "Empty your pockets."

His godpower licked the air to emphasize the threat. Sera's own zmeya tensed in something like exasperation—the bastard dragon was evidently unimpressed, but what else was new?

Sera fought back a sigh and turned out her pockets. His eyes met hers. "You expect us to believe you're out for bread? Without a single coin to pay for it?"

Her heart thudded inside her ribcage as she thought of the silvers hidden within the lining of her coat. The last thing she wanted was for him to find them and accuse her of being part of Vitaly's insurgency. Drag her away to prison, no doubt with someone curious enough to look up her old sedition charge.

"My sister owns the shop, Your Magnificence," she offered with a gesture. "It's just down the road."

Before he could respond, one of his fellow soldiers called his name. "There's talk of a detainee two streets over. Let the woman go get her bread, Yarik."

Sera exhaled as the soldiers left. It was a sobering reminder of why she had sent Galina to the palace, why she needed to finish the panacea.

She plunged deeper into the Black, its velvety darkness wrapping around her in a shroud. The Old Smoke Tavern loomed ahead, sandwiched between towering tenements and narrow alleyways, where families huddled together desperately for survival. But the alurean landlords showed no mercy, and those who couldn't pay their debts were arrested and taken to wither away in the coalfields up north.

Sera crossed the street, watching a group of young men eyeing her with interest. She revealed the knife tucked inside her coat. The group's leader flashed a grin, doffed his hat, and allowed her to pass.

The thick plumes of factory smoke danced around Sera as she neared the row of taverns on the thoroughfare. Every establishment was already half-filled with patrons seeking warmth from the biting cold.

Sera paused outside the Old Smoke Tavern, the fading light casting an eerie glow on the crumbling brick facade. A gaggle of scruffy street children scampered playfully on the other side of the road, their laughter a symphony of innocence amidst the grime. She signaled to the eldest, who glanced at the others with a hint of reluctance, but approached her cautiously.

Sera held up a coin, the silver glinting in the dim light. "I need you to run into that tavern and fetch a man for me," she said. "And if you do it quick, I'll give you this."

The young rapscallion shot her an appraising glance, his nose crinkling up as he scrutinized her with the skepticism of someone twice his age. "Reckon you have more than one coin on you."

The little shit.

Sera gave him a withering look. "And what extortionate fee do you charge for a favor?"

He tilted his head, revealing several missing teeth. A testament to a life lived on the streets. "Two silvers."

"You drive a hard bargain for—what are you, six?" He just grinned. Sera rolled her eyes, digging into the hidden lining of her coat for more money. "Fine. Take these."

She pressed the coins into his tiny palm, provided him the name, and off he went.

The other children kept a watchful eye on Sera as she leaned against the grimy wall, her gaze fixed on the smoke billowing out from the chimney of the seedy tavern. The scent of ale and sweat hung heavy in the air. A chorus of ribald laughter erupted from within, the kind that made you wonder if the patrons were cracking jokes or breaking bones.

Sera briefly entertained the idea of going in for a pint but quickly dismissed it. This business was best done without an audience.

Vitaly emerged from the pub, his black hair tousled in the wind, collar turned high against the relentless chill. Her chest constricted as she watched him cross the road, her fingers curling into fists to keep from touching him.

"Sera," he said, his voice a caress. His gray eyes were sharp when they met hers. "*Ra drí khork.*"

His casual use of Zverti, even after the authorities had arrested dozens of people since his announcement in the broadsheets, instantly crushed any tenderness. Now all she wanted to do was strangle him with her bare hands.

"Find us somewhere we can talk in private," she demanded instead of returning his greeting.

He scrutinized her for a moment, as if assessing her intentions, before gesturing for her to follow. Sera trailed behind Vitaly as he led her down a narrow alley, the cobblestones slick with ice and shadows clinging to the walls. He pushed open a rickety door, revealing a dim passage between two structures that provided seclusion.

Before he could even blink twice, Sera pinned him against the wall, her blade drawn and pressed firmly against his throat, the steel a cold kiss.

Vitaly's entire body stretched taut with pleasure, and he let out a low laugh. "*Vorovka,*" he drawled, "if you wanted to play this type of game, I would have been more than happy to indulge you in my bed."

A flush of desire crept up her cheeks. She fought to maintain control as her god purred in response to Vitaly's nearness. The damp alleyway air did little to cool the fire burning within her.

"Don't toy with me," Sera hissed at Vitaly, her knuckles whitening as she gripped the hilt of her blade, willing her deity to subside. "Explain why I shouldn't slice you from gut to gullet right here and now."

Vitaly's lips twisted into a wry smile, the dim light casting shadows across his face. "Is this about the article?"

"You blew up one of your men, you insufferable prick," she said through clenched teeth.

Vitaly scowled. "Ivan was a grown man. He knew the risks. I didn't force him to enter that square."

"And he could have taken *us* out with him," Sera shot back.

A quiet breath escaped him, and his words caressed her skin like a ghostly touch. "It was your explosive design for close-range combat. I'd rather die than let any harm come to you."

Sera snarled, refusing to acknowledge the way her heart skipped at his declaration. "What about the people by the gates? Didn't they cross your mind?"

"I'm a criminal and a villain. I never claimed to be a virtuous man, remember?" Vitaly held her gaze without flinching, each word spoken with unyielding conviction. "My morality begins and ends with you. It's always been that way. Always will be."

Sera snorted and took a step back, lowering her blade. "The article and the bomb at *obryad*? You did that to provoke the alurea, not for me."

"No." Vitaly's eyes sparked with a newfound ferocity. "I did it to show those assholes we're not afraid, and I'll do whatever it takes to crush them. Call me cruel, call me ruthless, I don't give a fuck. I'm both, and I own it. But we can't afford another war, not with fifty million dead from the last one. Could I live with myself if I lost you?"

Sera growled under her breath and averted her gaze, her voice trembling. "Don't."

"You've always been the selfless one." Vitaly didn't let it go—he was incapable of letting things slide. Whenever he spoke in Zverti, it revealed his emotions with such clarity. His confidence made Grand Imperial seem lacking. "Smarter than Irina, more compassionate than both of us combined. You're the one who should be leading the faithless. So why are you still hiding?"

Sera's body went rigid. "I'm right here in front of you."

"Right here in front of me." His voice was an icy whisper, his gray eyes glinting like frost-touched steel. "Speaking the language of our oppressors."

The scorching ember of shame snaked through her belly, but Sera didn't let it show. Who was he to lecture her? To judge?

"I don't appreciate your insinuation." This time, she spoke in Zverti, her tongue wrapping around the staccato vowels.

She'd hated using their language in Dolsk; it reminded her too much of him and all the things she'd left behind. Just hearing Galina speak it had made her chest seize with pain so sharp it could cut glass.

"You shouldn't," Vitaly replied, his expression unyielding. "Because I can't help but wonder why you went to *obryad* twice. Why you abandoned the faithless, talk to me in Grand Imperial, and want nothing to do with me. And why a woman who witnessed her mother being burned alive by the empress isn't by my side, demanding vengeance. Remember, my brother was on that platform beside Irina. When the wind picked up, I could feel their ashes in my eyes."

"*Enough*," she hissed.

They had both been in the crowd that day, watching the execution. Sera had gone to stop Vitaly, afraid he might try to rescue his brother or get himself caught.

Vitaly made a noise, almost a weary sigh. He reached for her, his rough fingers brushing a curl from her nape, and Sera shivered at his touch. A part of her wanted to sink into his embrace and tell him every truth she had hidden in the dark. But she couldn't let herself be vulnerable.

Not now.

Never.

"What happened to you?" he breathed, his voice velvet-soft.

"I watched my mother die," she said, throat tight. "And we've been apart for too long."

"Too long," he repeated bitterly, releasing her. "I thought of you every damn day."

Sera searched his face. "You asked what happened to me. What happened to *you*, Vitalik?"

A spark of fury ignited in Vitaly's gaze. "I watched them murder my brother," he growled, mirroring her words. "And the night you fled to save us both, I lost the only person left who mattered to me."

He turned on his heel and walked away, and Sera's skin still burned with the heat he had left behind.

17

KATYA

Katya was kneeling before the empress, pressing her fingers into the monarch's aching feet, when a sharp rap echoed through the gilded door.

Isidora discarded a crumpled letter with an exasperated sigh, the room's already brittle tension threatening to shatter like the fragile porcelain adorning the shelves.

"Here is someone else undoubtedly about to demand my time," she muttered. Despite her annoyance, she called out, "Come."

A maid entered. Her gaze remained fixed on the lush velvet carpet, not daring to look at the monarch. "Forgive me, Your Imperial Majesty." She dropped into a curtsy, her silk skirts rustling as she waited for permission to rise.

Isidora regarded her with contempt. "Yes?"

The poor girl twisted her hands together even more tightly. "Your Imperial Majesty... Galina Feodorovna is ill."

Katya's heart thundered in her chest. Galina had been absolutely fine just a few days ago. What had happened since she left for Sera's? Since then, the empress had kept Katya locked by her side without so much as a minute of fresh air.

The palace walls were pressing in on her.

"Alurea are impervious to illness," Isidora said with cold finality.

The maid trembled with fear, her delicate lace collar quivering. "Of course, Your Imperial Majesty. I never meant to imply—"

"So you either implied it or lied," the empress hissed. "Which is it?"

The girl's gaze flickered toward Katya, a silent plea for aid in weathering the monarch's storm. Her breathing quickened, coming in short, panicked gasps.

Please don't let me die for this, Katya thought. She would bargain with any god listening if she had to.

The room constricted again, squeezing—opulent walls that were little more than her cage. The air was difficult to breathe through.

"*Suvya,*" Katya murmured, bracing herself for Isidora's fury. It was her role, after all, to withstand the empress's anger. She would pay for it later. "We haven't checked on Her Radiance since *obryad.*" She forced her voice to sound as calm as a summer breeze. "The guards are eager to express their gratitude for her bravery."

The monarch's harsh features softened. "What a kind girl you are, Katenka," she said. She returned her attention to the maid. "Bring Galina Feodorovna to me."

Katya's relief was short-lived. The girl's terror radiated from across the room. "She's confined to her bed, Your Imperial Majesty. She can't leave her chambers."

Empress Isidora's eyes blazed with a ferocity that had reduced untold victims to ash. "Fetch my slippers," she snapped at Katya.

Katya's hands shook as she slid the empress's slippers onto her feet, tying the ribbons.

The empress stood and seized the maid by the throat, her nails digging into the girl's flesh. "Never interrupt me again," she growled.

The girl's screams sliced through Katya like a jagged knife. When the empress finally released her grip, the girl's neck bore the ugly, scorched mark of Isidora's hand—a reminder of her transgression that would last a lifetime. Katya longed to offer some comfort, some solace, but there was nothing she could do.

She trailed after the empress as they wound through the labyrinthine corridors of the palace, the staff scurrying out of their way. They all knew this mood too well: the empress's thunderous expression, how she stalked the palace halls with fire in her eyes. When Isidora was angry, her godfire burned bright, her wrath on a hair trigger.

Upon arriving at Galina's chambers, the empress shoved open the door. The maids inside gasped and curtsied, their movements clumsy with fear. The empress paid them no heed, focusing solely on the ailing Galina. Katya trailed behind, pulse racing with apprehension.

The stench of vomit and stale food hit Katya like a punch to the gut. When they reached Galina's bedside, she bit back a gasp. The woman's skin was clammy and pale, her lips tinged with blue. Sweat soaked through her sheets, and her hands clutched the blankets in a white-knuckled grip.

Empress Isidora's expression was unreadable as she looked down at Galina. "How long has she been like this?"

One maid hesitated before answering. "She mentioned feeling unwell yesterday, Your Imperial Majesty, but she's been ill since this morning."

The empress's lips thinned with disdain. "What you're seeing is the result of overindulgence. The fool clearly drank herself into a stupor last night."

The maids hastily nodded, but Katya struggled to conceal her shock. She had served the empress for six years, learning to read the monarch's moods as a matter of survival. Beneath the rigid exterior, she detected a hint of fear in Isidora's voice.

Why was the monarch afraid?

"Leave her," the empress ordered the maids. "She'll be fine by tomorrow. Come, Katenka. I want to rest."

A lump formed in Katya's throat as she considered Galina's labored breathing. She needed help, and quickly. "With your permission," she whispered hesitantly, "I could attend to Her Radiance while you rest. I could prepare some tea from the kitchens to ease her discomfort."

The empress's lips pressed into a thin line. "Let one of the other maids tend to her," she snapped. "Your place is at my side."

Those words pushed against Katya's chest like a stone, squeezing until she couldn't get in any air.

"They're not as trained in tending to an alurea as a handmaiden is, *suvya*," she implored, hoping to quench the empress's fury before it exploded into a conflagration.

Empress Isidora glared down at her, the room blazing with a power that could snuff out her life in an instant. She grasped Katya's chin, the searing heat from her fingers like a brand. "Don't make demands and sugarcoat them with endearments."

Katya averted her eyes as she tried to calm her racing pulse. "I'm sorry, Your Imperial Majesty. I only want to help."

Isidora exhaled, her shoulders relaxing as the anger dissipated. "Your heart's too tender, *knesí*," she said softly. "I often wonder how you would have fared outside my protection. So many people would have hurt you by now."

Katya gritted her teeth, holding her tongue against the memories of the countless times Isidora had inflicted pain upon her. Her bones ached from the memory of brutal blows, and her skin tingled with the remembered sear of the empress's power. Yet Isidora tried to sweep all those agonizing moments aside with the balm of sweet endearments and pet names.

Katya could recall each one with aching clarity.

The empress sighed once more. "Very well. Stay with the girl—but I expect you to attend to me when I wake."

Katya maintained her vigil by Galina's bedside for the next hour, her breaths shallow and measured. She coaxed the other woman into sipping water and placed ice between her parched lips, watching it melt within seconds. Galina's feverish mutterings filled the room, her body wracked by the relentless heat.

"Sera," she rasped, her voice barely audible as she weaved in and out of consciousness.

Katya wiped the sweat from Galina's brow with a cool cloth, her heart constricting with fear. "You have to get better," she whispered, hoping her words could somehow anchor Galina back to the world of the living. "If anything happens to you, my future is lost."

No sandy beaches, no boundless skies overhead, no hope of freedom. Only the weight of ownership etched into the cuffs around her wrists and ankles like a branding iron.

A lifetime of servitude, awaiting a brutal death to claim her.

Galina shook with panic, her movements frantic.

Katya rose to her feet, steeling herself against the grim reality of their situation. "Galya, it's me, Katya. You're safe. You're going to be all right."

But as soon as she touched Galina's skin, the heat of it seared her palm. Katya staggered backward with a gasp as red welts formed on her flesh. The temperature radiating from the bed intensified.

Katya hurried to the door, barking orders at the first maids she spotted. "You two! Fetch buckets for each hand and pack them with snow outside! And you!" She pointed at another maidservant. "Find someone to help you bring up pails of cold water for the bath—don't heat it!"

She returned to Galina's bedside, her heart pounding. The other woman's skin was a feverish red, and she was delirious with pain.

As the line of attendants bustled into the room with buckets filled with ice, Katya's mind raced with strategies to save Galina's life. "Help me," she said to the maids. "Use your aprons as gloves."

Between them, they carried Galina—bedclothes and all—into the water closet.

"Gently," Katya ordered, her voice thick with fear and urgency, as they lowered Galina into the frigid bath.

The other woman let out a shuddering breath, and for a moment, it seemed as if the water would offer some respite.

But then Galina's body contorted in agony.

Katya watched in horror as the liquid started to boil. Steam rose in dense, choking clouds.

A vise of desperation clamped around Katya's heart. The future of freedom she'd promised to herself evaporated with every passing second. Galina's orders were clear—*get Sera.*

"Watch over her," she told the maids. "Make sure none of the other servants know about this. Let no one into this room, and don't touch Her Radiance. I'll return in a few hours."

The maids gave a fearful nod.

She raced down to her closet in the empress's apartments. She gathered her silvers and penned a note to Sera, concealing it within a hollowed-out coin. Then she intercepted a guard in the hallway. "Her Imperial Majesty will crave something sweet when she wakes; take these and fetch the little cakes from Anna's Confectionery in Khotchino. Leave the rest on my desk. Go as fast as you can."

With the guard dispatched, Katya grabbed her simplest cloak. The message alone would not be enough. She would have to go to Sera in person if she wanted to save Galina's life.

18

SERA

The jingle of the bell above the door announced Sera's arrival at Anna's Confectionery.

She paused, letting the pleasant aroma envelop her senses as she surveyed the interior. Nestled in the heart of the Khotchino district, this place attracted a particular breed of customers who flaunted their wealth like peacocks showing off their feathers.

Thanks to Katya's connections, Anna's had the privilege of receiving a royal order from Empress Isidora to sample her sweet delicacies, a blessing in disguise that led to a substantial increase in patronage and revenue.

And the empress's insatiable fondness for sweets provided the perfect cover to launder messages from the palace.

Anna glanced up from the till. "Good afternoon, Serafima Mikhailovna. How are your neighbors in Ardatovo?"

Sera froze, recognizing the coded message signaling trouble. "Well enough, thank you," she replied, striding over. She drummed her fingers on the counter, waiting for a customer to pick up their cake. "Just the usual," she said to Anna.

It was all an act of normalcy. But Sera was the only one who noticed the barely perceptible glint of concern in Anna's eyes.

She retrieved a small, square gingerbread cake from under the counter and presented it to Sera. The cake was stamped with intricate designs, serving as a clever way to convey Katya's note without arousing suspicion. Sera handed over the requisite amount of silver in exchange.

"Come back again soon!" Anna chirped.

Another message. That could only mean one thing: Emil had given Anna the intel on where Vitaly was producing his bombs.

They would go on a hunt tonight.

Sera settled at a table, carefully examining the gingerbread cake. Anna had artfully arranged various shapes and symbols across its surface, decorations that doubled as signs to guide Sera in reconstructing Katya's missive.

With delicate precision, Sera sliced the cake into individual segments, arranging them on her plate until the dispatch took shape: *EAST HARBOR UNDER THE BRIDGE BEFORE SUNDOWN GALINA URGENT.*

"Fuck," Sera muttered under her breath, drawing the notice of a nearby patron.

In a panic, she grabbed a handful of small pieces and shoved them into her mouth, destroying the dispatch. The sweetness of the gingerbread exploded on her tongue, but she couldn't savor it. There was no time to waste.

She quickly wrapped the remaining slices in a cloth napkin, stuffing them into her pocket as she hurried out of the shop. Katya had sent an urgent message only once before—but Irina was captured before Sera intercepted it, and her execution was scheduled.

She could only pray the warning hadn't come too late this time.

Sera huddled beneath the East Harbor bridge, watching as twilight brushstrokes painted the sky in shades of orange and blue. Her breaths crystallized in the air, her shivering limbs and heavy overcoat barely keeping her warm in the biting cold. Beyond the dark, choppy waves of Tumanny's bay, the silhouetted peaks of Sundyr's mountains were dusted with a pristine blanket of snow.

She knew that in each of the other alurean nations on the continent, kings and queens were sharpening their blades and preparing for war. It was only a matter of time before their lands were plunged into a maelstrom of steel, blood, and magic.

And if Galina died, the Blackshore would fall, and the country would burn.

Sera paused at the sound of boots crunching through the frost. Her hand moving to the concealed dagger in her coat, the blade whispering as it slid from its sheath.

Her grip on the weapon loosened when Katya emerged from the bend, a tattered woolen cloak whipping around her in the biting wind. Her brown hair lashed her face, snarled and tangled by the merciless winter gusts.

When Katya's dark eyes met Sera's, she seemed momentarily taken aback, her gaze flicking briefly to Sera's shorn and dyed locks.

"Your hair is lovely," Katya said, ducking under the shelter of the bridge.

Six years had passed since Sera last saw Katya. They had first met in Liesgau—Katya newly appointed as a handmaiden to Empress Isidora. Her delicate, sweet features belied a survivor's fierce intelligence and determination.

Sera had spied the flicker of discontent beneath Katya's practiced smile in the markets, and had quickly seized the opportunity to pose as a trader, drawing information from her like a skilled thief.

But Katya was no fool; the empress had murdered fifteen handmaidens before her, and she had only one means of escape. Instead of sounding the alarm, she began passing messages to Sera.

Over the years, she became one of Sera's most closely guarded secrets.

"Are you safe?" Sera's gentle inquiry cut through the air.

Katya rarely left the palace grounds, and Sera feared that any deviation from routine might provoke the empress's infamous wrath.

"For now," Katya replied, her features etched with apprehension. "A footman let me out through a lesser gate while the empress took her midday nap. I have to return before she wakes."

Sera frowned. She hated having to rely on unknown people who could easily betray them. "Can you trust the person who let you out?"

Katya's nod was swift and resolute. "None of Zolotiye's staff would risk taking my place."

Sera recalled the whispered rumors of what went on behind closed doors in the palace. Handmaidens were playthings used to entertain visiting alurean nobles. The alurea were known for their cruelty and debauchery, and Sera shuddered at the thought of what Katya had endured.

But Sera couldn't dwell on Katya's safety. Her mind was consumed by the question troubling her since she read the dispatch.

"How's Galya?" she asked, her voice barely audible against the wind.

"She's sick." Katya clutched her skirts in a hard grip. "The empress won't let anyone near her except the maids, and none of us can tell what's wrong. When I saw Galya this morning, her fever was so high that I had to put her in an ice bath. That's when I sent the message. I don't know what to do."

Sera's breath caught as she thought of the day Galina had received the first injection, her face withering in pain as her body shook with spasms.

She couldn't let anything happen to Galina. Not now, not after everything they'd already been through. She'd never forgive herself.

Sera pulled a box from her pocket. "This has a syringe inside with an antidote to the serum I tested on Galya. Once you give it to her, get out of the room. I don't know how her zmeya will react." Sera hesitated before adding, "Just keep her safe. We can't let the empress think she's weakened."

"The empress won't hurt her." Katya took the injection from Sera, her fingers trembling as she slipped it into her cloak. "Not while Tumanny is on the brink of war with Sopol. Princess Vasilisa's absence is causing doubt among the empress's allies, and she needs Galina's godfire to reassure them."

Sera's curiosity got the better of her. "What's the word on Princess Vasilisa?"

The rumors of the missing princess had grown wilder by the day in the underbelly of Blackshore, and they were all grim. People wondered whether the empress had murdered her daughter for the sake of power, in a fit of grief over her late husband, or simply out of sheer, unbridled rage.

"There isn't any," Katya replied, her voice tinged with unease. "She's barricaded herself in a separate palace wing for three months. No one in or out, except to deliver meals."

Sera remembered seeing the princess on the royal balcony by the empress's side—proud, defiant, determined. Vasilisa was twelve when she first displayed her power for the public: the godfrost, a lethal ability that was as dangerous and rare as her mother's godfire.

As she grew into adulthood, Vasilisa took extended tours of Sundyr and Tumanny, granting audiences to her people as heir to the throne.

But the princess had vanished like a wisp of smoke since her father's funeral. She was absent from her mother's side at *obryad* and failed to address the brewing conflict with Sopol.

How could the future leader of an empire just disappear like that?

"What do the staff say?" Sera inquired.

"The staff don't know what to think. Her meals are eaten, and she occasionally summons the maids for a request. Two months ago, she had a shipment of seeds and clippings from Sundyr sent for her glasshouse, but none of the servants saw Her Imperial Highness. She's a recluse."

"Strange," Sera mused. "And nothing else, only the seeds?"

"Some books." Katya's face scrunched in thought. "A maid tried reading the titles, but Her Imperial Highness is fluent in nine languages."

Sera pondered Princess Vasilisa's puzzling behavior. The Durnovs were known for wearing two faces—one in public, the other in private. It was uncharacteristic of the princess to abandon her duties when whispers of conspiracy swirled around her.

"Keep me updated," Sera said, her voice strained as she swallowed down her fear for Galya's safety. "And if anything... happens to Galya."

Katya softened. "I'll care for her as if she were my own sister."

19

GALINA

Galina's body was ablaze with pain.

Every touch scraped her raw nerves—the scratchy lace of her nightdress, the cold press of the bathtub's edge against her lower back. The god snarled, its voice reverberating through her bones. It rattled the cage of her ribs, scales grinding against her flesh with each breath. The Exalted Tongue was a maelstrom in her mind—a furious litany that she struggled to comprehend.

But through the haze of agony, Galina understood the zmeya's commands with alarming clarity: *Wake up. Wake up.*

WAKE UP.

But her eyes were too heavy.

And she had no strength to fight off her memories.

Galina stood in the dimly lit room, the flickering candlelight casting long shadows over the stonework. Her senses were inundated with the musty scent of mold and decay, making her feel as if the walls were closing in.

The only touch she felt was the firm press of Irina's hand on her shoulder, an anchor dragging her into dark water. A man, a stranger to Galina, was strapped to the chair before her, gaze wide with fear and panic. Galina was Irina's secret—her weapon.

"Vmekhva," Irina said. The endearment was a lie, one she always used in her manipulations. "Do you know what this man did?"

Galina shook her head, prompting a disgusted noise from Irina. "He betrayed us. He sold our enemies information that led to the slaughter of our allies. What do you think we should do with him?"

The man in front of them squirmed against his restraints, his muffled protests futile against the coarse fabric of the gag.

"Burn him," Galina whispered, her voice soft and weary, like a petal falling from a dying flower. She had done this before, and Irina had a list of enemies to deal with.

"That's right," Irina said. "Burn him, Galechka."

A tender touch landed on Galina's arm, drawing her back from the abyss of unconsciousness. She opened her eyes, glimpsing a woman with brownish hair kneeling by the bathtub's edge. Galina's mind was foggy, and she couldn't recall who the woman was or where she was. The room was unfamiliar, its walls adorned with vivid mosaic tiles that formed intricate patterns. The memories were hazy, like trying to catch smoke.

"Give me your arm," the woman said, soft and gentle. Galina struggled to remember her name, but it eventually surfaced. *Katya.* The familiarity offered a sliver of comfort amidst the chaos. "This will make you feel better," Katya assured her. "You're going to be all right, Galya."

"Sera," Galina croaked, her throat aching. "I want Sera."

She needed her sister, the only person who knew everything about the nightmares that haunted her. The things that chipped away at her soul.

(The deaths you're responsible for.)

Katya placed a hand on Galina's forehead, her cool touch a balm against the heat. "I know. But she gave me something that'll help you. Hold still for a moment."

Galina felt a sharp prick at her arm, and then a torrent of agony erupted inside her.

The serum coursed through Galina's veins, scorching every nerve ending. The pain was unbearable, unrelenting.

She shook as her body struggled to contain the god and its power. The screams that tore from her throat were drowned out by the deafening roar of her blood pounding in her ears.

Darkness. Galina focused on the idea of it, imagined it enveloping her in its shroud—a place where pain and sound could not reach her.

"Come on," Katya whispered, her voice finding Galina in the black.

She helped her out of the tub, her strong arms supporting Galina's weakened body. She stripped off the drenched clothes and dressed Galina in dry ones. Galina winced as the fabric grazed her tender skin, but she was too weak to fight back.

Finally, Katya guided Galina into the sanctuary of the bed, tucking her in with gentle hands. "Sera told me to leave once I gave you the antidote," Katya murmured. "You'll be all right, Galina. You'll be all right."

Galina let the memories take her away.

"So fast, Galechka," Irina said in appreciation. "You're getting better at the godfire every day." A noise drew her attention to the door. "Oh, Simochka. *Welcome home."*

Sera's eyes darted to the scorched walls and ash-covered floor, her face contorting in anger with each passing moment. "What have you been doing to her, you sick bastard?" she snarled through gritted teeth.

Irina's expression twisted into a frigid mask. "What needed to be done. Make sure Galina eats something. I need to see someone in the Black."

Once Irina departed, Sera kneeled and gently cupped Galina's cheeks, fingers cool against her feverish skin. Her sister's voice came out low and unwavering. "I won't let her break you. Not ever, do you understand?"

Galina awoke to a whisper caressing her ear, coaxing her from the depths of unconsciousness. "You're going to burn this entire place if you don't pull yourself together."

She struggled to focus her blurry vision and saw Princess Vasilisa looming over her.

Pretty eyes, Galina mused. They were the color of the Lyutoga Sea in Olensk at sunset.

"The blankets are on fire," Vasilisa said.

Galina lifted a hand, mesmerized by the wild flames that danced across her skin.

Vasilisa sighed and seized Galina's arm, extinguishing the godfire with the icy sting of her godfrost. "That's it. You can't stay here. Get up," she commanded, determination lacing her words. "We're going to my wing. Say goodbye to your cell."

As the princess assisted her in getting out of bed, Galina whispered, "Tea." Her voice was raspy and strained from disuse. "You gave me tea."

Vasilisa arched an eyebrow in amusement. "Are you suggesting I slipped something into your tea? Didn't you bother to read my note? I assure you, I know the difference between my poisons and non-poisons."

Galina shook her head, her hair falling against her feverish skin. "No. Can't leave the tea. You gave it to me."

The princess laughed, low and rich. "Oh, you delightful lunatic. How can I resist a request from such a charming madwoman?" Vasilisa used her godpower to create a door and slid her arm around Galina's back. "I'll have a servant bring your tea in the morning. Now, walk with me through the portal, and please, for the love of the gods, try not to incinerate me."

20

KATYA

"Steady, Katenka."

The scent of candle wax filled Katya's senses as she inhaled painfully. She'd made a single demand of her empress—to care for Galina—and now she served as Isidora's living footstool, paying the price for her audacity.

But despite the crushing weight of Isidora's boots on her back, Katya refused to yield. She was a survivor, and she wouldn't let the empress crush her.

"Stay still," the empress hissed.

Isidora's foot pressed down harder, as if trying to crush Katya into the earth. It was a punishment she knew all too well, designed to break the spirit of anyone who dared show even a flicker of defiance. This twisted monster could do nothing to her that she hadn't already endured.

She clung to the image of freedom: blue skies and the sound of waves crashing against sun-kissed sand, the feeling of weightlessness as she soared above it all. She wanted to fly.

The air crackled with tension. Empress Isidora was seething over Galina's disappearance during the night.

But Katya couldn't help the envy that bubbled up. Galina could open doors that would have allowed her to escape the empress. She could be miles away before anyone noticed.

Katya struggled to rein in her emotions. Time was slipping away like water through her fingers, and she was powerless to stop it.

The empress tapped impatiently on the armrest of her chair, her gaze fixed on the frosted window. "You spent hours with her yesterday, Katenka. What did she say to you?"

Katya kept her eyes down, studying the intricate pattern of vines and gold threads on the carpet. "Her... condition was acute, *suvya*. She could barely ask for water."

Katya's hands were still trembling, the skin on her palm raw and blistered from the burns inflicted by Galina's godpower. Even with the antidote, Galina needed time to recover from the failed panacea.

Had she truly gone without saying goodbye? Did she abandon Katya?

"If that girl fled because she was a spy," the empress growled, "I'll hunt her down, tear open her throat, and rip out her spine."

Katya kept her breathing steady, praying the empress's anger wouldn't turn on her. She'd seen the aftermath of Isidora's rage before, the carnage left in its wake—the pools of blood, the ash-soaked carpets.

She couldn't be another footnote in the monarch's history of violence.

Blue skies. Calm ocean waves. Birdsong in the air. Somewhere warm. Her mind sought solace in the freedom that seemed to slip from her every minute.

A knock on the door interrupted the tense silence. A guard entered, standing stiffly in his polished armor as he waited for permission to speak.

"Yes?" the empress snapped. "Have you found her or not?"

The sentry hesitated, his eyes flickering nervously between Isidora and Katya. "Her Imperial Highness offered a room to Her Radiance in the Glasshouse Wing."

The empress's face twisted in anger, her lips flattening into a thin line. "I see."

"Would you like me to—"

"No," the empress cut him off sharply. "Get out."

The guard practically tripped over himself in his haste to leave. Isidora removed her feet from Katya's back and rose, bracing herself against the window frame as she stared at the bleak, snowy landscape beyond.

"Vasilisa has been nothing but trouble," she murmured, her voice low and fierce. "Say something, Katenka. I'm tired of your silence."

Katya spoke carefully. "Do you want my advice, *suvya?*"

The empress waved a hand in dismissal. "No. I have enough arrogant advisors who think they're smarter than me. But I know the truth. The faithless are as much of a danger as Sopol. And with my daughter's absence from court, the situation with our allies is only getting worse."

Katya kept her gaze fixed on the intricate carpet, her mind racing. She understood that leaders across Sundyr would scrutinize the empress's decisions. An alliance with Sopol might expand their territories, but rumors of a new courtier with godfire had already spread like wildfire. The other royals would undoubtedly suspect that the empress had started these whispers to keep her enemies at bay while an uprising brewed within the capital city.

"A united front with your heir would help to quiet the gossip," Katya suggested.

"Vasilisa can't be the future empress," the empress said flatly. "She's not suitable. When the time comes, I'll choose my successor. Until then, I have no heir."

The shock that rippled through Katya threatened to topple her. It was unheard of for the sole child of imperial rulers—one bonded to a god as powerful as her mother's—to be deprived of her rightful place on the throne. Declaring the Tumanny empire heirless was an incomprehensible decision with catastrophic implications.

If that news left the room, the country would lose its allies long before Galina and Sera's strategy had a chance. Courtiers would protest—and the gods only knew what they would do. An attempted coup wouldn't be out of the question—many already favored Princess Vasilisa over a foreign empress who married into the Durnov line.

"You're quiet, *knesi*." Empress Isidora's regard was sharp as she studied Katya's face. "I've shocked you."

"It's not my place to comment, Your Imperial Majesty," Katya whispered. "I'm satisfied being your footstool for today."

Katya knew how to bow and scrape to appease Isidora. She hid her true feelings about the woman who had killed her sister behind a mask of servitude. Every lie was a hidden blade. Yet, she remained poised and demure, a picture of the perfect servant.

In five more hours, Isidora would sleep, and Katya could breathe.

The empress let out a heavy sigh. "Stand up. Speak freely. I don't need a footstool right now."

Gritting her teeth against the pain, Katya rose to her feet, her limbs stiff and uncooperative. She kept her expression neutral.

"*Suvya*." She clasped her hands in front of her. "I'd like to understand your reasons."

Isidora's eyes blazed with a fierce intensity, the embers of her godpower smoldering under the surface. "What's there to understand?" she demanded, her voice cutting through the air. "I've spent my life being passed around like a parcel of no consequence. My mother gave me away to my uncle, and my uncle to Yuri Nikolaevich Durnov. I sat on the lesser throne for thirty years while my weaker husband used *my* god to expand his empire. And now that he's dead, people expect me to cede my power to Vasilisa and let her take what's mine?"

Frustration simmered beneath Isidora's words as she pressed her hand against the wallpaper, the heat of her godpower causing it to curl and smolder. "They all saw me sitting on that inferior throne and believed I was weak. But I'll prove them wrong."

Katya needed to steer her before she did something catastrophic. She had to buy Galina and Sera more time before an invading army arrived on their shores; her life depended on it.

"It would be wise to quell the rumors," Katya said, gaze fixed on the carpet. "Show our allies that Tumanny's empress isn't to be underestimated. Win them over before they defect to Sopol."

The empress arched an eyebrow. "Diplomatic visits?" She shook her head. "We're in mourning for Yuri. My court is supposed to be in somber reflection."

Katya hesitated, the weight of mourning protocol heavy on her shoulders. But she knew they couldn't afford to wait any longer. "I'm sorry, *suvya*," she whispered. "But Sopol showed no respect for our grief when they marched into contested territory."

Isidora fell silent, her mind a battlefield as she weighed her options—the choice between protocol and survival. A year of court mourning was too long.

"Go on," she finally said, her voice tight with resolve.

Katya's stare lingered on the scorched handprint marring the once-elegant wallpaper, a testament to the empress's fury. She chose her words with care. "Let them see Galina Feodorovna and Her Imperial Highness. Show them the strength behind Tumanny's new ruler."

Empress Isidora approached, her steps measured. Her blue eyes danced with the barely contained fire that smoldered within her. To those in Sundyr, she might appear to be a vulnerable queen, but Katya knew better. Isidora was the first monarch in centuries to hold the godfire, and that power had once conquered the continent.

"You want me to invite potential enemies into our midst? Alurea, whose gods may be able to build doors into my palace."

Katya's grip tightened on her skirts, the fabric crumpling under her clenched fingers. Every minute that passed was a minute closer to death.

"Yes, *suvya*," Katya replied, her voice measured. "I'll instruct the staff to renovate the rooms and hallways after they leave. You've said before that enough cosmetic changes can obscure the mental image to thwart that godpower."

Isidora nodded, her expression inscrutable. "You're a clever girl, *knesi*. Sometimes I wish..." She trailed off, features tightening for a moment before smoothing out again. "I'll give the order. And I want you by my side when they arrive."

21

GALINA

Galina jolted awake to a stretch of glass arched above her.

Her mind swam in the fog, trying to make sense of her surroundings—so far removed from the gilded prison she'd called home for the last month.

The sweet scent of flowers and the verdant hues of leaves surrounded her as she lay sprawled on a chaise in an immense glasshouse. Sunlight glimmered through the crystalline walls, casting fragmented light over the ground.

Memories of the previous night came roaring back—Princess Vasilisa's commands, her voice lilting and firm.

That's it. You can't stay here. Get up. We're going to my wing. Say goodbye to your cell.

Galina's bare toes met the cool, dewy grass beneath her as she rose from the sofa. Vasilisa had brought her here, but why?

Her eyes were drawn to a nearby table with intricate lab equipment scattered across its surface—vials, tubes, and glass vessels filled with an array of bright liquids. Sera would have instantly recognized their purpose.

Raising her head, Galina searched the dense foliage for Vasilisa. Before she could take another step, a firm grip seized her shoulder, sending a jolt of heat through her veins.

Galina turned and met Vasilisa's eyes.

And it was like a spark on tinder.

Galina's god blazed to life at the other woman's touch, unleashing an uncontrollable display of godfire that threatened to reduce everything to ashes. The spectacle of flames would have been magnificent—breathtaking even—if it wasn't so terrifying.

But Vasilisa wasn't fazed. Her own zmeya crackled with electricity, and the surrounding air sparked as the two opposing forces collided, each refusing to give an inch. It was a clash of opposites, a surge of raw power coursing through Galina's veins as her god fought for dominance.

"Don't even think about burning down my glasshouse," Vasilisa warned, a hint of amusement lacing her voice. Her piercing blue eyes glowed with the immense energy of her deity. "I spent five years germinating that *dem gre*."

Galina exhaled shakily as the frost extinguished the flames, her breath misting in the frigid air. An almost imperceptible shiver ran through her—her god captivated by its adversary.

Don't do that again, you menace, she told the dragon.

"I'm sorry," she said to Vasilisa.

"I just hope your zmeya isn't about to pitch a fit," the princess remarked, loosening her grip on Galina's shoulder and flicking away the last vestiges of godfrost with practiced ease. "The powerful ones don't take kindly to being smacked on the wrist."

Galina struggled to swallow the lump in her throat, sensing something far more disconcerting than anger from the beast beneath her skin.

Interest.

"Not at all," she murmured, trying to calm her deity.

But Galina couldn't help but admire every inch of Princess Vasilisa—from the constellation of freckles that graced her nose and cheeks, to the glint of something inscrutable hidden within her eyes.

The princess returned her look with a slow grin. "If you keep staring at me like that, I'll have no choice but to blush."

Galina dropped her gaze immediately, unsure of how to react. Her face burned with the heat of embarrassment. Clearing her throat, she feigned interest in the glasshouse and its vast greenery.

"Wondering which of these plants are the lethal ones I use on the irritating guests?" Vasilisa inquired, and Galina couldn't help the bubble of laughter that threatened to escape her. "Ah, I see a smile forming."

That mirth vanished instantly, replaced with tension in Galina's shoulders. The day would come when she'd have to wield her god's power against Princess Vasilisa—and she couldn't afford to let her guard slip, even for a moment.

Vasilisa heaved a dramatic sigh. "And just like that, the smile's gone."

Galina ground her teeth, her resolve hardening. "You said you didn't want me here, remember?"

The princess shrugged. "I said I didn't want you lurking in my room without permission. This is my wing of the palace, and I've invited you in this time."

Galina snorted, scanning the opulent surroundings with mistrust. "Why?"

"Why?" Vasilisa echoed, canting her head to the side, her dark hair cascading over her shoulder. "I thought you might enjoy a change of scenery from your cozy cell. But if you prefer the smell of charred wood and stale air, I'll have the guards escort you back. I'm sure the burned remains of your bed will make for a delightful ambiance."

The princess held Galina's gaze for what felt like an eternity, and Galina could almost feel those pale eyes threatening to unravel every secret she'd ever kept buried.

"So if I wanted to leave..." she asked, trying to keep her voice steady, "you'd let me go?"

Princess Vasilisa shrugged. "Of course. Who am I to stand in the way of a dramatic, burning desire to be locked up in a palace suite?"

Galina knew she had a choice to make. Sera would tell her to stay, to gather valuable information for their cause. The princess's sudden disappearance from society was still a mystery, and Galina had the chance to earn her trust.

"And if I stay?" Galina inquired, her pulse racing.

Princess Vasilisa leaned a hand against the table. Galina's notice lingered on her fingers—graceful, like those of a master pianist. "Then do as you please," Vasilisa said, her voice smooth as silk. "Twenty-three rooms to enjoy, a solarium, a glasshouse, my private garden—and my company, which I'm sure you'll find most charming. I'm excellent at conversation."

Galina raised an eyebrow. "You threatened to kill me the last time we met."

Vasilisa's laugh was contagious, mischief glinting in her eyes like sunlight on glass. "Oh, that's just my way of greeting people. It's like saying, 'Hello there, did you know my god can freeze your balls off in seconds?' The usual pleasantries."

Galina snorted. "Must have missed that part of the etiquette book."

"It's in the appendix," Vasilisa replied sweetly. "Right next to 'How to Deal with Spies in Your Boudoir.'"

"I wasn't spying," she countered. "But I can't help but notice your own affinity for luxurious prison cells, since you've secluded yourself in this wing so long everyone's talking about it."

The princess's mirth vanished. "That's a bold observation."

Galina refused to back down. "And you won't answer why before I stay with you?"

"Decline," Vasilisa said evenly. "Unless you intend to tell me every detail of your upbringing? I'm curious about an alurea raised by supplicants who appeared on the scene just as Sopol invaded. Are you willing to offer all *your* secrets so freely?"

Galina felt her pulse quicken. This woman was too sharp, a razor that could slice through her guise and expose her in a heartbeat.

A sudden knock on the hothouse door jolted them both. Princess Vasilisa didn't break eye contact with Galina as she spoke. "What is it?"

"Your Imperial Highness?" A servant's voice came from behind the door. "Her Imperial Majesty requests an audience in your solarium."

"Always the damn solarium," the princess muttered under her breath. To the servant, she replied, "Tell her I'm coming."

Once the footsteps faded, Princess Vasilisa said, "Choose a room. Don't go into mine."

Galina bit down on her lip. "What will your mother say if I stay here?"

"Leave it to me. And keep those fingers away from any locked doors."

22

VASILISA

Vasilisa stumbled out of the glasshouse, her body wracked with pain.

She clenched her jaw and scanned the empty corridor, acutely conscious that she was no longer alone in the Glasshouse Wing. With a shaky hand, she retrieved the cane she'd stashed in the closet beneath the stairs. Galina's visit had drained her more than she expected.

"Stupid girl," she berated herself in a whisper. What in the name of Smokova had possessed her to allow that woman into her private sanctuary?

But Vasilisa hadn't been thinking—that was the problem. She'd been distracted.

By the beautiful woman who had built a door to her bedchamber, seeking refuge from the suffocating confines of the palace. The desire to see Galina again had kept Vasilisa awake, stealing her sleep and, evidently, her sanity with it.

So she'd used her godpower and opened a short portal from the Glasshouse Wing to the Royal Wing.

Channeling her zmeya had come at a high cost. The god had flexed its muscles, tearing through her bones like a caged animal. If any courtiers or servants had seen her, they would have known the reason behind her prolonged absence.

Vasilisa, heir to the Tumanny throne, was unwell.

Now, because of Vasilisa's notorious weakness for women with a glint of sorrow in their eyes, she'd made idiotic choices.

The world could fall apart around her, but she couldn't resist the allure of a pretty face.

As for her deity? Ugh. No better. At the mere touch of Galina's skin, the zmeya felt an inexplicable urge to grapple her god into submission. Pathetic, really.

Cursing herself for being a simpleton, Vasilisa trudged up the stairs, each step feeling like a fresh dagger plunged into her flesh. On the worst days, she could barely reach the floor above her without needing to stop and catch a breath, gritting her teeth against the agony gnawing at her muscles and bones.

Every inhale was a battle.

Every step, torment.

That morning, Vasilisa had brewed a tincture to dull the pain that wracked her body. Even godpower couldn't heal the degenerative disease that ran through the alurean bloodlines.

Stories whispered of it being caused by thousands of years of caging gods—forcing the zmei into a cycle of bonding and imprisonment that slowly killed them. But no one dared speak of it aloud, not when it signaled the end of their existence. Not when royal families refused to acknowledge the illness at all; children born with it were quietly disposed of under the guise of "accidents."

Empress Isidora had only one name for it: *the misfortune.*

Gasping for breath, Vasilisa approached the solarium.

She propped herself against the doorframe, observing Empress Isidora's disdainful survey of the shabby sofas, their upholstery worn and faded.

Like most chambers in the Glasshouse Wing, the room's

furnishings were more suited to comfort than elegance. The space was bright and inviting, and on days when Vasilisa's pain was manageable, she relished reading there.

Those were rare—Vasilisa's illness had progressed to a point where even walking was a challenge.

Her mother had forbidden her from revealing any vulnerability to the public. The pressure was suffocating, and Vasilisa had paid the price. She was barred from marrying or bearing children, destined to live a life of isolation long before she had retreated to the Glasshouse Wing.

Vasilisa suppressed the urge to let out a sigh. "*Vuabo pue.* What a pleasant surprise."

The empress's gaze flickered over Vasilisa's face before settling on her cane. Her scrutinizing stare seemed to assess the weight Vasilisa placed on the mobility aid, determining the extent of the internal damage that necessitated its use.

The empress had dedicated years to finding a cure for her daughter's affliction, secretly summoning alurean healers from Sundyr. Yet all of them gave the same grim verdict: the *síbnya* plant would put her to sleep, and she'd feel no pain in the end.

Vasilisa couldn't help but wonder how many alurean children had perished under similar circumstances. How many had shared her illness and were offered the same "mercy" of death?

When the healers had given their damning prognosis of Vasilisa's illness, Isidora had sent them away with threats to burn them alive if they dared utter a word about her daughter. That had been years ago.

Nowadays, the empress seldom spoke to Vasilisa, aside from the occasional visit for proof of life.

Isidora perched delicately on the couch like a bird of prey, ready to strike. Her dress was ostentatious even for the occasion—a battle armor of silk and lace. Gone were the days when she would rush into Vasilisa's chambers in a panic with only a nightgown and disheveled hair, whispering prayers while gripping her daughter's hands tightly.

"You look well," Isidora murmured finally.

"Well enough." Vasilisa settled into her chair, setting aside her cane. "But I suspect you didn't come just to admire my health. What do you want, Mother?"

Empress Isidora's expression twisted with irritation. "You know why I'm here. You have one of my courtiers, Vasilochka."

Vasilisa snorted. "Oh, do I? I wasn't aware that I'd taken a courtier from you. I thought I'd stolen a prisoner."

"You're in a mood," Isidora said sharply. "I don't like it. Your time in the Glasshouse Wing has affected your comportment."

"I'm not your handmaiden or servant, *vuabo pue*," Vasilisa replied, her voice low. "Don't tell me how I'm supposed to behave."

Her mother's eyes flared as she abruptly reached for her tea. "It's too dangerous to let that woman stay here. You know that." She gestured at Vasilisa's cane.

"How I handle Galina Feodorovna is my business," Vasilisa said. "And you didn't lock her up in the Royal Wing for my benefit."

"She *claims* she was raised by supplicants, but no one can vouch for her. She could be a Sopolese spy."

Vasilisa had suspicions about Galina, but she'd be lying if she said she didn't want to kiss her senseless, anyway. Because Vasilisa was unhinged and spending too much time alone with her plants.

As she poured herself a cup of tea, Vasilisa struggled to steady her trembling hands. "Keep her confined, and you'll only make her more sympathetic to Sopol. You haven't given her a reason to be loyal to you."

"I didn't come here to debate," the empress retorted.

Vasilisa gave a dry laugh. "No, you're here to give orders. There's a difference."

Her hand shook as she brought the teacup to her lips, and

Empress Isidora's hawk-like regard didn't miss a thing. She'd been watching Vasilisa's illness since infancy.

Isidora's jaw clenched. "Galina Feodorovna's bed has been replaced. I'll grant her some liberties. A daily walk."

"One walk a day?" Vasilisa smirked. "How generous of you."

Vasilisa thought of the woman in her glasshouse. When their eyes met, desire surged through her, and her thoughts were reckless.

I won't let my mother have you.

I want you just for me.

"Good." The empress looked relieved. "Then I'll have the guards escort her—"

"No," Vasilisa said before she could even think.

Isidora's cup clattered on the table. "If you're bored, I'll send a courtier I trust to keep you amused."

A spy, she meant. "I'm not interested in entertaining one of your insufferable lackeys," Vasilisa retorted. "I took Galina Feodorovna out of that room because her god was so volatile that it had already burned through her blankets."

"She wasn't feeling well. She drank too much wine."

Vasilisa glared at her mother. "Is that what you told the servants?" Her mother's expression gave it away, and Vasilisa scoffed. "You held a god like that captive for a month. What did you expect would happen?"

"She received several meals each day, more dresses than she had ever seen, and a suite larger than most supplicants' entire homes," Empress Isidora responded. "Some would consider that kindness."

"Paint a cage in gold, and what are you left with?" Vasilisa asked tiredly. "A prisoner has no use for gold."

Isidora let out a breath, the lines around her eyes deepening. "What's your intention with her, Vasilochka?"

Vasilisa lifted a shoulder. "Some breathing room, someone to talk to, and a way to stop her torching down a palace wing by accident."

The empress softened, a reluctant smile tugging at the corners of her lips. But the amusement faded as quickly as it came, replaced with the stern countenance Vasilisa was all too familiar with.

"And if she finds out about your misfortune and hurts you?" the empress pressed, her voice edged with concern. "You might be letting an assassin live down your hall. What then?"

Vasilisa's gaze drifted toward the window, scanning the private garden beyond the solarium. The high stone walls offered her a refuge where she could move unencumbered by her cane or the need to hide her limp. The Glasshouse Wing was a haven where she could be herself, without pretense.

And she worried about the encroachment on her sanctuary by a woman with eyes like the sky at twilight and a voice like smoke. Vasilisa clenched her jaw, worry gnawing at her gut, but she wouldn't give her mother the satisfaction of knowing.

"Then you'd have less to worry about, wouldn't you?" Vasilisa murmured, fingers tapping absently on her cane.

"Don't," the empress said, her tone a warning.

Vasilisa sneered, baring her teeth. "What's the matter? Did you forget what those healers told you? I've heard of my younger relatives dying in secret. Parents handing their children a blade or some poison and a stern demand for the good of the alurea. They all chose their status first."

Isidora didn't look away. "I chose *you* first, Vasilochka."

Vasilisa shifted, a jolt shooting up her leg. Her mother may have spared her life, but she never spared her suffering. Forced to perform in public for years to mask her pain, Vasilisa slowly faded away, a mere shadow of herself.

It was a slow, agonizing death of the soul.

"If that's all, I have things to do," Vasilisa said, her tone tinged with bitterness.

"Not yet." The empress's demeanor changed from motherly concern to a regal distance. "Sopol's army is progressing through Kseniyevsky, which means our borders won't be safe for much longer. After Yuri's assassination, our allies are getting skittish."

Vasilisa's grip on her cane tightened. "Because I've avoided the public."

Isidora nodded. "I suppressed the rumors of his murder, but the closed casket at his funeral only made people suspicious, and your absence raised more questions. Some believe Galina Feodorovna's godfire is a desperate lie to cling to power." She spoke bitterly. "And if Sopol invades, they'll find our citizens hate me as much as they do."

"So what's your plan?" Vasilisa asked.

"I'm summoning our allies to Zolotiye," the empress replied. "We need to reaffirm their loyalty. They'll see that Galina Feodorovna isn't a rumor, and Tumanny has two alurea wielding godfire and one with godfrost leading our armies."

Vasilisa's head snapped up. "You want me to attend? I thought we were supposed to be in mourning."

"It's war, Vasilochka," Isidora reminded her, her tone heavy with the weight of their situation. "Sopol won't wait for us to finish grieving. And if allies hear even a whisper of your disease, they'll defect to our enemies faster than we can blink. Understand?"

Vasilisa gritted her teeth, remembering the countless injections Isidora forced on her to maintain appearances. It started as a treatment every few months but soon became a daily regimen—morning, noon, and night. The drugs were a blend of painkillers and stimulants designed to mask her illness and keep her on her feet. But it was a steep price to pay. Each event took longer and longer to recover from.

A year ago, she decided she'd had enough.

Vasilisa drummed her cane against the floor, her impatience growing by the second. Her mother was asking her to put on a brave face again, to lie and smile and pretend everything was just perfect when her insides felt as if they were being ripped apart by a pack of bloodthirsty wolves. All for the sake of politics.

"And what happens when they suspect something?" she asked. "When you don't pair me off with someone worthy of the godfrost? When I don't have any children?"

The empress looked away, but not before Vasilisa caught the flicker of fear in her eyes. "We'll deal with that after the war."

"Fine," Vasilisa said, her words clipped and cold. "But next time, I don't think you'll choose me first."

Her mother did not contradict her.

23
SERA

The buildings loomed like menacing giants, their dark windows casting ominous shadows on the narrow streets.

Sera raised an incredulous eyebrow at Anna. "That tenement looks one gust of wind away from becoming a pile of rubble. You're sure this is the place?"

"This is where Emil said." Anna shrugged nonchalantly. "What did you expect? We're in *Zatishye*."

Sera rolled her eyes. "If I get crushed by a falling building, I'm blaming you."

The tenement was the perfect cover for Vitaly's illicit operations—no one would have suspected it to be an explosives manufacturing facility. The grime and soot on its stone walls made it blend effortlessly with neighboring structures. Next door, the unassuming Tsindel Woolen Mill provided an ideal front for smuggling.

The two women arrived well after midnight; the laborers had left hours ago to rest or drink their worries away. The tenement and factory were silent except for the occasional creak of a loose door flapping in the wind.

She had to admit, this was exactly the kind of place where one could commit a bunch of crimes in the dead of night without consequences.

"Emil said the supplies are sent from Sundyr through a little village in the south named Oreksa," Anna murmured. "Their wool shipments cover their operation. Not all of it's for explosives—written materials, too."

Shivering against the winter chill, Sera regretted not wearing more layers. "Is the boss of this shithole factory aware that his dump is being used for smuggling a bunch of munitions?"

Blackshore bosses were mainly commoners—known loyalists, propped up by the power structure that allowed for negligible social or economic mobility. Laborers toiled for a pittance, trapped in their circumstances for life.

"Doubtful. Vitaly's men strip the crates and stockpile the supplies in the basement of that tenement." Anna tilted her chin toward the closest block. "They make all the bombs there. It's an easy way to move their goods without drawing attention. And if they get caught, Tsindel Woolen Mill takes the fall. From what I hear, the mill's boss is a mean son of a bitch. Abuses his workers. Vitaly knew what he was doing when he chose his target."

Clever. Vitaly always did love making his enemies complicit in his crimes.

Sera peeked around the corner, checking the road for any sign of trouble. A few ruffians were scattered along the pavement, their muffled laughter echoing through the street. The only other sound was the distant roar of the waves crashing against the docks at the shore. Though the adjoining building to Tsindel Woolen Mill was dark, Sera still couldn't verify its emptiness. Vitaly's operatives could be inside, constructing explosives for an impending assassination attempt.

The next time they tried, Galina might not be so lucky.

Sera began unbuttoning her overcoat. The cold pierced through her thin shirt underneath, and she gritted her teeth as she passed the garment to Anna.

"We have to be quick and precise, Anya," Sera said, grabbing the leather bag she'd brought. She pulled out a dusty coat. "No room for error. Understood?"

"I'm not an amateur," Anna said, rolling her eyes.

Sera scowled as Anna handed her the military cap. She had to appear as a Blackshore municipal alurean guard, but it didn't mean she had to enjoy it.

Anna snickered at Sera's outfit, her laughter echoing through the narrow alleyway. "That cap suits you, Sera. You look like a proper prick in it," she said, struggling to contain her mirth.

Sera shot her a glare. "Shut it. And stay here until I call you."

She buttoned up the coat she kept for occasions like this, stolen from an unsuspecting sentry. Impersonating a guard was a capital offense, but Sera had no other option. She might have to confront some henchmen.

Sera strode across the pavement, her black coat fluttering in the frosty breeze. A group of miscreants loitering further down the way noticed her and gaped.

"Move it, you louts! Inside, all of you!" Sera barked, channeling her inner asshole. City guards never talked to anyone with an ounce of decency.

Shattering glass filled the air as the ruffians scrambled into the nearest building. Sera didn't even pause as she approached the door of her target, examining the heavy lock. Its intricate design intrigued her. With practiced precision, Sera withdrew a lock pick from her trousers and got to work, deftly maneuvering the tool until...

Snap!

The lock pick broke in half.

"Damn," she muttered.

Clenching her jaw in exasperation, Sera drew out her blade and sliced open her forearm. The pain was searing, but it didn't matter. She needed to get inside that tenement.

"Godpower," she murmured to her dragon as it stirred. But it wasn't impressed; it snarled and recoiled from Sera's offering.

You ungrateful piece of shit.

"How about now?" she growled, making another shallow slice on her arm for good measure.

The zmeya seemed to consider her tribute, nudging at the two cuts until blood ran freely down Sera's arm. Finally, it rumbled its approval, sliding its rough tongue along the raw, exposed flesh. Sera's fists clenched as the god took what it needed before the wound healed.

It then spoke a simple word in the Exalted Tongue through Sera's lips.

With a satisfying click, the lock gave way, granting Sera access to the dilapidated structure. A rush of musty air escaped through the crack, assaulting her senses with the pungent smell of stone and coal fire—and something else.

Explosive powder.

Sera crept forward, guided only by the shafts of moonlight through the windows above, footsteps muffled by the broken floorboards. The voices below grew louder, speaking in the rolling tones of Zverti.

She addressed her god, a whisper in the dark. "One more door. If you have any objections, do it now."

The zmeya responded with a last probing lick over her healing wounds, a gesture of reluctant approval.

Sera took a deep breath, the adrenaline coursing through her veins. With a fierce determination, she charged down the stairs, godpower pulsing around her.

The door exploded off its hinges with a deafening crash, sending splinters of wood flying in all directions. The five men inside looked up in shock, their eyes widening as they caught sight of Sera's uniform and silver insignia glistening in the dim light.

"*Sva non vmonkt blu!*" one of the men shouted in Zverti,

ordering his companions to flee. But one of them, brave or foolish, lunged for her with a furious shout.

Dodging his attack with ease, Sera's movements were fluid and graceful. With a sweep of her leg, she took out his kneecap, the bone shattering beneath her boot.

The man howled in agony. His friends scrambled for the door, their desperate retreat echoing through the corridor.

The ruffian limped toward her, fists raised in a clumsy attempt to fight back. Sera sidestepped again and slammed her fist into his jaw with a satisfying crunch. Lunging forward, her blade flashed in the dim light, nicking him across the side and drawing blood.

A quick distraction.

Godpower surged through her, delivering a blow that left her opponent motionless on the floor. Sera grinned triumphantly.

With practiced ease, she straightened her overcoat and sheathed her knife. Then she darted up the steps and whistled for Anna.

"You had to have all the fun, didn't you?" Anna said as she entered, seeing the hapless victim lying on the ground. "You couldn't even leave one for me to kick in the balls?"

"We don't have any time for that."

Sera surveyed the room. The walls were laden with crates, while tables displayed assorted components: tin casings, timing devices, clocks, and containers sealed with unstable compounds. Different explosives were in various stages of construction, granting glimpses into the assembly process.

"You designed all this?" Anna inquired, picking up a half-finished mechanism.

"That's my simplest invention." Sera heaved a crate with a grunt. "It just requires sealing a volatile mixture in a container, along with some fuse wiring and a clockwork timer set to the desired time lag. When the timer goes off, it'll ignite the fuse, sparking the mixture and causing a bang that'll leave your ears ringing for days."

"I understood about thirty percent of that."

"It's a box that goes boom," Sera simplified. "Now, help me with these crates."

Between the two of them, they spread every container across the tables.

"So, what's the plan?" Anna asked, eyeing the various supplies scattered before them.

"I'm going to blow it all up," Sera said, her tone casual.

Anna's eyes widened. "Are you insane? That's your plan? And where are we supposed to be when this goes off? You'd better not say 'right here.'"

"I have this under control."

She was about sixty-five percent certain she had it under control.

"Coming from you, those words make me shit bricks," Anna said.

Sera forced a smile, bravado barely masking her unease. Her god stirred in its cage, demanding another sacrifice—blood she wasn't sure she had the strength to give it. But she needed to manage her zmeya, or she and Anna would die in minutes. With a sharp inhale, she drew out her blade and cut herself deep.

Blood dripped onto the floor, and Sera's voracious dragon rumbled with pleasure.

"Stand back," Sera told Anna.

The other woman retreated toward the door, doubt etched in her expression. And no wonder—Sera was now fifteen percent less confident in their plan than when they started.

Closing her eyes, Sera summoned her godpower, created a spark, and ignited the powder.

The explosion hit her like a punch to the gut, sending jolts of electricity through her veins. Her barrier shuddered under the force of the shockwaves and threatened to crumble—but Sera refused to let it shatter. Not with the weight of their mission resting on her shoulders. Gritting her teeth, she siphoned away the oxygen fueling the flames, smothering them until all that remained was a choking veil of smoke clinging to the air.

The dragon withdrew its defense with a rumble that communicated it was through for the night. What a bastard.

Sera stumbled against the worktable. Her entire body was shaking, the adrenaline wearing off, replaced with a stabbing pain that made her wheeze. A firm grip on her shoulder brought her back to reality—Anna.

"Thanks for not killing us," Anna said wryly, handing Sera a cloth from the table to press against her bleeding forearm.

Sera managed a weak smile, knowing full well she looked like a walking corpse. "You're welcome."

A low groan filled the room, and their attention was drawn to Vitaly's bruised and battered goon trying to rise, blood gushing from his wound.

Anna stormed over and pushed him down. "You used your blade on him?"

"I had no other choice," Sera replied, kneeling beside him. "I had to put him down fast, and he had the weight advantage on me."

Anna muttered a curse under her breath. "Unbelievable."

"Be quiet," Sera told her sternly, her focus on the injured man. She delivered a sharp slap to his face, and his eyes fluttered open. "*Vdre dilp*," she commanded him. He jerked in surprise at her use of the forbidden tongue. "Good," she said, sensing his tension ease when she spoke Zverti. "*Ra.*"

The man blinked at her in confusion. "How—who?" he croaked.

"*Shh*," Sera soothed, ripping a piece of fabric from her shirt and pressing it to his wound. She deftly wrapped the cloth around the man's torso. "It's the best I can do," she told him, rising to her feet. "*Lífche*," she added apologetically before turning to follow Anna out the door.

24

VITALY

The Black reeked of coal smoke and putrid fumes.

Vitaly drank it in reverently—this was his home, after all. He was raised in the shadows and gutters of the inner city, fostered by criminals and thieves who taught him everything he needed to know to survive.

Vitaly negotiated the dark like an old friend; years of life on these streets gave him a familiarity bordering on omniscience. The labyrinthine tangle of alleys seemed a thing out of a nightmare, stretching for miles under an unforgiving sky; winter brought an unrelenting chill that could freeze even the bravest man's heart to ice.

Still, the Blackshore endured—as it always would.

Snowflakes swirled around Vitaly as he prowled through the darkness. Across the way, people huddled beneath doorways and archways, seeking whatever scant refuge they could from the cold. He saw them, too: souls teetering on death's edge, their frames half-buried in fresh snowdrifts. He'd offered them food and shelter in the tavern earlier, but they'd declined with a stern word. After all, pity only served to comfort the weak—and they had too much damn pride to take it.

Vitaly shook his head as one of the men blew into the hole-ridden gloves on his hand, knowing full well it wasn't enough to keep the creeping fingers of frostbite at bay. In this city, the only sure thing was death.

A simmering rage brewed in his gut. He'd seen alurea in gilded carriages toss morsels to the starving masses and watch them fight for food like rats. He remembered being among those desperate souls, his tongue raw from licking scraps off the cobblestones just to taste sugar for the first time.

But not anymore. Now, Vitaly Sergeyevich Rysakov prowled these grim streets with a new resolve.

He'd see the empress and her courtiers burn.

The raucous laughter and merry-making reached Vitaly's ears long before he arrived at the Old Smoke Tavern.

A welcoming warmth enveloped him as he pushed through the doors. The rich aroma of burning coal and wood mingled with the heady scent of beer that flowed freely throughout the tavern. Tankards were raised in his direction from many familiar faces he had encountered over the years, and he returned the gesture with a broad grin.

But it was short-lived. Pyotr, Vitaly's second-in-command, intercepted him at the door. Once the leader of one of Blackshore's most prominent street gangs, Pyotr had challenged Vitaly for power after Irina's execution four winters ago, only to be beaten in a brawl that had seen him break two ribs. Though an uneasy alliance had since been forged between them, both knew it would be tested should Vitaly ever overthrow the alurea.

"Got a visitor, boss," Pyotr said.

"Who is it?" Vitaly asked, barely concealing his irritation at being interrupted during his much-needed rest.

"The Merchant," Pyotr replied, nodding toward the back room where Vitaly conducted all his business dealings with his informant.

Vitaly sighed inwardly, but didn't argue—the Merchant rarely visited.

"Come with me and wait at the door," he told Pyotr.

Vitaly had no name for his spy; he was dubbed only by his profession, a cover to sneak in contrabands to fuel the rebellion. The Merchant was an essential cog in this machine. Smuggling pamphlets, weapons, explosives, and anything that would keep the faithless alive against the oppressive alurea. The rarest merchandise he supplied were the books inscribed in Zverti. The Merchant was making a pretty penny from his dealings.

But it wasn't just smuggled goods the Merchant provided. He also offered invaluable intelligence that had allowed Vitaly to arrange the assassination of Emperor Yuri and strike a significant blow against their oppressors.

The back room of the tavern was shrouded in darkness and smoke, the only light coming from the flickering flames of the hearth. A hooded figure sat in the shadows, with only a single strand of black hair visible under his hood.

"*Ra vzda,*" Vitaly greeted, settling into the seat across from the informant. "Can I offer you a drink?"

"Can't. Ship's leaving port tonight. I have things to do before then." The Merchant's voice was deep and ragged, expertly disguised to conceal his identity. One could never be too careful in his line of work.

Vitaly nodded in understanding. "I'll send my men down to the docks with you. Signal them when you're ready. Usual payment?"

The Merchant leaned back in his chair and considered for a moment. "Double."

"I don't think so, you sly bastard," Vitaly growled.

The Merchant's lips curved into a smirk within the darkness of his hood. "It's risky business, *stsot,*" he said. "I've got the Sopolese army breathing down my neck on the route, and I still have to pass inspection on your shores."

Vitaly raised an eyebrow, unimpressed. "And why should I care about your little problem? There are plenty of other smugglers out there."

"Because those smugglers are *also* getting squeezed by the Sopolese army, who have more weather mavens on their side," he said. "With their recent capture of Bogdanovo, your empress's troops are pinned down by their storms until reinforcements arrive. Tumanny can't afford a supply shortage, and if you want your bombs, you'll have to pay up."

"Fucking alurea," Vitaly muttered under his breath, knowing the Merchant had him over a barrel. "Thirty percent more, and that's it."

"I'm not one for negotiations, *stsot*," The Merchant replied. "But I'll offer you information to sweeten the deal."

Vitaly's eyes narrowed. "What sort of information are we talking about here?"

"First, let's settle on the deal."

"Fine," he said through gritted teeth. "Double."

The Merchant's hooded figure chuckled in response. "I caught some rumors on the docks in Akra. Word is, your empress plans to gather her allies for a grand ceremony to showcase her new courtier and win allegiances. The rulers of nine countries and their courts all converging on Zolotiye."

"When's it happening, and for how long?" Vitaly asked, his mind already racing with potential strategies and outcomes.

Monarchs from so many nations rarely gathered; if they did, it was always under heavy security. Every ruler was a target, and the chaos of such a gathering could be ripe for exploitation.

"A week hence, and only one night." A pause and another laugh. "Worth double?"

Worth more than double, if Vitaly was honest.

He had some assassinations to plan.

Vitaly kicked off his boots and shut the door of his upstairs suite. He exhaled as he relished the momentary silence of his apartment, tastefully decorated with items he'd never come by honestly. The antique globe he'd stolen one arrogant evening, the leather furniture he purchased with the silvers lifted from an unsuspecting alurean courtier in Sgor. In the corner, a luxurious bed fit for a lord beckoned him to rest.

But there was no rest for the wicked.

He built a fire in the hearth and uncorked a bottle of imported brandy he'd filched from the same place he'd scored the globe. Just as he was about to begin his strategies, a knock rattled the door.

Vitaly groaned, rubbing his bloodshot eyes. Why couldn't they leave him alone for a minute? "Enter."

Pyotr stepped inside, his face dark with concern. "Raid tonight in Zatishye. An alurean guard found our explosives."

Vitaly's response was immediate and forceful. "Is there any chance we can retrieve it?"

The other man shook his head. "No. The lads escaped with their lives, and that's the only good news I can offer."

"How'd they find it?" Vitaly asked, swallowing back a curse.

Pyotr hesitated, as if weighing the consequences of his words. "You were with a woman outside the tavern a few days ago. The tall blonde?"

Vitaly scowled. He ought to have been used to people not minding their business in the Black. "What about her?" he demanded, his voice sharp.

"Lev mentioned the sentry matched her description. She patched him up and let him live. Not something a typical alurean guard would do."

Vitaly couldn't help but smile. Serafima was something else entirely—he loved it when she played games like this. He leaned back and grinned at the thought of her caring for his injured agent in that no-nonsense way he found so charming.

"*Serafima.*" His grin grew wider by the second as he plotted his next move. How he could tease her, tantalize her, and make her squirm. "Sera, Sera, Sera," he repeated with reverence.

He couldn't contain his laughter. Sera had always been his most formidable sparring partner, both in and out of bed.

Pyotr looked at him with confusion, but Vitaly couldn't be bothered with his lackey's bewilderment. The other man knew nothing about the ways to seduce a woman like Sera. With bombs and knives, the games they played, the strategies they employed, and the fierce kissing in the darkness. It was all part of their courtship.

"I'll see you in the morning," he said, his thoughts already consumed by his plans for Sera and the alurea.

His wife had always been his favorite challenge.

25

GALINA

The sunset bathed the Glasshouse Wing's garden in silver and gold.

Galina closed her eyes, savoring the freedom granted to her by Princess Vasilisa. She crept into the garden every dawn, where the solitude and the towering walls ensured no attentive guards watched her. The princess's residential wing was reserved strictly for private use.

But Galina couldn't help the nagging feeling that something was off with the princess. She'd gone two days without seeing her. Was Vasilisa avoiding her? Galina managed to push that thought to the back of her mind, but it left a sour taste lingering in her mouth.

A prickling sensation pulled her gaze up—and there she was, Vasilisa peering down through a window. Galina's heart thundered at the sight of her, but Vasilisa's expression was a mystery—she could have been pleased, or she could have been plotting Galina's death by poison.

Candlelight played across Vasilisa's features, lovingly caressing her skin. Galina yearned to follow that flickering light with her fingertips.

Come out and show yourself, Galina thought, a reckless desire clawing at her.

Come out and make me blush like a fool again.

But Vasilisa retreated into the shadows of her bedchamber, leaving Galina alone with a yearning that twisted in her chest.

She withdrew to the palace, her thoughts filled with a thousand illicit images. Galina needed a distraction, something to pull her mind away from the woman who haunted her every moment. She'd explore more of the Glasshouse Wing, take refuge in its dusty, silent rooms and empty halls. With trembling hands, she pushed open the last door in the corridor.

The sight stole her breath.

Galina stood before endless bookshelves, their towering heights stretching toward a second level accessible only by a spiraling staircase. The scent of aged parchment and leather bindings wafted through the air, beckoning her closer. She brushed her fingers across the textured spines. The shelves were packed with thousands of volumes—literature, religion, philosophy, history, and mathematics.

The weight of the information within those pages was worth more than gold to her. After the Blackshore University riots, the libraries were closed, and the imperial ministry censored the news. Only the wealthy could afford books, and even then, they risked their lives to acquire them. Commoners were prohibited from accessing alurean records now.

Only an imperial princess could have access to texts like this. Perhaps, hidden in one of these thousands of tomes, Galina might find what she needed to help Sera.

She snatched up the alurean history volume and hurried to her room, clutching the book like a thief.

After a few hours, she slammed the book closed with a thud. No luck. The documents hadn't gone back far enough—she'd have to keep searching.

Galina reentered the library to see the hearth ablaze and the lamps dimmed. Shadows and light flickered over the walls.

And then she saw her.

Princess Vasilisa, reclining on an oversized sofa, arm covering her eyes. Galina's breath snagged at the sight. The princess's dark waves tumbled down her shoulders, and she wore a soft lawn shirt with rolled-up sleeves that exposed her graceful forearms.

Stop staring and get out of there.

Hoping to slip away unnoticed, she edged forward to return the book to its place among the towering stacks. She selected the shortest pile, tilting the volume so it appeared like a careless afterthought.

She was about to make her escape when Princess Vasilisa's voice sliced through the silence.

"Find anything worth stealing?" Her tone dripped with amusement.

Galina cursed under her breath. "I thought you were asleep," she said, as if that would excuse her sneakiness.

"Wouldn't that be nice? At this point, sleep is more aspirational than a real possibility."

Galina turned to face the princess, and her skin prickled at the sight of those eyes—keen and piercing, honed to a lethal edge. Despite the princess's delicate appearance and stunning beauty, her true nature was anything but harmless. She was just as perilous as the empress.

One misstep could mean Galina's undoing.

"I'm sorry, Your Imperial Highness. I didn't mean to disturb—"

"Shhh," Vasilisa interrupted, raising a finger to her mouth. "Listen. Do you hear something?"

Galina only heard the crackling of the fire. "No."

"Perfect. Then you can drop the ridiculous title," Vasilisa said, settling back into her pillows. "Call me Vasya. I won't tell anyone, and I promise not to bite." She smiled slowly. "Unless you ask me to, of course. I'm always open to new experiences."

Galina's eyes widened in disbelief. This was the imperial heir, a woman raised to the highest station in the realm, inviting her to address her by a diminutive name—like a friend. It was too familiar.

And—gods above—Galina couldn't help but imagine the pleasure of Vasilisa biting her during a kiss.

(And it's just like you to ignore the reminder of who she is, and what her family did to you. You're so used to burying things.)

Galina clenched her jaw as that intrusive thought snaked past her barriers—because she couldn't deny its truth. "Vasilisa Yurievna," she conceded tightly.

Princess Vasilisa wrinkled her nose. "Really?"

"Or Your Imperial Highness. Your choice."

"So eager to please. It's no wonder Mother kept you locked up like a prized pet."

Galina's heart skipped a beat. Had she fallen into a trap? But before she could respond, Vasilisa spoke again. "Calm down. I won't have you groveling at my feet. Unless that's another one of your unusual interests. Why are you awake at this hour?"

Galina swallowed. She had to be careful with her words. "I have trouble sleeping."

"Really? How interesting," Vasilisa said, arching an eyebrow. "It just so happens that I do, too."

Galina stepped closer, studying the princess. The weariness etched into her features was impossible to miss.

"Are you in pain?" she asked with concern she had no right to feel.

Vasilisa gave a bitter laugh. "You're too perceptive. It would be irritating if I didn't find you so charming. But you artfully dodged the question: why can't you sleep?"

Galina intertwined her hands as she contemplated her response. She couldn't confess to the princess how she avoided sleep to escape nightmares of Olensk. When she drank alcohol, she didn't dream—and that silence was a beautiful thing, considering all she had been through.

But in Zolotiye, she couldn't stifle her memories—not of her parents, her village, the people Irina forced her to kill, or the priest and priestess she'd burned alive. In this place, her mind was sharp as a knife, and every recollection was a thousand cuts. She couldn't drink to numb herself.

She wouldn't permit it.

"Taking your time with an answer, aren't you?" Vasilisa said.

"Decline," Galina whispered.

Vasilisa's eyes sparkled with a mischievous glint. "Ah, there it is. The word you're finally learning to say. But don't stop there. Dare to ask for more."

Galina felt a sudden rush of boldness, her back pressed against the bookshelf as she looked at Vasilisa. This woman had a way of making her feel both terrified and exhilarated.

"Why are you hurting?" she asked, the words tumbling out of her before she could stop them.

The princess's expression shifted, momentarily caught off guard by Galina's question, before breaking into a soft laugh. Galina found herself frozen in place, a foolhardy thought surfacing in her mind: *She's so beautiful.*

"You're more dangerous than my mother gives you credit for," Vasilisa said in amusement.

Galina felt a flutter in her chest, tamping down her growing admiration for the princess. Despite her better judgment, she was starting to like her. "Maybe I am," Galina replied, her tone measured. "Perhaps you are too."

"Oh, I know I'm dangerous. I take immense pride in it." Vasilisa gestured to the chair opposite her. "Sit—unless you intend to loom there all night?"

Galina's hands instinctively balled into fists. "Is that a *command*, Your Imperial Highness?"

Show me that monstrous god inside you and remind me why I came here. We are not friends.

We are not friends.

We are not friends.

Vasilisa grinned. "When you get riled up, your zmeya pushes at me like it wants a fight." Galina was taken aback by the remark, but before she could react, Vasilisa continued, "I think it's charming. My god wants to dominate yours too."

Galina's anger evaporated in a burst of shock. "My god does *what*?"

She hadn't noticed the heat coursing through her veins. Her dragon thrashed with anticipation, eager to demonstrate its power against a worthy adversary.

"Our zmei don't differentiate between a challenge and an attraction." Vasilisa leaned in, her voice low and suggestive. "They're opposites, and they can't resist each other." With a playful gleam in her eye, she raised her hand. "Should we let them have their game?"

Vasilisa's hand was an invitation, slender fingers curling in a tempting beckon. A flush spread through Galina's body, the heat of desire urging her to reach out and take that hand, to unleash the full might of her god. What could happen if she did?

But reality came crashing down, shattering the moment like a fragile vase. Vasilisa was not an ally.

She was the enemy.

"I'm more exhausted than I realized," Galina said quickly, attempting to mask her unease as she backed toward the door. "I think I'll try to sleep again."

Princess Vasilisa's knowing smile didn't go unnoticed. She dropped her hand. "Of course. Sweet dreams."

Galina returned to her room and collapsed onto her bed, her heart still pounding.

26

SERA

"You've sliced yourself too deep, you foolish nitwit," Anna snapped at Sera. "All that bragging about your god healing you against its will, and now look at you."

It had been a properly shit night. After dealing with Vitaly's explosives, Anna and Sera had to take a long, winding path to the Khotchino district, avoiding the places where the faithless were most active—a precaution that may not have been wholly necessary, but Sera's face had been etched into the memory of every lowlife in that chamber. If they didn't hunt her down tonight, they'd be lying in wait for her.

By the time the women reached the underground annex, Sera was ashen and unsteady from the blood offerings to her god. The cloth wrapped around her injury was soaked through.

"My zmeya used up its godpower to contain the explosion," Sera explained, lounging in Irina's desk chair while Anna threaded a needle with nimble fingers. "If you stitch it together, it'll mend quicker. And quit bossing me like an old lady."

"You need someone to boss you," Anna grumbled. "Four years without someone to boss you, and now you're a mess."

"I already had a mother," Sera retorted, her eyes fixated on the desk cluttered with stained notes and crumpled papers, a result of countless sleepless nights spent researching panacea.

"A shitty one," Anna muttered under her breath.

"*Anna Borislava.*"

Her friend just shrugged, pulling the skin of Sera's arm taut as she began the painful process of stitching up the cuts. "Stop fidgeting," she said. "I've only got two hands, and I can't fix you if you're wriggling around like an infant."

Sera let out a sharp hiss as Anna's needle pricked a sensitive spot. "Ouch, damn it. That hurts."

Anna's lips curved in a smirk. "Poor baby."

Sera shot her a venomous look. "You're loving every minute of this, aren't you?"

"Just trying to be delicate," the other woman said with a shrug. She worked the needle in and out of Sera's skin with practiced ease. "Wouldn't want you looking like you got in a knife fight with a bear."

"What's the point? When the god heals me, there won't be a trace of it left. And even if there were, it's not like I need to impress anyone."

"You *do* have a husband," Anna reminded her. "But I suppose he'll be less than thrilled when he finds out we destroyed his explosives stockpile."

Sera rolled her eyes. "The man's deranged. He'll probably think I'm flirting with him."

"Don't sell yourself short. You're *both* deranged," Anna said with a snort. She finished sewing the wound, smearing a poultice of Irina's herb collection over the gash. "Looks like shit, but it's done." She washed her hands in the basin she'd set out upon their arrival. "You ought to pay me for what I put up with."

"Pay you with what? I buy your desserts."

Anna cast her a withering look. "And in return, you have the best little cakes in the city. So what do I get?"

"You get to poke me with needles as punishment, and I don't even ask you to go easy on me." Sera hopped out of the chair and pulled her sleeve down. "I'll be in my room. Come wake me in twenty minutes."

"You need more rest," Anna called out as Sera walked away.

"Twenty minutes," Sera hollered back.

"Idiot," she heard her friend mutter.

Sera staggered into her bedchamber, slamming the door behind her. She struggled to catch her breath as she collapsed onto the cot, breaths coming in ragged gasps as she tried to calm herself. The explosion in the basement had left her a tangled mess of shattered nerves and frayed thoughts.

Her body was a fragile mechanism, overloaded from the sheer concentration it had taken to stay alive. If she had let her focus slip for even a fraction of a second, she and Anna would have been nothing but blood and bone splattered across that grimy basement floor.

Sera yanked the blanket over her head, blocking the glow of candlelight from the wall sconce. The stillness draped over her like a warm cloak, a soothing balm to the relentless chill of the annex's stone walls.

But her moment of repose was short-lived. A searing pain ripped through her skin as her god scraped against her flesh. Scales, wings, teeth, claws, all of it a punishment. She knew it was intentional—a subtle, wordless hint of its loathing. It seemed to take pleasure in tormenting her, in asserting its dominance.

Sera gritted her teeth, pushing against the zmeya. "*Enough.*"

The god slunk back, but Sera was furious at the violation. At the space inside her body that had been stolen to cage this creature that despised her. At its unwelcome presence in her mind. Worse, it was just as angry with the arrangement as she was. Just as trapped.

Just as powerless.

Weren't they the same? Two spirits confined within the same vessel, waging war for their own insufficient slice. Hating each other. Hurting each other.

With the zmeya banished to its corner, Sera relaxed. Her breathing steadied, and she shut her eyes. Sleep was a cherished respite.

"Sera?"

Her eyes opened at Anna's voice, muffled by the door. The world was blurry and disorienting, like someone had scrambled her brains and tried to fit them back into her skull. She couldn't have been out for just twenty minutes. That was a lie.

With a grunt, she pushed herself up from the bed, dislodging the tangled sheets. The floor wobbled beneath her feet as she stumbled to the door. She swung it open to find Anna standing there with a small box.

She glared. "That was *not* twenty minutes."

Anna made a face. "You needed sleep."

"You're too fussy, Anya."

"And you're too bitchy." She lifted the box. "This came for you at the confectionery."

Sera glanced at it. "Katya?"

"Not sure. It was left on the doorstep, and it's too light for even your smallest explosive designs." Anna shoved the item into Sera's hands. "I have to head back to the shop. Get some rest, Serafima."

Sera nodded and closed the door behind her friend. She brought the box over to her desk, scrutinizing its corners for any possible hazardous residue, but found none.

She took a deep breath before opening the lid—and froze.

Embedded in the soft wool lining was a plain band she had worn years ago. At times, she still remembered the weight of the ring on her finger and its absence when she pulled it off and gave it to—

This belongs to you.—Vitalik

PS: Nice work patching up Lev. My thanks for not killing him.

Sera snorted and ripped the note into shreds. Then she placed her wedding band on the desk. She sat there for what felt like an eternity, mulling over its fate—whether to pawn it or discard it. Her marriage had crumbled the day she left. So what purpose did this ring serve?

Just when she thought she had made up her mind, Sera reconsidered. Instead, she fastened it to a cord and wore it around her neck, hidden beneath her shirt, where no one could see.

Where she could always feel it against her skin.

27

KATYA

That morning, Katya was roused from sleep with the empress's decree: "Today, you're my pet."

Pet. The word echoed in her mind like a taunt as she perched at the base of the empress's throne in the receiving room—ornate with polished walls and shimmering pillars designed solely to impress the emissaries that visited through portals. Katya's throat and ankles jingled with the bells that marked her shame; today, she was lower than a servant, lower than a piece of furniture.

It was a fate worse than death.

The atmosphere hummed with power as Isidora channeled her god. Shadows twisted on the walls, a collision of light and darkness. The portal she crafted sliced through the center of the room—a delicate veil bridging the distance between Tumanny and the other countries of Sundyr.

These gateways were the keys of the court, allowing emissaries the chance to come and go—accepting or rejecting the empress's invitations to her ball.

Creating a door was a task that required precision and immense strength. The receiving room was stuffed with furniture that could be moved and shifted. The servants worked tirelessly, redesigning the chamber after every visit, making it difficult for potential spies to form the perfect mental image needed to create their own portals.

The dark slit of a portal undulated as Emissary Igor of Samatsk stepped through, flanked by two guards resplendent in their crimson uniforms. The threads of scarlet and gold on their attire gleamed in the chandelier light.

Igor's eyes scanned the room, locking onto Katya with a flicker of surprise as he noticed her subservient position at the empress's feet. Typically, handmaidens were not privy to delicate discussions, but Isidora was hardly known for her subtlety. Katya was little more than a symbol of the empress's power, a convenient target should these negotiations sour.

Isidora, catching his gaze, reached out to stroke Katya's hair, a gesture that made her stomach churn with revulsion.

She kept her expression neutral, steeling herself against the rising tide of anger and humiliation that threatened to overwhelm her.

"Welcome, Emissary Igor," the empress said. "Please convey my thanks to your monarch for accepting my invitation. It took courage and trust to accept my door, and I hope she's had ample time to consider my offer."

Emissary Igor's face was as inscrutable as ever, but Katya could sense his discomfort. She couldn't blame him. Isidora had a way of making even the most seasoned diplomats squirm with unease.

"She wants to know the nature of your gathering, Your Imperial Majesty."

Isidora's fingers continued their languid exploration of Katya's hair, a mockery of affection that made her skin crawl. "I'm hosting a ball to debut my newest courtier, Galina Feodorovna," she said smoothly. "And to celebrate with Tumanny's allies, of course. Will Yelena attend?"

Katya felt the tension in the air as Igor hesitated, clearly reluctant to deliver bad news to the empress. He looked like a man with an open wound in the company of hungry vultures.

Finally, he spoke, his voice strained. "Her Majesty is honored to receive your invitation, but she's expressed some hesitation after the *very* recent death of her uncle."

Isidora's expression turned frigid, her grip on Katya's hair tightening almost imperceptibly. "I'm aware of when my husband died," she said. "And I don't need a reminder of Yelena's relation to him. If our cousins in Sopol had shown me the same courtesy during our mourning, I wouldn't require her audience."

The tension in the room tightened like a noose as Emissary Igor cleared his throat. "My queen has a request if she is to attend."

A demand, he meant.

Isidora's lips twitched—a clear sign of her displeasure. It was a brazen move to make a request during a royal visit, especially one presented as a condition of attendance. But Yelena of Samatsk wasn't known for her subtlety. She commanded the largest army of alurean soldiers within Sundyr, and an alliance with Sopol could tip the balance of power in her favor.

"I'll consider it." Isidora's voice was deceptively calm. "Tell me what Yelena wants."

"To witness the lady's godfire for herself," he said. "She found it interesting that a foundling with such a rare ability would be abandoned in a Tumanny village and raised by supplicants."

Katya gritted her teeth as the empress's nails sank into her skin, drawing blood. "Don't play games with me," Isidora snarled. The glint of fire in her eyes was a warning signal, and Katya knew better than to make sudden movements. "Your queen is calling me a liar."

The memory of her sister's brutal death after an envoy's failed mission flashed through Katya's mind, and she fought to keep her composure. She couldn't afford to let this be what killed her.

Not now. Not when the stakes were this high.

Emissary Igor's lashes dipped low, indicating he was gathering his thoughts.

Katya recognized the gesture as a defense mechanism of alurean diplomats bonded to weaker dragons. If the empress unleashed her godfire, he would be utterly defenseless.

Finally, he spoke. "Her Majesty wishes to renew her alliance with Tumanny. She believes a demonstration of the godfire by your newest courtier will dispel any doubts or speculations among her court. She asks this favor only to reassure her subjects."

Isidora released her hold on Katya, who winced as a drop of blood trickled down her skin.

"What a smooth tongue you have," Isidora drawled. "Inform Yelena that my new courtier will demonstrate the godfire. Once she does, I expect your queen to honor her agreement with my husband." She waved a dismissive hand. "Now, get out of my sight."

After Emissary Igor departed, the empress seethed. "Can you believe the insolence of that man, Katenka?"

Katya could feel the intensity of the empress's anger bearing down on her like a storm front. She held her breath, knowing any misstep could lead to a swift and brutal end. The empress had already proven herself more than willing to kill anyone who crossed her, no matter how capable or loyal they might have been.

Her sister Sofia had learned that lesson the hard way.

Katya felt a wave of dizziness wash over her, the pain from the wounds on her neck still raw. "He confirmed Queen Yelena's doubts. You'll gain their trust at your gathering."

"Hmm." The empress focused on Katya's neck. A sound escaped her as she extended her hand to graze the injuries, painting her fingertips in crimson. "*Knesi*," Empress Isidora murmured. "I've harmed you."

Katya clenched her jaw, resisting the urge to snap at the

empress. She knew the woman's contrition was fake. Katya was just a toy to her.

"It'll heal, *suvya*," Katya said, her voice devoid of emotion or pain. The hurt inflicted by the empress ran deeper than any cuts or bruises.

The empress reached out to stroke Katya's hair, her demeanor shifting from anger to cloying instantly. "What can I do to make it up to you? A gift? What would you like?"

Katya shook her head. She didn't want the woman's trinkets or baubles. "No gift, *suvya*. But if I may be so bold, could I rest while you complete your invitations?"

Empress Isidora considered Katya's request, her gaze lingering on the injuries she had caused. "Yes, *knesi*. Take the evening for yourself."

"Thank you, Your Imperial Majesty," Katya replied, grateful for the slight reprieve.

Isidora's dismissal gave Katya a moment of respite, a chance to escape the empress's suffocating presence. She retreated to the only space in the palace that belonged to her—a small closet adjoining Isidora's suite.

She pressed her back against the door, shutting her eyes. Every minute spent in the empress's service was like a knife to her soul, a reminder of her sister's fate and her own impending death.

The scratches on her neck were just the start. She knew the empress's cruelty had no limits and that each day brought with it the possibility of more violence, more abuse. And in the end, what would become of her? Perhaps her ashes would join her sister's in the palace woods where the servants had buried her remains.

She used that moment in the dark confines of her closet to gather herself. To savor every breath as it heaved through her shaking frame.

Then she left to clean the blood from her skin.

28

VASILISA

Vasilisa's pulse thrummed like the relentless beat of a war drum. The agony of her god's suffering reverberated through her mind, its piteous whimpers a constant reminder of her affliction.

It felt like a thousand knives were stabbing at her brain.

"Stop shouting," she growled at the writhing zmeya. "I'll fetch it."

Summoning every ounce of her willpower, she clawed herself from the bed, her hair matted to her forehead with sweat. The room spun around her in dizzying madness, threatening to swallow her whole. She groped for the nightstand, finding the vial and tipping its bitter contents onto her tongue.

Ten minutes. That's all she needed to dull the jagged edges of her torment.

Twenty minutes. Her thoughts would fade like smoke, an escape from her god's agonized pleas.

Thirty minutes. The pain would become bearable.

She clenched her jaw and grasped her cane, rising shakily to her feet. The Glasshouse Wing was eerily quiet as she limped out of her room.

Earlier, she'd heard Galina pacing in the corridor outside her bedchamber—and Vasilisa had held her breath, waiting for the knock on her door. She dreaded wearing a mask of composure to disguise her illness; pain had robbed her of several nights' sleep despite her treatments.

But Galina's footsteps disappeared down the corridor, and it was strange how relief and abandonment warred within Vasilisa in equal measure. She *wanted* to see Galina—but she couldn't. Not like this.

Vasilisa made her way across the hall to the glasshouse. Its sweet and musty aroma wafted through the corridor, beckoning like a siren's call. A refuge.

Inside, she savored the familiar fragrance that filled the air. The night-blooming *io scispol* near the door was particularly aromatic, evoking summer nights from her youth. Continuing toward her worktable, she was greeted by the heady perfume of *ab scienvio*, a well-earned reward for her tireless devotion to its stubborn needs.

But Vasilisa's work in the glasshouse wasn't only a hobby—it was a matter of survival. Her illness had once threatened to cut short her existence, but her medicines had given her a reprieve. This was the battlefield where she fought for every precious moment of life.

Her deity was a fickle one, demanding constant attention and dedication. But in the glasshouse, she had found a way to keep the zmeya satisfied. Her godfrost was no longer a weapon of war but a tool for nurturing her fragile flora. Achieving a harmonious balance was crucial, but one she had learned to master over the years.

Working methodically, Vasilisa tended to the plants on her worktable before moving on to the *cíob hílne*. Utilizing her godpower to extract the creamy white substance's medicinal properties was a meticulous process, requiring all her skill and concentration.

But as she worked, she felt the familiar buzz of the drug

wearing off. The pain was still there, lurking just below the surface. She needed a fresh dose, and she needed it soon.

The *ciob hilne* was addictive, and Vasilisa knew it. The euphoria was a dangerous lure, tempting her to take more and more until she lost herself in its hallucinatory embrace.

But tonight, she had to be careful. The correct dose would ease her agony, allowing her to breathe again. But too much could lead to disaster.

With a steady hand, she measured the precise amount she required, the drops hovering in the air like liquid stars. She would worry about the consequences later. For now, all that mattered was the relief it offered.

"Your Imperial Highness?"

The voice was as soft as a thief's footsteps. Vasilisa glanced over to find Galina standing in the doorway. Her delicate features were half-hidden in the shadows, but as she edged closer, the light revealed every tantalizing curve and blush of her skin. Vasilisa's heart quickened as a wave of desire pulsed through her. She knew the danger of such temptations, of letting her guard down around someone like Galina.

It didn't help that her god was clawing at the back of her mind, eager to dominate its rival. Her zmeya grumbled, scales scraping against her flesh.

Stop that, Vasilisa snapped at it.

She's not for us.

She couldn't afford to give in to her desires for Galina. In the cutthroat world of the alurea, vulnerabilities were a death sentence—and she'd have to be ready for the day her mother chose power over her daughter's life.

Vasilisa dragged her blade across the flower's pod, carving a precise incision. She avoided meeting Galina's gaze. "We agreed to use my name. Don't tell me we're regressing now."

"Vasilisa Yuryevna," Galina said with a wry smile.

"Improvement," she replied, a hint of satisfaction in her voice. "Sleep was elusive again, I assume?"

As she prepared to extract the milky essence from the pod, her zmeya's godpower thrummed. The pounding in her head eased. These minor power uses were harmless, yet effective, in nurturing the dragon's abilities. The glasshouse was her haven, allowing her to hone her talents without the irritating stares of simpering courtiers.

"Sleep and I aren't on the best terms," Galina said. "But I wasn't here for that. Does your library have alurean records? I need to know more about my lineage."

A faint whisper of sympathy brushed across Vasilisa's heart. This woman had so much to learn if she wanted to understand her place within the alurean court—where bloodlines meant everything. Alurea raised those with the strongest abilities with even more pressure to perform. Their alliances could dictate the fate of entire nations.

"How refreshing to see you bold enough to request instead of snatching my tomes like a nocturnal bandit," Vasilisa said, flexing her fingers to draw the milk from the pod. As the substance floated in midair, she concentrated, synthesizing its properties with her unique talents. "The records you want are hidden in the dustiest section of the upstairs library." Vasilisa smiled at Galina. "They're so dull, they'll probably cure your insomnia."

Galina's lips lifted in amusement, but she made no move to enter the glasshouse.

"Come now," Vasilisa chided playfully, "what are you waiting for? An engraved invitation? Or are you scared of what my god might do?"

A delicate flush rose in Galina's cheeks, a sight that Vasilisa found utterly captivating. "I'm more afraid of what my own god might do."

Vasilisa laughed in surprise. "Don't be shy. You know where I live if you ever change your mind."

The color on Galina's face deepened, and for a moment, Vasilisa entertained a reckless thought of following that blush with her lips.

"I'm enjoying your garden," Galina said quietly, diverting the conversation from danger. "Thank you for letting me have it."

Vasilisa's breath hitched in her throat as she recalled the image of Galina standing outside her window—her hair illuminated in a golden halo, head thrown back in pure satisfaction. Vasilisa couldn't help but entertain the most dangerous thoughts.

Come inside.

Let me make you blush.

"You're welcome." Vasilisa's body strained with the urge to move closer. "Next time you visit my garden, try coming in the evening when the *cegre pleddaus* blooms in winter moonlight."

Galina's gaze locked onto hers. "Will you join me?"

Vasilisa went still.

Not for you, she thought.

But the words escaped her lips before she could stop them. "Yes, I'll come."

And the smile that spread across Galina's face—the first one Vasilisa had ever seen—was worth everything. Every single risk.

Then those eyes shifted, sweeping across Vasilisa's worktable. "You're not using godfrost here, are you?"

"Some of these plants benefit from the freezing cycle I replicate with godfrost, but my zmeya has other minor talents," Vasilisa spoke as she cut open another pod. "Control over the wind and air. A knack for playing with flames. And if you want to be dazzled, I could tell you the location of every scrap of metal in the room, down to the shape. Like the key in your pocket or the sharp, stabby pin hiding at the back of your dress."

Galina laughed. Damn, but it was even more gorgeous than her smile, resonant and lovely. Vasilisa was a goner if she kept this up.

"Quite the amusing trick," Galina remarked.

"Put me on the streets, and I'd make the best pickpocket who ever lived."

Her smile remained, and its warmth spread across Vasilisa's skin. "So what are you doing, if I may ask?"

Vasilisa plucked a few leaves to add to her bowl. "Most of the plants in this glasshouse have medicinal properties. I extract the ingredients using godpower and regrow what I've used. The pain treatments are sent to the Blackshore's doctors to alleviate the supply shortage from Sundyr."

Despite the toll that tending to the glasshouse took on her body, she was acutely aware of the inequality in the Blackshore; too many people couldn't afford medicine, and hospitals were always overcrowded. The lack of resources during the winter months made the situation worse. Her glasshouse provided only a modicum of help to those in dire need.

Galina's expression flared with surprise. "You send medicine to the Blackshore?"

"To a select group of alurean healers and doctors," Vasilisa answered softly. She tenderly traced the petals of a large purple flower on her worktable. "*Cíob hílne* is the key ingredient in a powerful painkiller, but the prolonged winter has led to a shortage in the southern regions. Boloto is the only other suitable location for its cultivation, but since they share a sea with Sopol, their shipments have to pass through the northern channel, leading to significant delays." Vasilisa shrugged. "I do what I can."

Galina's regard was sharp as she studied her. Vasilisa never cared for the fickle opinions of courtiers and alurea, but she yearned for this woman's approval. She wanted Galina to comprehend that she longed to leave a legacy in this world that wasn't defined by the bloodshed and conquest that dictated her lineage.

The air between them grew heavy and still.

Galina made no move to step forward, and her fingers curled tightly at her sides.

Vasilisa couldn't stand the silence any longer. "Are you sure you wouldn't like to come in?" she asked, trying to sound casual. "I promise I'll make my god behave itself."

A burst of fire illuminated Galina's irises—a spark of hunger. The other woman's zmeya pushed at Vasilisa's skin in a pleasurable conflagration. Vasilisa couldn't resist the enticing pull, her own dragon responding with a shuddering purr of need. She wanted to experience that heat, that rush of power—a clash of lips and teeth.

But just as quickly, the blaze receded, leaving Vasilisa feeling breathless and wanting.

"Decline," Galina breathed softly. "I should try to sleep again," she added, composing herself. "Consult a dusty tome and cure my insomnia."

Vasilisa longed to feel their hands interlocked as their gods collided in a fiery or destructive battle. She ached to discover why Galina couldn't sleep.

Vasilisa was frustrated by the lack of answers, but at least she could offer Galina some relief in her dreams.

She tucked her cane behind the worktable and approached the door, picking a few violet flowers. Despite the earlier treatment, pain coursed through her limbs as she pushed herself to walk naturally, hiding any sign of discomfort.

Curiosity flickered over Galina's features as Vasilisa presented her with the delicate purple blooms.

"What's this?" the other woman asked.

"*Bei io*, the lunar night." Vasilisa dropped the blossoms into Galina's hand. "It's a moody flower. Only found in one location in Tumanny, just outside Likhvin. She needs constant tending: too much water, too little water, and she dies without warning. But she also requires a regular cycle of freezing and thawing, or she won't blossom. The flowers hold no perfume, and while it's lovely, I have others that are less fussy and far prettier."

Galina's brow furrowed with confusion. "Why keep it if it's so difficult to care for?"

"Pride, at first," Vasilisa murmured. "I don't like failing, and on the surface, *bei io* seems so resilient. Her tiny thorns caution any creature that might cause her harm. But she's at the mercy of the climate, the elements, and the soil. So many things that could be her downfall. Yet, she thrives in her corner of the world, flourishing under the moon's glow, where she hides her secrets."

Galina's gaze flicked back up to hers, and Vasilisa's heart gave an unexpected lurch. "What secrets does she keep?"

For a moment, Vasilisa felt like gravity had left her body altogether; like every atom was unbound from earth and fire and sky. She yearned for contact, perhaps more. Much more.

Not for you.

Vasilisa's reply was sharp and quick as she retreated. "Her petals bring the sweetest dreams and deepest sleep. Try adding them to your tea if the dusty tomes don't work."

"Vasilisa Yuryevna," Galina's voice was soft.

Vasilisa steadied herself against her table. "What is it?"

"Why don't you take the *bei io* if it can help you sleep?" Galina inquired.

Pain seared through every inch of her weary body. She had to maintain the pretense a moment longer. A whisper left her lips as she turned away. "Goodnight, Galina Feodorovna."

Vasilisa heard Galina's dress rustle down the corridor as she left. Silence descended once more. A tremor shook her frame as she fought to regain her balance, to compose herself.

She was afraid to want things she couldn't have.

29

VITALY

Vitaly despised being rushed, especially when planning.

The Merchant's intel had been correct—alurea from all over Sundyr were arriving at Zolotiye Palace for Empress Isidora's grand ally ball. Blackshore Bay was practically overflowing with ships, while supply carts clogged up the roads as they made their way to the palace. Vitaly's people had been keeping tabs on their arrivals.

The faithless complained bitterly about the opulent wares: wines from Alempois, beers from Sasnis, and exotic fruits from Ardincaple. Servants scurried about, hunting game to sate the hunger of hundreds of alurea, while commoners were left to choose between bread and sausages stuffed with sawdust to fill their bellies. Some of his men suggested raiding the carts under the cloak of nightfall.

Vitaly discouraged such reckless notions. Assassinations required precision and planning—there was no room for error. It had been ages since alurea from the most powerful ruling families had gathered in one place, and this was the first time the faithless had intercepted their plans.

This was his chance. He couldn't afford failure.

Perched atop the creaking stairs of a rundown tenement cellar, Vitaly surveyed his crew as they assembled the bombs. Even after Sera's meddling, the Merchant's shipment was more than enough to cause chaos at Zolotiye.

"You sure you don't want any backup, boss?" Pyotr piped up, scratching at his unkempt beard.

"Fewer hands means fewer fuck-ups," he muttered, more to himself than to Pyotr. "And besides, we don't need any more loose lips. There's a traitor among us."

"And if that woman sticks her nose in our business again?"

The question scraped against Vitaly's already frayed nerves, but he bit back an insult. None of his close associates knew Sera was his wife. Even Pyotr, who had been with him for years, considered her another enemy. But Vitaly couldn't abide anyone calling her "that woman." She had pulled his ass out of the fire more times than he could count, and he was forever in her debt.

"Let me handle her," Vitaly said firmly, his tone brooking no argument.

Pyotr scowled, sensing the finality in Vitaly's words. "I could take her out. She's always with that confectioner. I know how to get to her."

"No." Vitaly's voice was quiet, but it carried a weight that could make even the most hard-nosed criminal hesitate. "She's not to be harmed."

"If she gets you captured or killed—"

With lightning-fast reflexes, Vitaly drew his knife, pressing its tip against Pyotr's throat. The other man was built like a bear and known for taking a beating, but Vitaly was no stranger to fighting dirty. He'd clawed his way up from the gutters, surviving by besting enemies twice his size.

The alurea who had hunted him four years prior had learned this lesson the hard way. Their skulls had been generously introduced to his daggers.

"I said," Vitaly's voice was dangerously low, "no one touches her."

"Your little game with this woman is going to put our entire operation at risk," Pyotr growled.

"Track down whoever is leaking information to her," Vitaly commanded, pressing his blade against the other man's neck until the skin split. Blood pooled under the sharp edge. "Make it your top priority. But if I discover her lifeless body, Petya, I'll gut you and feed your entrails to the city's dogs. Understood?"

Occasionally, Pyotr needed a reminder of who had the power here.

The other man's expression remained carefully neutral. "Yeah, I comprehend," Pyotr said through gritted teeth. "But for a man who talks about risks, you seem all too eager to take them."

Vitaly made a soft, dismissive noise. "Not your business. If I succeed at Zolotiye, we'll convene a council and let the people pick their own leaders. Until then, you'll follow my orders or fuck off."

Pyotr's mouth twisted in a scowl. "Then I'll track down the rat bastard myself. And when I do, I won't wait for your blessing to take him out."

"Fine," Vitaly said, retracting his blade and slipping it into its secret sheath. "And I'll ensure the alurea don't make it past the winter."

The sun had barely crept above the horizon when Vitaly began his journey from the streets of the Black to the comparatively prim and proper lanes of Khotchino. As he ambled through the winding alleys, he couldn't help but feel out of place in the orderly world of the east Blackshore. The twisted passages of the Black, with their shadowy corners and whispered secrets, were his natural habitat—a sanctuary that had saved his skin when he was a fugitive. He could blend into their darkness like a phantom, invisible to all but the most discerning eyes.

But today, he had personal matters to attend to.

His network of street urchins—all eager for a few coins—had tipped him off when his quarry surfaced in the bustling lanes of Khotchino. He'd kept his distance, watching her every move like a wolf on the hunt until she arrived at her destination.

As Vitaly pushed open the confectionery door, a tiny bell tinkled overhead. The warm, sweet air inside mixed with the aroma of cakes and pastries, enveloping him in a cloying scent that made him want to gag. While some might find it pleasant, the smell was overwhelming for Vitaly, triggering painful childhood visions of scavenging for scraps in the streets.

He almost turned and left the shop—until he saw her.

All his defenses crumbled. The memories faded as he drank in her presence like a fine liquor. There she was, his Sera, carefully assembling a ginger cake with precision. Always so meticulous, that woman.

He couldn't help but notice how her cropped blonde hair fell across her forehead. He yearned to bury his hands in those silky tresses and make her scream his name as he plunged deep into her, just like he used to. Gods, he missed how she laughed in bed and whispered filthy nothings in his ear.

So many evenings he might never have again.

Sera's expression was inscrutable as she finished arranging the ginger cake, inspecting each piece with an almost obsessive attention to detail before popping a small slice into her mouth.

Vitaly watched her with his breath held, his desire for her growing stronger with each passing second. As she closed her eyes and savored the taste, he nearly lost control. The urge to take her right then was overwhelming, but he managed to rein it in. For now.

He dragged a chair over and sat across from Sera.

Her gaze shot up to meet his, and the look of contentment vanished. Her heart was a fortress, impenetrable and guarded, but Vitaly was determined to sneak inside. He had scaled those walls before, and he would do it again.

"Serafima," he said with a smile. "*Ra spe.*"

"My morning *was* good. Then you showed up." Sera replied. "You've slunk pretty far from the Black today, haven't you?"

Vitaly relished that sardonic timbre. She made nothing simple for him, always a challenge to conquer. He was dying to know how she destroyed his entire explosives cache and only left behind a scorch mark on the floor.

"I've got some business," he said.

Sera bit into another piece of ginger cake. "Don't bother telling me what it is. I'm not interested."

A sharp pain hit Vitaly in the chest. This was not the same woman he knew—the one he'd tangled with in the shadows, who'd watched his back and shared his bed. Together, they'd once been a fierce storm, a collision of wind and ice.

But that Sera was gone, and in her place sat this woman with a stare colder than the deepest winter—a stranger he didn't recognize.

"You used to be so damn curious," he said, emotions hidden behind a mask of calm.

"Back when I gave a shit about what you did. I have better things to occupy my time now."

Vitaly feigned a wounded gasp, clutching his chest. "That hurts me, *vorovka.*"

She snorted. "Which part? Your conscience? I wasn't aware you had one."

"I thought I had something that passed for a conscience once, but its voice sounded suspiciously like yours, Serafima Mikhailovna."

Vitaly wanted her defiant. Wanted to feel the press of her knife against his jugular with that fiery glint in her eyes. In the Black days ago, she'd been all fury and flames, vibrant and alive. Apathy didn't suit a woman like her; it was tantamount to a death sentence.

"I'm not interested in playing your moral compass," she told him.

"Oh, don't lie. It thrills you to be the sole voice of reason guiding the best thief in the empire. I don't think twice about anything except the disapproving look on your face."

"The *best* thief in the empire?" A faint smile tugged at her lips. If he couldn't have her anger, amusing her would suffice. "Is that what you're calling yourself these days?"

"Damn right it is. My skills justify the title."

She laughed, and Vitaly savored the sound, a thing utterly rare and beautiful. "I nearly forgot how arrogant you are."

"You know it's the truth. Lock away something precious, and I'll steal it. It's only a matter of time." He leaned in close and whispered, "If you need to protect your heart, I understand, but that's just going to be my greatest heist yet."

Her mirth evaporated in an instant. "Did you come here to annoy me?"

Gods, he adored her.

"I came here to see if you got my gift," Vitaly drawled, flashing her a wicked grin, "but annoying you is always a delightful bonus."

Sera reached into her shirt and yanked out his ring on a cord around her neck. She dropped it onto the table between them, the clatter of metal akin to a death knell. "Keep it."

The crude ring, wrought from the hands of a Zmeiny blacksmith, seemed to mock him as it lay there, a specter of a simpler time. He'd once agonized over whether to give her one when they'd exchanged their vows.

It's only jewelry, Vitalik, he imagined she'd say. *Not important.*

But Vitaly wanted Sera to have a memento from him as they traveled across distant lands like Sgor, Sopol, and Akra. He'd entertained audacious schemes of breaking into the palace and plundering alurean gems for her—just to see the look on her face when he handed over some garish, ill-gotten ruby.

But a ring like that drew too much attention.

So he'd asked for a simple band etched with geometric shapes—a thing a woman could wear when she moved through the world like smoke.

Four years ago, when they were running from sentries, she'd kissed him softly and said, *I'll lead them away from the city. When I do, you escape to Sundyr. Understand?*

No, he'd replied. An automatic response. He wouldn't part from her.

I have someone else I need to get to, she told him, but she didn't say who. Instead, she'd pressed the ring into his palm, the metal still warm from her skin. *Keep this for me. I'll come back for it sometime.*

Now she'd returned.

And she didn't want it.

"When I took this from you, I never intended to keep it," Vitaly said softly. "You told me to hold on to it until you returned. Or did you misplace that memory when you decided I was no longer worthy of you?"

"It was years ago," Sera replied through gritted teeth. "And I don't have time for this. I have things to do."

She got up from the table and left the shop.

Vitaly jammed the band into his pocket and stalked after her. Snow kissed the cobblestones outside, a blanket of ice and cold that mirrored the harshness of their conversation. Sera stuffed her hands deep into her coat pockets, her expression tight and annoyed.

"Go home, Vitalik," she said without looking at him.

"But why would I do that when I'm enjoying a leisurely stroll with my lovely wife?" he asked.

Sera's jaw clenched at his words. "Not your wife."

"Yes, you are. We never got around to getting a divorce."

"Only because I'd have to go to court, and you know why I can't do that," she snapped.

A few alurean sentries across the road lifted their eyebrows at their bickering, and Vitaly remembered why it was always wise to keep a low profile in Blackshore; even the slightest infraction could lead to detainment.

Sera paused. Then, with a watchful eye on the guards, she raised her hand and brushed it gently over Vitaly's cheek.

Her meaning was clear: *we're just two lovers having a passionate moment—nothing to see here, move along.*

Vitaly's breath hitched as her thumb softly skimmed his lower lip. It had been over a thousand days since he last held her, a thousand days since he felt the softness of her skin against his. Time had dulled the memories, but not the need; it burned hotter than godfire.

But the sentries were still staring at them, as if they had all the damn time in the world. Vitaly ground his teeth together, willing them to look away.

Sera was done waiting. She grabbed him by his collar, and her lips collided with his. At first, it was just a show for the sentries—a clever cover for their argument. But then their kiss shifted from performance to something deeper and more desperate. Four years of deprivation spilled out in a single moment. Pain bled into pleasure as Sera tangled her fingers in Vitaly's hair and yanked him closer.

Dimly, Vitaly registered the sentries' amused laughter as they finally departed.

Sera pulled away. Their breath clashed together in the biting wind.

"Kiss me again," Vitaly said, his voice low and urgent. "And don't ever stop."

Sera answered with a hunger equal to his own. She seized him by his coat and dragged him into the shadows of a nearby alley. He barely had time to react before she slammed him against the wall and claimed his lips with a ferocity that consumed him.

The rest of the world went quiet. Nothing else mattered to him but Sera, her scent drugging his senses and shattering his restraint. Vitaly's grip around her waist tightened, fingers digging in with urgency. He wanted her every moment of every day.

"Let's go to my apartment," he breathed.

"No," she replied in a soft hiss.

But then her lips found his again, nipping with teeth. He loved her like this, wild and feral. He wanted all of it—fucking needed it like his next heartbeat.

"No?" Vitaly asked as he slid his hand between her thighs. He pressed his fingers against her core, smiling as she shivered against him. "When was the last time someone made you scream in pleasure, *vorovka*?"

Her silence was a victory. No one since him.

No one since you, either.

Vitaly spun their positions so her back was to the wall. He reveled in the dominance he shared with her—a constant give and take between them.

"Stay in my bed tonight," he purred into her ear, "and I'll make you forget your own name."

She shuddered against him, her breath rasping through the alleyway like a blade dragged across stone. On the cusp of surrender—just where he wanted her.

"Come home with me," he whispered.

Wrong thing to say.

She pushed him away with a force that took him by surprise. Her chest heaved. Her eyes were steel when she looked at him; iron walls had reforged around her heart.

"Don't pretend you're here about us," she snarled. "You're here about the explosives."

Vitaly leaned against the wall. The warmth from her body still clung to him, and he yearned for it again. "Is that so?"

"Call off your dog, Vitalik," she said. "If I catch him spying on me again, his life is mine."

The words hit him like a punch to the gut.

His jaw tightened as he ground out the next question. "What did the bastard look like?" If it turned out that Pyotr had acted outside of Vitaly's orders, he would have him flayed alive.

"Menacing," she replied with a roll of her eyes. "It wasn't subtle. If you're going to send someone to spy on me because I ruined your precious bombs, at least make sure he's not as big as a damn bear."

So Pyotr had followed her, not one of his lackeys. Relief warred with fury within Vitaly. "I didn't send him."

Her expression remained unchanged. "But you know who he is?"

He gave a slight nod. "If he makes any move against you, come to me. Understand?"

"Why?" Sera's features were stone-still and unreadable. "I'm not one of your faithless. I'm not part of that anymore."

Vitaly's fingers curled into a fist, and something inside him shifted—like the snarling awakening of an old beast trapped deep in his bones. His brother's execution had stoked hatred into a cold, unyielding fire in his gut. The fury was his armor now. He wielded it with deadly intent.

"Have you become a loyalist, then?" he asked, his voice a soft hiss of venom.

Her eyes went even colder. "That's all you think in terms of—loyalist or faithless? Supplicant or alurea? Not everything is so simple."

"Answer the question, *vorovka*."

Had Sera forgotten so much? The alurea had abandoned the Blackshore to suffer in squalor and desperation, leaving them to resort to thievery and deceit to survive. The gods they prayed to were worth less than dog shit.

"Just because I'm not a member of the faithless, doesn't mean I'm a loyalist," she gritted out. "Maybe I have my own plans."

Vitaly stepped forward, closing the distance between them until their breath mingled. "Then tell me the plans. Why were you at *obryad* twice in a row? And what were you doing watching that new courtier like she can solve all our problems? She's not one of us."

"Galina Feodorovna was raised as a commoner," Sera replied tightly.

Vitaly's composure shattered. "I don't give two shits if she grew up in the gutter or crawled out of a ditch. She has a zmeya inside her, and I'll kill them all, starting with her."

Galina Feodorovna. Even the most ruthless denizens of Blackshore whispered her name in hushed tones of reverence, all because she wasn't raised with a silver spoon up her ass like the rest of the monsters. She symbolized the fragility of his cause—proof that people would always choose the easier path.

"Then that's it," she said. Those sharp words sliced through Vitaly like shards of glass. "Our paths don't align. One day, I think you'll find your blade in my gut and my blood on your hands."

Vitaly's heart constricted in a clenched fist. The distance between them seemed as vast as an ocean. A mere few inches might as well have been a thousand miles.

"Don't ever say that," he whispered.

She turned her head. "Go home. Don't come looking for me again."

With a dull ache in his chest, he stepped forward. She flinched at his touch but didn't pull away. He placed the metal ring in the center of her palm and closed her fingers around it.

"Then keep this. It's still yours, even if I'm not."

30

GALINA

Galina had been wandering the Glasshouse Wing's library for hours.

She had lost track of the twists and turns, the stairs she'd climbed, following a series of winding paths until she found herself in a forgotten corner, covered in dust and cobwebs.

The shelves loomed over her, groaning under heavy leather-bound tomes that hinted at thousands of years of alurean secrets. Undeterred, Galina scanned the spines until she discovered what she sought.

Births, deaths, and godpower records.

With each page, the information stacked on top of her. Her pulse raced as she devoured the book's contents, each entry hinting at mysteries and revelations long hidden. When she stumbled upon the notation for Princess Vasilisa's birth, Galina knew she had to share it with Sera immediately.

Galina rose from her seat in the nook, a surge of power coursing through her veins as she channeled her god. The door to the underground annex tore through the room like a dark mouth beckoning her.

But something held her back.

A memory of the night she and Vasilisa spent together at the glasshouse filled her mind, the princess's dark hair glinting in the candlelight. *Bei io* blossoms pressed into her palm, blue eyes meeting hers with a gaze that could set a city on fire.

At that moment, Galina felt alive.

And later, she'd put the flowers in her tea and slept. She'd dreamed of the Lyutoga Sea, of midnight waves crashing against the shore. Dreams of a world without war, without death, without pain.

Her mind was unsettled now. She needed Sera. Sera always managed to calm the chaos inside her.

Galina swallowed and stepped through the door into the annex, her boots resonating off the cold, damp walls. As she made her way to Sera's study, she couldn't help but pause at the door to Irina's dark interrogation room. The flickering hallway lights barely illuminated the space. The memory of the horrors that had occurred within that chamber flooded her thoughts—the mangled bodies, the tortured screams—shattering pieces of her soul like ash scattered across the walls. Vasilisa gave her a reprieve from those nightmares.

A gift she hadn't had in years.

Approaching footsteps echoed down the corridor. She heard her sister's voice. "Galya? Are you all right?"

Sera's arms enveloped her in a warm embrace, and for a fleeting moment, Galina savored the familiar comfort of her sister's presence. It reminded her of her loyalty, of the reason she was in that palace. Doubt was dangerous, and Galina didn't want to feel like this—she didn't want to yearn for Vasilisa.

Galina forced a smile. "I'm fine," she lied, noticing Sera's disheveled appearance and bloodshot eyes. "Have you even slept?"

Sera shot her a withering glare. "Is that a polite way of saying I look like shit?"

Galina refrained from answering that question truthfully and instead opted for, "Who's been taking care of you in my absence?"

Sera let out an exasperated sigh. "Anna's been up my ass more than usual," she replied before sizing up Galina with a smirk. "You, on the other hand, look lovely. Nice dress. How's your prison cell treating you?"

"I'm not locked up anymore."

Sera jolted. "You're not? Where has the empress put you, then?"

Galina couldn't explain the irrational desire to keep the Glasshouse Wing hidden from Sera, even with all the knowledge she had gained from the library gnawing at the back of her mind. She tried to dispel the fantasies that plagued her—of Princess Vasilisa, of running her fingers over her skin, pressing her lips to the princess's neck and inhaling her scent.

But as she stood before the doorway of the dark room where she had slain countless of Irina's enemies, she knew she couldn't lie. Not to her sister. Not after everything they'd been through.

With her back straight and voice resolute, Galina said, "I'm in the Glasshouse Wing now. Princess Vasilisa Yuryevna invited me."

Sera's head snapped back, disbelief etched across her features. "*Invited* you? You've actually met her? Katya told me the princess has been mourning since her father's death. Said she's a recluse."

Do they still think I'm shut away here wallowing in grief, incapable of donning a dress and performing for them like a pet on a lead?

Galina nearly smirked at the memory of Princess Vasilisa's dry wit, but she kept those thoughts to herself. The princess's words were a private indulgence.

"She came to me after Katya administered the reversal agent," Galina said, her fingertips tracing the rough surface of the interrogation room's doorway. "I almost set my room on fire."

Sera's expression softened. Galina hoped her sister wouldn't pry further into why Princess Vasilisa sought her out.

"Gods, I'm sorry," Sera muttered.

Galina waved her off. "Don't be. The Glasshouse Wing's library is immense, and Vasilisa granted me full access. I risked coming here to tell you I managed to get my hands on some of the old alurean records."

Sera's eyes narrowed in interest. "Records? Like the kind Irina once accessed at the university?"

"Yes. Birth and death registers of the royal families," Galina replied, her thoughts turning to the tangled web of ancestry she had uncovered. "It's a cesspool of inbreeding, but what's fascinating is the ancient godpower the nobles once wielded. Future sight, metal manipulation, and healing so potent that it could raise an entire army from the dead. Their zmei were so strong." She paused, a weight falling over her voice. "Sera, I think the alurea are losing godpowers."

Sera's eyebrows shot up. "*Losing* it?"

"If Irina was correct with my summoning marks and I really am bonded to the same god as Empress Maria was, then we have proof some zmei don't die once their alurean host does. They return to Smokova and can be summoned again. But the dominant dragons the alurea used to be bonded to aren't coming back. Maybe they weakened with each cycle and died eventually."

Her sister's face twisted in shock. "That's... you're sure?"

"Not sure, but I believe so." Galina edged closer, her words low and tight. "Because there's something else. Records reveal a surge in alurean youth deaths, some directly linked to the royal lineages in Tumanny and Sundyr. Tumanny entries are marked with a single line and false cause of death—like when they tried concealing Yuri's assassination."

She didn't mention Vasilisa's name was among those struck through with that same dark line. However, unlike the others, the princess wasn't dead. So what had killed them? What did the markings signify?

Her sister mulled over Galina's words. "Any other details from the foreign entries?"

Galina shook her head. "No. Just the death records. They didn't have the marks like the Tumanny entries did."

"Maybe the rulers are keeping something from each other and the public—a vulnerability? Something killing off the zmei in their bodies so they can't return?"

Galina's thoughts drifted back to Princess Vasilisa and the inky scar that disfigured her name. The weight of the scratch had almost pushed through the page, as if the person who'd marked it couldn't bear the act.

"I don't know," she said, voice strained.

Sera watched her closely. "Is that all you found?"

Galina exhaled sharply and tore her gaze away, swallowed by guilt and regret. She wanted to tell Sera everything—how Vasilisa had reached out and stolen a corner of her heart. Comforted her. How she yearned for more.

Hated herself for it.

"That's all," Galina muttered, the words almost getting stuck in her throat. "I have to get back." The shame of lying to her sister clawed at her.

But as Galina channeled her god to return her to Zolotiye, Sera asked softly, "What about Princess Vasilisa?"

Galina went still. "What about her?" Fear constricted her chest like a noose.

"You didn't tell me how she treats you. Whether I should brandish a knife at her in your honor. The usual."

Galina's fingers curled into a fist as the image of the ink slashed across the record book rose once more from her memory. *Vasílisa Yuryevna Durnova*, struck through like a verdict—a mark of death.

"I don't think she poses a threat." She measured every syllable that slipped from her lips.

Sera countered her with a sharp look. "Of course she's a threat. She has the godfrost."

Galina thought of Vasilisa brewing medicine from her flowers. A small gesture, but an attempt to use her destructive godpower for something good. Not like her mother.

"Empress Isidora remains our priority," she said.

"And what happens if the princess finds out about you?" Sera's voice was soft, but there was an edge to it that could slice steel. "Will she let you break her godbond without a fight?"

Galina stayed silent.

"Nothing changes," Sera continued. "If the panacea works, use the lustrate to expel the deity from her. Until then, they're both a danger to us." She hesitated before continuing, "Please be careful at the alliance ball. Not just with the alurea. Anna's informant said Vitalik might try something."

Of course Sera knew about the ball—Katya must have sent her a missive.

Galina couldn't help but feel grateful for her sister's concern. "I will," she promised.

As night descended, Galina stood in her room, fingers tracing the black mark seared onto the page next to Princess Vasilisa's name until the pen's grooves seemed etched into her skin. Her thoughts roiled with an unrestrained tumult.

She cursed herself for wondering what those judgments meant.

For even giving a damn.

Cradling the book against her chest, Galina gazed through the window at the walled garden bathed in moonlight. She was being absurd; what she felt for Vasilisa was nothing more than a false sense of security in enemy territory. Sera was right—the princess *was* as deadly as her mother.

With determination, she crossed the dimly lit corridor to return the volume to its place—a symbolic gesture of finality.

She didn't want to care about those dark marks.

But when she opened the door to the library, she found Princess Vasilisa lounging on her overstuffed sofa, surrounded by towering stacks of leather-bound tomes. A strange pleasure coursed through her, leaving her just as unsettled.

I can't have you.

Stop making me want you.

Before she could escape, Vasilisa looked up from her book. "Sneaking away again?" she teased.

The fluttering in Galina's chest became a discomfort. Who was this woman to disrupt her life? To change her in ways she couldn't explain? To make her lie to Sera, the one person who had always been there for her?

She didn't want these feelings—yearnings that betrayed her sister. Her village. All the people she made promises to during sleepless nights.

But her god didn't care. It stirred, eager to engage. Scales writhed under her skin, itching for connection. Wings flapping as if aching to fly.

"Seems like you're occupied," Galina said curtly, pushing the deity back into its corner. "I'll leave you alone."

But before she could take a step, Princess Vasilisa's voice stopped her in her tracks. "You're upset with me," she said with a hint of puzzlement. "Did my *bei io* give you a lousy dream, or did staring at alurean records bore you all night?"

Galina clenched the leather cover of the book she held, trying to control her emotions. "I'm exhausted."

The princess let out a snort. "Of course you are. You've been reading that dreary tome for hours. I told you it wasn't worth your time. Now turn around." When Galina complied, Princess Vasilisa gestured to a nearby chair. "Sit. Talk to me. What's really bothering you? Is it the alliance ball where my mother plans to toss you to a pack of wolves?"

Galina's temper flared at the reminder, and she made no move to sit. "Maybe it strikes me as odd that the empress isn't as keen on showing off her daughter with the godfrost. You're just as much of a prized possession as me. The Tumanny heir. And yet you spend your days here, not seeing anyone but me."

Too many emotions flitted across Princess Vasilisa's face for Galina to identify. "Watch your words," she warned.

Their gazes locked. Galina recalled the ink stains on the book she held, and she couldn't shake off the thought that this princess would someday suffer the same fate as the others—a death hidden behind a veil of lies.

And gods, but that hurt to even consider.

"Why are you hiding in this wing?" Galina asked.

She had to know. If Sera's panacea worked and forced her to judge this woman, she wanted to understand her. Why would Vasilisa take refuge here instead of sitting beside her mother's throne like she was born to?

Why did someone write that black slash through her name like a condemnation?

"Decline," Princess Vasilisa spoke in a low voice.

That word pounded in Galina's ears as she settled in the chair across from the princess and placed the record book on the table between them. The gilded letters and red leather gleamed in the firelight. She noticed an imperceptible tension in Vasilisa's shoulders, a sharp inhale that indicated she knew precisely what Galina had seen. But she said nothing, as if waiting for the inevitable question.

What does the black mark mean? Are you going to die, Vasilisa Yuryevna?

Or will you decline to tell me that, too?

Galina kept quiet, offering something more reckless and terrifying than questions: an outstretched, open hand. Her intrusive thoughts tried to slither forward, sowing seeds of doubt, but she shoved them back. Took control.

She wanted certainty.

Show me something real—that can't be hidden behind lies.

Vasilisa's gaze fixed on Galina's palm as godpower surged between them. The air thickened with the scent of smoldering embers and the piercing chill of frost.

As Galina braced for rejection, Vasilisa's hand slipped into hers.

Contact—immediate and electrifying.

Galina inhaled sharply as sparks of electricity slid across her skin and crackled through the room, the zmei responding as if recognizing one another. Vying and battling, godfire and godfrost clashing. Seething heat met biting cold, forming steam that twisted around them. The elements glided together like they were made for each other. Flames licked at icy tendrils while frost crept over burning embers, creating an intricate, mesmerizing pattern.

Not a war—a meeting of wills, a test of strength. The women entwined their hands, their godpower intermingling and sparking in a collision of domination and surrender.

Galina's thoughts scattered. Her heart raced as desire pounded through her in an overwhelming crash of heat.

"Does it feel like this with—"

Vasilisa shook her head, her gaze unwavering. "No. Only with you."

Galina couldn't find it in her to hold on to anger—not when Vasilisa grinned at her like that. It was a genuine smile, not the kind that concealed a thousand daggers.

The dance of elements continued, a breathtaking display of beauty and force that seemed to pulsate with the rhythm of their heartbeats.

Galina felt herself swallowing hard, compelled by a desire for honesty. "I don't know how to behave tomorrow at the ball."

Vasilisa arched a brow. "Is that your way of asking me for advice? Because it's known among courtiers from Tumanny to Akra that the daughter of Empress Isidora is a wicked, wicked woman with no manners."

Their eyes met, fire and frost playing like old lovers.

"What makes you so wicked?" Galina asked.

Vasilisa's lips curved into a playful smile, her fingers tracing Galina's palm. "Ah, now that's a question, isn't it?" she said. "What makes me so wicked? Some would say it's my naughty wit. Others might point to my penchant for mischief. And some swear my alluring nature makes even the strongest will crumble. They say I'm quite the charmer."

Galina snorted despite herself. "Is that so?"

"True as the day is long," Vasilisa said with a grin. "Just look at you. I had a spy in my bedchamber, and I've already wormed my way into her good graces."

Galina couldn't control the heat that blazed across her cheeks.

Even her god seemed content with its nemesis.

"I've managed to charm the woman who once threatened to kill me with poison," Galina countered. "I think I win."

Vasilisa laughed, delighted by the game. "Galina Feodorovna, are you flirting with me?"

"Wouldn't dream of it." Galina's words were light, but her heart was heavy with tomorrow's expectations. "But I don't think I have the luxury of playing games at the ball."

Vasilisa's smile vanished like a snuffed candle. She threaded their fingers together, and Galina shivered at the added contact.

"This is all that matters tomorrow," Vasilisa said, her voice haunted by an unfamiliar gravity. "You have something they want. Power. And they'll display you like a prized animal to be gawked at and paraded around. They'll be cruel if given a chance."

Galina stilled at the severity of the princess's words. "And what does their cruelty look like?"

Vasilisa's jaw clenched. She didn't answer, but her godpower surged through Galina like a knife's edge, a biting cold that seared her skin. It was an act of dominance that sent a jolt of unexpected pleasure through Galina's own god, which yielded in temporary submission.

"I can't protect you at the ball," Vasilisa said, her eyes blazing with a fierce intensity. "But I promise you this. If anyone touches you, I'll consider killing them for you."

Galina's heart skipped a beat at the tenderness in the other woman's expression. "Vasilisa Yuryevna, are *you* flirting with me?"

Amusement flickered over the princess's features. "Every damn minute," she murmured. With that, she released Galina's hand. "Get some rest. Tomorrow, we both perform for the wolves."

31

KATYA

Katya sat at Empress Isidora's feet on the dais, feeling like an animal in a cage.

The orchestra's tune filled the ballroom with a dissonant melody that failed to drown out the incessant jingling of the bells fastened to her wrists, ankles, and neck with every movement. Each metallic tinkle proclaimed her as the empress's property to all in attendance.

Katya balled her fists at her side, her nails digging into her palms. She wished she could rip the bells from her body and throw them into the deepest ocean.

Her clothing was no better. In a cruel mockery of supplicant customs, she had been forced to wear a traditional sarafan. Her delicate dress and chemise were embellished with a mosaic of embroidered flowers, standing out in contrast to the glittering gemstones and silks of the surrounding royals.

She was meant to be noticed. Humiliated.

Every decision, from the bells to the wardrobe, was a silent permission for any noble to leer, touch, and covet her. A noblewoman approached the dais and ran her fingers through Katya's hair, treating her like a lapdog.

I hate you for this, she thought at the empress, who sat on her throne and wore clothes adorned with lustrous jewels.

The noblewoman left and joined the other alurean royals and courtiers as they danced, chatted, and sipped from their long-stemmed glasses. Every ruler from every corner of Sundyr had brought their retinue of attendants, courtiers, and guards, all bedecked in the vibrant hues and precious gems of their homelands.

The silver gowns of Akra shimmered in the light, while the ochre and ultramarine threads of Liesgau were embroidered with intricate designs that caught the eye. The mauve and cobalt of Samatsk stood out against the sea of colors, and countless smaller nations, allied with Tumanny and its empress, dripped in diamonds, emeralds, rubies, and sapphires from head to toe.

The spectacle was almost blinding, an atmosphere of power that made Katya feel as if she were surrounded by ravenous predators. Walls closing in on her. Pressing against her chest until she struggled to breathe.

No escape.

Isidora watched her guests, her features going cold as Queen Yelena of Samatsk approached the dais. Mauve silk rippled against her slender figure as she moved, her crown sparkling with a thousand gems.

"Isidora." The accented voice was calm and collected, but hostility lurked beneath the honeyed words. "It's been years. You're just as lovely as when I last saw you. My condolences for the loss of your husband."

Empress Isidora maintained her composure, but Katya could feel the tension in her body. She was like a coiled snake, ready to strike at any moment. "Yelena. How wonderful of you to come."

Katya felt the storm brewing between them, a deadly animosity that could spark conflict between Samatsk and Tumanny with little more than a single breath.

Queen Yelena scrutinized Katya. "And who is this?"

Isidora's hand tightened around Katya's nape, claiming her in full view of the court with primal possessiveness. Katya's stomach roiled at the contact. "Yelena, permit me to introduce Ekaterina Isidorakh. My handmaiden."

The queen's regard swept over Katya as if trying to decide whether to make a purchase.

But even as humiliation burned into Katya's cheeks, resolve grew with each passing moment. She would never be treated this way again. She clenched her fists and envisioned the destruction of these royals—the whole court.

"Just as lovely as the one you brought to Samatsk," the queen said, tone dripping with a sickly-sweet venom that made Katya's stomach churn. "That one had the most beautiful voice I'd ever heard."

Katya fought to hide her flinch. Samatsk was her sister Sofia's last trip with Isidora before she was brutally murdered.

The empress's lips thinned at the mention of Sofia, and the surrounding air seemed to crackle with unsaid words. "Sofia Isidorakh is gone now. Ekaterina is her sister."

Queen Yelena reached out and took Katya by the chin. "Smaller than the last," she mused. "Does she sing, too?"

Don't move, she told herself, curling her nails into her palm. *You will survive this.*

Empress Isidora's face betrayed nothing, but Katya sensed the embers of her godfire were barely contained. "Gifted with the most beautiful voice I've ever heard," she said tightly.

The queen made a noise that could have been anything and released Katya. "My handmaiden's singing is dull," she drawled, gaze fixed on Katya like a hawk eyeing its prey. "Have this one perform instead."

A wave of revulsion washed over Katya as the words echoed in her ears. But Katya kept her face neutral.

Empress Isidora nudged the bells at Katya's neck, their jingle a stark reminder of her status as Isidora's possession. "Remember your place, cousin. She'll sing for us all."

Queen Yelena inclined her head in acquiescence. "Very well—but where is your new courtier? Queen Marianne and I were looking forward to seeing her demonstrate the godfire."

The message was clear: if Galina failed to show her power, Samatsk and Akra would turn against Tumanny. No matter how powerful Isidora was, the godfire wouldn't be enough to save them from the combined might of multiple monarchs and armies.

Empress Isidora's eyes smoldered, fire and fury radiating from her petite frame. "My dear cousin," she said, her voice sweet but laced with malice. "Please enjoy yourself. You'll meet Galina Feodorovna, and later, Ekaterina Isidorakh will sing for you."

As the queen departed and disappeared into the crowd, Isidora's smile vanished. Katya watched as the empress gripped the armrest of her throne so tightly that her knuckles turned white. The faint odor of burning ore filled the air as the gilt began to warp and twist beneath the heat of her palm, a testament to the raw power that simmered within her.

Under the empress's composed exterior, her seething anger threatened to boil over at any moment.

Her survival depended on calming that storm.

"*Suvya*," she whispered, her voice as fragile as the wings of a moth, barely audible above the orchestral din of the ballroom.

Empress Isidora curled her hand into a tight fist, leaving molten proof of her strength behind. "I'm sorry, *knesi*," she said through clenched teeth. "No one should hear you sing but me." She waved a hand. "Go fetch Galina Feodorovna. Make sure she's ready."

Katya nodded in obeisance and left the dais.

The palace was alive with activity in the corridors. Servants hurried back and forth between courtiers gathered in the halls. Dukes and duchesses sipped their wine and ate various sweets made to impress royalty. There were the *blini*, delicate pancakes topped with sour cream, honey, and wild berries gathered from the imperial estates. Others nibbled on *medovik*, a sumptuous cake with thin layers soaked in sweet cream. It was a cacophony of scents, sound and motion, yet the palace seemed eerily still beyond that noise. Most staff had congregated around the ballroom to cater to the whims of the hundreds of guests.

Katya released a breath of relief as she crossed into the Glasshouse Wing. She tugged off the strings of bells from her wrists, ankles, and neck before shoving them into her pocket—a brief reprieve.

Katya knocked on Galina's door.

The other woman opened it and let her in with a relieved expression. "Katya. Gods, I'm glad to see you."

Galina was a celestial vision in her gown. Myriad twinkling gems were scattered across the fabric—stars on an ebony sea. They glimmered and shifted with her movements, casting prismatic shadows that danced along her skin. And the headdress—a crown resplendent with a thousand diamonds and pearls.

"Is everything all right?" Galina asked, her fingers brushing the gown as if to soothe its shimmering facade.

Katya hesitated. "The other rulers and courtiers have arrived," she said carefully. "They're eager to meet you."

"Your face tells me this isn't good news."

"Tensions are high," Katya admitted. "If they're not pleased, they'll ally with Sopol. Empress Isidora asked me to escort you to the ballroom."

Galina nodded in resignation, but then paused as if remembering something important. "And Vitaly? Any sign of him or the other faithless?"

"None so far," she replied. "But I haven't been able to leave the empress's side." Reaching inside an inner pocket,

Katya retrieved the bells, each tinkling sharply. Her shoulders slumped at their song; minutes without them were never enough. "Help me with these?"

Galina was silent as she fastened each link around Katya's neck and wrists, a look of steely determination crossing her features as she worked. "These aren't part of the traditional sarafan."

The weight of the bells made Katya feel like she was sinking.

Tears stung her eyes, but she blinked them back. She refused to cry—not here, not now. "They're the mark of the empress's pet."

Galina clasped the last link into place and stepped away to observe her work. "One day, you'll be free of this. I'll make sure of it."

"I don't want to be saved, Galya," she said, voice low. "I'm helping you so I can tear these bells off myself."

32

Vasilisa

The drug cocktail Vasilisa used to manage her pain was synthesized from the compounds of fifteen rare plants. From godpower to injections, she knew the ins and outs of pain management better than any doctor.

The price of that relief was steep—the next few days would be a blur of agony. Her god may have been powerful, but it was utterly useless at healing.

So she'd spent years perfecting the treatments she needed to keep herself up and moving.

That didn't mean it was easy. The dancing alone required a dose of the cocktail that she swore she would never give herself again. Too much, and her mother would have the servants scraping her corpse off the ballroom floor.

Vasilisa remembered the last time she'd endured this misery, and her skin crawled as if it had been only a moment ago. Her father's funeral. She'd secluded herself in her room, throwing up everything she ate, while Isidora ordered the maids away from her chamber.

If only they'd seen the pitiful state of the empire's precious heir, they'd know the alurea weren't really immune to illness. When her body finally cooperated, Vasilisa had dragged herself to the Glasshouse Wing, desperate for a shred of normalcy and weary of the endless charade.

She just wanted to be left alone.

Of course, that would never happen. Not when you're the ruling bastard's only daughter.

A soft rustle of paper from the darkened corridor pricked her ears, and then a note slid beneath her door—the age-old method of servants passing along the empress's missives. Hurried footsteps echoed through the Glasshouse Wing as the dutiful attendant returned to the ball.

Vasilisa snatched up the cursed message.

Your presence is needed in the ballroom. Now.

Closing her eyes, she crumpled the note in her white-knuckled fist and hurled it into the fireplace. Where it belonged.

The pain that shot through her body was swift and excruciating. The drugs she'd taken only numbed the worst of it; her head felt like it was drifting, detached, while her gut churned in turmoil. Eating was out of the question once the nausea of her injection took hold.

Her dress, a heavy black silk shroud for a grieving daughter, only added to her misery.

A maid had come to her earlier, fussing and tugging at her laces, the bone-lined corset pulling taut against her aching flesh. Courtly beauty standards demanded too many sacrifices—a torturous union of aesthetics and pain. But other courtiers could cast off their trappings at the end of the night. She couldn't.

Just a bit more relief, Vasilisa thought.

Vasilisa eyed the vial of *cíob hílne* on her bedside table, her fingers twitching with anticipation. She knew the injection she'd created years ago wouldn't ease her current agony. She needed something stronger to soothe the raw ache that seared through her body.

The god shifted, sensing her distress.

"I'm sorry," she told it.

She snatched up the vial and yanked off the cap, inhaling the sickly-sweet scent of synthesized ingredients. Her stomach roiled in protest, but she ignored it. The *cíob hílne* was all she had left to dull the sharp edges of her pain. It wouldn't banish her suffering entirely, but it would leave her too numb to care.

The drugs would silence her zmeya for a time, but it would feel only a fraction of her agony.

Just like her.

Vasilisa let the cloying liquid settle on her tongue, her eyes closing as she savored the taste of the drug. It was bitter, but she welcomed it all the same. She tipped her head back and waited as the treatment took hold, drowning out the screaming in her veins. The god inside her shifted restlessly, but she barely noticed.

Finally, her thoughts swam in a haze of numbness, and the pain that had been her constant companion for so long retreated to a dull throb.

And she left to give her performance.

Vasilisa's mind was awash with a dizzying array of sensations as she approached the grand staircase.

The courtiers and staff milling about in the upper hall were a swarm around her, a chaotic symphony that stung her ears. The drugs distorted everything into a murky fog, a suffocating mire. As if she were sinking into a dark, churning sea.

Vasilisa took measured breaths as the announcer bellowed her name to the assembled guests below, his voice echoing through the cavernous room.

Like a pack of hungry wolves, the entire ballroom turned to gawk at her.

All those predators in military finery and sparkling gowns—faces without names, names without meaning. More than she could ever be bothered to recall.

Her eyes stung as she descended into the throng.

The chandeliers cast a harsh light on the polished marble floors and glittering jewels. It was an unforgiving atmosphere, more akin to an executioner's chamber than a ballroom.

Show them nothing. Show them nothing.

Vasilisa held her face still, the vile cocktail of drugs raging through her veins. The ballroom was hushed as she took step after agonizing step. Though her pace was slow out of necessity, her deliberate descent had the added effect of ensnaring their rapt attention.

She swallowed back a sigh. *I loathe you all for this.*

Vasilisa kept her head bowed low, showing shallow respect to the pompous rulers of Liesgau and Akra and their entourage of fawning courtiers—a flock of carrion birds preening themselves.

The only thing more menacing than the room's oppressiveness was Vasilisa's mother. Her features were severe as she watched the display from her position on the emperor's old throne, the ostentatious gilding and jewels threatening to engulf her petite frame.

The empress's eyes locked onto Vasilisa. With a curt nod, she told her daughter she had passed this twisted mockery of normalcy.

Vasilisa executed a practiced curtsy. "Your Imperial Majesty," Vasilisa intoned as she inwardly seethed with contempt.

Isidora was an empress before all else—a mother only in title.

"Vasilisa. Sit beside me."

Isidora gestured toward the smaller throne at her side—the seat she had once filled as her husband's consort.

The unspoken implication stung; Vasilisa would never occupy the grander throne. Once the tensions with Sopol abated, she and her mother would have to confront the uncomfortable truth of Vasilisa's illness and the persistent inquiries regarding her lack of a husband.

But for now, sitting at her mother's side was enough to still the whispers surrounding Vasilisa's absence.

She settled into the chair, suppressing a grunt of pain as her exhausted body protested.

And then, as the empress gestured for the waiting throng to advance, she hissed softly for Vasilisa's ears alone, "You're late."

"I'm on fifteen different drugs," Vasilisa said through clenched teeth. "You should praise whatever gods are listening that I can even move."

The empress's regard was sharp. "You appear to be in good health." The words were cloying.

Vasilisa wanted to rip that sweet smile right off Isidora's face.

A fawning nobleman came forward, pressing his lips to the ring on Isidora's hand before doing the same to Vasilisa. She ignored him as the empress spoke with poison-tipped carelessness. "Your cousin, Friedrich Heinrich, has requested a dance. And several other suitors. I expect you to indulge them all."

Fury scalded Vasilisa's throat. "Remember this every moment I'm out there. Remember what it costs me and how much I hate you for making me do it."

But Isidora only turned away, giving another courtier one of her false smiles.

33
GALINA

Galina's breath came in shallow gasps, strangled by the weight of her dress. It was a monstrosity of silks and brocades, threatening to drag her down with each step. But the towering headdress was worse—an abomination of gems and gold that bowed her neck in submission.

She knew what awaited her at the ball—the blood-soaked intrigues masquerading under a veneer of luxury and glamor. But even so, the grandeur of the ballroom halted her in her tracks. It was a beacon of opulence and power, pulsing to its own heartbeat.

The room was ablaze with light, displaying wealth and status in every corner. Noblewomen wore gowns dripping with precious stones, while their male counterparts strutted in military garb. All donned sashes studded with medals boasting battles that claimed countless innocent lives.

Galina surveyed the crowd with gritted teeth, watching those privileged few flaunting their power earned through centuries of senseless violence and savagery. Olensk. Dolsk. Mere names on a map to these bastards, testimonies to their blood-soaked conquests.

"Galina Feodorovna Kolenkina!"

The announcer's voice echoed through the grand ballroom, a clarion call that summoned the attention of the bloodthirsty audience. Their eyes fixed upon her, ravenous creatures ready to devour their prey.

She refused to show weakness.

Katya whispered behind her. "Take a deep breath, Galya. I'll see if there's any sign of Vitaly Sergeyevich. Good luck."

Descending the staircase was a journey into the jaws of beasts. Heads inclined toward each other, lips moving in silent conspiracies. The air was thick with the stench of godpower, a clammy fog that licked at her skin.

These were not mere people—they were predators wearing cloaks of respectability and civility. Feral gods hidden in human shells. They appeared harmless amidst their velvety gowns and polished uniforms, but Galina knew better. Their medals were not just for vanity.

They held destruction within them, born with a thirst for conquest in their veins. And she was only another tool in their insatiable search for power.

Let them think I'm easily used.

Let them think I'm the queen's puppet.

Whispers swirled around her. She was an unwelcome presence in their midst, a stranger disrupting their delicate hierarchy. Yet, for all its menace, one face in the crowd shone with kindness.

Princess Vasilisa.

Their gazes locked across the room, a silent understanding passing between them. From her perch on the dais, Vasilisa tilted her head in a welcoming gesture that said, *Welcome to the wolf's den.*

Galina raised an eyebrow, an unspoken message of her own: *I'm ready.*

The moment was all too brief as she settled her full concentration on Empress Isidora.

Galina sank into a deep curtsy, playing the role of a humble supplicant who didn't know any better. Courtiers gasped at the sight; no alurea subjugated themselves like that—not in this court of hidden knives.

The murmurs ceased as Galina's voice echoed through the chamber. "Your Imperial Majesty. I'm grateful for your invitation this evening."

The empress rose from her throne and descended the stairs, the fabric of her black gown glistening like sunlight on the surface of a dark sea.

Silence swallowed the room until Isidora finally spoke. "Welcome, Galina Feodorovna."

Galina slowly straightened.

The empress signaled for the orchestra to resume their performance, and music filled the ballroom. Courtiers continued chatting and dancing, weaving intricate patterns across the floor.

Isidora hooked her arm around Galina's, her grip like an iron shackle hidden beneath the silk of her gloves. Galina's god bristled at the contact, but she quickly pushed it back. *Behave.*

"Come," the empress said. "Walk with me."

From the corner of her eye, Galina saw Vasilisa take the hand of a young nobleman as he led her to the throng of dancers. The princess sent a pointed look Galina's way.

Her message was clear: *watch yourself.*

To walk through the court was to be put on display, paraded as if she were a prized animal before the leering eyes of the alurean nobles. Galina caught a sympathetic glance from Vasilisa, who must have known all too well what it was like to be a trophy for courtiers who thought they owned you.

But this was an unfamiliar experience for Galina. Her god refused to stay backed into its corner amid so many threats, its raw energy surging through her veins. Courtiers prodded and poked with their godpower as if she were an exotic beast in a menagerie, whispers trailing her like tendrils of smoke.

The heat rose from Galina's skin, and the surrounding air shimmered with the force of her dragon's response.

"Control it," the empress said. "I haven't given you permission to unleash the godfire."

Galina sucked in a sharp breath, her body trembling as she fought to contain her zmeya. "Forgive me, Your Imperial Majesty," she muttered through gritted teeth.

"Spare me your apologies. I want obedience. I'm about to introduce you to someone who will prod at your zmeya like an iron poker." She gestured toward the approaching royal. "Queen Yelena of Samatsk, may I present Galina Feodorovna Kolenkina? You were eager to make her acquaintance."

Queen Yelena was an imposing figure whose intimidating presence was rivaled only by the empress. Her mauve gown whispered against the marble floor, reflecting the room's subtle glow.

The Queen of Samatsk commanded a god with cerebral abilities—not as cataclysmic as godfire but lethal in the hands of someone without mercy.

"Your Majesty," Galina murmured, lowering into a deep curtsy.

"Galina Feodorovna," Queen Yelena replied. "What a pleasure to finally meet you."

Her gaze was like a predator's, honed with a deadly focus. With the swift, sure strike of a hunting animal, she grasped Galina's arm.

Galina's instincts screamed at her to pull away.

Empress Isidora gave a terse shake of her head. *Let her touch you.*

She forced herself to stay put as Yelena gripped her arm. The queen's eyes went obsidian black, and the Exalted Tongue slipped between her lips. The power of her god slammed into Galina's mind and raked with talons.

Galina's zmeya snarled in a threat. *Back off.*

The queen jerked, startled. "Quite the beast." Galina's muscles tensed as Yelena kept sifting through her mind. "And you have no memory of your lineage? Who sired you?"

Her god thrashed, sharp claws and teeth raking beneath her flesh as it felt threatened by Yelena's presence. The lies she'd been instructed to tell were at risk of crumbling under the monarch's scrutiny.

"Feodorovna was the name given to me by my foster mother," she said, fighting to maintain control. "I was raised in Rontsy from infancy."

Princess Vasilisa glanced over from her position in the line of dancers, her expression creased with concern—until she noticed Queen Yelena's hand still firmly gripping Galina's arm.

A crystalline rage flickered over Vasilisa's features, the protectiveness of someone prepared to march through fire, shield at the ready, sword poised to kill. It sent a tantalizing thrill through Galina's body.

But the rush was short-lived as Queen Yelena probed her mind once more. "Pushing past your deity and seeing into your memories could be intriguing. I haven't been challenged in years."

Galina stiffened, bracing herself for impact. She had no experience against a dragon like Yelena's, didn't know the shape of her godpower.

She had seconds to acquire that knowledge.

Seconds to prepare.

Before Queen Yelena could delve into Galina's mind and pluck her secrets, Vasilisa abandoned her partner mid-dance and sauntered forward with a slow, deadly grace.

"Cousin Yelena," she said with thinly veiled contempt. "I don't recall it being basic ballroom etiquette to use godpower on guests, but Galina Feodorovna is not your toy."

"*Vasilochka*," Isidora hissed between her teeth.

Yelena's irises shifted from black to pale blue as her godpower receded. "This is no ordinary ball, and she isn't an average guest. Shouldn't I know how much she can withstand in battle? King Maksim, after all, has some skill in warding off mental intrusions."

Vasilisa's features tightened imperceptibly. Godfrost crept across her gloves, dark silk shifting to gelid white. But just as quickly as it came, she composed herself. The frost dissolved into the fabric, leaving no trace.

"Mother. You were about to request that Galina Feodorovna show her godfire to your guests, weren't you? Maybe she should conserve her energy for that instead."

Empress Isidora gave a curt nod of agreement. "Yelena, wasn't that a prerequisite for your attendance tonight?"

Queen Yelena scowled, but she released Galina's arm. "Fine, let's get on with it."

The empress signaled to the orchestra, and the music ceased. Dancers paused. All focus shifted to Isidora.

"Vasilochka," she said, "take Galina Feodorovna to the center of the room. Let everyone see her."

As Galina followed Vasilisa through the throng of onlookers, she tried not to stare. "I thought you couldn't protect me today," she said in a low voice.

"I made an exception." A muscle worked in Vasilisa's jaw. "I didn't like the way she touched you."

Galina's heart skipped a beat. "Would you have killed her for me?"

Their eyes locked, and everything else melted away. "You're so damn dangerous for my control," Vasilisa breathed. "I would have just started a war for you. Now, finish this before I do something foolish."

Galina had never felt this want. It was bottomless. She wished they were alone.

She leaned in closer. "Missing your glasshouse?"

Princess Vasilisa's smile was small. "Especially when you're with me there. Come find me later."

With that, she disappeared into the swirling mass of people.

And Galina braced herself for what was to come.

34

VITALY

Vitaly and Pyotr stood on the lookout point, buffeted by a biting wind that tugged at their clothes. Zolotiye Palace's spires loomed in the night sky, the opulent facade glistening like a golden mirage against the bleak cityscape.

"How many alurea reported?" Vitaly asked.

Pyotr's face was grim as he replied, "Ten nations, maybe more. Two hundred nobles, all told. Even if you don't slaughter the lot of them, an attack could make them defect to Sopol."

"If we succeed tonight, Sopol will have its own faithless to deal with."

They'd arm their allies with bombs and set them free to unleash righteous hell on their oppressors.

The royal residence was a festering sore on the hill, a nauseating reminder of the gulf between the alurea and those who lived in misery beneath them. It revolted him to imagine those pompous bastards gorging themselves on fine wine and delicacies while the common folk starved in the streets. They were monsters, every single one of them. He wouldn't allow them to continue their games of war and politics, sacrificing countless lives for their own gain.

No, Vitaly would make them pay. He'd tear down their golden tower, brick by fucking brick, until they were left with nothing but the rubble of their arrogance.

The citizens of the Blackshore would rise up and take what was rightfully theirs.

Vitaly scanned the landscape, his ears pricking at the distant strains of music carried on the wind—a mocking reminder of the decadence within the forbidden grounds.

"*That woman* is going to interfere," Pyotr muttered, his tone grim. "I traced the source of her information to Emil when he sent a missive to the confectioner in Khotchino."

Vitaly hadn't known Emil well, but betrayal still stung. The faithless couldn't afford disloyalty.

"Did you deal with him?"

Pyotr's eyes glinted in the moonlight. "I can't abide traitors," he said simply.

Vitaly gave a curt nod. There was no room for fucking about here. Not with so much at stake.

"What do you plan to do about *that w*—" Pyotr began, but Vitaly cut him off with a sharp glare.

"I'll take care of it," he snapped.

"You really are soft on her," Pyotr said, his expression hardening. "Just because you want to stick your cock in her, doesn't mean she's not a liability. And I've already handled two problems tonight. Now I'm not sure I trust you with the third."

Vitaly's eyes narrowed. "What did you do?"

"Emil was sending intel through the confectionery," Pyotr replied coolly. "So I made a logical choice and dealt with the confectioner."

"*Fednezno it*," Vitaly hissed, knowing nothing could be done about it now. The music from the palace reached a crescendo. He had to act. "We'll argue about it later. If I'm not back within forty-eight hours, assume the worst."

"Good luck, boss," Pyotr said, his tone neutral.

"Eat shit, Petya," Vitaly shot back as he left the lookout spot, his mind focused on the task ahead.

He wouldn't rest until the alurea were brought to their knees.

Vitaly crept along the palace's perimeter, sliding his fingertips over the fortification. He sought the slightest irregularities in the rampart until he felt it—an invisible barrier of godpower weaved into the stonework.

The first line of defense for the palace.

But even the most potent layers of godpower had weaknesses, and Vitaly knew how to exploit them. The person who built the protection was only as good as their knowledge, and he was willing to bet that the empress had overlooked a few key details.

She thought in terms of empires, not criminals and confidence artists; of grand strategies and forced entry instead of nimble thievery. In other words, she'd never think like him.

A thief with nothing to lose.

Vitaly gritted his teeth as he ran his palms over the godpower's unforgiving surface. It was known throughout Blackshore that the barrier Empress Isidora had placed in the palace walls was impenetrable. You couldn't go through it.

But Vitaly was not one to be deterred by a little nuisance like impenetrable godpower. So he'd just climb over the damn thing.

Scaling the palace walls, Vitaly couldn't help but chuckle to himself. Luck was on his side today. The guards who usually patrolled the grounds were too busy protecting the pampered royals inside, leaving the exterior unguarded. It was a practical move, but one that left the place wide open to a skilled thief.

The muscles in Vitaly's arms and back burned beneath his coat as he climbed, but he gritted his teeth and pressed on. Each stride and hold was muscle memory from years of thieving in the Blackshore, an instinctual response to the looming architecture. As he boosted himself up using the weathered pockmarks on the wall, he felt exhilaration overcome the bitter cold seeping through his skin. Only the godpower that scratched his flesh served as a reminder that this wasn't just another night-time climb.

He reached the top, heart pounding. The descent was often more treacherous than the climb up, but Vitaly couldn't allow himself to hesitate.

He slid his hands into his pockets to warm them. "Don't be a coward," he muttered to himself. "Finish what you started."

Vitaly let himself down over the edge of the wall and plunged feet-first into the snowbank below. A sharp sting shot through his legs as they sank deep into the powder. He fought off an unpleasant shiver as he struggled to rise out of the drifts, pushing against them until he could stand.

Vitaly fastened his gloves, preparing for what awaited. No more scaling walls—he'd breach the palace gardens on foot.

As he crept through the vast estate, he kept to the forest, veiling himself from sight. The falling snow covered his tracks with each step. The music swelled as he advanced, the melody filling the air. Finally, the manicured garden came into view, illuminated by the blinding lights beyond the arched windows.

He spotted the silhouettes of courtiers, guards, retainers, and busy servants. Vitaly pressed himself to the shadowed hollows of the hedges.

Crouching low, he waited patiently for the perfect guard to come his way. He needed someone to help him lay his trap.

Vitaly's senses were alight as he surveyed the scene. The winter chill was no match for the heat pouring out of the ballroom's doors, surrounding the garden in a blaze of warmth. He was drowning in opulence—the glinting gemstones on the alurean dresses, the shimmering military medals and livery threads, everyone drinking from long-stemmed glasses brimming with some bubbling concoction he'd never tasted.

And the smells—fuck, it was enough to make a man weak in the knees. A heady mix of perfumes, flowers, and food wafted on the breeze, teasing his nose and making his stomach grumble. Succulent cuts of exotic meats, adorned with spices so colorful and fragrant they'd put a spice merchant to shame. Delicate pastries filled with creamy fillings, crowned with fresh fruits and sweet syrups.

The scent of it all was overwhelming, and for a moment, Vitaly was transported back to the days when starvation gnawed at his insides. When his pockets were empty and his gut was hollow. When he didn't know where his next meal would come from. He could smell some savory meat roasting, but he couldn't even identify the animal it came from—yet his stomach throbbed with a hunger he thought he'd left behind.

Vitaly wasn't hard up for silver like the desperate souls in the Black. But he remembered what it was like to live on the brink—one meal to the next.

The glittering realm of wealth ignited a cold fury in his gut. This was a world built on the backs of its citizens, where monsters held all the power.

But not for much longer, Vitaly vowed as he spotted his mark.

A lone sentry, bedecked in the colors and finery Vitaly recognized from Alempois, strolled to the back of the garden for a quick smoke. The burn of the paper lit in the darkness.

Vitaly followed him and struck.

The cigarette went flying as he clamped a hand over the guard's mouth, preventing any chance of godpower being used. The sentry bucked and struggled against him, but Vitaly's grip was unyielding.

This guard was his only way into the palace's interior.

Vitaly reached into the depths of his coat pocket and retrieved his device. The man's body went rigid as he snapped the metal shut and engaged the locking mechanism.

"Listen here," Vitaly spoke calmly, his voice hinting at danger. "I'm going to take my hand off your mouth, and you won't make a sound. Not one scream, not one word in the Exalted Tongue. This collar's loaded with enough explosive powder to turn your skull into a fucking bowl. Got it?" The sentry whimpered in response. "Good. I knew you'd understand."

As soon as Vitaly released him, the man turned, fear etched into his features. "What do you want?" he asked in a hoarse whisper.

"Your assistance," Vitaly replied nonchalantly. He dug into another pocket and pulled out fifteen small devices, each no bigger than a coin. "Take these trinkets and scatter them around that fancy ballroom. Plant them on a table, in a vase, or even up your ass. I don't care where, just do it right, and you might live to see morning."

The guard's mouth opened and closed a few times. "I—I can't. You can't ask me—"

Vitaly scowled. "I'm not asking. Let me make it clear. The collar you're wearing is rigged to blow in forty-five minutes. Any second you waste not doing what I ask is on you. But if you want to keep your head attached to your neck, you'll put these in the ballroom and return here once you're done. Got it?" The guard's breaths quickened, but he nodded in agreement. "Good."

As Vitaly turned to leave, he remembered something he needed to add. Not because he gave two shits about morals, but because Sera would be furious with him if he didn't. He still had to win her over, after all.

"One more thing," he drawled. "If you come across any servants, tell them the empress commanded them to head down to the kitchens."

The palace was massive, and the kitchens were deep down in the bowels of its foundation. With a bit of luck, it was enough distance from the blast radius and Sera wouldn't carve him into tiny pieces by tomorrow.

At least, he hoped not.

The guard seemed bemused. "For what?"

"Because I said so, and you've got my bomb attached to your neck," Vitaly snapped. "Make something up. Now, off you go. Your time has shrunk to forty-one minutes."

The sentry hurried off. His movements were as cautious as one would expect from a man wearing a bomb and lugging around fifteen more.

Enough to annihilate every alurea in the ballroom.

35

SERA

Sera's boots crunched against the rocky shoreline as she scoured the beach for any trace of Emil's intelligence drop.

Anna's informant sent word he had information on Vitaly's plans for the alurean ball. Sera's sabotage in Zatishye hadn't seemed to rattle her husband—but Vitaly always had contingencies. He was quick to adapt.

Katya and Galina were as good as dead unless Sera could retrieve this missive—fast.

She didn't give a shit about the royals, but the innocent people caught in the crossfire of her husband's schemes deserved better.

She gnashed her teeth and followed the path between two craggy landmarks that Emil had referenced. She dug at the sand with her bare hands, scraping until her nails were muddied with soil. But she found nothing.

"Damn it," she muttered.

Maybe Emil had mixed up the coordinates in his rush? Sera strained her eyes against the blackness, scouring for other markers she could use to pinpoint the drop location.

The glacial wind nipped at her fingers, numbing them as she shoveled away at the snow and sand. Until—

Something brushed her knuckles.

Sera's heart plummeted like a stone in water as she unearthed a pale hand. "No," she whispered, her breath fogging in the frigid air.

She dug frantically until broad shoulders emerged from the drift—cloaked in gray wool that matched the stormy sky above. Skin marked by frostbite, a cruel kiss from the cold. Sera swallowed hard, knowing what she'd find when she uncovered his face.

He looked like he was sleeping, with dark lashes curled against his ashen cheeks. But bruises marred his jaw and bloodstains slashed across his torso from stab wounds, the violence a jarring contrast to the serene sound of the waves crashing against the shore.

Sera's stomach churned as she read the note pinned to his body, written in Zverti.

Don't interfere. The same goes for your friend.

"Anna," Sera whispered, her heart clenched with dread.

She set off through the streets of the Blackshore, her breath heaving in ragged gasps as she dodged down alleyways and snaking lanes. A single thought pounded in her head: *Hurry, hurry, hurry!*

The slick cobblestones made it difficult for her to maintain her footing, but she pushed on until she arrived at the bustling main street. The harsh smell of smoke assaulted her senses, and she spotted the glow of flames flickering in the distance.

Coming from Anna's Confectionery.

A gust of wind tore at Sera's coat as she burst through the door, screaming Anna's name. The heat of the inferno enveloped her like an angry, living thing. Haze choked the air. She couldn't see.

"Anna!"

A faint sound caught her attention, and she rushed toward the establishment's rear, struggling to navigate through the thick smoke and searing heat. The fire chased her, eager tongues licking hungrily at her coat.

An agonized whimper cut through the chaos, and Sera dropped to her knees, crawling through the wreckage of shattered glass and burning debris. Beads of sweat dripped down her face as she inched forward, tracking the trail of a muffled cry.

Then, she finally spotted a patch of dark hair beneath a table.

Anna was tied up with a gag so tight not even the gods could hear her screams. But at least she was still breathing.

Sera crawled closer, swiping at her sweaty forehead with a sleeve singed by the flames.

Her hands shook as she sliced through the ropes that bound Anna's wrists, the knife glinting in the flickering firelight. She moved on to her ankles, working quickly to free her friend.

"Sera," Anna whispered, her voice hoarse.

"I've got you," Sera promised. "Hold on."

She cut through the final rope.

Sera seized Anna's hand and dragged her out the front door. The sudden slash of frigid wind provided a welcome reprieve from the oppressive heat. They stumbled out onto the street as the roof collapsed behind them.

Sera led Anna away from the growing throng of spectators, guiding her toward a quiet alley where she could regain her composure.

She eased the other woman into the snow and tilted her chin up. "Are you hurt? Do you need anything?"

Anna shook her head, her eyes ablaze with fury. "I'm going to murder someone."

Sera's mouth twisted. "My husband, I presume?"

"Someone else. A maniac behemoth who called me a nuisance."

"Employed by my husband, then," Sera muttered. "The same giant who's been tailing me since Zatishye. He's trying to stop us interfering with their plans tonight. He killed Emil before I could get the information drop."

Anna flinched and swore. "Then go," she said, pushing Sera away. "Get to Vitaly before he kills Katya and Galina."

"Can you make it on your own?"

Anna rolled her eyes. "Stop fussing over me, Sera. I'll be fine. Now go!"

With a sharp nod, Sera bolted. Her breath came in ragged gasps as she sprinted through the moonlit streets, her boots pounding the frozen earth. She raced up the hill toward the palace, determined to reach Galina and Katya before it was too late.

They had thrown themselves into the lion's den to aid Sera in her mission. Failure wasn't an option. Not after the promises she'd made.

The fortress walls loomed in the darkness like a towering monolith. And then Sera spotted it—Vitaly's footprints, almost hidden under a fresh blanket of snow. The sneaky bastard had scouted out the weak points in Isidora's defenses.

Following the trail, Sera arrived at a section of the wall that was pockmarked and cracked, perfect for scaling. Vitaly had the mind of a thief.

Sera swore softly and began to climb. Though she couldn't match Vitaly's feline grace, Sera had enough experience with covert operations to handle the physical rigors of the job. Her muscles burned with the effort of ascending the stone barrier, but she gritted her teeth and persevered until she cleared the top.

The cold bit at her exposed skin and sweat dampened her coat as she dropped onto the snow-covered ground within the compound.

Faint strains of music wafted on the wind, mingling with laughter from the palace's guests. Sera darted through the dense trees, her eyes scanning for signs of danger.

Boots crunched through the ice—sentries doing their rounds.

Sera melted into the shadows of the palace walls, her breaths coming in shallow gasps. The two guards walked past her, so close their thick coats brushed against her cheek.

With a fortifying breath, Sera dashed toward the unlit windows of the east wing. Her fingers traced the protective layers of godpower placed by Empress Isidora within Zolotiye's facade and foundations, a clever double-layered defense for those with the clearance to enter the building.

Although Sera didn't possess godpower as strong as Galina's, she had a plethora of strategic skills at her disposal. The basic godpower granted by her dragon proved incredibly useful during her Sundyr missions. They allowed her to infiltrate places where even the most skilled faithless spies couldn't gain access.

Sera did what any spy worth their salt would do—she searched for weaknesses in the barrier. Fortifications of godpower were no different from physical walls. It had texture, hairline fractures in its construction, and the occasional exploitable vulnerability. It was like feeling for cracks in masonry or examining a suit of armor for faults. Every protective godpower required periodic maintenance to keep its integrity.

Sera yanked off her glove and ran her fingers along the godpower's intricately woven matrix. The craftsmanship was admirable, but Sera had no time to waste. She needed a way inside.

She traced down the lines of power. "Hurry, come on," she muttered under her breath.

Then she found it.

A crack in the godpower's architecture. An exploitable flaw. Sera reached for the blade concealed under her coat, rolled up her sleeve, and made a long, thin gash across her arm. Her zmeya nudged at the wound, debating whether to comply. Deciding if she had bled enough for this one task.

"More later if you get me in there," she gritted through her teeth.

Her dragon shifted, scraping the underside of her flesh as if to say, *You'd better.*

The stubborn bastard growled the Exalted Tongue through her lips, exerting a small but forceful bit of power that shoved against the fracture and created an opening for her to pass through.

She quickly wrapped her handkerchief around her bleeding arm, grateful for the servants who had opened windows to counter the intense heat of the gathering. Hundreds of bodies with powerful zmei had elevated the temperature of the palace to a level resembling that of a summer heatwave.

Sera chose a darkened room, forced open the window, and clambered inside.

Then she set out to find her husband.

36

KATYA

Katya strode down the corridor, scanning for any sign of the faithless. She knew every nook and cranny of Zolotiye Palace, every servant's face and name, and every visitor who had ever crossed the threshold.

It was a skill she had developed out of necessity, honed during her years as a handmaiden. The empress prized her memory, but Katya wielded her knowledge of insignificant details like a lethal weapon, ready to strike at a moment's notice.

Sera and Galina needed her.

So she kept a vigilant watch, scouring the faces of the royals and courtiers who entered the ballroom. She noted their clothes, their ribbons, their colors—all the superficial markers of prestige that mattered in this godsforsaken world.

Servants hurried back and forth, fetching drinks and food for their masters and mistresses. The bells on their collars chimed like a twisted symphony, marking them as property. Katya's face burned with fury as she watched one handmaiden struggle under the weight of a plate of desserts, her eyes glazed with pain. She had been there before, forced to carry out the most demeaning tasks under threat of punishment.

Then Katya noticed someone dressed in the livery of a Liesgau servant slip through the corridor.

"Sera," she breathed.

Katya wasted no time. She strode toward Sera, grabbed her by the arm, and pulled her into a dark alcove. "What are you doing here?" Katya demanded. "And where did you get these clothes?"

Sera winced. "I didn't harm the woman I took them from—"

"*Godsdamn it,* Serafima." She hardly ever cursed, but tonight she was unraveling at the seams. "Does Galina know you're here?"

"No, but I had to come. Vitalik's here. I saw his tracks in the snow."

Katya edged out from the alcove, taking note of the guests and staff as they scurried from the ballroom. "I haven't spotted any unfamiliar faces," she murmured. "And the secondary ward built into the palace architecture should've barred anyone without clearance. You had help from your god, I assume?"

"Vitalik doesn't need a god," Sera replied. "He's crafty and ruthless enough to break through any protection. One of his men murdered a spy and almost killed Anya this evening. They won't miss this chance."

Katya reeled. "Is Anya all right?"

Sera's features tightened, but she breathed out slowly. "She's alive. But we can't just sit on our asses. Keep searching."

Katya tried to steady her nerves and strategize. "If Vitaly Sergeyevich is planning something catastrophic, you have to leave."

Sera squared her shoulders, determination etched on her face. "I won't let you and Galya put yourselves in danger. If you see Vitalik, don't confront him. Just get back to me as fast as you can."

She nodded reluctantly and left Sera in the alcove. As she hurried through the corridor, the orchestra's music from the ballroom only added to her growing panic, every note like a countdown to her impending doom.

If Vitaly lay in wait inside the palace—

A guard from Alempois stumbled out of the ballroom, his eyes wide with terror. A crude metal collar encircled his neck, devoid of jewels or decoration. None of the other sentries wore one like it; during a ball where appearances were everything, no one would dare.

Katya caught up to him. "Your Magnificence," she said, bowing respectfully, as any servant would. "May I get you anything?"

The man's throat bobbed frantically against the collar as he swallowed hard. "No, nothing," he croaked, his lips barely moving. "Her Imperial Majesty has ordered all staff to report to the kitchens immediately. Please pass the message on to any servants you encounter."

Alarm crashed through Katya's mind. She hadn't spotted servants since she'd emerged from the alcove. Her gaze returned to the device around his neck—a metallic contraption with a locking mechanism at the front.

"May I inquire about your collar?" Katya asked, keeping her tone soft. "I've never seen anything like it, and Her Imperial Highness, Princess Vasilisa, has a remarkable ability to detect metals. I'd be delighted to tell her about it. Can I ask where it came from?"

"No." He stepped away from her, desperation in his voice. "Please, just go to the kitchens—"

Katya grabbed his arm, an action that contradicted her training and protocol. But she had no time to waste. "Did someone put this around your neck? Tell me now."

His breathing hitched as he swung his head wildly. "Please—please go."

She gripped him harder. "Come with me. I know someone who can help you."

Katya didn't care about the sentry or his situation. She was more worried about the people who would die if the bomb went off. Herself included.

"No one can help me."

"I'm not lying to you. If you want that thing off, come with me."

The guard allowed Katya to lead him to Sera, who remained tucked away in the shadows. She jolted with alarm—until she spotted the collar around the sentry's neck.

"Oh, for fuck's sake," she muttered under her breath.

"Can you help?" Katya whispered urgently.

"Don't move," Sera commanded the sentry, as forceful as an empress. She studied the device, examining every inch of it. "He put this on you?"

The guard nodded, his mouth quivering. "And he said—"

"I have a good idea of what that asshole told you." Sera scowled, fingers tracing the edges of the metal box. "How many bombs did you plant?"

The guard's panic returned, his words coming out in a jumbled mess. "I—I didn't—"

Sera cut him off, her voice as sharp as a sword's edge. "He gave you little devices to put around the ballroom. Might have looked like coins? How many?"

"Fifteen," he breathed quietly.

A string of expletives erupted from Sera's lips. "When were they set to go off? Or did he have a trigger with him?"

"I don't—please—"

"Shh, calm down," Sera murmured in a gentle tone. "Let me look."

The guard trembled, each second stretching into eternity.

Sera cursed under her breath and lowered her hands. "If I had my tools, I might be able to take this off, but the design is foolproof. If I apply too much pressure, it'll detonate. If I try to crack it open, it'll detonate. The only way to get it off is with a key."

"He has a key." The guard's fear was palpable. "He said he'd take it off if I did what he wanted."

The edges of Sera's mouth pulled taut. "Where were you supposed to meet him?"

"The gardens. He said he'll wait for my signal."

"He won't get your signal," Sera said. "You both go locate the bombs. It's standard tech, so you can disable them once you're there. Find the locking mechanism and turn it off. I'll deal with Vitaly."

Katya nodded in agreement and nudged the guard out of the alcove. "Be careful," she whispered.

Sera leaned in and breathed, too low for the sentry to hear, "When he shows you where the explosives are, you and Galina get as far away from him as possible. Do you understand me?"

Katya's heart thundered in her chest as she comprehended what Sera was saying—there was no way to disarm the bomb on the sentry's neck.

She held her breath as she returned to the ballroom. Death might await her, but she refused to be afraid. She was a survivor.

And she would survive this, too.

37

GALINA

Hundreds of eyes watched Galina.

She wanted to hold her head high and stare back at them in defiance. But that wasn't the role she'd come to play. She needed to wear the mask of docility—a marionette at the behest of her monarch.

Her fingers trembled with affected unease, her shoulders heaving in feigned submission. Let them believe she was a timid mouse.

She would prove them wrong.

"A simple demonstration, please," Empress Isidora told Galina, pacing at the edges of the gathered throng. Her voluminous black dress rustled with her movements. "So we can all get back to our dances."

But Queen Yelena stepped forward, her glittering mauve skirts catching in the light. "I didn't come all this way for some trifling display," she said, eyeing Galina with cold calculation. "We're not supplicants here to genuflect at your throne, Isidora."

The other monarchs and courtiers nodded in agreement.

Though they appeared calm on the surface, their faces were ravenous, hungry for what Galina could offer.

The gentle hum of conversation echoed through the room, whispers of ambition and greed. If they could defeat Sopol in a war, it would mean greater spoils for all of them: vast expanses of land, increased power and influence, and hordes of new devotees flocking to their respective thrones.

As if they *wanted* this war.

Empress Isidora's eyes blazed with fury, but her voice was sweet as she inquired, "What would satisfy you, Yelena?"

The words sounded innocent, but it was a clear warning: *don't overstep your bounds.*

Queen Yelena summoned Queen Marianne of Sasnis to her side, and the women conferred in quiet consultation, much to Isidora's apparent displeasure.

After a moment, the queens separated, and Yelena resumed speaking. "You want us to trust someone with an unknown lineage. So we need to know her abilities. Her god's strength is impressive, but I won't jeopardize my kingdom by relying on a courtier who can't control it."

The jingling of bells reverberated through the chamber—a delicate razor cutting through the stillness. Galina spotted Katya slipping into the ballroom, her fidgeting fingers betraying her anxiety.

Before Galina could contemplate its meaning, Queen Yelena's expression shifted as if she had just had a revelation.

"I remember your mastery of godfire was legendary, Isidora," Queen Yelena remarked casually. "Weren't you known for tormenting your enemies by burning them until the brink of death and then resurrecting them for another round? An impressive skill. Does your protégé share it?"

"Yes." Isidora didn't seem amused. "Get to the point, Yelena."

"I humbly request that your new courtier showcase her talents on your handmaiden," Queen Yelena declared with a twisted grin.

Galina's blood turned to ice in her veins. She'd vowed

never to use the godfire power of resurrection again—not for any reason. But here she stood, cornered by a pack of wolves, every promise she ever spoke exposed as a godsdamned lie. Killing priests and priestesses. Ordered to employ the torture Irina had honed in the interrogation room, one that made Galina regret even surviving Olensk.

If she failed, Empress Isidora would have no use for her. Worst of all, Katya would be dead.

Queen Yelena was requiring nothing less than a display of raw strength—irrefutable evidence that allying with Isidora was worth it, even if it meant going up against Sopol. She was staking her throne on whichever side she chose.

Empress Isidora's expression went cold. "I thought you wanted Ekaterina Isidorakh to sing for you, not use her to make threats."

Queen Yelena's lips stretched into a smile. "I'd be happy to listen to her sing later. Surely your handmaiden will survive? Or do you doubt your courtier's ability to control her godfire?"

The implication was clear: if Isidora didn't trust Galina, why should they? The fragile alliance between them was based on power, not loyalty. The queen's vast armies could easily tip the scales in Sopol's favor.

Calling her demand a request was being too generous.

Isidora's expression turned sour. "Ekaterina Isidorakh," she said, gesturing toward her handmaiden. "Come forward where everyone can see you."

Galina watched as Katya drifted closer, her chest heaving underneath her vibrant dress as her usual composure deserted her. The melodic tinkle of her bells was at odds with the suffocating tension in the chamber.

Empress Isidora approached them. She leaned close to Galina and said, low and deadly, "You won't wait until her last heartbeat. Do you hear me? Pull back before that."

Galina's zmeya could only heal burns caused by its flames; it couldn't bring the dead to life. She nodded solemnly. "I will."

"Good," the empress murmured, her voice as smooth as a serpent's hiss. "Don't rob me of my handmaiden." And with that, she faded into the crowd, leaving Galina to do her grim work.

Galina understood the message: *fail me, and I will ruin you.*

(*Like you used to fail under Irina's orders. That interrogation room is covered in the ashes of your mistakes.*)

Galina's fingers dug into the fabric of her skirt as she shoved that insidious, unwanted thought beneath a grim determination that anchored her in place. No. Death might be inevitable—but not tonight, not for Katya. Not while Galina still had a breath left in her body. She'd performed a resurrection before, and she'd do it again.

The air hung heavy with the scent of the handmaiden's terror. Galina almost wished for Irina's deceitful tongue to spin pretty lies.

There was no comfort to be found in the presence of the wolves. They worshipped power, and they demanded their due.

Galina's god stirred—and she let it take over. Her muscles tensed, and she exhaled in ragged gasps as the godfire built inside her. The courtiers watched her, their whispers silenced by awe.

But Katya trembled with fear, her bells chiming an eerie tune. Remorse gripped Galina's chest, and sweat slicked her palms as heat prickled beneath her skin.

"I'm sorry," she whispered.

Words in the Exalted Tongue formed at the back of her throat—a jagged slash of godpower against her mouth.

Galina extended her arm and released the blast. Godfire exploded in a brilliant display of light and heat, an intense mix of color that filled the room with a brilliance that was almost blinding. Waves of crimson and gold swept outward, followed by shimmering streams of orange and yellow that crackled through the air like lightning. It burned hotter than any blaze, a conflagration that could reduce the world to ashes.

It was beautiful, and it was terrible.

The room shook with the force of the power that Galina had unleashed. Marble shattered and windows cracked as the godfire devoured everything in its path.

Katya's screams were swallowed up by the roar of the inferno, a desperate cry that was quickly silenced.

Galina squeezed her eyes shut, but the image of Katya consumed by godfire would be permanently seared into her memory. She could still feel the heat radiating from the blaze and smell the acidic stench of burning flesh.

It reminded her of Olensk. Of the way she had huddled in the cellar and prayed for the flames to pass her by.

Yet, this was different. This was *her* god. *Her* power. There was no one else to blame, no distant figure on a hill to curse. The zmeya writhed in pleasure—a beast reveling in destruction and chaos.

Galina refused to let it consume her.

She was not a monster.

And she would not let her god turn her into one.

Galina still clung to the memories of the girl who had hidden while the world burned around her. She could feel the weight of that fear and helplessness even now, as Katya crumbled to ash.

Bring her back, she told the god. *Bring her back now.*

More godpower spilled from her lips, piecing together the shattered remnants of the body before her. Ash reformed into bone, bone into muscle, and blood into organs and flesh. Every stitch was woven with pain. Galina fell to her knees, gasping for air as the god's strength coursed through her.

Katya's nude form lay lifeless on the ground, her clothing devoured by the flames. Her eyes flew open, and her mouth twisted in a silent scream of agony as the godpower took hold.

Galina crawled to Katya, ignoring the gasps and whispers of the onlookers.

"Katya," she rasped. "*Katya.*"

The other woman shuddered, a whispered word slithering from her lips so softly that Galina had to strain to hear it. "Bombs... here."

Galina's head snapped up, and she locked gazes with Vasilisa. Something in her expression must have given her away because the princess surged toward her—

BOOM!

The ballroom shook, the walls quivering from the force of the explosion. Smoke and debris filled the air. Galina felt a sharp sting slice across her arm.

"*Galina!*"

Vasilisa's voice reached her through the chaos. The princess threw herself at Galina, godpower bursting from her—a shield to protect her and Katya.

But there was no time. Another bomb detonated and the blast tore through the room.

38

SERA

Sera's footsteps pounded against the gravel as she charged into the gardens.

When she saw the explosive device she had designed, she knew the poor bastard with the bomb strapped to his neck was as good as dead.

But she couldn't predict the guard's reaction to the imminent threat of his demise. Would he lash out and hurt Sera and Katya? Trigger the bomb? So she kept her mouth shut and lied about a key that didn't exist. Let the sentry believe he had a shot at survival when Vitaly had sealed his fate.

Her husband would be on the run, eager to view the carnage from a safe distance.

She intended to hunt him down.

The gardens were deserted, all the alurea flocking inside to watch Galina's godfire display like she was some kind of trained animal. If Katya didn't locate those bombs...

"Get Vitaly," Sera muttered as she charged down the garden walkway. "Find the bastard."

Sera raced through the gate and into the woods, her gaze locked on the footprints in the snow. The weather had already put Vitaly at a disadvantage, and she aimed to capitalize. With a burst of energy, Sera charged through the trees, guided by the blazing lights of the palace that illuminated the path and the silhouette sprinting ahead of her.

"*Vitalik.*"

Her husband froze and turned sharply. "Sera." Her name fell from his lips like ash in a dying fire. "What are you doing here?"

"You rigged that sentry's neck with explosives," Sera snapped, closing in on him. "One of your lackeys killed my informant and almost murdered my friend. You don't have the right to demand anything from me."

Vitaly reached out and gripped her arm tightly. "Follow me. Now."

"So you can set off the bombs on your way out? I'd rather swallow a sword, you witless hack. Hand over the detonator before you mess everything up."

Vitaly didn't say a word. He tightened his grip and tried to drag her through the forest. Sera's other fist shot up and hit hard on his side. With a grunt, he released her.

"For fuck's sake, Serafima. Can't you ever—"

Sera charged at him again, throwing punches. He responded in kind, but his stance was more protective than combative. He wasn't looking to hurt her.

But Sera had no time for this. She drew out her dagger and grasped it tight—readying for a brawl.

"Hand over the detonator," she snarled, "or I'll make you regret it." Let him think what he wanted; that she had betrayed his cause and was an alurean loyalist. She didn't care. "*Give it to me*, Vitalik."

He seized her wrist as quickly as a striking snake, his silver eyes flashing in the darkness. "That's what I've been trying to tell you. They're timed, and they're set to go off—"

The explosion shook Sera's bones.

Sera whirled to see smoke rising from the palace—a plume of destruction in the night sky.

The first bomb.

Vitaly's grip on her arm was tight enough to bruise as he yanked her toward the cover of a nearby tree. They both knew what was coming next. He might as well have tried to hold back a storm.

Fifteen. Vitaly had that guard plant fifteen bombs. They were out of time, out of options. Sera could hear the countdown ticking in her head.

If all those devices went off, the forest would be no protection from this.

Sera didn't hesitate. She wrenched free from Vitaly's grasp and stepped in front of him, her blade gleaming in the moonlight. This was the only way to keep her god compliant for the amount of godpower she needed.

She plunged the dagger into her gut.

Vitaly's shout stung Sera's ears as she gripped the hilt tight, blood spilling between her fingers. But the power of her god was a wildfire, burning away her fear and doubt.

The countdown hit zero, and the world exploded around them.

Sera refused to break. She stood tall, ablaze with a surging energy that hummed through her veins. Her godpower raged inside her, an unstoppable tempest finally unleashed.

The shockwave smashed into her like a physical blow. Sera pushed back, pouring all her strength into a shield of pure light. It crackled and spat as it met the blast, holding against the force of the explosion.

She felt it in every inch of her body—her frame jolted, and her blood dripped onto the ash-covered snow at her feet. But Sera did not falter. She held fast, determined to protect what she loved.

And then it was over.

The silence was deafening, the surrounding trees solemn witnesses to the devastation. Sera sank to her knees, gasping for breath as the power within her slowly ebbed away.

And Sera's god slithered between the hollows of her bones, licking hungrily at her wounds. She had asked the zmeya to save her, and now it exacted its cruel price.

Her quivering fingers dug deep into the crimson-stained snow, her mind struggling to find clarity in the enveloping darkness. She had aimed with precision, hoping to avoid striking any vital organs. But in the end, it may not matter.

Someone must have seen her. The maid she had stolen clothes from would soon be discovered locked in one of the rooms. The alurea would be hunting Sera again; this time, she might not be so lucky.

"Sera." A gentle touch on her face pulled her out of her daze. Her vision swam. "Sera."

"They'll be looking for us," she whispered, falling forward into Vitaly's arms.

As she lost consciousness, she felt the god stretch and lick her blood from its claws.

"Don't you dare close those eyes, Sera." The words echoed through her mind as she fought to stay conscious.

The skeletal trees swayed above her as she was jostled from side to side. Vitaly was carrying her, shoving his way through the snowdrifts. She could barely hear the shouts in the distance over her heartbeat.

She shut her eyes again, too tired to keep them open.

"Serafima." Her husband's voice was thick with emotion as he lowered her gently to the ground, his gloved hands warm against her skin. "Open your eyes. *Open them.*"

She forced her lids apart to see his beautiful face, pale in the moonlight and etched with worry. "*Vorovka,*" he said. "I'm going to go up the palace wall, and I need you to hold on to me. Can you do that?"

Sera's teeth chattered as she nodded, too spent to speak. With a swiftness that belied his size and strength, Vitaly hoisted her onto his broad back and secured her arms around his neck.

Every muscle burned during the arduous ascent. Her vision blurred in and out of focus, nausea bubbling from her stomach to her throat. When she began to slip from his grasp, he steadied her without breaking his climb.

The next time Sera opened her eyes, they were on solid ground, and Vitaly was carrying her away from the palace walls.

"Why bother saving me?" Sera muttered weakly into his shoulder, her body wracked with pain. "You know what I am."

He would never have wed her if he knew; he would have snuffed out her life without a second thought.

Vitaly shot her a withering glare, his features momentarily illuminated by the moonlight filtering through the trees. "Stop asking foolish questions."

He picked up the pace, each jolt sending shudders through her aching bones.

"Carrying me like a sack of fucking turnips," she gasped.

He grunted in response. "Next time I'll be sure to bring a cushion for your delicate ass. Keep those eyes open now."

But the darkness was swallowing her vision once more. "Just let me sleep, and maybe I won't slit your throat," she breathed, her voice fading into a whisper.

"You can't kill me if you're dead."

"What if I promise to wake up?" Her words were faint now, evaporating into the frigid air.

Vitaly's head turned slightly, his features barely visible in the blackness that cloistered them both. "You'd better keep that promise, Sera," he murmured, before the void claimed her once more.

Sera woke slowly.

Agony rippled through her body, setting every nerve ending ablaze. She knew the feeling all too well. She had pushed her godpower to its limits and was paying the price.

Through hazy senses, she registered laughter blending with distant chatter, woodsmoke-scented air, and the harsh scratch of a wool blanket against her skin.

Sera eased her eyes open. Light pooled at the foot of sun-faded curtains, spilling into the spartan room. She shifted on the bed, taking in the collection of mismatched furniture alongside fancier pieces, like an antique globe across the chamber that indicated ill-gotten wealth—her husband's extravagant taste. Typical.

Sera winced as she propped herself up on her elbows, biting back a curse as she gingerly lifted her shirt to assess the wound on her midriff. The gauze and bandages suggested that someone had tended to her with utter care. Had Vitaly patched her up?

The click of the latch made Sera hastily feign sleep.

Footsteps approached, and a gruff voice broke the silence. "I know you're up, Sera."

She ground her teeth, refusing to look at him. "Go away. I'm avoiding you."

Vitaly snorted, and she felt his calloused hands lift the hem of her shirt, exposing her injury.

Sera's eyes snapped open. "What are you doing?"

He ignored her as he peeled back the dressings to inspect the stitches. A herbal ointment had been applied to the wound. "Checking to make sure it hasn't gone septic. Bonesaws told me you'd be thrilled to hear you didn't nick any of your organs."

Anger flared in Sera's chest. "You brought a doctor?" Sera hissed.

She could have taken care of herself. Anna could have sewn her up and whined about it. Now she had to worry about some stranger who had seen her face.

"My wife was bleeding out in front of me. Yes, I fucking brought a doctor," Vitaly snapped impatiently. "And I had to bribe the bastard with a pile of silver to forget he saw you."

"I didn't ask for help—"

"No, you sure as shit didn't," he retorted, affixing the clean bandage in place. "Seeing as you were unconscious after plunging a knife into your stomach like a damn idiot." His stare locked onto hers. "Why?"

Sera studied the sharp angles of his cheekbones, each line honed like a blade. He was a creature forged in ice and tempered by frost, but she'd peered beneath that armor before. She had felt the heat of his lips against her own each night.

Her perusal drifted over the lines etched into his forehead, down to the broad span of his shoulders, taking in the imposing figure that dominated the cramped room. She swallowed the lump in her throat. He was still the most beautiful man she'd ever seen.

Vitaly made a faint noise. "I can't think when you look at me like that," he said softly.

Sera collected herself. "Thank you for patching me up," she said, attempting to slide past him.

His grasp was gentle yet firm as he clamped onto her arm. "Don't even try it. You're in no condition to move."

Sera's attention fell to his hand. And there it was—the ring she had given him. The piece of scrap metal she had scavenged from the shore, a clockwork part from an old, rusted-out mechanism that a blacksmith had repurposed into a band—a reminder of what they had lost, what they had sacrificed to survive. Despite everything, he still wore it.

"You didn't answer my question last night. Why did you save me?" she asked. "I would've bled out and died in those woods. Or frozen to death. Why did you bother?"

Vitaly's expression hardened. He plucked at the chain hidden under her shirt, his hand moving so fast that she had no time to react.

"Strange that you'd wear this when you know your husband so little," he said. His ring landed heavily against her chest as he released it. "I told you not to ask foolish questions."

Sera clenched her jaw. "You also told me you'd kill anyone with a god inside them. I kept it as a reminder."

With a light shove, she pushed past him, limping toward the window. She ripped aside the curtain to reveal a view of the palace in the distance. From her vantage, she could make out some of the destruction wrought upon Zolotiye—though most of it lay hidden away behind those high walls.

"What have you heard from the alurea?" Sera asked, struggling to keep her voice steady.

Did you kill my sister? she wanted to demand. *Did you kill Katya?*

Their marriage was already in shambles, but if anything happened to Katya and Galina, there would be no way to fix it. She'd stake a claim on Vitaly's life without a second thought. She had saved him more than once, and perhaps he owed her: her life to give and hers to take.

Vitaly came to stand next to her. "Worried about your Common God?"

"Don't fuck with me," she snarled. "What have you heard?"

He let out an exasperated sound. "The news is being throttled, but the empress and your precious Common God were seen on the temple balcony." His words dripped with bitterness; his plan had failed.

Sera's relief was so intense it almost knocked her off her feet. She reeled back and steadied a hand against the antique globe to keep herself upright.

"What about the empress? Was she with someone else? A petite woman with dark hair? Her handmaiden?"

Vitaly's gaze sharpened with suspicion. "She was. Care to explain why you're asking?"

Sera wouldn't have to kill him, not yet. She could give him another day.

Galina and Katya were alive. Thank the gods.

"I don't have to answer your questions. I said I have no interest in associating with the faithless."

His lips pressed into a hard line. "Well, isn't that too bad? We're already associated. The sentries are massing at the gates to sweep the streets. Rumors are swirling that a woman and a man fled the scene. The woman was bleeding out from a stab wound. Accompanied by a man with black hair who bears an uncanny resemblance to the one who escaped them four years back—"

"Stop explaining," she snarled. "They're looking for us again, and your stupid plan failed."

He got up close and personal with her face. "It wouldn't have failed if someone hadn't warned our enemies about it."

Sera's expression turned to stone. "So you're calling me a traitor."

"I'm calling you a spy," Vitaly growled. "And I'm an idiot for trusting you and bringing you here."

"You think I'm a *spy*?"

Vitaly stepped closer. "I know what I saw at the palace. I had to move quickly and use the retaining wall for cover if I wanted to survive, but then you were there—and I felt... I felt your..."

Sera clenched her fists so hard her nails bit into her flesh. "Just say it," she whispered, thick with an emotion too dark to name.

"What, that you're an alurea?" The room seemed to contract as Vitaly's rage filled the air. "I've known you since I was fourteen years old, Sera. You've seen what those bastards can do, and you've saved my ass from them more times than I can count. And you didn't say a word."

But there was more in his expression than fury—hurt beyond imagining, pain over everything she had kept hidden for so long. Secrets etched bone deep.

Sera had built her life with Vitaly on a foundation of lies, and it was all crashing down.

"If you had realized what I was the day we met, what would you have done with me?" she rasped. He looked away. The answer he gave required no words. "Right. Then what do I deserve: to be denounced or killed? Maybe I should give your ring back now."

"Do you want me to end your life, or do I have the right to ask questions first?" Vitaly asked tightly.

Sera arched a brow. "Why bother? You've already convicted me of being an alurean spy and a liar."

His sudden grip on her chin was gentle, yet his eyes shifted like molten steel—dangerous and unstable. "Was there ever any truth in our relationship? Or was it all just pretend? Were you manipulating me the day my brother and Irina were murdered?"

Sera's mouth twisted. "Is that what you believe? And where does that leave me in your revised version of the last four years? Have I spent it in alurean luxury while you toiled away in Sundyr?"

Something dark filled Vitaly's features. "Did you?"

Sera slipped out of his grasp and stared at the ancient globe. It was a relic of a bygone era, marked with nations that had long since been swallowed by more powerful alurea, conquered, and consumed in bloodshed. She'd fled to some of these places as a fugitive.

"I see," she said wearily. "You don't trust your memories. You want the truth from the beginning, then? I'll lay it out for you." She had kept so many secrets, so many unsaid things. "I'm bonded to a dragon so broken and angry it wants me dead. The day we met on the beach, I would have drowned myself if you hadn't shown up."

Something stricken passed through Vitaly's features. "Gods," he rasped.

"We both did what we needed to survive, remember? I patched you up and kept you alive through every mission we ever took." Her voice softened. "Am I really such a bullshit artist that you think I'd orchestrate all that just to dupe you?"

"*Vorovka*," he whispered. A prayer this time—or maybe a damnation. Right now she couldn't tell which.

"I was always afraid of losing you," she told him. "And I was always afraid you'd hate me when you learned the truth."

He didn't reply. Instead, he shifted behind her, his heat suffusing through her body in sharp contrast with the chill of memory. He'd last held her four years ago.

Before they split apart like sparks scattered in the wind.

Vitaly's forehead rested against her nape. "I could never hate you, Serafima Mikhailovna," he whispered. "You could stab me in the heart and still be the only person I give a damn about."

A trembling exhale left her. Those words buried themselves deep. So deep that she could feel their warmth in every part of her. "I lied to you in the alleyway after *obryad*," she said. "When I fled the Blackshore, I didn't leave you. Not by choice. If you believe nothing else, believe that."

His breath caught in his throat. Long moments passed where only silence lingered between them. Then his fingertips swept along her shoulder blade. "I spent years looking for you."

Sera's fingers curled into her palms, resisting the urge to touch him. "Where?"

He reached around her and spun the globe, stopping at the southern edge of Tumanny. "Udinsk, first," he said. The port where Zverti pamphlets were dispatched. Again, he rotated the map, focusing on the continent of Sundyr. "Tikhmenevsky. Krestov Brod. Dzheb. Nikolskoye. Dozens of little towns and villages and countries, more than I could remember. Whenever I heard of a woman traveling alone, I followed the rumors. It was never you. Where did you run?"

Pain stabbed through Sera's chest. Galina had been another secret she couldn't chance revealing—another risk that had set him off on a wild hunt with no hope of success. He had searched for one woman and never realized he might have found her if he'd sought two.

Exhaling deeply, Sera took his hand and turned the globe until it paused. "I hired a cart from Gorodetsk," she began quietly, guiding his finger along the narrow portion of the Dark Sea until it stopped. "I knew a smuggler in the village willing to take me on his vessel across to Sundyr." Her touch slid down a thin waterway and stopped at a small coastal village below the border of Samatsk. "Mysovaya was where I got caught by the city sentries after someone reported me. I shook them off by escaping on a passenger boat downriver." She moved his hand up. "The port in Pribrezhny, for a few weeks, until a storm cleared up. Then I crossed the Bṛzatī Mountain Range when I heard rumors of guards looking for a fugitive. We crossed the border into Akra, and in Starapolė, I dyed my hair and kept it short."

Vitaly stilled. "You went to Akra?"

Sera nodded. "It seemed safer to stay among Tumanny's enemies. Empress Isidora couldn't exploit her allies' resources. That was six months after we said goodbye."

She felt his warm breath on her nape. "I was in Belazari kiai. At the same time."

Belazari kiai, Akra's capital city—and a mere twenty minutes by cart from Starapolė. The name was like a weight on her chest. What if he had found her? What if he had shown up at her cabin door with hope for their future? She might have crumbled under his touch, forgetting all the reasons she chose to stay away.

Sera swallowed, regaining her composure. "I stayed in Starapolė until I heard Voroski needed people with medical knowledge during a city outbreak."

The thump of Vitaly's heart was steady as he moved closer. "I went to Voroski. Two years ago."

Her eyes stung. She wanted to turn in Vitaly's arms and press her face to his shirt. Breathe in his scent. Find comfort in his solidity after so much time apart, with nothing but memories.

But in the end, she blinked back tears. "I lived in Dolsk after that. By then, enough time had passed. I had a little cottage there. They'd stopped looking for me."

And so had you.

She could feel Vitaly's grip on her tighten. "I resurfaced in the Black and hoped you'd hear about it and come home. How long were you in Dolsk, knowing I was still alive?"

Sera withdrew from Vitaly. "Does it matter? I couldn't keep lying to you. And I'm not an alurean spy—for whatever it's worth." Walking over to the bed, she slipped on her overcoat, preparing to face the cold outside. Just as she was about to leave, she paused, the truth burning in her heart. "When we were married, every moment was real."

39

GALINA

Galina's memory of the explosion was a blur of shattered glass and darkness. She remembered being dragged from the mayhem by a sentry as she struggled to locate Katya and Vasilisa amidst the debris. Screams of agony rang in her ears as her eyesight dimmed.

She woke in her bedchamber in the Glasshouse Wing, her dress caked with soot and her body aching from the godfire. The maids who tended to her trembled in fear, their voices hushed. Galina finally found the voice to tell them to take the night off.

Then she lay motionless on her bed, numb with shock and drained of all energy.

When the sun peeked through the windows hours later, another maid dressed her in a plain black gown and buttoned it up to Galina's neck, the fabric as tight as an iron collar.

Her duty was clear: stand beside Empress Isidora and smile for the restless crowd outside. Show them that their ruler lived and their Common God remained unharmed.

Relief rippled through Galina when she saw Katya standing by Isidora's side on the balcony. Memories of the handmaiden engulfed in godfire and reduced to ash flashed through her mind, and she couldn't help but wonder if Katya would see her as a monster. But when their eyes met, a spark of understanding passed between them: they were both alive, and their plan was still in motion.

The empress's voice was brusque. "Wave to the supplicants, then return to the Glasshouse Wing with the guards."

With her brief appearance over, Galina retreated to a dusty bedroom at the end of the Glasshouse Wing—the only chamber that offered a view of the destroyed section of Zolotiye. From the window, she watched the palace staff carry the bodies in white sheets and lay them in the snow, where the cold would preserve the remains until they could be transported to their home countries.

Thirty-three at her last count.

Earlier, the maid who dressed her mentioned finding unexploded bombs in the ballroom. If any of the rest had gone off...

Galina shuddered and crossed the corridor, pausing outside Princess Vasilisa's door. She pressed her ear to the barrier, listening for any sign of life beyond it. The silence was suffocating, as if the air had been sucked out of the hallway, leaving only the heavy drum of Galina's heartbeat.

She'd seen Princess Vasilisa collapse on the floor but couldn't recall seeing any visible injuries. The uncertainty made her uneasy; she couldn't just walk away. What if the princess needed help? What if she was hurt?

Summoning her courage, Galina rapped lightly. "Your Imperial Highness?" Her words went unanswered. She tried again, this time with a whisper: "Vasilisa Yuryevna."

Still nothing.

Dread gripped Galina, and she pushed open the door, overwhelmed by the medicinal smell permeating the chamber. She walked toward the bed, where Princess Vasilisa was hidden under the duvet, her breathing heavy and uneven.

"Vasilisa Yuryevna," she murmured, her voice barely a ghost of a sound.

The room swelled with an oppressive silence. Only Princess Vasilisa's shallow gasps filled the air, each one a thread threatening to snap. Galina's unease deepened as she drew closer. The princess was so still, her skin as pale as the sheets.

Worry clawed at Galina—was Vasilisa hiding some kind of injury beneath that nightdress? Why hadn't anyone sent a healer yet?

Galina went motionless at the thought. The woman in that bed had become her undoing. Making Galina question her mission, her past, and her present—every moment of anger she'd ever held. It all crumbled at the mere thought of Princess Vasilisa dead because of Vitaly's bombs.

A whisper of sound broke the silence: "Galina Feodorovna."

It felt like a bolt of lightning to Galina's heart—her name on the princess's lips sounded like something forbidden. "Vasilisa Yuryevna?"

But the princess's eyes remained closed. Was Vasilisa dreaming? If so, then...

She dreamed of Galina.

A strange, overpowering emotion surged through Galina. An urge to stroke Vasilisa's hair and settle her head against her shoulder, to fuss over her with a tenderness only lovers could share.

Madness.

But then she repeated it: "Galina Feodorovna."

Galina's name wasn't muddled by the daze of sleep this time. It was crystal clear and laced with bewilderment.

Galina looked up to find Vasilisa's eyes open, her regard like a scalpel cutting through the darkness between them. How had she forgotten how intense the princess's attention could be?

"I came to make sure you weren't dead," Galina said, a thousand wants and desires clashing in her thoughts. "When I saw your food hadn't been touched—"

A sly smirk played at the edges of Vasilisa's lips. "You fretted over me?"

Galina's confession was locked behind gritted teeth. *And I was fully prepared to throttle my sister's worthless husband if he'd done anything to harm you.*

A mild panic roiled in her gut at the thought. "Do you need water? I'll get you water," Galina offered, avoiding the question.

Vasilisa let out a breathy laugh that seemed to contain equal parts pain and amusement. "No, I've never been better," she said, pushing herself into a half-sitting position. "A beautiful woman snuck into my chambers in the dead of night just to fret over me. I can't think of a nicer way to wake up. Are you courting me, Galina Feodorovna?"

Galina's thoughts scattered.

She thinks I'm... beautiful?

Her face burned at the confession. She swallowed hard, her throat dry. "You told me you'd poison me if I ever came into your room uninvited again."

"Guess I changed my mind," she replied.

"Is that so?"

The princess's sharp gaze swept over her, studying her features with keen interest. "I've decided you're always welcome in my bedchamber. Anytime, day or night. An open invitation."

The words fluttered against Galina's skin like moth wings. She imagined their limbs tangled in bed, soft kisses stolen in the dark.

"Are you courting me, Vasilisa Yuryevna?" she whispered.

Vasilisa's eyes held such tenderness that Galina felt fragile enough to break apart at any moment. "Do you want me to stop?"

Her hand lay so close, their fingers nearly touching. "No," Galina murmured. "I just wish I didn't like it so much."

If only Vasilisa were more like the empress. Loathing enemies was second nature—so effortless. But resisting Vasilisa was as impossible as mending the shattered fragments of her soul.

The princess shifted, and Galina noticed her subtle flinch. "You're in pain."

"I'm used to it," Vasilisa said simply. Her eyes were warm in the dark, as soft as fingertips to Galina's nape. "You're unharmed?"

"Thanks to you," Galina replied, focusing on Vasilisa's pallid complexion and glistening forehead. "But you didn't answer my question earlier—were you hurt in the ballroom?"

The princess's reply was like the strike of a blade. "No."

Galina's throat constricted with a thousand unanswered questions. Why did she feel any sympathy for the daughter of the empress who razed her village to the ground? Who'd taken the lives of countless innocents? It was idiocy. Princess Vasilisa would tear her apart when the truth came out.

But Galina couldn't bear the thought of Vasilisa hating her.

Why did she care?

"Good. I'm glad you're not hurt," she said, turning to leave.

But Vasilisa's grip on her wrist halted her, the touch like a searing brand. Her god flared to meet the princess's. This time, it was different; pleasure and want entwining, a pull so intense that it threatened to drown her.

"You didn't ask," Vasilisa said, her voice a whisper of velvet over steel.

"Ask what?" Her question betrayed none of the desire that burned through her, a need that knew no end.

The princess's fingers slid from Galina's palm. A spark passed between them, their zmei reaching out to each other like lovers. Vasilisa's thumb lingered on the pulse point of her inner wrist—by accident or design?

Galina couldn't be sure.

Princess Vasilisa made an indiscernible noise. "Why I've been in this bed for two days if I was uninjured. Why I said I was used to it."

"Maybe I don't consider it my business to know."

"And yet here you stand, risking death by poison, just to enter my room without permission—all out of concern."

Galina swallowed, the question a weight on her tongue. "Would you answer if I'd asked?"

Vasilisa's response held a somber gravity. "Yes." She hesitated for a long breath, then ventured, "If I asked about your past, would you tell me?"

"Yes," she whispered, her voice barely audible.

Their hands clung together for one last tender moment before Galina pulled away. Her zmeya writhed with disapproval at the loss of contact. Longing pierced her, but she could not—*would not*—allow herself to succumb to it.

The ache in her chest lingered. "But I can't bear the thought of how you'll look at me when I do."

40

KATYA

Katya watched from the empress's suite as the staff carried the corpses from the palace to the gardens and readied the bodies for transport.

Vitaly's explosives had done more than destroy the ballroom; they had demolished the foundation of Sundyr's social hierarchy. Noble corpses lay in pools of blood amidst the shattered walls and debris that littered the floors of the once magnificent chamber.

Entire empires were upended in a single evening.

She took small comfort in Vitaly's twisted sense of mercy—he had spared the servants from his deadly massacre, aiming only at the nobles. Those caught in the crossfire were fortunate to walk away with only minor injuries. Katya couldn't help but acknowledge her own good fortune in escaping the ball with her life, but the memories haunted her. She woke in the middle of the night, drenched in sweat and plagued by nightmares of being engulfed in flames and dying in the bombing. Too many close calls for one day, reminders of how fragile her time was.

The alurean survivors were far from unscathed. Healers were still working tirelessly to mend the victims' broken bones and torn flesh. Even the most experienced were hard-pressed to keep up with the influx of the wounded.

The high-born casualties were staggering in number; their absence would leave a gaping hole in Sundyr's political landscape. The fatalities included Queen Yelena of Samatsk, Queen Marianne of Sasnis, two princes, four princesses, two dukes, and a duchess.

As the healers attended to the injured, the earth and air mavens in the court used their godpower to reconstruct the shattered sections of the palace. When Katya and Empress Isidora had last surveyed the ruined wings, the mavens had already cleared the debris from everywhere but the ballroom. They had even erected a temporary barrier to safeguard the interior halls from the frigid winds.

An annoyed huff broke Katya's reverie—Isidora pacing the room like a caged beast. Two men, dressed in the crisp military garb of Tumanny, sat across from her—the general of her guard and her royal adviser. The empress gripped the back of her settee, her expression as hard and unyielding as stone.

That she could stand at all was a testament to the godpower of three devoted healers. The blast had spared her life, but not her body—her arm had been shattered in several places, ribs cracked, and a fracture along her skull. Even the most skilled alurean menders couldn't have saved her if she had been more damaged.

Bitterness burned in Katya's chest as she stared at the empress she despised—still breathing, while two monarchs and countless others lay dead.

A thought twisted through her mind. *I wish it had been you.*

Isidora scowled at her advisors. "How is it your soldiers haven't apprehended these criminals?" she snarled at her general. "It's been a day. You said the woman was wounded, General Vasilchikov. How far could she have gone?"

Katya fought an urge to flinch, a thousand frantic questions raging in her thoughts. Had Vitaly done anything to help Sera? Were they safe somewhere, or had Sera died in Blackshore's grime-splattered alleys? Had Vitaly killed her? Nowhere to find out—not when Anna's Confectionery lay in ruins. With the increased security, sending a message from the palace was an unspeakable risk.

Meanwhile, Katya had to be more careful than ever around the increasingly unhinged empress. The walls seemed to shrink in and crush the air from her lungs. The future she once envisioned slipped further and further out of her grasp, like trying to hold on to smoke.

"We tracked them to the Black, Your Imperial Majesty," General Vasilchikov said, shifting uncomfortably. "But the supplicants there are..."

Empress Isidora's eyes narrowed. "They're what? Speak up."

"They're not very forthcoming," he finished, clearing his throat with a delicate cough.

Empress Isidora scoffed. "So now you're telling me mere commoners have outwitted an alurean general? Are the factory workers and thieves in the Black so cunning?" She glanced pointedly at her adviser. "What do you think, Nikita Ivanovich? Are they so talented?"

Katya watched as Zubov wilted beneath the empress's stare. He opened his mouth, then closed it again. Eventually, he croaked, "The people of the Black are... stubborn," he managed, voice quivering. "Our soldiers have found more graffiti on the walls in Zverti."

The empress's expression darkened into something colder than death. "And where would they scrawl their seditious messages without shelter?" she asked. "Where would they keep their traitors safe? Maybe you can tell me, General Vasilchikov."

Even the general was visibly shaken. "Your Imperial Majesty?"

The empress had never looked so monstrous. "My husband underestimated the faithless infecting this city. That incompetence got him butchered, pushed us to the brink of war, and led to our allies being slaughtered." The empress leaned forward. "I want to know where they're making explosives, where they hold their secret meetings. I want the names of every scum who plots against me and the names of their families. Set fire to this city until you root out every last traitor. Maybe then these commoners will think twice before protecting terrorists."

Katya's mind raced as the room warped around her. How could the empress so callously order the destruction of an entire city? Was there no concern for the lives of the people in it?

"It's the middle of winter, Your Imperial Majesty," General Vasilchikov said. "If you—"

The empress silenced him with a look. "If they want to protect the faithless, then let them freeze to death. Now go."

General Vasilchikov bowed and left in a hurry.

Zubov remained seated, his calm demeanor shattered. His hands trembled as he nervously clenched and released them. "Your Imperial Majesty," he murmured tentatively, "have you given further thought to staying in Arzalavat for your safety? I can send word ahead to have the servants prepare a room."

"No," she said. "I won't be driven out of my palace like a child and give the faithless the satisfaction of seeing me run. Focus on preparing the dead for transport."

Zubov hesitated, his eyes flickering with concern. "Our allies are demanding answers, Your Imperial Majesty. We shouldn't let gossip reach their ears before we respond. General Vasilchikov did his best to mitigate the rumors, but it won't be long before they spread across Sundyr."

Isidora's gaze hardened, and she leaned forward in her seat. "Then let them hear whispers," she said. "Let them hear rumors. Let them hear half-truths and lies. But don't allow it to be known that this was done by the faithless. If the

Tumanny Courier receives a statement from these terrorists, throttle it. If they print it, shut down the newspaper. The last thing we need is for our allies to align with Sopol because insurgents murdered their monarchs and courtiers."

"What story should I have them publish?"

Isidora's shoulders slumped, exhaustion etched on her face. "We're already on the verge of war, Nikita Ivanovich," she said. "Say the terrorists were aligned with Sopol, and our allies will rally their armies in vengeance. Even the supplicants in the Black might reconsider their loyalties if we say Tumanny's enemies committed the massacre." She waved a hand dismissively. "Now go. I want it printed in tomorrow's broadsheet."

With the men gone, Isidora moved to stand beside Katya at the window. Her hand settled on Katya's shoulder, a gentle weight that had the impact of solid stone. She felt like she was drowning in a suffocating current as she swallowed back her emotions—all of them kept coiled tight. Her fingernails curled into her palms as she resisted the urge to shake off the empress's touch.

Outside, the snow was stained crimson with blood—a horror-filled tableau that left Isidora unfazed.

"I worried about your death in that ballroom," she murmured. "If Galina Feodorovna had failed, I would have had to kill her."

A memory bubbled to the surface from the ballroom—flames shooting toward her, the feeling of her skin bubbling from her bones. The godfire had forced her to choke on her own ashes until she wondered if she'd die. But somehow, there was relief in that pain—because, for one blessed moment, a part of her soul had been liberated. And then her heart and breath had come back to life, and in that fire reforged determination. She refused to be free in death. She'd be free in life.

She stared down at the bracelets of bells adorning her wrists. Replacements for those that had melted under Galina's flames. It didn't escape Katya's notice that Isidora's first concern was not to console her, but to gift her with another set of shackles.

And yet... and yet...

"You were worried about me, *suvya?*"

Did this woman really care for her, or was it only pretend?

With a noise, Isidora took Katya's face in her hands, her gaze snagging on the scratches along Katya's hairline and the faint bruises on her cheek. "Little Katenka, of course I was worried about you. I can't bear to see my things broken."

Things. The word echoed in Katya's mind like a hammer striking steel, a stark reminder of a handmaiden's place in the empress's world. Belongings, not people; property, not family; Possessions, not sisters. Just bondservants owned by an empress who could choose to discard any of them if it pleased her.

And if Katya stayed much longer, she'd suffer the same cruel end as every handmaiden before her.

41

VITALY

Vitaly yanked another paper from a stone wall in the Black and shoved it into his overcoat.

The *Tumanny Courier* had published the drawing the day before, nestled snug between the palace's propaganda. They claimed agents from Sopol had tried to murder their empress, her heir, Tumanny allies, and scores of nobles, courtiers, and the precious Common God.

The palace howled for justice, and the *Courier* obliged. "Anyone with information on the whereabouts of these terrorists should contact our offices."

The artist's rendering, far too accurate for Vitaly's liking, depicted him and Sera—and now it papered the city from the Black to Antrea.

And then there was the reward: five thousand imperial gold pieces to whoever found them first.

That morning, Vitaly awoke in his cramped apartment and hurriedly packed a bag. He tore aside the ragged curtains to peer out the window, only to find Pyotr and a few lackeys loitering at the tavern entrance below.

Vitaly was no fool; five thousand imperial gold pieces

were enough to tempt even his most trusted allies. Everyone had a price, and some of his faithless had debts and large families to feed.

The men had conversed in hushed tones, too quiet for Vitaly to make out—but their hands brushing against hidden weapons told him everything he needed to know. He swung the leather bag over his shoulder and escaped by rooftop, leaving Pyotr and his cronies with an unwelcome surprise when they entered his room.

Now he had to find Sera.

Muttering curses under his breath, he yanked another artist's sketch off the wall and stuffed it into his coat pocket with the rest of his contraband. A mother and child stared at him incredulously across the street, taken aback by his profanity-laden outburst. He scowled and pulled up the collar of his overcoat, concealing his face as he slogged through the snow-covered roads. Resolve surged through his veins with each step—bringing him closer to Sera.

But then a shout caught his attention.

He crept closer, pressing himself against the shadows of an ancient tenement, and peered around the corner. His blood ran cold at what he saw: a woman surrounded by a half dozen alurean peace officers. The only reason for such a gathering was a raid, but Vitaly knew of no operation there. So why were they swarming a building inhabited by seamstresses?

"I don't know!" the woman shouted.

"Look again," the soldier barked, shoving an artist's sketch in her face. "Burn it into your brain. Have you seen this man or this woman?"

Cornered and terrified, the woman shook her head wildly. "*No.* I said no."

Vitaly's hands curled into fists. Plenty of people in the Black recognized his face. He controlled most of the territory. Every faithless in the city had heard his name, and in the Black, everyone knew at least one of his agents.

"Search the place," the soldier ordered his subordinates. He turned to the gathered rabble. "Tell me now if you've seen the man or woman in the papers. I'll also offer mercy if you have any information on where the faithless meet."

The crowd shook their heads—it wouldn't have been the first time the Black was threatened by a bunch of asshole sentries who thought they could come into these streets and take whatever they pleased.

A peace officer emerged from the tenement building. "Nothing here, sir."

His commander nodded, although the fury etched on his face conveyed more than words ever could. "Burn it all."

His partner looked taken aback. "Sir?"

The commander ignored him. Instead, he addressed the stunned crowd. "Anyone caught hiding these two, or any other faithless, will be branded traitors. Let it be known we'll tear torch every building until they're found. So either tell us where they are, or your city burns."

Smoke bloomed across the sky as officers fanned out with torches and began setting everything on fire.

The female tenant wailed her despair, her cries echoing off the buildings.

"Restrain her," the commander told an officer.

The muscles in Vitaly's body tensed like a coiled serpent poised to strike. He wanted to wrap his hands around the man's neck and strangle him, watch his eyes go wide and limp, hear the cracking of bones as he twisted and yanked them.

A word in the Exalted Tongue fell from the officer's lips, and blood burst out of the woman's mouth.

Vitaly darted out of the alleyway, weapon glinting at his side. "Heard you were looking for me," he snarled, slamming his fist into the guard's face. He reveled in the sickening crunch of shattered bones like a sweet melody.

He struck fast, plunging his blade through the gap in the guard's armor. Another sentry charged in from behind.

Vitaly spun away just before an explosive force of godpower ripped through the air where he'd been standing. Fragments of brick flew past, but he dodged to the side, slashing out and burying his knife in the second sentry's flank.

Guards bellowed from the building, their orders drowned out by the crackling of flames and the crumbling of stone. Smoke billowed into the street, obscuring his vision as he moved through the chaos.

Time to escape.

Stalking to the terrified woman, Vitaly tore one of the stylized buttons off his overcoat and pressed it into her palm. "Take this," he said breathlessly. "Show it to the priest at the old temple next to the boneyard on the shore." The pauper's cemetery. "He'll give you shelter and food."

Shouts cut through the air, and Vitaly glanced up and spotted alurean sentries thundering down the stairs from the tenement. Their godpower lashed out like lightning strikes.

Vitaly slipped away into a fog of coal smoke, a bitter blessing that served as cover—if he stayed ahead of them, it would hide him from their attacks.

They wouldn't catch him. Not in these streets. Vitaly had been bred in the gutters of this city, had hidden from the same guards that now scoured the alleys for him. He was schooled in every concealed alleyway and forgotten nook. He was born to die in the Blackshore—but not on their terms.

The shadows welcomed him as he darted into an alcove. His fingers eagerly dug into the pitted stone of the tenement's wall as he climbed, the building worn down by years of weather and neglect. Every dip and crack was etched into his mind from countless thefts, each narrow escape carved into his flesh as a reminder of what he was.

The crumbling architecture was his domain; this time, it would be his salvation. A smile played across his lips as he clambered onto the rooftop, shoving on his gloves as he scanned the street. The sentries below scurried like rats in the dim light of the alley.

"Those idiots never think to look up," Vitaly muttered with a shake of his head.

Then he leaped to the nearest roof—using the densely packed buildings to his advantage as he jumped from one to the next.

By the time he arrived at Khotchino, he had lost his pursuers.

Their fellow officers and sentries would be out in force, scouring every inch of the Blackshore from Khotchino to Svyatoy Krest, but Vitaly was a step ahead. He could watch the soldiers' movements from his vantage point high above the street without being seen.

As he reached a tenement on the main road, Vitaly noticed the scorched remains of the confectionery that Pyotr had foolishly set ablaze.

"*Fednezno it*," he growled under his breath.

Pyotr was a fucking imbecile. If he hadn't attacked the confectioner, Vitaly could have convinced her to give him information.

But now, nothing was left of the place but a charred husk, its interior blackened and twisted by flames.

Vitaly paced the roof as he considered his options—but a familiar brunette came out of a building below, and he couldn't believe his luck. The confectioner hurried away from the charred ruins of her shop and vanished into a side street.

He descended from the tenement like a predator on the hunt, fixed on his quarry. She moved with the grace of a feline, strides light yet purposeful. He quickened his pace to keep up. Vitaly didn't care how long he had to tail the woman until she led him to Sera—he'd follow her for days if he had to.

But then she abruptly darted into an alley and was gone. Vitaly skidded to a stop, heart thumping against his ribs as he scanned the shadows for any sign of her.

And that was when he felt it—a blade pressed against the small of his back.

"You're following me." The words sliced through the quiet street. "Why?"

Clever, clever. He hadn't expected to like the confectioner this quickly.

He gave a low chuckle and carefully lifted his arms in a gesture of surrender. "I thought it best to introduce myself," he said easily.

Her weapon still held its threatening point against him. "You should think twice before approaching random women. Some of us don't take kindly to unwanted attention. So we carry sharp objects."

Vitaly laughed again. "I see why my wife counts you among her friends."

The weapon withdrew, replaced by the solid grip of a hand that turned him roughly. Her eyes touched on his features, and her lips flattened. "Vitaly Sergeyevich Rysakov," she snarled, as if tasting poison on her tongue. "Even if you hadn't come into my shop a few days ago, I'd have known that face. Serafima told me you were a pretty one."

"She said that, did she?" He flashed his teeth in satisfaction. If his wife were present, he would have preened for her.

The woman ignored Vitaly's obvious pleasure at Sera's compliment. "Anna Borislava Smirnova," she introduced herself curtly. "Your godsdamn operative burned my shop to the ground."

Pyotr, you absolute prick. "I'm deeply apologetic for the actions of my imbecilic operative."

"He also murdered my informant."

Well done, Pyotr, you've really outdone yourself in fucking me over this time. "This morning, he tried to sell me out to the alurean authorities. Suffice it to say, we're not on good terms."

Anna lifted a lip. "Is that what passes for solace these days?"

"Not really. I was just pointing out that he's an exceptional breed of halfwit."

"And why should I believe anything you say? Serafima warned me you're a liar."

Vitaly placed a hand on his chest. "My Sera gives such flattering compliments."

She didn't react to his attempt at levity. "Tell me what you want, Vitaly Sergeyevich. I'm running short on patience."

Fine, then. He could be serious when he needed to be. Vitaly's smile faded, and he adopted a more solemn expression. "I need to speak with my wife. If you have any information on her whereabouts—"

"No." Anna's response was quick and decisive.

Vitaly couldn't help but think of the woman in the Black, stripped of everything she owned; of the alurean authorities, who could end lives as easily as one would snuff out a candle; of the soldiers dogging his every step, chasing him and Sera without mercy. They'd cause death and devastation, abandoning citizens to die in a brutal winter.

The alurea didn't give a shit. But Vitaly loved this grime-encrusted cesspit of a city; its people were as hard and unforgiving as its alleyways, but maybe that was why they were so capable of great kindness.

And he wanted his wife. No more passing each other like two strangers in the night. No more aimless wandering throughout Sundyr, scouring towns and villages, haunted by the thought of where she might be hiding—desperately wondering if she was alive or dead. If these were his final moments, he'd spend them with Sera, defying the alurea till their last breaths.

"Sentries are searching the city," he told Anna. "They won't stop until they find us and every member of the faithless."

Anna gave her head a shake. "Sera's safe. She can take care of herself. You certainly haven't bothered to do it."

"Listen to me," he hissed. "I just watched their sentries burn five tenements in the Black. Our faces are plastered on every wall in this city, and they'll terrorize its residents until they get what they want. Now, where is she?"

"Why should I tell you?" The confectioner crossed her arms. "Sera's an alurea. Why should I trust you're not going to kill her?"

Vitaly's mind drifted back to the night at the palace. The explosion and the fleeing were now distant memories; all that remained was the agony he felt at the thought of losing Sera.

Even so, Sera's deception had kept him up the whole night, fighting the dark sting of betrayal. Vitaly had never felt so vulnerable or so godsdamned exposed. Sera had lied to him for years, and he'd been too blind, too foolish, or too in love with her to see it. Every moment he'd held her in his arms, tracing the curves of her body with his fingers, every time he'd shared his secrets with her, whispered his plans in her ear—not once suspecting that she was an alurea. He could barely control the complicated mix of anger and hurt, but then he'd gazed at the wedding ring on his finger, and something fragile kindled inside him. A reminder: she was the only reason he could claim a shred of humanity. She was still his fatal flaw, his undoing, the only shining star in his abyss of villainy, and the only one he wanted in his bed. Nothing changed that—not time, distance, or the dragon within her.

Fuck it all. I just want my wife.

Vitaly held up his left hand, and the band gleamed on his finger. "I haven't taken this off since she gave it to me. When I said those vows to her, I meant them. I'd never hurt her."

Anna's expression tightened. "Pretty words for a known liar."

Of course Sera had to choose a stubborn friend. "I left the ring I gave her in a box at your shop," he said. "She could have thrown it away, but she didn't. She wears it around her neck. What does that tell you?"

The breath seemed to go out of Anna. She looked like she might regret her decision, but said, "In the Khotchino nameless cemetery, you'll find an entrance to the tomb where they kept unidentified alurean soldiers. The latch behind Soldier Twenty-Three will take you to an annex that once belonged to the old medical school. After the student purge, Sera's mother sealed off the university, and..." Anna pressed her lips together. "Used it for her own purposes."

Vitaly scowled. What else had Irina hidden from him? He'd never heard of any underground passage. But he didn't have time for questions. "Get out of the city while you can still travel," he warned her. "Leave Sera to me."

Anna gave a curt nod. "Have her send a coded message when she can. If she needs transport—"

"I'll tell her." Then, because he knew what it cost her to trust him: "Thank you."

Anna sheathed her blade in her coat. "Don't thank me. If you mess up after I've given you Sera's location, I'll hunt you down to the ends of the world, jam this knife down your throat, and watch you choke on your own blood."

Vitaly almost smiled. "I'll remember that."

42

VASILISA

Isidora waited in Vasilisa's solarium, her presence as unwelcome as it was inevitable.

Each step up the winding staircase was a harsh reminder of the crushing price Vasilisa paid for attending the ball. Her mother viewed it as nothing more than an inconvenience to be overcome, but Vasilisa was done with the endless struggle. She'd had enough of the constant façade of normalcy and the never-ending demands to push through the pain.

So. Fucking. Done.

By the time she reached the second floor, her breaths were labored and raspy, cheeks reddened with rage and exertion. She retrieved the spare wheelchair from the closet, a necessary tool to help her navigate a world that was hostile to her very existence.

The coming conversation between her and Isidora would be another battle, one that would leave her drained and exhausted. All she wanted was to be left alone, to rest and recover in peace, to be spared the constant demands of an empire ruled by power and vicious politics.

But that was too much to ask.

Relief washed over her as she settled into the chair, yet it couldn't compare to the agony still gnawing at her insides. And the anger? That was bottomless.

Vasilisa pushed herself to the doorway of the solarium. Her mother was lounging on the damn sofa, sipping her tea. But this time, her expression was different. Troubled.

Vasilisa couldn't blame her. The day before, she'd seen the bodies piled outside the palace—it was a political disaster.

Isidora's eyes shifted to Vasilisa's chair. Her countenance darkened further. Another visible reminder of Vasilisa's illness—something their enemies might exploit if they found out.

The Glasshouse Wing was no longer empty.

Now, Vasilisa didn't care. Galina had come to her room and asked after her, and Vasilisa felt like she'd been cast adrift. As if the world had tilted off its axis. She had wanted to kiss Galina, to pull her into the sheets and touch her everywhere.

You're alive, she would have whispered. *And you're mine.*

She couldn't read books or focus on anything except the woman down the hall. No one had expressed concern for Vasilisa in years.

Her mother was proof.

How many days had it taken for the empress to see her daughter? Three.

And where did she choose to visit? The godsdamn solarium.

Vasilisa tightened her grip on the armrests until her knuckles went white. "I've been in bed for days," she snarled. "You know those injections make me sick. And you still chose this room."

Isidora remained motionless beneath Vasilisa's glare. "If you wanted another location, you should have sent a note," she said, her voice even and measured. "I can't read your mind, Vasilochka."

Vasilisa let out a frustrated growl. "I shouldn't have to tell you. Maybe if you visited me more often, you'd understand that." She smacked her hand against the armrest. "This wheelchair isn't some decoration, *vuabo pue*. Neither is my cane."

Isidora's eyes flickered to the chair again, scrutinizing it like it insulted her. Vasilisa had commissioned the chairs against her mother's wishes, paying a fortune to a craftsman in Sundyr to keep his mouth shut.

"Have you even bothered to hide this from Galina Feodorovna?" Isidora spat. "Or is she someone I need to watch lest whispers reach Sopol?"

"Not all of us operate under the assumption that everyone is an enemy," Vasilisa said. "And she came to check on me before you did."

A muscle twitched in Isidora's jaw. "I don't have the luxury of ignoring potential threats, Vasilochka. We were nearly murdered in our own home. I lost several royal allies in that attack. I had more pressing matters."

More pressing matters than her daughter.

The silence was deafening as their unspoken thoughts clashed like swords.

Her mother's words reduced Vasilisa to a footnote in the grand scheme of Isidora's life. The throne was her everything, her obsession. It was why she would always prefer the solarium over a room on the ground floor, why she would always ask Vasilisa to dance at gatherings, and why she would always choose politics over the health of her daughter.

Vasilisa's hand trembled as she considered reaching for the cup of tea before her, but she knew it would only end up spilling.

"Who?" she asked, bracing herself for the coming tide.

Her mother let out a breath. "Queen Yelena. Queen Marianne. A number of powerful courtiers, nobles, and guards. Their countries will stand with us once they learn Sopol's allies are responsible."

Vasilisa looked up sharply. "You can't keep covering up crimes committed by the faithless. People will eventually notice the sudden influx of dead royals in Tumanny."

Isidora waved a dismissive hand and took a sip of her tea. "They won't need to speculate once I've crushed the rebels. Yuri did nothing about the faithless festering in the Black, and that's how we ended up with all those dead royals. But that's not why I'm here."

"Then why are you?"

Because it wasn't for the pleasure of my company, that's for sure.

Vasilisa gritted her teeth, steeling herself for the reason behind Isidora's visit. She hadn't come all this way to the Glasshouse Wing just to check her daughter's health. Her mother hadn't done that in years. Isidora considered Vasilisa broken beyond repair, and the physical distance and emotional barriers she had erected proved it.

To a monarch whose power and lineage were everything, *incurable* might as well have meant *dead*.

"Galina Feodorovna and I appeared on the temple balcony to reassure Tumanny's citizens that their monarch and Common God are safe." Isidora's words were brittle when she used the moniker. "Our people will want to hear from my heir, and our allies need to know you're alive."

"I'm not your heir," Vasilisa said flatly.

The empress's features tightened. "As far as the public is concerned, the future of the Tumanny throne was in that room when the bomb went off."

"Don't mince words with me. You're asking me to make more public appearances," Vasilisa said, her irritation simmering under the surface. "You told me the ball was the last one."

"And it would have been, if our guests hadn't been assassinated between the waltz and the mazurka," she snapped, before taking a deep breath and straightening up. "We can't afford to accommodate your desire for seclusion,

Vasilochka. As long as our allies believe Sopol was responsible for the attack, they'll go to war alongside us. The slightest hint of your"—she glanced at Vasilisa's wheelchair—"*illness*, and they'll know I'm a liar."

"Cover it up, then. Say I was injured in the blast and need the chair," Vasilisa replied, gritting her teeth with frustration.

Isidora's mouth twisted. "Showing weakness is never an option. Not with anyone who could use it against us. Do you think they'll see that chair and instantly feel sorry for your situation? Or will they believe the future of the Tumanny throne is too vulnerable to follow into battle?" She shook her head. "No. We only show strength and power to the public. We don't give them a reason to doubt us."

Vasilisa's skin burned. The empire would never accept her, never let her be who she was. "Please don't make me do this."

Isidora sighed and reached for her, stroking Vasilisa's cheek. "Do you think it pleases me to ask this of you?"

"No," Vasilisa whispered. "I just think you care more about your throne."

The empress's hand fell away, fingers curled into a fist of iron. At that moment, she looked more like a monster than a mother. "Prepare your treatments. The people will expect to see you soon."

Vasilisa knew Isidora had already made her choice.

The empire always came first.

Moonlight pooled in the hollows of the glasshouse, the spectral glow reflecting off Vasilisa's collection of flasks, tubes, and vessels that lay scattered on the table. The air was heavy with the scent of crushed plants, a mix of deadly poisons and exotic herbs. Vasilisa combined the concoctions that gave her life a semblance of control.

Footsteps echoed down the hall, interrupting her reverie.

Vasilisa could hear her mother snapping orders in her head. *Hide the wheelchair, Vasilochka. The table is large enough to conceal it. She doesn't go past the doorway. She won't see.*

But Vasilisa was done hiding from the world that wasn't built for her. She was tired of shrinking herself down to fit the impossibly small confines of her mother's expectations. Done with allowing others to dictate her fate.

She refused to cower away.

Galina gave a soft exhale. "Hello."

Vasilisa's zmeya stirred beneath her skin, scales rippling in reaction to Galina's proximity.

Well, that settled it. If her god was won over by Galina's voice alone, then Vasilisa was already halfway claimed.

More than halfway, if she was being honest.

"Hello," Vasilisa replied, turning her wheelchair to meet those beautiful blue eyes.

Her chest constricted as she braced for the onslaught of questions, the patronizing pity, the stifling discomfort.

But all Galina said was, "Working on your medicines again?"

Relief flooded Vasilisa, and she smiled. "Would you like to keep me company?"

The corner of Galina's lips curved as she stepped into the glasshouse, studying Vasilisa's chair. "You're all right?" she asked, lingering just out of reach. The question was more intimate than a kiss.

Vasilisa laughed softly. "I'm not dead, so that's a resounding yes."

Their gazes met. "That wasn't what I meant."

Vasilisa could sense the grip of Galina's influence tightening around her heart—and no part of her wanted to break free. She was ready to offer herself up to this woman. Every part of her, every sharp piece and broken bit.

"Still concerned about me?" she asked. "Why do I have this strange suspicion you like me?"

Electricity shimmered in the air between them. Vasilisa couldn't forget the memory of Galina's pulse beneath her fingertips in her bedroom, the staccato rhythm that had made her ache to kiss the pulse point and see how Galina would respond.

Galina's low reply obliterated any lingering doubts. "I like you."

A surge of fierce pleasure coursed through Vasilisa, intoxicating and sharp. "I'm glad to hear it," she said. "Because I think our zmei have decided they're not enemies."

"Is that all this is?" Galina asked quietly. "Us at the mercy of our deities?"

Vasilisa's voice whispered like a secret, shared only between them. "You know it isn't."

Drawing in a shallow breath, Galina gripped the table. Vasilisa ached to feel those hands tracing the curves of her body.

She wanted it all.

Galina remained silent, filling the air with a biting edge of tension. Finally, after what felt like an eternity, Galina spoke, opting for a safer topic. "I read in one of your books that the *ciob hilne* was a poison."

A smile played at the corners of Vasilisa's lips. "Have you been researching my flowers? Trying to figure out how many poisons I have in this glasshouse? The answer is three hundred."

Galina let out a startled laugh, and Vasilisa couldn't help but notice how her eyes sparkled in the candlelight like distant stars. "Godsblood, you could run an entire boutique for assassins. Should you add poison merchant to your secret life as a medicine supplier?"

"Every remedy can be harmful if taken in excess. And do you know why plants have toxins?"

"My research only got me so far as death within minutes," Galina replied. "But please continue."

Vasilisa found herself amused by the image of Galina ensconced in the library, book in hand, captivated by the secrets of noxious botanicals—an enthralling tableau.

"It's a defense mechanism," Vasilisa explained, lifting a flower with its milk-filled pod and admiring its delicate construction. "Plants are vulnerable, being anchored in place. So they've had to adapt. Some develop thorns or spines or thick skins. Others produce the chemical defenses that we call poison." Her eyes sought Galina's. "But the reason behind its evolution was the simple need to survive."

"So it hides its vulnerability by making itself unappealing," Galina said softly. "By driving everyone away."

Vasilisa felt a pang of recognition, a shared understanding with Galina that ran deeper than words. "Yes."

They fell into a comfortable silence, punctuated only by the rustle of leaves and the cadence of their breathing. Vasilisa gazed up at the sky beyond the glasshouse, drinking in the moon's light as it filtered through the panes.

"Did you ever see the *cegre pleddaus* in my garden?" Vasilisa asked. "The flower that blossoms at night in winter?"

Galina's breath caught in her throat, a sharp stutter of surprise. "No," she whispered, the word a fragile confession. "Because you promised to show it to me."

Vasilisa felt something shift beneath her ribs, a tangled thicket of emotions that left her breathless. "Well then. The moon is up, and the flowers will be out. Would you like to pay them a visit?"

The other woman smiled softly. "Let me get my coat."

Minutes later, they departed the glasshouse wing and entered the moonlit garden. Vasilisa propelled herself along the broad paths she had designed for her wheelchair. As they traversed the track, she couldn't help but steal glances at Galina, her breath hitching each time. Galina looked like a creature of winter, forged from moon-kissed steel and stardust; pale hair framed in an ethereal light.

At the garden's edge, Vasilisa led them to a wall where *cegre pleddaus* vines twisted over the stonework. The star-shaped blooms shimmered in the moonlight, surrounded by thorns resembling a fierce protective crown. The scent of their petals was soft and intoxicating, a haunting combination that reminded Vasilisa of Galina.

"Beautiful," Galina said.

"It's toxic to touch," Vasilisa warned. "But it has a lovely perfume."

Galina leaned in, eyes shuttering closed. An emotion stirred across her features. "Oh," she said on an exhale.

Something fragile squeezed inside Vasilisa's chest at the sight. "They say *cegre pleddaus* can bring forth memories. What does it remind you of?"

Pain rippled over Galina's face, written long ago on her skin. "Home," she whispered, then stepped back as if scorched by a flame. "I'm sorry. I have to go."

But Vasilisa couldn't let her leave, not yet. She caught Galina's wrist with shaking fingers, and godpower sparked between them.

"You're upset," Vasilisa said, pressing her fingertips to Galina's racing pulse. "What's wrong? Were you thinking about your mother in Rontsy?"

Galina's muscles tensed even further, and she seemed to withdraw from Vasilisa's touch. "No."

I want you.

I want to know you.

Vasilisa gathered the courage to take a risk. She lifted Galina's hand and placed a delicate kiss on her knuckles. "Tell me."

Their zmei embraced, godpower crackling through the air between them. An energy built beneath the stars, an unspoken bond that dragged them closer—a pull as powerful and inexplicable as gravity.

"My home is gone." Galina's voice was barely more than a whisper. "Why did you show me that?"

Vasilisa froze when she realized Galina's eyes were wet. "I thought you would like it."

"You thought I would like it?" Galina barked out a bitter laugh, the sound as brittle as broken glass. Like the memories had clawed at something raw inside her, an open wound that refused to heal. "You thought I'd like to remember my home, a place that no longer exists? You think I want to go back to my room and dream about the dead?" With a sharp noise, she tore from Vasilisa's grip. "I don't want this. Stop making me want you. Stop encouraging your god to bond with mine."

"*Galina Feodorovna*." Vasilisa rose, her legs aching with the effort, and reached for Galina's face. The other woman went motionless as Vasilisa's fingers landed on her cheeks. "Galusha," she murmured.

Galina's words were unsteady as she whispered, "That name..."

Vasilisa's expression softened. "Galusha." That intimate name, like a rune carved into the stillness—each syllable danced like embers in the air between them. "Our zmei understand us. They want what we want."

Galina laid her palms over Vasilisa's but didn't pull away. Her breath hitched, as if she were on the verge of confessing something—exposing herself, leaving herself bare. A trapped bird flapping its wings in desperation, mirroring the rhythm of her pulse.

But in the end, she only shook her head. "I know you're ill. In the alurean record books, there was a black mark through your register."

"Yes," Vasilisa said. She'd be the one to let go of her fear. Prove that this meant more to her than godpower or safety. "I have a degenerative illness passed through the alurea. The zmei in our bodies are growing sicker each time they're summoned against their will from Smokova. Caging them is killing them and us. We've successfully hidden it for centuries."

Galina went still, her hands tightening around Vasilisa's. Worry was etched across her features. "Will you die?"

She felt Galina's god flare, fierce and protective, sending heat shooting through her veins. Vasilisa's zmeya stretched its wings in response, perhaps longing to take flight with its chosen mate and soar among the stars.

"I can't tell you that. Every other alurea with my condition—"

"The secret had to be kept," Galina guessed as the knowledge dawned on her.

"Yes," Vasilisa breathed.

A ravenous, wild want plunged its claws into Vasilisa, a need too impossible to resist.

Vasilisa leaned forward and touched her lips to Galina's. She felt an answering roar through Galina's body—a reply to a question never asked. The other woman yanked her close, searing trails of kisses down her throat. Heat rushed through Vasilisa's veins, and she wanted nothing more than to be swept up by Galina, to be consumed by the flames between them.

Let the blaze take her.

Let it incinerate her.

Desperation clawed at them both as they fumbled with the fabric of each other's clothes. Then it happened—torrid fingertips scorched over Vasilisa's skin as Galina slipped a hand into her bodice and cupped her breast, dragging a thumb across her nipple. Vasilisa gasped—a desperate plea and command combined into one.

Not enough.

Give me more.

Give me everything.

Their zmei thrashed against each other, the fire between them a reflection of their human counterparts. They were locked together, fates intertwined, destined to bond.

Mine, Vasilisa thought.

She slid her palm down, reaching for Galina's skirts, frantic now. She wanted to taste and plunder every inch of her, to make her shiver with pleasure so strong even the cold winter air would be forgotten.

But as her fingertips brushed down Galina's thigh, Vasilisa was met with rough, scarred skin. A secret that had left its mark on Galina's body.

Galina tore out of Vasilisa's embrace, hastily straightening her clothes. Her god withdrew so fast that Vasilisa's zmeya whimpered at the loss of contact.

Vasilisa panted, swaying unsteadily. She sought purchase against the back of her chair as the frigid wind cut through her coat.

"I have to go," Galina whispered on a breath, ragged and threadbare. She scrubbed at her lips, as if she wanted to scour the memory of their kiss from her mind. "Please let me go, Vasya."

The diminutive name slashed through Vasilisa—a blade forged from pain and regret. "Galusha—"

What happened? What happened to you?

But Galina answered with nothing but a silent shake of her head. "Don't." The moonlight cast its baleful glow upon her anguished face. "You're like that flower. Reminding me of everything I want but can never have."

43

SERA

Sera's hands fumbled as she stuffed her clothes into her bag. She was no stranger to being hunted by sentries, but this time was different. It wasn't just her life—everything she and Galina worked for could come crashing down in seconds if she were discovered.

Then she heard a noise so faint it could be nothing. But Sera knew better than to ignore it. Her grip tightened around the bag's strap as she strained her ears to isolate the sound.

Footsteps. Soft but distinct over the endless drip of water echoing through the dimly lit corridors. Not Anna's confident strides or Galina's graceful steps. Slower, more deliberate, searching.

A stranger—moving down the main corridor toward her room.

Sera pressed her back against the peeling wallpaper beside the door, holding her breath as she listened again.

A lone guard, maybe. If she let him leave here, he'd bring others. Search the rooms.

Find all her mother's notes.

Sera reached for the knife in her sheath, fingers curling around its hilt as a figure stepped out of the gloom beyond her door.

She lunged.

Her weapon arced through the air, but before it could find its mark, strong hands seized her by the wrist and pinned her to the wall.

The dagger clattered to the ground.

Sera's heart pounded as she looked into the face of the man who had caught her—Vitaly, with his stormy eyes and slow, dangerous smile.

"That blade almost went through my throat," he said, amusement threading his voice like velvet. "You've improved."

"You're slower," she countered. "You should have dodged it. I would have stumbled after my swing."

Vitaly's hand found purchase on the wall beside her head as his gaze roamed over her body. "And what then?"

"Would have left my back exposed," Sera replied.

It took all her resolve not to lean forward and claim his lips. Their skirmishes had always been equal parts pleasure and violence—unspoken words of surrender burning between them.

"But you would have expected my tactics." His voice whispered across her, igniting sensations she'd only ever felt with him. "I had to disarm you first."

A smile crept unbidden over Sera's face, and she heard the catch in Vitaly's breath. She knew exactly how to make him weak, how to bring him to his knees before her.

"You're forgetting something, Vitaly Sergeyevich," she said, watching desire flare through his features. "I always keep more than one knife."

In a blink, Sera pivoted and swapped their positions, pressing the tip of her hidden dagger against Vitaly's throat. His gaze locked onto hers in a heady combination of arousal and amusement.

"Fuck, I've missed you," he sighed.

Sera forgot to breathe; his tender words had a way of creeping up on her hardened exterior. But she wouldn't let Vitalik see her break, so she forced herself to show no reaction. "And no wonder. You're out of practice and more careless than ever."

He laughed softly. "None of my operatives can match your skill and finesse."

She hardened her resolve. "What do you want, Vitalik?"

His hot breath caressed her cheek. "What do I want?" he repeated. "You, *vorovka*. But I'll settle for the smallest corner of your heart, if you're feeling generous."

The seconds ticked by in silence. The world dimmed to a narrow focus—the only thing that remained was the torturous rhythm of their synchronized heartbeat.

Her heart was like the glass shards of a broken window, sharp enough to wound her with every fragment that belonged to him. He owned more than the smallest piece—the whole damn thing was his. He couldn't steal what he already had.

She fought against the tide of emotions, trying not to break beneath the pressure. "Don't say that to me."

His expression softened. "Then I'm here for the pleasure of seeing you."

"How did you even find me? Did you follow me from the tavern? Can't I have a few days to be mad at you about those bombs?"

Vitaly's lips twisted into a sardonic grin, making it all too clear that he knew the effect he had on her. "You know I can't resist your charms."

Her lip curled. "Try again."

Vitaly shrugged nonchalantly. "Your confectioner told me."

"Anya?" Her grip tightened on the weapon. "What did you do to her?"

"I didn't do anything to her."

"Bullshit," Sera retorted, her voice low and dangerous. "That towering imbecile with the permanent scowl following me was one of yours, and he set her shop on fire. *With her inside.*"

"I didn't tell Pyotr to do that," he said.

"And who killed Emil?" she asked through her teeth.

He winced. "I might have known Pyotr would do that."

Sera withdrew her knife from his neck, the steel scraping as she slid it into its sheath. "Get out," she snarled. "I'll scold Anya later for telling you where I live. Don't come back. And tell your lackey to keep his distance, or I'll shove this blade through his face."

But Vitaly wouldn't budge. "Anna Borislava told me where to find you because the alurean soldiers were after us in the Black. She fled the city and trusted me to keep you safe. It's worse than the last time, Serafima. They're not just raiding the slums—they're burning buildings to hunt the faithless."

Sera's breathing grew labored as she stared at him. "But it's winter. Citizens will freeze to death—"

"They don't give a damn," Vitaly said. "They've plastered wanted posters of us on every street corner from Khotchino to the Shore. The Black is crawling with sentries."

Sera noticed the satchel slung over his shoulder. "You left the tavern."

A muscle worked in Vitaly's jaw. "It wasn't safe anymore," he said. His attention fell on her midriff. "Let me make sure you didn't irritate your injury when you attacked me."

"You won't stop pestering me until you see the wound, will you?"

"Not even a little."

"Then follow me." She led him into her cramped bedroom and sat on the bed. "Have a look."

His towering frame filled the room, looming like some imposing sentinel as his head almost brushed the ceiling.

He surveyed the bare walls and empty shelves. Nothing of interest except—

She froze as his gaze locked onto the seashell resting atop her dresser. The iridescent glow of the inner carapace shimmered in the dim light of the single lamp.

Vitaly reached out, his fingertips tracing his childhood gift. So many memories were embedded within that object—it was the beginning of them both. "You kept this."

Images crashed to the surface of her mind. That summer day eighteen years ago when they were children clinging to adolescence. The girl was twelve, still getting used to the god inside her. The boy was fourteen—already on the prowl, a cunning thief from the Black, scouring the Shore for soft marks to exploit.

Sera didn't care much for the beach; she only went for the sound of the sea. Her zmeya was restless from the start, howling like the caged beast it was. She sat in the sand, watching the undulating tides, and contemplated drowning herself.

Then along came Vitaly.

Sera wondered later if he saw her as another easy target, a gullible girl ripe for the plucking. Maybe he planned to lure her in with his dashing smile and that pretty seashell he offered.

But when he gave it to her, and his fingers brushed against hers, the god went quiet.

"What's it for?" she'd asked, rolling the seashell around in her palm, savoring the shimmering interior. The silence of her thoughts.

Sera would have seized on any excuse to prolong the conversation, to make him stay.

Vitaly shrugged, his bony shoulders rising and falling. Time would do its work, filling them out with muscle and sinew. "Just didn't want you to be sad."

Sera had stared at him and seen her future, a glittering horizon stretching before her.

But she should have known better.

Sera looked away. "It's still here from when I was a girl. Are you going to look or not?"

Wordlessly, Vitaly sank to his knees, taking his time with a slow perusal of her body. Sera held her breath as his calloused hands ghosted over her, lifting her shirt to expose the pristine complexion beneath. After removing the stitches, the wound disappeared without a trace of scarring.

Their eyes met.

"It never occurred to me before now that you never took a scratch during all those Sundyr missions," he said, fingertips skimming over her. "Perfect skin, no scars for me to trace, no bruises for me to kiss. Meanwhile I came out of those operations with more injuries than I could count."

Sera curled her fingers into her palms at the memory of the scars on his back, remnants of skirmishes with sentries. "Believe me, if my zmeya had a choice, I'd have bled out in the woods at the palace." At his silence, she asked bitterly, "Do I disgust you now?"

Vitaly lowered his head and kissed her ribs. One after the other. Softly, like petals falling on her skin. "I told you not to ask foolish things," he murmured, nipping gently. "And you never answered my question back in my apartment. How long you were in Dolsk communicating with the Blackshore when you knew I was alive?"

"The whole time," she replied quietly.

Vitaly held his breath before leaning over Sera, planting his hands on either side of her. A flame sparked to life in his gaze. "Did you think of me at all while I was searching for you?" he asked, his words sharp as arrows. "Did I haunt your dreams like you did mine?"

"No." A lie so small it slipped from her lips without thought.

"No?" His voice was soft, but there was an underlying edge of anger. "*Vorovka pro fse ku*, you're a better liar than any confidence artist I've ever met. But every time I kiss you, you look like you're drowning."

Her jaw tightened. "Stop."

It was useless to resist Vitaly. He had a knack for finding and exploiting the least defended parts of her heart. What good was armor when he knew where her weak spots lay? Her walls were nothing but scraps of paper; they crumbled whenever he touched her.

Even her zmeya was hushed, straining against her. Aching to assert some claim on him just as much as she was. He'd tamed the untamable.

His lashes lowered. "Fine." As he pulled away, the chasm between them felt as vast as the ocean. He noticed her bag on the floor. "You were leaving."

"Yes." There was no point in denying it.

"Where?" His voice was rigid with carefully disguised emotion.

"One of Irina's safe houses. I still have business in the Blackshore."

"With the alurea? Your Common God?" A spark of temper flashed in his eyes. "Why would she give a shit about you?"

Sera's emotional wall crumbled entirely, shattered into a thousand tiny pieces. She was done keeping secrets.

"Come with me," she said with a resigned sigh. "I need to show you something."

Vitaly trailed after her down the dark passageway, scrutinizing the lines of Zverti the old university students had inscribed on the stonework. Each one was a grim reminder of oppression, of what would happen if she failed.

Sera led him to where Irina made Galina into a weapon.

"Here." She gestured to the scorched remains of the place where her mother had ruthlessly interrogated and murdered enemies. "Go ahead. Have a look."

Vitaly stepped into the charred chamber. He turned slowly, surveying the bare room and its blackened stone walls. "What is this?" he asked quietly.

Sera snorted softly, her lip curling in disdain. "An interrogation room. Or, if you prefer, an observation room. Where Irina conducted her sick experiments."

He froze. "What experiments?"

"First, I want you to understand how many failed uprisings she witnessed," Sera said. "How many commoners died despite any weapon they could obtain or construct. They can't stand against an army bound to the zmei."

"Alurea aren't immortal," he snapped. "Plant a few bombs in the right place—"

"Let's not forget, you tried that before. How did it turn out?" She let out a harsh exhale. "My mother was one of the last scholars at the university before the purge. She discovered ancient texts describing how zmei were bonded to humans against their will. Once they were caged, there was no way out for them. The first alurea to summon gods from Smokova and trap them were commoners used as experiments by the ruling class. Irina planned to replicate the tests and call a zmeya with enough godpower to break any connection between humans and gods."

Vitaly stiffened. Did he think about the temple archways, the carvings of zmei hovering over the door? Winged beasts snatched from a distant world and imprisoned in human bodies? Their wings pinned down so they could no longer fly?

"What did you just say?" His voice came out strangled.

"The alurean texts had everything," she said. "The notes describing how they forcibly summoned the zmei, how they primed people for the bond, the plants they needed, and the ages of their chosen survivors. Once they perfected the process and bore children naturally bonded to deities, they destroyed all the ingredients and hoarded the power. Irina spent decades searching for the plants believed to be extinct. That's what she did to me, Vitalik. I wasn't born an alurea."

Vitaly's hand trembled as he reached out to touch her cheek. "Wait, she used their secrets on you? Her own daughter?"

"Children were the only ones who survived the process." Sera couldn't hold back the acrid bitterness that laced her words. "So she took one look at me and thought, why not her own flesh and blood?"

"That insufferable piece of shit," Vitaly snarled. "If I had known, I would have—"

"Stabbed her in the neck?" Sera asked with a slight smile despite herself. "Anya wants to bring her back from the dead just to throw her into the sea."

"I would personally detonate each limb, savoring every excruciating moment, and then gift the remnants to Anna Borislava for her own amusement," he replied.

Such a gentleman.

"Creative," she said.

A peculiar lightness floated in her chest, the weight of her long-buried secrets vanishing with his responses.

"I have a knack for artistic violence when the mood strikes me. Irina actually tortured you as a child to summon a fucking dragon?"

Sera's grip on her composure nearly faltered at his blunt question. "She caged the wrong god. My zmeya demands a blood sacrifice for its power."

His expression turned even darker. "So what you're telling me," Vitaly said, scanning the dimly lit chamber, "is that a well-executed explosion would have been too merciful a fate for her. Because it's clear you weren't your mother's last attempt."

"No," she replied in a hollow voice. "The Blackshore municipal hospital took in a lone survivor whose village was decimated by the godfire. She was left with no family. She wanted revenge. Irina convinced the girl to volunteer for her sick experiments and trained her to infiltrate the palace."

Realization washed over Vitaly, softening the hard lines of his face. "Galina Feodorovna," he murmured. "She's the reason you went to *obryad*. And she was who you were after on the day we parted ways four years ago, wasn't she?"

Sera nodded. "Galina's my foster sister. She has the godfire but can't break godbonds. Irina guessed she miscalculated in her serums, that Galina's body wasn't primed enough for the zmeya. She designed a panacea to bolster their bond, but the empress executed Irina before she could finish it."

"Why didn't you tell me about her?" Vitaly made a low noise, gesturing to the scarred room. "About any of this?"

Sera wanted nothing more than to feel her husband's arms around her, to be swallowed up in his embrace, but the words wouldn't come. Too much time had passed; too much had happened.

"No one could know about Galina," she replied. "Irina's plans depended on it. And you would have exploded her limb from limb, remember?"

"But Irina was dead four years ago," he said quietly. "She's not why you stayed in Dolsk and never sent me word."

Her fingers dug hard into her palms until they hurt. "You despise the gods, and I couldn't keep lying to you. I stayed in Dolsk because I didn't want you to have to kill your wife."

A fire in his gaze sparked to life at that. "I told you not to say foolish things," he whispered. He swept his thumb across her wet cheek. "You know me better than that. I'm a bastard and a villain with no sense of morality or decency. Except when it comes to you, god or no god." His expression was tender. She missed that. She missed *him*. "I've belonged to you since the day we met on that beach."

The last of Sera's defenses crumbled under his words. He was her match in every way, igniting a fire in her that no other could. He was fierce, he was brutal, but he was hers.

Sera kissed his palm, and she savored how his breath shuddered in response. But as quickly as the moment came, it was gone. Vitalik's head jerked up, his gaze alert. He tapped a finger to his lips, urging her to silence.

"Three sets of footsteps," he whispered.

Sera paused to listen. "Four. They're coming down the main stairwell."

Vitaly kept her body tucked against his as they pressed to the wall and out of view. "Anyone you know?"

"Definitely not. I sense godpower."

He drew a knife from his coat. "Any chance there's another way out of here?"

"Just the one." She held up her blade. "Ready to fight some sentries?"

Vitaly's lips brushed against her forehead in a fleeting contact that left her yearning for more. "Just like our missions in Sundyr," he murmured. "Lead the way, *vorovka*."

Sera let herself smile.

44

GALINA

Galina's footsteps echoed as she trailed the guard through the winding corridors of Zolotiye.

"In here, Your Radiance," he muttered, ushering her into the mangled wreckage that was a beautiful ballroom mere days ago.

Galina surveyed the devastation. Shards of chandeliers littered the ground like fallen stars, while snow dusted the shattered remains. Curtains were charred and stained, and snowflakes drifted through gaps in walls and ceiling. Ash covered everything, and the harsh air filled her lungs, making breathing a challenge.

Empress Isidora and Katya stood silently among the debris.

Galina flinched as she met her friend's gaze. No matter how hard she tried, she couldn't shake the memory of Katya's screams echoing in the chamber as she was immolated in the godfire. She'd tortured Katya at that ball, and bringing her back from death's doorstep had done nothing to absolve her guilt. And now they were forced to pretend nothing had happened.

Galina's attention fell on the delicate chains of bells adorning Katya's limbs. Her godfire had melted down those adornments—it had only been days, yet the empress had already replaced them. Galina had to repress an urge to incinerate Isidora until she was reduced to dust.

Isidora appraised Galina with a calculating look. "Galina Feodorovna," she said in greeting, dismissing her guard.

Galina bit down on her tongue, dipping into a deep bow. "Your Imperial Majesty," she mumbled, keeping her eyes glued to the scorched marble at her feet.

Isidora stalked around Galina, the rustle of her dress like serpents slithering through the grass—the twining vines embroidered into the black silk only added to the image of a predator stalking her prey. A chill swept through Galina's veins.

"Following the ball," Isidora said, "I never got to compliment your display—though corpses can't speak, I imagine Yelena and Marianne would agree." The empress's words were dry as she referred to the assassinated queens of Sasnis and Samatsk.

The memory of the bloodbath—the ballroom decimated and corpses littering the floor—consumed Galina's thoughts.

She sucked in a deep breath and forced her hands together to still their trembling. "I'm honored by your compliments, Your Imperial Majesty."

"I've been giving your circumstances some thought. My investigators have yet to discover proof of an alurean infant escaping notice. We keep such meticulous records, even when enemies produce children. Illicit unions aren't as rare as one might think."

Galina fought against the urge to look at Katya for reassurance; the handmaiden understood precisely how these subtle changes in Isidora could be a warning sign that things were going south.

"Your Imperial Majesty, I..."

"It no longer matters," said the empress with a mocking twist of her lips. "In some ways, it's almost a blessing you were born an orphan. Had you grown up as my daughter, surrounded by courtiers and sycophants, I would have been forced to hand you off like a prize to some sniveling king in exchange for alliances. So many alurean women are used to bolster their husband's power. It's revolting. My mother taught me back in Liesgau that I would be just another man's weapon. Did your late mother tell you the same?"

Galina thrust her fists into the folds of her dress to mask her fury.

No, she wanted to say. *She didn't get the chance to teach me anything about marriage because you murdered her. You left me with nothing but anger and scars.*

"No, Your Imperial Majesty."

Katya shook her head ever so slightly in warning, and Galina realized with a jolt that her friend had caught the hint of rebellion in her words. She forced herself to smother the emotions stirring inside her with an iron will.

Galina lowered her gaze to the floor. The drums of vengeance beat a furious rhythm in her heart. When the time came, Isidora would learn what it was like to have her entire world crash down around her.

"No," the empress repeated. "Then you understand I won't yield my power again. Not to Sopol, and certainly not to some upstart commoners with bombs. Yes?"

"Yes, Your Imperial Majesty," she replied through gritted teeth, willing herself to be patient. The empress would lose everything soon enough.

"Good. I'm glad you agree," Isidora said with a smug smile.

A bitter wind roared through the shattered chamber, whipping snow in frenzied circles. Isidora had a blazing gleam in her eyes as she surveyed the damage. Rubble and timber littered the floor, remnants of the blast that had nearly claimed their lives.

Galina remembered the sound of the explosion, the way the walls had shaken and trembled. It had been a miracle that they'd survived.

Isidora gestured to the devastation before them, her voice low with rage. "Remember this place whenever you think of sympathizing with those who raised you. A few soft words and commoners will murder you without a second thought."

Galina clenched her jaw, keeping her expression blank and guarded. Why did the empress ask her to come here?

"We can't undo the chaos and political anarchy this bomb caused," Isidora said with a bitter edge. "Two rulers are dead, and their kingdoms are struggling with weakened replacements." The empress turned to Galina with a cruel purpose in her eyes. A feral desire that Galina couldn't comprehend until Isidora added, "If we act, Sundyr can be brought together under one rule, just like it used to be."

Fear ran through Galina as she stared at the empress—as if she was eight years old again, spotting this woman on the hill outside Olensk. Waiting for the fire to rain from the sky. But there was no running this time. No hiding. No escape.

"How?" she asked, relieved that her voice held steady.

Isidora reached for her. "Give me your hand."

Galina hesitated, eyeing those fingers stretched in offering—a grotesque counterpoint to Vasilisa's tender touch. Galina dreaded what her god would do when faced with the prospect of merging its godfire with Isidora's. Would it prefer the empress over Vasilisa?

Our gods want what we want, Vasilisa had said.

Please let that be true.

Galina had no choice but to comply, and as her hand trembled in Isidora's grasp, a jolt of electricity surged through her. Her zmeya roared in protest, teeth and claws scraping against her bones as it struggled against its cage. Her dragon despised this. Sparks of energy spat across her skin as if their gods were trying to repel one another from a forced union, threatening to ignite a full-blown war.

From the corner of her eye, Galina saw Katya flinch, startled by the sudden flare of heat and hostility in the frigid chamber.

"Our gods hate each other," Isidora said. Her voice was calm, but Galina could see the strain on her face as she fought to contain her own zmeya.

This was nothing like with Vasilisa. There was no pleasure, no desire, no shiver of want—only aggression that licked at Galina's senses. Her god was almost frenzied with violence. Heat shimmered between them, godfire threatening to rise to the surface.

Galina sucked in a desperate breath, her dragon howling inside her in warning as she spoke. "I'm sorry, Your Imperial Majesty."

Thank you, she thought to her god. *Good dragon.*

"Zmei are animals at their core," Isidora said. "They don't take kindly to threats." She paused, her eyes searching Galina's face. "Bonded pairs are rare, and I've often wondered if yours might have been mine."

Galina remained silent, unable to admit her zmeya only answered to one woman—Isidora's daughter.

The fine hair along Galina's neck prickled as her god growled with an insidious rumble beneath her ribcage that signaled its eagerness for battle. It had made its choice, and the empress wasn't it.

Then the empress waved a hand. "It's not important. We control them, and they can be forced to work together even when they don't like each other." She nodded at the surrounding room. "Use the godfire with me."

Galina swallowed, her throat dry. "Here in the—"

"The room is already destroyed, and the mavens will just rebuild it. I want to see what we're capable of."

There was no way out of this. No way to avoid speaking those words in the Exalted Tongue and summoning her god.

The zmeya rose, stretched its great shape through her bones, and gave its call of destruction.

The godfire erupted, blazing with a furious intensity. The searing heat melted the snow, splitting stones and pulverizing the rubble to nothing but ash and dust.

Galina and Isidora destroyed walls with a single exhalation, reducing the progress that had taken the mavens and servants days of labor to rebuild. The havoc they could unleash was beyond her comprehension. It made her wonder what would happen if they let the godfire run rampant through the villages and battlefields of Sundyr.

The stench of smoke and charred wood assaulted her senses, and the howling wind ripped through the chamber, sending dust and embers into the air. Sepulchral evidence of violence that threatened to bring back too many memories of Olensk. Of being pulled out of the rubble and finding her village reduced to dust.

She had walked out of the ashes to become the thing in her nightmares.

Dread twisted in her gut at the thought of what would happen if Sera's plan failed. Katya seemed to sense it too, a visible shudder passing through her that did not escape the empress's keen eye.

"You're trembling, Katenka. Was it our godpower?"

"I'll adjust in a moment, suvya," Katya said, her expression neutral despite the tension in her shoulders.

Isidora glanced at Galina. "If you ever take a handmaiden, you should be aware they're fragile things—easily broken by mistake or accident."

Galina's zmeya stirred at the empress's words, and a wave of heat surged across her skin as she struggled to keep her anger in check. She remembered Katya's warning: Isidora had gone through fourteen other handmaidens before her—all murdered in fits of rage. The alurea had always treated commoners as expendable, just bricks in the empire's foundations.

Galina lowered her head. "Yes, Your Imperial Majesty."

Her zmeya thrashed against her hold—godpower threatening to ignite—and it took all her strength not to lose her composure.

Calm down before she notices, she commanded the dragon.

Just in time, a uniformed man strode in, his expression unreadable as he surveyed the devastated ballroom. He bowed low, the medals on his uniform shining in the broken light streaming through the shattered ceiling.

"Your Imperial Majesty," the man murmured, an eagerness in his voice that made Galina go still. "May I have a word?"

Isidora must have caught the same spark of anticipation. "Please tell me you have news of our fugitives, General Vasilchikov."

Gods above. Galina held her breath.

The general's nod was swift. "We spotted the man in the Black this morning, and my sentries tracked him to Khotchino. We'll have both traitors captured by nightfall."

Galina's nails dug into her palms as her dragon thrashed harder now. She and Katya locked eyes, a silent exchange passing between them. The stakes were too high, and they couldn't afford to betray a flicker of their fear. This place was a den of vipers, and if they wanted to save Sera, they had to keep their guard up.

Galina's chest heaved with the sheer effort of reining in her god. *Stop. We'll save her, and we'll get our revenge. I promise.*

The zmeya settled back in its cage with a snarl, but obeyed her orders.

Isidora smirked at General Vasilchikov. "I want to hear the instant you have them in custody."

"Yes, Your Imperial Majesty." General Vasilchikov bowed once more and hurried out of the room.

Isidora turned to Galina. "My staff tells me the supplicants have taken a liking to you—that they've named you the Common God."

Galina's throat seemed to close on itself. "My apologies if—"

A dismissive wave silenced her. "I'm not interested in apologies. I'm aware this country despises its empress. Newspapers might refer to these traitors as Sopolese agents, but all citizens will see is a foreign empress executing people from their streets. As much as I'd love to slit the throats of every rebellious commoner, I have an easier solution."

Fear pricked at her skin. She had a sinking feeling that whatever Isidora planned would be executed with the same cruelty she was infamous for.

The empress stepped closer to Galina. "Let them witness their Common God give her endorsement. Your presence may calm the more unruly ones."

Betray her upbringing. Betray her people. Betray everything she stood for. She already had two kill counts in the empress's name and had been forced to use her godpower on Katya. How much more blood would she spill to keep up her ruse?

Galina's response was measured. "You want me to stand by your side."

Isidora's smile faded—replaced with something far less pleasant. "I want many things, but when I say them, they're not a whim."

"Yes, Your Imperial Majesty," Galina said. "If your general says the prisoners will be in custody today, may I rest before their sentencing?" If she didn't get away from the empress now, she wouldn't be able to maintain her performance.

"Fine," she said with a curt nod.

"May I have your handmaiden attend to me?" Galina hid the shake in her voice. "I'd like to be as composed before the public as possible. A favorable impression might help the crowd understand the severity of the crimes these terrorists committed."

The empress's expression soured, but she relented with a nod. "I'll let you borrow Ekaterina Isidorakh for the afternoon. But if you remain in my court, you'll find a servant of your own." Isidora glanced at Katya. "Go with her, *knesi*. I'll send word to have her dressed when General Vasilchikov returns."

Katya curtsied low. "Yes, *suvya*," she said, her voice barely above a whisper.

Galina and Katya walked through the twisting passageways toward the Glasshouse Wing. The distance was vast, and with each passing moment, Galina's fear amplified. Katya's bells jangled with each step, a mockery of their predicament.

She couldn't help Sera within the confines of Zolotiye.

By the time they arrived at Galina's bedchamber, a plan had solidified in her mind. She strode to her wardrobe. "Keep watch while I'm gone. I need to get to Sera. I'll open a passage to the tunnels—"

"No," Katya said. "If they've been discovered, the sentries might recognize you. Your face is plastered on every window in the Blackshore."

"Then I'll open a door close to there," Galina snapped as she threw clothes onto the bed. "The guards will clear out the streets to make their movements easier. I need to reach Sera before they do."

Katya shook her head, her fingers deftly unfastening the clasps of Galina's dress. "If someone sees you—"

"I have a few modest black gowns that'll suffice, and I'll keep my hair covered."

Katya yanked at the stays of the gown, tugging the cumbersome silk fabric from Galina's petite shoulders. "It's too dangerous."

"I won't let my sister die, and I won't let you rot here."

Katya shut her eyes tight and Galina watched emotions war across her face. It was like she'd told her before—her time was running out. Some other handmaiden would take her place and meet the same fate—an endless cycle of women trying to break free from the chains that no one could escape until death.

They could stop that cycle.

Katya seized the black gown and handed it to Galina. "Then I'm coming with you this time."

45

SERA

Sera and Vitaly crouched in the inky darkness of the tunnels. Their enemies were close, heavy footfalls echoing down the claustrophobic passage.

"My research is in the study," Sera breathed into Vitaly's ear. "We need it for the panacea."

Vitaly mouthed a string of curses, his grip tight around the hilt of his blade. Despite the gravity of their situation, Sera's lips twitched at the prospect of battle. They had come close to death more times than they could count during their days as smugglers in Sundyr. Still, an excitement thrummed through Sera's veins. She and Vitaly had always been a force to be reckoned with.

"Time for a distraction," she muttered, rolling up her sleeve and pressing her knife against her arm.

Vitaly grabbed her wrist. "Do you have to hurt yourself whenever you call on it?"

Sera swallowed at the ferocity in his question. "Unfortunately."

Vitaly's expression twisted with emotion. Was it hatred? Disgust? She couldn't tell. "I don't like that."

Sera gave a bitter half-smile. "Neither do I." Then she sliced the blade across her skin. The zmeya's power surged, an overwhelming force that threatened to burst out of her.

Her husband's gaze fell on the wound, and then he lifted her arm and pressed a gentle kiss below the trail of blood, his lips warm. "Is your dragon listening?" he asked softly.

Sera swallowed. "Always."

It always listens to you.

"Good," Vitaly said, low and dangerous. "We're going to have a little chat sometime. Me and it. If it keeps hurting you, it'll have to answer to me, and I don't tolerate anything causing you pain. Ever."

The zmeya froze, pinned by the heat in his words, and a rumble vibrated in Sera's chest, scales shifting under her skin. Was that a begrudging agreement?

Sera scowled. This little shit of a god would rather listen to a murderous brigand with a pretty voice than the human it was supposed to be bonded to?

Unbelievable.

As if to make its point, the zmeya flicked its tongue beneath Sera's wound before speaking its language through her lips. The command, sharp as a serpent's bite, rang out as the enemy troops advanced toward the split in the main corridor of the tunnels. Her pulse of godpower created a slight sound—just a rattle of noise that snap-cracked from the other direction, but it was enough to send the guards scrambling in search of the source.

She signaled to Vitaly and led him through the dimly lit hall to study.

With Vitaly's help, she gathered notes and various materials, shoving them into one of Irina's well-worn leather satchels. She frantically combed through her records, feeling the weight of time bearing down on her as she struggled to decide which ones to take and which to leave behind. Every scrap of information seemed crucial to her now.

"Sera," Vitaly whispered urgently. "We have to leave."

"Not yet."

"We don't have the time for this, *vorovka*."

"We'll make time," she said firmly, ripping pages from the journals without considering their delicate condition. Her plan felt so fragile, like one wrong move could break it apart. "This panacea is too important."

Sera moved around the study, grabbing small vials and her test samples with Galina's blood and hoping the containers wouldn't shatter in her bag. There was no time to secure them properly.

Where would she even work on the panacea next? There weren't many laboratories in the Blackshore, certainly not for a wanted criminal with a reward of five thousand imperial gold pieces on her head.

Vitaly hovered by the door, monitoring the intruders' movements from the hall as Sera scrambled to gather the disordered paperwork that comprised a month's worth of her efforts.

"*Serafima*," her husband hissed.

"This is everything I've worked on," she explained, her voice tight. "All my information on the serum. We can't go without it. It's our best shot at overthrowing the empress."

There was too much to leave behind, too much to risk losing to the enemy.

Vitaly jolted from his post at the door. "They're coming. We have to move."

Sera's pulse lurched. These tunnels had been her home, but at that moment, they might as well have been a death trap. Vitaly's gaze met hers, and the tenderness in his winter-gray eyes was almost enough to make her forget the danger.

He stepped close, cupping her cheeks in his calloused hands, his lips brushing her forehead in a fleeting caress. "I won't let you die here, *vorovka*."

He reached into his coat and produced a small coin Sera recognized as her smallest explosive design.

It was time to go. Together.

Sera took the device from Vitaly and set it on the desk. She pressed the timer's button and snatched the satchel.

Vitaly clasped her hand and pulled her into the corridor, the clatter of pounding boots echoing behind them. Shouts echoed through the annex. A sudden burst of golden light blazed in the darkness as the sentries' godpower flew past.

They sprinted faster, the ground vibrating under their feet. Chunks of rock and debris exploded around them, but Sera pushed forward. The searing heat of godpower brushed her overcoat, and the fabric ignited. Flames licked at her arms and shoulders, but Sera gritted her teeth and used a pulse of power to douse the blaze, refusing to let the pain slow her down.

If they emerged from the tunnels too quickly, the guards would be on their heels. They had only one chance to shake them off—the ticking bomb in the study, primed and ready to detonate.

Sera slammed to a halt, her boot soles shredding on the stone ground. "Take this." She thrust the satchel at Vitaly. "Hold it close. No matter what."

"Sera. What are you—"

She swiped her blade across her forearm again, drawing deep. There was no time to check if Vitaly's earlier threats to the obstinate god had worked. "Take the bag. Get it to Galina."

But he seized the lapels of her coat, his expression fierce. "I told you, I'm not leaving you to die."

"*Vitalik.*"

"Do what you need to do to make that damn dragon listen," he whispered, his eyes meeting hers. "But I stay."

She remembered the day she met Vitaly, how even the crash of the sea against the rocks couldn't muffle her god's roar. It only responded to violence and… him.

He's ours, she told the bastard god, her thoughts a snarl. *You understand, you stubborn fuck? He's ours to defend.*

Sera cupped his cheek and pressed her lips to his, her other hand outstretched toward the guards as they thundered down the corridor. And her mind went quiet. The zmeya stilled, the brutal beast soothed by that one point of contact. A kiss it once savored. The silence it craved as much as she did. They communicated through Vitaly, a bridge between them; her words were as clear as a temple bell.

Listen now.

Listen to me.

Sera unleashed her godpower at the same time the bomb went off. The tunnels exploded around them.

Gripping his coat in desperation, Sera pulled him closer, her lips seeking refuge in his. His touch ignited her, allowing her to channel the blast's power and redirect its full force on their pursuing enemies.

The zmeya thrummed through her bones, feeding off Sera's blood offering, thrilling at the kiss. A clash of dominance and lust, savagery and longing. The god was satiated, yet it craved more—more contact, more acknowledgment, more submission, more of everything.

Sera's desire for Vitaly burned just as fiercely. She clung to him, finding solace in the familiar scent that evoked memories of their past. All the years they'd spent together.

As the surrounding tunnels crumbled and shook, Sera channeled the power of the zmeya and held the debris at bay.

"What do you think?" she murmured against his mouth. "More chaotic than Ardatovo?"

Vitaly's eyes gleamed with amusement and wicked delight as he surveyed the floating rubble and bloodied bodies of sentries. "Definitely. And we kiss better than we did in Ardatovo."

Then he took her by the hand, and they escaped into the city before the explosion brought more guards.

46

GALINA

Galina's godpower cracked open a door into a shadowed alleyway just off the underground annex.

Brick-and-mortar storefronts flanked the claustrophobic street, their façades adorned with intricate carvings and weathered domes, more suited for commerce than living quarters. This part of Khotchino was deserted in the afternoon, abandoned by all but the rats and roaches that skittered through the gloom.

Beside Galina, Katya trembled, the handmaiden's anxiety scrawled across her pretty features like a jagged scar. The clomping of boots nearby sent unease snaking through Galina's veins.

She dragged Katya into the shadows, praying they hadn't been seen.

"Now what?" the handmaiden whispered.

Galina hastily daubed the grime onto her clothes and smeared it over her face, gesturing at Katya to do the same. "We don't pass for factory workers at the end of their shift. We may not be who they're hunting, but we don't want them taking a second look at us."

The guards' footsteps echoed closer, giving them no time to plan. Katya quickly copied Galina's motions, smudging charcoal over her cheekbones and wiping it away in streaks, leaving dark trails in their wake. When she was finished, she stood back for Galina's appraisal.

Galina sighed and adjusted her headscarf, hiding her blonde locks. "Our dresses aren't convincing, but if we're lucky, they'll be too busy tracking Sera and Vitaly to pay attention to us."

They hurried down the narrow lane with skirts swishing in a frantic cadence. Galina spoke over her shoulder as they fled. "Irina had safe houses all over the city—Sera could be in one of them."

"How many?" Katya panted, struggling to keep up.

Before Galina could answer, the guards burst into the alley, godpower licking through the air. Alurean sentries were bonded to lesser gods, but authorities were trained to use the godpower of their zmei against rebellious supplicants.

"You there!" a guard barked, his voice ricocheting off the walls.

The women froze. Galina's pulse skittered. From the frantic rise and fall of Katya's chest underneath her cloak, she knew the girl was every bit as terrified.

The sentry advanced, the sound of his steel-shod boots ringing off cobblestones like a death knell. Galina felt her zmeya stirring beneath her skin, ready to unleash a swift and immobilizing blast of godpower.

Katya must have sensed it; she seized Galina's wrist in a hard grip. "*Don't,*" she hissed as the guard drew closer. "Let him do his job before resorting to your godpower. We don't want to leave a trail of unconscious guards behind us. Now, curtsy."

They both dipped low as the sentry stopped in front of them. "Your Magnificence," they intoned together.

Silence filled the air. The sentry gripped Katya's chin, forcing her face upwards. He scrutinized her features, searching for any trace of the fugitives he sought.

Then he rounded on Galina, and she barely had time to slam her god back into its cage before his rough fingers found her skin. The zmeya seethed and hissed at the contact, aching to be unleashed.

Galina's pulse quickened as the guard's stare lingered, the weight of his suspicion tangible.

Her black shawl, a standard garment for factory workers, did little to conceal her identity. Her visage was all too familiar across the Blackshore. Galina held her breath as the guard studied her, barely daring to blink. She wanted nothing more than to melt into the shadows.

I'm nothing, she projected at him. *No one. I'm a supplicant who fears you.*

The guard sneered as though he could hear the desperate plea in her thoughts. "Get out of here," he spat, releasing her chin.

Galina took Katya's hand and hurried away from the guard.

"How many safe houses did Sera's mother have?" Katya asked again, her voice barely audible above their quickened breathing.

"That's the problem. She wasn't exactly forthcoming about all of them. Sera knew of a few, but—"

An explosion tore through the district, shaking the ground beneath them. Shouts and thundering boots reverberated from nearby.

The guard sprinted past them in a blur, his yell echoing after him. "Get off the streets! Now!"

Dread knotted Galina's stomach. "That sounded like it came from near the tunnels," she told Katya. "Sera must have set them to blow. She'll be on the run."

The handmaiden looked shaken. "Do you think we should intercept her?"

Galina shook her head. "Not together. Irina had a hideout in the abandoned hat shop nearby. It's close enough that Sera might go there until this mess dies down." She rattled off quick directions to Katya. "When you're inside, take the stairs to the old storage room. Move the blue trunk out of the way, and you'll find a hidden staircase to the cellar. If Sera finds you, tell her to stay put. Wait for me."

"What are you going to do?" Katya asked as Galina led her to the end of the alley.

"I'll search for her in the streets and try to lure the sentries away. Now go. Quickly."

As Katya vanished into the labyrinthine alleys, Galina found herself alone amidst the chaos. The buildings seemed to close in around her, as if trying to swallow her whole.

Galina shook off the fear and focused on her task. She hurried in the opposite direction to Katya, hoping to reach her sister before she went to the secret apartment beneath the hat seller.

But as she emerged onto the next road, she cursed under her breath, watching the flood of guards sprinting past. The city was a heaving mass of bodies and noise, with the towering edifices of the district jutting from the landscape like jagged knives. She had no chance of finding her sister in this chaos. Not with the countless alurean sentries patrolling the streets.

She needed a diversion—and a signal to Sera.

Galina broke into a run, her boots pounding through the slushy snow. She focused on the proximity of the buildings, the layers of stone and mortar—the nooks and crannies where Sera could hide.

Nothing.

Galina skidded to a halt outside the crumbling ruins of an old candle merchant's shop—a little collateral damage, but no risk of casualties. Galina had done worse in her time.

With a steadying breath, she closed her eyes and let the

zmeya flex through her bones. The dragon stretched beneath her ribcage, its power surging through her limbs.

And then she unleashed it with a thunderous roar.

The shop facade exploded in a shower of bricks and dust, the blast echoing across the city skyline. Galina felt the rush of air against her face as the shockwave slammed into her.

She didn't hesitate—she turned and fled down the serpentine alleys, her feet barely touching the cobblestones. She knew the guards would come, but she wasn't worried. They wouldn't find Sera. Galina wouldn't permit it.

She had walked these streets countless times before, the memories etched deep. Alongside Irina, she had mapped out every corner and crevice, tracing the lines of the city's architecture until they bled into her veins. Now, as she sprinted through the twisting lanes, dodging broken glass and crumbling walls, she relied on her intimate knowledge of the district's weaknesses.

Find Sera.

The words echoed in her mind like a prayer, driving her forward with relentless fury. Galina knew she risked everything to rescue her sister, but she didn't care. Sera was her family.

And Galina would do whatever it took to protect her.

She didn't hesitate as she tore through every abandoned shop she found, leaving behind trails of wreckage as she went. She moved like a blur, her black clothes blending into the expanding darkness. Nothing would stop her from getting to her sister.

And then she heard it—a piercing whistle that cut through the chaos like a knife.

Galina stumbled to a halt, relief washing over her in a wave. She clung to the wall for support, her body shaking with exhaustion. Sera emerged from the shadows of a nearby rooftop and dropped onto the street.

Galina collapsed against her sister and finally allowed herself to breathe.

47

VITALY

Vitaly's gaze lingered on Sera as she tightly embraced the other woman.

"*Vítsví*," his wife softly murmured, almost like a prayer.

He stepped back, keeping an eye on the entrance of the dark alley. After escaping from the tunnels with Sera, they climbed onto the rooftops to flee.

Sera had planned to seek refuge in one of Irina's secret apartments, but before they could make it, an explosion jolted the ground beneath them, sending plumes of dust into the air. Vitaly's brow furrowed in confusion as Sera turned to him with a question in her eyes. But he shook his head, denying any involvement.

"It's Galya," Sera had said with a snort, almost amused. Another boom caused the tenements to rattle and groan in protest.

Sera had insisted on climbing down to meet her, and now Vitaly unexpectedly found himself watching a sisterly bonding experience.

It was a privileged peek into a world that Sera had kept

hidden from him all these years—one she had guarded with ferocity and refused to share with him. But who could blame her? He had proven himself untrustworthy countless times, with two attempts to murder her sister standing as testament.

"I can't believe you came," Sera said. "You've got more guts than sense, and that's saying something."

Galina rolled her eyes. "You don't get to lecture me on the bravery–stupidity conundrum. Remember when you came for me in Dolsk?"

"Not the same. We weren't on a secret mission then. Stop trying to change the subject."

"Then quit picking fights," Galina said. "Katya's waiting for us in Irina's safe house beneath the hat shop. You can scold me there."

Sera shot Vitaly a glance. He shook his head, expressing what he couldn't say aloud: how could they be sure this woman wasn't luring them into a trap? He didn't know who this "Katya" was.

Vitaly was a man of few confidantes. But Sera... she was an exception. These other women? He wouldn't know them from a street vendor hawking rotten fruit. Nothing personal, but he wasn't about to let his guard down.

"Katya's my informant inside the palace," Sera told him. "The empress's handmaiden. That's why I asked if she survived the ball."

Oh. Shit. Had he almost killed two of his wife's operatives? That queasy sensation in his gut was something like regret. He hated that feeling.

"Sometime," he said carefully, "you're going to tell me how the empress's handmaiden became your spy, but that doesn't mean I'm eager to rendezvous with her in an unfamiliar flat while we're running for our lives."

Galina's piercing gaze bore into him with all the gentleness of an animal attack. It was like being on the receiving end of Irina's rage when he'd absconded with Sera. Hell, even rebel leaders had standards. They didn't take kindly to infamous criminals fucking their daughters. That was the look that said he was a dirty rat, unworthy of breathing the same air as the woman he called his wife. And he couldn't argue with that, not really. He was a filthy bastard through and through.

But that didn't stop him from taking what he wanted. A thief's moral code was a fluid thing, after all.

"You're lucky I'm saving your life after you tried to kill me," Galina told him. "But I can also leave you here if you'd rather take your chances with the guards."

Sera made an impatient noise. "We don't have time for alternatives, Vitalik. Even sentries aren't so stupid that they won't start to search roofs."

Vitaly felt a gnawing sense of uncertainty, the urge to bundle up his wife and haul her to safety, to rely on their cunning and wits. But one look from Sera shredded those plans, an expression conveying that perhaps the stakes were too high this time.

He relented with a curt nod.

They darted down the narrow alleyway, the shadows swallowing them whole. The day workers had long gone home, and the night crept upon the city like a death shroud. They had to hurry before curfew.

When they reached the end of the alley, Vitaly motioned for the two women to halt. He peered around the tenement wall to survey the adjacent road. A few guards trotted past, but once their footsteps faded, he gestured for Sera and Galina to move on.

"East route goes through the alleyways," Sera whispered as they hastened to the next street. "They'd struggle to squeeze more than a handful of sentries that way, and it'll be easier to bolt if we're spotted."

Vitaly gave her a skeptical look. "More residents mean more eyes in the tenements. We take the Dells, where the hanging laundry can hide us from above."

"And keep us blind."

"I never said it was a perfect solution, Serafima."

Sera let out a derisive snort. "There's a difference between a flawed plan and a pile of steaming shit."

"Then conjure up a less shit one. I'm all fucking ears."

"As entertaining as this is," Galina whispered sharply, cutting through their bickering, "can we just make a damn decision?"

Sera wrinkled her nose and muttered, "Fine. The Dells it is."

Galina shifted forward. "Then I'll check the street. Wait here."

As soon as Galina was out of sight, Sera peeled off her overcoat. Vitaly stared, unable to tear his eyes away from her body, as usual.

"I must admit, watching you undress is always a pleasure," he said.

Sera fixed him with a wicked smile. Then she flipped her coat inside out, revealing a vibrant green design instead of the previous black. This trick had saved them four years ago when they were transporting arms to Akra's capital city. The wardrobe change had bought them crucial seconds when sentries were looking for anyone matching their original description—seconds that could mean the difference between life and death.

"Ah," Vitaly said. "I see you're still using that ruse from Mechetnaya."

"This won't be like Mechetnaya," Sera replied.

The faithless uprising had crumbled there, and the region had fallen into the hands of the alurean army. To make matters worse, their enemies had intercepted their intelligence. But they had survived.

Vitaly knew their past like the scars on his back, tracing the lines of their existence in his mind since he spotted the troubled, beautiful girl on that beach when he was fourteen.

When her eyes first met his, the world shifted beneath his feet, and he knew he was hers.

Always.

Galina reappeared, motioning frantically. "Clear," she said, taking in Sera's coat. "Always one step ahead, aren't you?"

"Hid us for four years, didn't I?" Sera replied with a smirk.

As they navigated the winding streets of the Dells, Vitaly's instincts were on high alert—attuned to every sound, open window, and blind spot in their journey. Even in this wretched corner of the city, he couldn't shake the feeling of being watched—an army of unseen eyes upon him.

He prepared himself for sudden attacks, knowing they were venturing into dangerous territory. The deeper they went into the district, the more his disquiet grew. They should be hearing the shouts of guards, the snapping of orders. They should be hiding out of sight every few steps.

Vitaly finally halted and shook his head, unease crawling up his spine. "I don't like this."

Sera gasped for air, her chest rising and falling with each ragged breath. "No sentries?"

"Not as many as there should be. We've been running for several streets now with no sign of anyone trying to stop us."

Galina's expression darkened. "When Katya and I were still with the empress, the general of the guard was convinced he'd find you. I expected we'd have to fight our way through just to get anywhere near Irina's apartment."

Sera's jaw clenched. "Then we're playing right into their hands." She turned to Galina. "Can you make a door to the hat shop?"

"Irina never took me there," Galina said. "So I can't picture it. I only know it from her maps."

Vitaly's heart raced as his mind conjured up memories of the faithless purge four years ago. The sight of Irina's followers being herded like cattle haunted him, their screams still ringing in his ears. He knew firsthand what the alurean military could do, and it wasn't pretty. If he didn't come up with a solution fast—

CRACK!

Godpower surged through the air, crackling with force as the nearby structures shook and crumbled. Bricks rained down from the sky, shattered stone spraying out like shrapnel. Fissures crawled up the walls of the surrounding shops, expanding at a breakneck pace as if some vengeful deity had decided to level the alley.

And the mavens of the Tumanny military were at the heart of it. The entire street was about to come down on their heads.

Without hesitation, Vitaly shoved Sera. "Run!"

Their footsteps pounded against the pavement as they tore down the narrow lane. Behind them, buildings gave way and collapsed with ear-splitting crashes. The ground shook beneath Vitaly's feet in sharp tremors as walls on either side groaned with strain.

But they couldn't stop; they wouldn't make it out alive if they did.

A second *crack!* filled the air as another building fell, and Vitaly knew they were being herded like cattle. The smoke and dust were so thick he could hardly see, and the stench of burning rubble choked his senses. They had to keep moving, had to find a way out.

A chunk of glass flew toward them, and Vitaly lunged forward just in time. He yanked Sera into his arms, sheltering her from the deadly shard as it smashed into the pavement behind them.

Trapped. Hemmed in. Ambushed. They were cornered, with no egress in sight. Everywhere Vitaly looked, he saw only collapsing walls, soldiers closing ranks. He gritted his teeth, a surge of panic rising in his chest. He'd been in tight spots before, of course. But this felt different. This was final. He could hear them drawing nearer, tightening the noose.

Think, he told himself.

The rooftops were out; the alleys were blocked. Every path was a dead end. Every street was a gauntlet. Vitaly cursed under his breath, trying to push past the fog of pain in his skull.

He wouldn't go down without a fight.

Through the haze of dust and smoke, shouts of soldiers rang out from all directions. They'd been expertly corralled here, like animals herded into a slaughterhouse, and there was no way out.

To these bastards, alurea held more value than a thousand supplicants. They didn't care how many lives they had to sacrifice in the search for their fugitives. They didn't care who they hurt, who they killed, who they trampled underfoot.

But Vitaly knew one thing for sure. He wouldn't let them take Sera. Not while he still had blood in his veins. Not while he still had a breath in his body.

A plan ignited in Vitaly's mind. "Cut through the lower marketplace," Vitaly said between tight breaths. "There's a narrow passage between two buildings that leads out to the street near the hat seller's shop. I'll create a diversion."

Sera wiped her brow, her gaze flitting between him and their pursuers, whose shouts had grown closer with each passing second. A daring glint settled in her eye. "No. Give me an explosive," she said, her tone low but determined. "I'll use my godpower."

Vitaly stalled, his thoughts racing as he racked his brain for an alternative. "I don't think this is—"

"Just give it to me," she commanded, and he reluctantly fished one of his devices from his pocket and placed it in her hand.

They didn't have time for debate, for hesitation—they had to act fast before the guards closed in on them.

Sera yanked back the sleeve of her coat and set her blade to her arm, slicing open the flesh beneath with a single stroke of the knife. Her wound from earlier had healed, leaving only dried trails of scarlet behind on her skin. Fresh crimson spilled down her forearm like ink seeping across paper—another offering to the damn god Irina had summoned. And he couldn't even retaliate against the dragon for hurting Sera without risking her life.

"Get ready," Sera murmured, like a predator preparing for the kill.

Gods above, she was a vision, fierce and untamed, with eyes that blazed with an otherworldly glow. Her god growled the Exalted Tongue through her, the words tumbling out in a guttural snarl—a feral beast roused from its slumber. The atmosphere came alive with an energy that set Vitaly's nerves on edge.

The explosive device hung in the air, suspended by Sera's godpower. With a grunt of effort, Sera hurtled the godpower toward its target, shielding it within a corona of light. Vitaly felt the jagged edges of her zmeya's power rasp against his skin.

Sera's focus wavered for a moment, fatigue bending her shoulders, but then she rallied. With a last heave of her godpower, she unleashed the bomb.

The explosion ripped through the street, smoke and debris raining down upon them.

"Now!" Sera shouted over the din.

The ground shook beneath their feet, and Vitaly's lungs burned as he sprinted away from the crumbling storefronts. Dust billowed around them, filling his nostrils with the tang of crushed stone and destruction. Sera stumbled, but Vitaly caught her before she could collapse.

Galina's voice sliced through the chaos. "Over there!" She pointed to a faded sign ahead.

They barreled into the building, only to be met with silence so thick it smothered the sound from outside. Vitaly strained to listen for signs of danger, but all he heard were faint groans from nearby shattering structures. He hoped the hat shop wouldn't become their tomb.

"This way," Galina said.

Vitaly's arm encircled Sera's waist, steadying her as Galina led them into an aged storeroom. Hats, trunks, bolts of cloth, and dyes littered the teetering old shelves. The sharp scent of chemicals made Vitaly's nose itch—or maybe it was the pulverized stone covering their clothes.

Galina kicked at a chest that had seen better days, uncovering a hidden stairwell leading down to the murky depths beneath Khotchino.

Vitaly took Sera's hand and stepped onto the staircase that spiraled into the shadows. Galina strained to push the trunk back into place before they ventured further underground. The stairs seemed to stretch forever, snaking downward until they finally reached a bleak and dreary apartment. The furniture was sparse and laden with dust, the only proof of life was a newspaper from six long years ago.

But then a shadow stirred in the corner—a woman shot up from her seat as soon as she saw them. Relief flooded her expression when she recognized their faces.

The empress's handmaiden—and Sera's palace spy.

"When I heard the explosions, I thought—" She cut herself off, staring at the trio. "My gods, what happened?"

"Sentries," Galina said. "Sera had to use her godpower near its limit." She gave her sister a worried look. "You need to rest. You're not invincible."

"Can't rest," Sera said. "We can't stay here. They'll tear this city apart to find us."

Vitaly moved quickly, helping her into a chair and pulling a handkerchief from his leather bag to press against the wound on her arm. He glanced at Galina. "Sera mentioned you can create doors. Can you build one from here?"

His sister-in-law nodded. "It'll take more godpower with multiple people, but I can get you both as far as the Shore."

"No." Sera stirred. Her gaze was unfocused as she settled her head against Vitaly's shoulder. "I have to finish the panacea."

"Outside the city, Sera," Vitaly insisted. He wanted to keep her somewhere safe.

"I can't leave yet. I need more ingredients, and the only place to have them imported without getting caught is the Blackshore's port."

"This is your life we're talking about," Galina whispered. "Remember what you told me? No serum is worth dying for."

"There are people in Khotchino who are dead because of me," Sera said sharply. "I owe it to them to stay."

Galina sighed, running her hands through her hair in frustration. "Fine. Then we'll wait until nightfall and find another one of Irina's safe houses deeper in the city."

Vitaly's gaze dropped to Sera, and his throat constricted. She was pale from the overuse of her power, and he knew she was teetering on the brink of collapse.

"*Vorovka,*" he whispered, "take a rest. I'll carry you."

Sera shook her head, her jaw hardening with stubborn determination. "No. You need your hands free to fight off sentries. I'll manage."

"You can barely stand."

Her lips flattened. "Then I'll crawl."

Galina's gaze met his—an alliance forged by desperation and shared purpose: *protect Sera. Get her through alive.*

His sister-in-law hesitated before speaking. "I know of a place where we might find the ingredients Sera needs, and the guards won't think to look for you there. But it won't be easy, and you won't like it."

Vitaly didn't give a damn where it was, as long as Sera could rest. "Where?"

She exhaled slowly. "The Glasshouse Wing in Zolotiye. It's where Princess Vasilisa has me staying."

Fine, so maybe he gave a damn where it was. "Absolutely not." When Sera remained silent, Vitaly said, "I'm not entertaining this ludicrous suggestion."

Katya cleared her throat, the sound echoing in the tense silence. Her gentle voice added, "I understand the risk of keeping you so close to our enemies, but Galina's right. It's the one place in the Blackshore they won't demolish in their search."

"And it has a glasshouse filled with medicinal plants and twenty-two unoccupied chambers that the staff never enter," Galina chimed in. "At the very least, Sera can sleep there before we move her."

Vitaly's mind went into a revolt at the mere thought of being in proximity with the empress and her band of sniveling alurean courtiers. And to top it off, having Sera next to those violent assholes while she was still weakened.

"And Princess Vasilisa?" he asked. He couldn't believe he was even asking. "I think she might have a problem with a couple of faithless fugitives sheltering in her home."

Galina's gaze dropped. "She won't be a problem."

Vitaly let out a scoff. "Trust a royal alurea? You might as well trust a knife-wielding lunatic with your throat. I wouldn't depend on them with my own life, let alone my wife's."

Galina's glare was sharp as she spoke through gritted teeth, "Considering you tried to kill me twice, *your* life is hardly a priority for me." Her attention shifted to Sera. "Do you trust my judgment?"

Sera was silent for a moment before slowly nodding. "Yes, I do."

"No, I don't," Vitaly cut in sharply.

Sera gripped his arm. "We don't have an abundance of options, Vitalik. I won't run from the Blackshore again. Are we going to be apart for another four years? Will you spend every night wondering where I am and whether I'm alive or dead?"

Vitaly hesitated as he stared at her wound and the blood-soaked bandage clumsily wrapped around it. His rationality with Sera was flawed, but he couldn't permit his protective instincts to blind him to what she needed to do. She was his wife, his partner.

He closed his eyes briefly, gathering his resolve. "Fine. We'll go to the palace."

48

VASILISA

Vasilisa's head lifted as a faint disturbance drifted down the corridor.

Her senses sharpened with the thrill of anticipation. She had given Galina her space for days, but the mere thought of the other woman sent a shiver of longing across Vasilisa's skin. It was like standing on the edge of a precipice, balanced on the cusp of madness.

And those scars on Galina's thigh? Vasilisa had to know their story, how someone bonded to a zmeya could have those marks. Then she wanted to trace every ridge and indentation with her fingertips until she knew Galina's skin more intimately than her own.

Gods, she was infatuated.

As voices filtered from Galina's chamber, Vasilisa leaned on her cane and approached the door. Just as she was about to knock, a young woman stepped out of the room—the empress's handmaiden. Vasilisa quickly hid her cane behind her back and out of sight from the servant.

Vasilisa's voice was soft as she spoke. "Hello."

Ekaterina froze like a cornered animal, her panic

morphing into a deep curtsy in seconds. "My apologies for not seeing you, Your Imperial Highness. Please, let me beg your forgiveness."

A spark of pity lit in Vasilisa's chest as she remembered Isidora's cruelty to her handmaidens. "Ekaterina Isidorakh, isn't it? No need to worry." She smiled reassuringly. "Is Galina Feodorovna still in her room?"

"Yes, Your Imperial Highness. Would you like me to get her?"

Ekaterina remained in her position of prostration. Isidora was infamous for teaching her handmaidens to stay like that for hours; Vasilisa heard she'd once murdered a servant who failed the task.

"Please stand," Vasilisa said gently. "Return to my mother. I know how angry she gets when servants keep her waiting."

A flicker of emotion crossed the handmaiden's face. "Thank you, Your Imperial Highness."

Her bells trilled as she hurried down the looming corridors, eventually fading into the shadows.

Vasilisa exhaled a long breath as she leaned her weight on her cane, feeling the ache in her bones. By the gods, that was too close for comfort. The servants were strictly forbidden from entering her private chambers for a reason. She never left her rooms without a mobility aid—and while a cane could be easily concealed, a wheelchair couldn't.

Thankfully, Vasilisa's pain levels had been manageable that day, enough for a trip to the garden. But her guilty conscience refused to give her peace. She'd made Galina uncomfortable, and needed to do whatever it took to make amends.

So Vasilisa raised her hand, steeling herself before rapping on Galina's door.

The sound of rustling came from within, and then the door opened and revealed a stern-faced Galina. She stepped out of the room and sealed the chamber behind her with a firm click. "Your Imperial Highness," she said, her voice strangely reserved.

Galina's greeting cut through Vasilisa with brutal precision, tearing away her protective layers. How could they go back to titles when their hearts had thrummed in unison just days ago? The burn of their kiss had haunted her dreams for nights—and now Galina's tone was telling her that it could never be repeated.

Yet Vasilisa's memory insisted on replaying their intimacy, each time a little more vibrant, a little more intimate.

She cleared her throat and spoke softly, trying to bridge the rift between them. "Back to that, are we? Not Vasilisa Yuryevna, but Your Imperial Highness. The other night, I enjoyed being Vasya."

Something almost painful flickered in Galina's features—a thing too fragile to grasp—before she bowed her head and adjusted the folds of her dress. As if the very action could build an invisible wall between them. "Vasilisa Yuryevna—"

"Better, but still sending a clear message that I messed up. I'm sorry for upsetting you."

"Don't," Galina murmured. "There's nothing to apologize for."

But Vasilisa refused to let it go. Even though she was far from the royal wings and the twisted games of power, her title cast its long shadow over every conversation she had—an irrefutable power imbalance. Two nights ago, she'd forgotten herself.

"Yes, there is," Vasilisa insisted. "I pushed too hard, and my behavior was completely inappropriate." Her voice thickened with self-loathing. "As if anyone could tell the daughter of the empress no. As if any courtier could."

Galina's hand cupped her cheek, as tender as a secret shared in the dark. It sent sparks through Vasilisa's veins, igniting an understanding born of solitary moments and whispered secrets in the Glasshouse Wing.

"I would have declined if I didn't like it," Galina said softly. "You taught me how, remember?"

The memory stirred a longing in Vasilisa that was as familiar as it was dangerous. Then there were the scars. Markings that spoke of brutal violence, of unspeakable agony. Not something a woman bound to a god should bear.

Mysteries she still wanted to unravel.

"But you left," Vasilisa said, barely whispering the words. "You ran. And now you're back here, 'Your Imperial Highness'-ing me again."

Galina's hand slipped from Vasilisa's cheek, leaving a lingering warmth behind. "I liked what we did that night too much."

An ache pulsed in Vasilisa's chest. "Would you like to see something else?" she asked.

"Yes," came the soft reply.

Vasilisa felt a weight lift from her shoulders as she led Galina to the glasshouse.

The door creaked open at Vasilisa's gentle push. "Eyes up," she murmured in Galina's ear, a lover's promise.

Galina obeyed, and a gasp escaped her lips. The domed ceiling was a dazzling tapestry of a thousand shimmering gems, arranged into star patterns Vasilisa had witnessed during her travels, a sky stolen from distant lands—a million points of light.

Vasilisa had spent the entire day directing her zmeya with precision to ensure the stars shone in the right arrangement. It was a gesture of contrition, a tribute to the woman who had kindled feelings within Vasilisa that she never knew existed.

Emotions burned across Galina's beautiful features: yearning... and something too painful to name. Vasilisa went still at the sight.

"You look sad," she said. "I've misread the situation again."

Galina shook her head, focused on the gemstones overhead. "No. I can see my home in these constellations."

"Rontsy?" she asked, puzzled. "Some of these aren't visible this far south."

Galina's expression iced over, like a frozen lake beneath a winter sky. Vasilisa comprehended how little she understood about the other woman's past—all the mysteries, all the secrets hidden in shadow. A mosaic of memories, only ever half-pieced together.

"Tell me," she said, taking Galina's hand and drawing her deeper into the verdant darkness of the glasshouse. "Tell me what this reminds you of. Because that's the second time I've heard hurt in your voice when you talk about your home."

Amidst the vibrant shrubbery and foliage, it was easy to forget they were inside the oppressive walls of the Zolotiye. They could have been transported far from the frostbite of Tumanny to a place where they could be whoever they damn well pleased.

Just Galusha and Vasya.

Two hearts intertwined by a thousand unknowable paths.

"During the winter festival," Galina began, reverently, "we had bonfires each night to ward away the cold and endless darkness. We wore evergreen wreaths—whatever we could find in the snow." A wistful smile grazed her lips as she gazed back up at the glass canopy. "The skies were so clear it seemed like the stars were made from diamond dust. I used to gaze at them for hours. The stars aren't as bright here in the Blackshore."

"Not Rontsy, then," Vasilisa breathed.

"The north," Galina replied, as if that single word contained every secret she'd kept locked inside her fragile heart.

Vasilisa's thoughts churned like a storm-tossed sea, each question threatening to pull her under. "I thought you grew up in Rontsy."

"You're clever enough to understand that the story I gave the empress isn't true. I left the north when I was eight."

Vasilisa held her ground like a galleon in a tempest. She spoke carefully, as if each word was an anchor keeping her afloat. "Do you miss it?"

"Yes," she replied flatly. "The Blackshore is harsher than my village. People there had never seen an alurea until Sgor invaded."

The memory was a jagged knife in Vasilisa's heart, a sharp reminder of the monstrous deeds her mother had committed to safeguarding Tumanny's borders. Vasilisa had been nine years old when her mother razed entire villages, slaughtering thousands of innocent citizens to deprive Sgor's troops of resources. To sit on the Tumanny throne was to rest on the bones of the dead.

"So you weren't lying when you said you knew little about alurean history."

A lock of hair fell across Galina's cheek. "And you weren't lying about the dusty tomes."

Vasilisa couldn't resist brushing the strand away. "Told you they were boring," she said teasingly. "There are reasons my mother relegated those old books to a forgotten corner of the palace."

She felt the spark at her fingertips, a path of flame along Galina's skin that threatened to burn right through her. The air between them crackled with a tension that begged to be broken. She wanted to touch more, to feel Galina pressed against her, to watch as she surrendered to ecstasy.

"I spoke to the empress yesterday," Galina said, her voice a breathless whisper.

"Oh? And what did she want with her glorified prisoner?"

"She was curious about how our gods would react to one another. She wondered if our zmei were..."

"A mated pair?" Vasilisa growled, a fierce surge of possessiveness clawing at her insides like a starving beast.

Mine, she thought fiercely.

Mine, her god seemed to echo.

Galina nodded slowly. "She explained that bonded pairs are rare. But so is the godfire. It only makes sense that our zmei might be companions."

Vasilisa's body tensed, consumed by a primal urge to declare Galina as her own. The desire to leave her mark on Galina's skin, to hear her scream in pleasure. "And how did it go?"

Galina arched an eyebrow. "Vasya, are you jealous?"

She was jealous enough to ignore the pain radiating through her bones, march into her mother's chambers, defying custom and consequences to assert her claim. She was ill, but her dragon was a beast to rival the empress's.

"Depends on how it went," she replied tightly.

Galina leaned in, her breath warm against Vasilisa's skin as she nuzzled her cheek. "Our gods hated each other."

Vasilisa's zmeya coiled inside her, purring with dark satisfaction. And Vasilisa? She was no better. Practically preening at the realization that this woman was still hers.

"Oh, that's too bad," she said, her tone too cheerful. "Terrible news. For my mother, I mean. Great news for me."

Galina's laughter quickly faded as a more serious thought crossed her mind. "Would you have to marry someone else?" she asked quietly. "Even if we were bonded?"

Vasilisa pressed her teeth together. "Not a concern. My mother won't allow me to pass on my illness."

Galina scowled. "I thought your illness was from the zmei being caged too many times?"

"It is. But the alurea would never acknowledge weaknesses in their bloodline. So there's no chance of me inheriting." Her eyes gleamed with a hard, fierce light. "Maybe my mother thinks you should be her heir instead. I wouldn't put it past her to kill me off."

Galina's gaze was as intense as the heart of a wildfire, and at that moment, Vasilisa feared her words had been too sharp, too full of barbed wounds from a life spent alone.

Then Galina moved closer, her soft lips claiming Vasilisa's in a desperate collision of heat, like the first touch of sunlight on a frostbitten morning. She gasped, nails digging into the fabric of Galina's dress as their kiss deepened.

They stumbled back until Vasilisa rested against her worktable, every inch of Galina pressed against her, breath fanning across her cheek like a secret whispered in the dark. Galina shivered, boldly exploring the dip of Vasilisa's waist before she took Vasilisa's hand and slid it beneath her skirts.

Galina's body was an undiscovered terrain that Vasilisa yearned to explore. She touched each crescendo and valley, mapping the topography under her fingertips until she felt as if she knew every feature by heart.

Galina pulled away, her forehead resting against Vasilisa's. "I won't let anyone take you from me. Not the empress and not the faithless. Do you understand? No matter what happens, I'm yours."

49

SERA

Sera rested against the pillows in Galina's luxurious bed, her zmeya purring with sheer delight. Whether it was from feasting on her blood, basking in the warm glow of its godpower, or her near-death experience, she couldn't say. The little bastard enjoyed toying with her—pushing her to the brink of demise and then slinking back to the shadows to watch her squirm.

But in the fleeting moments of repose that followed, when their bond was at its strongest, Sera found solace in the synchronous rhythm of their heartbeats and the pattern of their breaths. It was the only time the dragon stopped fighting her.

With her god satisfied, Sera scanned Galina's chamber. The opulent palace room was a testament to extravagance, exuding a stillness that came with being away from the clamor of carriages, factories, and shops within the city sprawled at the bottom of the hill.

The walls were lined with gold mirrors that reflected shimmering light around the room, and fabric draped luxuriously over furniture so polished it glimmered. Every piece was intricately carved, trimmed with intricate floral motifs, and fashioned from woods so rare they probably cost more than Sera's soul. This level of opulence came at a price only the alurea could afford, paid in blood and sweat and tears, wrung from the backs of their citizens.

Vitaly ran a finger across gilded furniture and studied the objets d'art lining the walls with such intensity that she couldn't help but find it amusing. His gray eyes darted across every corner of the room as he paced—she knew from experience that the man could build mental maps of a location that put even the most experienced thieves to shame.

"You on the prowl for something to steal?" Sera asked.

Vitaly shot her a wicked grin. "Would you judge me if I were?"

"I'm your wife. Judging is in the marriage contract."

He let out his beautiful laugh, resonant. "If I didn't always have one eye trained on potential acquisitions, would I even be the man you married?"

"I'll give you credit for that antique globe in your apartment, just based on the sheer size and skill it must have taken to liberate it from its owner. You didn't drop it out a window, did you?"

Vitaly winked at her. "*Vorovka pro fse ku*, some things are better left secrets, even between husband and wife."

Their banter served as a welcome respite, though Sera could feel exhaustion creeping up on her. She clung to consciousness with an iron grip.

"So what are you stealing?" she asked him, shaking the blurriness from her vision.

"The tiniest gold piece is all I'm taking," Vitaly said. "The rest of it is the ugliest cesspit of decadence I've ever seen. Are all the rooms as nauseating as this one? As if they needed more proof they had money to squander?"

"Money can't buy taste," she said with a sly grin.

"Well, it sure as shit can buy *someone* who's got it."

Sera lounged against the pillows. "When did you become an expert on home decor?"

"I'm a man of versatile skills, with a particular talent for collecting and dealing in luxury goods," he said.

He halted before a garish figurine bedecked with precious stones, scowling at it as if it had personally insulted him. Sera didn't have to guess what was going through his mind: the thing was utterly useless, a frivolous trinket only good for showing off one's wealth.

"You could throw it at an intruder," Sera suggested, breaking the silence. "Crack their skull open. Knock their teeth out."

Her husband's lip lifted in disgust. "A blade is more practical."

"What even is it?" Sera squinted, eyeing the bulbous shapes on the monstrosity. "I can't make out the details from here."

"It's a revolting, chubby infant made by someone who's probably never seen a real baby before in their life."

"I see rubies. Fence it."

"No one with a shred of sanity would pay for it, even with the rubies."

"Well, if it's not worth selling, it's a weapon. Imagine being attacked by a knife-wielding bandit, and all you've got is that ugly thing. What do you do?"

Vitaly approached her, ticking off items on his fingers. "There are still candlesticks, books, the clock on the mantel, a chair in a pinch, and—" Vitaly fell into the bed beside Sera, sending a jolt of arousal through her as his hand brushed down her thigh. "And my wife never travels without her knives." He yanked the dagger out from her concealed ankle sheath and brandished it with a flourish. "Problem solved."

Sera's heart pounded with a savage yearning. So much time apart, so many places since—Krestov Brod, Starapolė, Dolsk—and his smile still held her in its thrall. Years ago, he could walk into their Antrea apartment with that smile, and she'd go weak in the knees instantly.

Vitaly's expression flared with desire. "You're not thinking about weapons anymore, are you?"

Sera took the blade from him and placed it on the nightstand. "I enjoy playing with new toys. Who's to say I'm not?"

"Liar." Vitaly's fingers slid along the curve of her hip, leaving a trail of heat in their wake. Then he brushed his lips against her throat and whispered, "If you want me to fuck you, all you have to do is ask."

Fire blazed across her skin. Vitaly had always been direct, especially in bed. He knew how to use that honesty to devastating effect.

"We're in the enemy's palace," she pointed out. "You never had appropriate timing."

"And I never will," he said with a devilish grin. "Who cares about timing? We're fugitives. We seek our pleasure wherever we find it." He swept a lock of hair away from her face. "Ardatovo, remember? I'll take you any time or place you demand."

Sera's fingernails dug into the blankets. Ten years before, they'd supplied weapons to an uprising in the capital city of Samatsk, only to be stranded in Ardatovo when the alurea attacked the faithless. Vitaly and Sera had found shelter in a dilapidated barn at the city's edge.

Then, with the fierce urgency of two people who feared it might be their last day alive, they had torn at each other's clothes. Vitaly had taken her hard and fast against the rough wood of the barn door. She'd pressed her teeth to his skin and marked him as hers—something to remember her by in case she didn't survive.

But they had.

They married after Ardatovo.

"I remember," she told him softly.

Vitaly's thumb slid over her cheek. "You fed me a lie back in the tunnels," he said. "When I asked if you ever dreamed of me."

Sera's lips trembled as she spoke. "Yes."

"Tell me," Vitaly said with a fervent intensity. "What did you dream about?"

Sera sighed, settling her arms around his shoulders. "I kept a little cottage in Dolsk, away from the village. Every time I thought of you in it, you never seemed to fit—it was too quiet, too small, too tranquil. I had this image of you standing in our apartment in Antrea, looking out over the Blackshore like it was your kingdom. I'd picture you there and wonder if I'd ever see you like that again. But I said so many lies within those walls. Sometimes, I wondered if it was better for both of us if I stayed gone."

Vitaly was silent for a beat before asking, "If we survive this, will you stay or leave the Blackshore?"

She heard his unspoken words.

Without me.

"I don't know. What would you do if I left?"

He let out a soft breath. "I'd crawl across the fucking world for you," he said, voice low. "Scour every inch of Sundyr, bleed my feet raw chasing your shadow, if that's what it took. I won't stop you from leaving me, Sera. It's not in my nature. But if I found you in another lifetime, I'd hold you in my arms until the gods themselves tried to tear us apart."

Sera's chest squeezed. "Don't spend your life chasing my shadow, Vitalik."

He raised his head and met Sera's gaze. His molten silver irises burned into hers. "I'd rather spend an eternity hoping we cross paths again than resign myself to a single moment without you. I'll always belong to you, until my last breath. In this life and the next."

What they shared transcended language. When they were together, Sera's mind emptied, and every part of her was filled with pieces of him—comfort and belonging, an old story that was engraved in her heart, a past that spanned more than half her life.

They knew each other in ways that no one else could.

Sera inhaled a breath so sharp it could split stone. She dragged Vitaly toward her, her lips seeking his with an urgency that bordered on savage. He tasted of salvation after years in the dark, the kind of craving that could carve its way through bone. But as they kissed, something twisted at the edges of their need, sharpening into a desperate, clawing hunger. She'd almost forgotten what desire felt like—the insatiable longing after years of deprivation.

She ached. She needed.

When Vitaly touched her, Sera was alive. She burned. Every nerve ending ignited beneath his hands as he traced her curves through the fabric of her shirt, exploring the map of sensation beneath his palm—the dip of her hip, the long slope of her stomach. Every secret inch of her was his to rediscover.

Sera tore at the buttons of her trousers, guiding his hand between her thighs. Right to where she wanted it. Vitaly understood her desire. He always did. He had learned the skill of pleasuring her by asking what she liked, how she satisfied herself.

His fingers slid inside her with practiced ease, and Sera arched into it, biting back a sharp cry as the surge of pleasure stole the oxygen from her lungs.

He spoke into her ear, hunger seeping through each syllable. "Did you think of me while you were gone? Did you pleasure yourself and imagine I was the one touching you?"

The heat rose in her cheeks. "Yes."

His mouth was inches from hers as his fingers plunged in and out. "How many times?" he demanded. "How often did you imagine me fucking you?"

"Every night," she gasped.

Vitaly's lips crashed against Sera's, consuming her in a kiss that was equal parts passion and urgency. It matched her—a need that was so fierce it was almost violent. Never enough.

She clawed at his shirt as release tore through her—a long, shuddering ache that left her trembling. His kisses swallowed every sound until all that remained was his name on her lips—a whisper that sounded more like a plea.

They were resting when Galina returned to the room. Sera lifted her head. "Is everything all right?"

Galina hesitated, her features obscured by the shadows. "I think so. I looked through the glasshouse; it should have most of the ingredients. We'll go in after Vasya goes to sleep tomorrow, so you have more rest."

Vitaly shifted behind Sera. "*Vasya*, is it?"

Galina's jaw clenched, her eyes narrowing into a glare. "Just tell me what you need, Sera."

Sera got out of bed. She rummaged through her satchel, muttering, "An actual lab would be perfect. Synthesizing is—"

"Worry about it later," Galina said, pacing. "We'll have to hurry with the supplies. You can't stay here long."

Sera nodded and resumed her task of separating the small vials. "Before Katya left, I gave her a message for Anna," she said as she placed one of Irina's notebooks on the floor. "She can arrange transport and a safe house once we leave the palace."

"How is Katya supposed to get a note to Anna? I heard some maniac"—Galina eyed Vitaly—"set her shop on fire."

"I didn't set her shop on fire," Vitaly replied. "I just happen to know the maniac who did. We're not on speaking terms, if it helps."

Galina looked unimpressed, so she turned to Sera. "What's the plan?"

"Anna and I have an emergency system in place," Sera said. "Katya will send an obituary to the *Tumanny Courier* with a coded message, and Anna will do the same when she's ready. I'll give you the code names to keep an eye out for." She pulled out a bunch of items from her satchel—papers, notes, and her mother's journal entries. "Some of the plants I need are rare, so you better hope the glasshouse has them."

"It'll have them," Galina said. "And in the meantime, we'll find you another room. I'll get you when it's time."

50

KATYA

Katya trudged through the ashen ruins of Blackshore, her gray cloak billowing out behind her.

She gazed at the destruction wrought on the city, her heart heavy as the empress surveyed the carnage with the detached gaze of a butcher admiring her handiwork. The once glorious metropolis lay in shambles, its roads pockmarked and shattered by the sentries' relentless pursuit of Sera and Vitaly. Angry shouts and despairing wails of Blackshore citizens rippled through the air like a dirge, a symphony of suffering and loss.

"We'll rebuild it all, Katenka," the empress said, her voice as cold as the winter winds that whipped through the ruins. "Seeing the waste outside the palace gates doesn't please me."

Katya gritted her teeth, her fury simmering just beneath the surface. How could the empress stand there, so callous and unfeeling, when her orders led to this destruction?

She bowed her head in feigned submission and forced out two words. "Yes, *suvya*."

The empress's troops worked tirelessly in the aftermath of the chaos, rounding up anyone who challenged the monarch.

Those who burned the empress's effigy in the streets or protested outside Zolotiye were dealt with harshly, their screams muffled by the sounds of crumbling buildings and the rumble of soldiers' boots.

By all reports, the city's prisons overflowed with those waiting for punishment.

The few tenements still standing had become makeshift shelters for the desperate left homeless by the empress's siege, but no one was safe even there. The alurea had ferreted out more than a few faithless factions in their search, and those caught were shown no mercy. The only law that mattered was the empress's will.

And with each discovery, her cruelty grew more pronounced.

Katya stared at the gruesome sight of desolation, a tattered graveyard belching smoke and death in its wake. Everywhere she looked was charred ruin, broken glass, and crumbled stonework. Bloodied corpses were strewn along the wreckage. The streets were unrecognizable from the tidy boulevards that Katya had once known, reduced to a wasteland of twisted metal and scorched earth. Only the blackened remains of signs offered any indication of what had once thrived here.

And somewhere, buried beneath the rubble, lay the hat shop with Irina's hidden apartment. If Galina hadn't suggested the Glasshouse Wing as a refuge, Sera and Vitaly would have been captured or killed by now.

Empress Isidora looked sideways at Katya, too perceptive. "My weather mavens will clear this in short order, *knesi*. I hate to see you so unhappy. You've been quiet for days."

Katya's attention drifted to the smoldering remains of a dressmaker's shop. The empress picked her way daintily over the half-burned bolts of fabric strewn across the street, oblivious to the limp hand of a corpse protruding from the rubble.

Katya kept her emotions tightly leashed. "You honor me, *suvya*."

The words tasted like ash in her mouth, scraped raw by years of rote repetition. The script had been pounded into her head since childhood, and despite her attempts to choke it back, she felt herself slipping with each passing day.

The time would come when her skill in deceit would desert her.

Possibly, it already had; Isidora saw through Katya's carefully crafted facade. "You're upset with me," she said.

I hate you so much that every minute at your side kills a small part of me.

Katya sealed off these thoughts behind a mask of civility that she had worn for years. "You were right before, *suvya*. It upsets me to see the city like this."

The empress halted, signaling to her swarm of attendants to stay put. Katya's nerves frayed as Isidora lifted a palm and settled it gently on her cheek. She fought against the revulsion at the touch. The ruler's skin burned hot against Katya's face, her godfire simmering beneath the surface.

"Dear girl," she murmured, as if Katya were a child. "Tell me what I can do to make you smile. Ask me to clear up this mess, and I'll have it done. What else? A new frock? A bauble? Anything."

There was blood splattered on the stonework nearby, corpses half covered in the wreckage—gruesome sights that the empress disregarded as if they were nothing. She'd heap bodies throughout the Blackshore without batting an eye and try to rectify things with her handmaiden by tossing her trinkets and trappings.

"I want nothing, *suvya*," Katya said. "I'm sorry for being unfocused."

"You're fragile, *knesi*. You've seen so little of war and death." Isidora withdrew her touch and put on a smile. "Later, you'll sing for me, and we'll forget what we've witnessed here. Agreed?"

It was remarkable how easily the empress discarded any remembrance of the horrors she put Katya through. Like so many other servants, she'd once been tasked with the gruesome duty of cleaning up Isidora's murdered handmaidens. She'd been at executions where people were burned alive, and godpower was used to snap bones like twigs. But when it came time for the empress to recall these events, she hardly seemed to retain any grisly details.

Katya swallowed hard, steeling herself. "Of course. It would be my honor to sing for you."

As they resumed their procession up the road, the empress swept past the rigid formation of soldiers and guards. Their threads and buttons denoted their ranks, each adornment glinting in the noon-day sun.

The monarch's thunderous expression made clear what she thought of their incompetence. After days of futile searching, her royal retinue had failed to find Sera and Vitaly. Those who had seemed promising from the artist's rendition in the *Tumanny Courier* had all proved false leads.

General Vasilchikov clicked his heels and bowed at his monarch's approach, his stoic exterior betraying no hint of emotion or fear despite her growing rage—a rage that could turn into an inferno at any moment.

Empress Isidora's hands clasped tightly behind her back, her small stature belying the immense power that emanated from her. Her body was wreathed in an aura of heat, a reminder of the destructive force beneath the surface. She regarded her general with a stony expression of displeasure.

"General Vasilchikov," she said with a dangerous edge. "You have two hundred soldiers at your disposal, and my fugitives still slipped through your grasp. Are these traitors cleverer than you, or are you just that incompetent?" She took a step closer, her anger simmering. "And if that's the case, what good are you in your position?"

General Vasilchikov stood rigidly, the twitch in his jaw betraying his agitation. To be dismissed from his post in such a humiliating manner would bring him nothing but shame and ostracism. He would be cast out from the circles he once ran in; his children would be denied entry to the courts.

"Your Imperial Majesty—"

The empress cut him off with a swipe of her hand. "I'm not finished." She lifted her chin, scanning the line of military officials stretched along the road, flanked by ruined shops. "Yesterday, you assured me that the terrorists were confined to Khotchino. And here we are, with the market in ruins and our fugitives still at large." She spread her arms wide. "So, General Vasilchikov, I must ask you again: why have you failed me? Speak."

The general's knuckles went white around the hilt of his sword. "We believe they had help, Your Imperial Majesty."

Isidora scowled, disgust etched upon her features. "Help? Oh, how gracious of you to point that out, General. Your zmei may not be impressive in my court, but against a mere supplicant, there's no comparison."

The general stood a little taller. "Someone may have assisted their escape, Your Imperial Majesty."

The empress latched onto his chin, her nails digging into his flesh. He winced. "I don't care if a hundred someones helped them. I withdrew the best mavens from my military, when they should have been fighting Sopol. Your ineptitude is putting my empire at risk, General."

Katya's heart slammed. She didn't need to see the future to know things were about to go south. The tiny bells of her ankle jingled in tension as she shifted her posture, drawing the notice of a nearby sentry.

Katya knew that look too well; it said he recognized her from somewhere else. And not for her role as a handmaiden.

She froze, fear gripping her chest.

The empress noticed the soldier's intense focus. "Your officer seems to have a sudden interest in my handmaiden, General. I'm not sure I like it."

"Explain yourself, Ilya Ivanovich," General Vasilchikov said sharply.

The soldier swallowed thickly. "Forgive me, Your Imperial Majesty. But I've seen her before."

Katya took another step backward as terror whispered in the back of her mind.

Six years.

Six years.

Her days had expired weeks ago. Yet, here she was, on borrowed time, waiting for the end to come crashing down on her shoulders. The bells chimed as she moved—a cruel mockery of her impending doom.

"Stay put, Katenka," the empress barked, fingers like talons around Katya's arm. Her touch seared through Katya's coat as she squared off against the soldier once more. "You've seen her with me at *obryad*, haven't you? Or in my carriage."

"No, Your Imperial Majesty," he said, respectful but firm. "When the two fugitives fled from us, I saw her running through Khotchino, near the embankment."

The empress's hand dug into Katya's flesh, leaving behind a searing trail of pain. "Ekaterina Isidorakh, my dear," she said. "I don't recall ever giving you permission to leave the palace grounds."

Struggling to think quickly under such intense scrutiny, Katya tried to recover the situation. "He must be mistaking me for someone else. The smoke in the streets—"

"I always remember a face," the soldier said firmly. "And yours is too pretty to forget."

Suspicion crept over Isidora's features, twisting them into a severe mask. Katya felt like an animal in a cage; cold steel bars held her captive as Isidora loomed over her, a feral beast ready to devour its prey.

"Was she alone? Or did she have another woman with her?" Isidora asked the sentry, her eyes drilling into Katya's.

Galina. She wanted to know if Katya had betrayed her with Galina.

"No, Your Imperial Majesty. She was by herself, disguised as a commoner."

Isidora's grip branded Katya's skin. She let out a pained gasp, but Isidora held fast. She was a storm, a natural disaster made flesh and given purpose. Katya's instincts buckled beneath the weight of her stare. She'd been the empress's puppet for too long, the strings of servitude carving grooves into her soul. Bone-weary, practicality giving way to a desperate urge to flee.

"I was helping the maids in the east wing," Katya said, trying to keep steady.

Isidora's eyes were unyielding daggers that pierced through Katya's facade. To the empress, Katya was a tool to be used and discarded, a handmaiden marked for death—just like all the ones before her. The ghost of each woman haunted her every moment.

A prophecy of what was to come.

"Where are they, Ekaterina Isidorakh?" The empress snarled, her voice a lethal whip crack.

Isidora spat Katya's name as if it were a curse—Ekaterina Isidorakh. Not *knesí*. Not Katenka. The empress had passed her verdict, and Katya's fate was sealed.

There was something different about the way Isidora looked at her now—a look of fury and betrayal, one that could strip flesh from bone.

Still, Katya tried to plead with her. "*Suvya*—"

"I'm your empress, and you'll address me as such." She pushed Katya toward General Vasilchikov. "Take her, General. Lock her up in the palace hold. Extract the location of the faithless out of her. Use whatever methods you must."

The general's grip was like iron as he dragged her away. The bells on her limbs jingled their cheerful tune.

51

GALINA

Galina's nerves were frayed as she led Sera and Vitaly to Vasilisa's glasshouse.

She pushed open the door, greeted by the shining jewels above—still arranged in the constellations Vasilisa crafted. The air was thick with the fragrance of exotic blooms and heady perfumes, but Galina had no time to admire the scent.

All that mattered was getting Sera what she needed to finish this—and then maybe, just maybe, Galina could square her debt with Vasilisa.

But as she thought of the princess, the guilt was a noose around her neck that squeezed. She wondered if she even deserved the princess's kindness.

Violating Vasilisa's safe place was like a desecration.

Vitaly let out a low whistle, his voice an unwanted intrusion in the fragile space. "Imagine having the luxury of caring for this many flowers while the city burns."

Galina's eyes narrowed at her brother-in-law. She was fiercely protective of Vasilisa and the bit of peace the princess had managed to carve out in this hellscape of a royal court.

She couldn't explain to Vitaly that the glasshouse was more than just a courtier's whim; it was the only thing keeping Vasilisa from becoming another nameless corpse in the alurean records.

"Only touch what Sera needs for the panacea," Galina said. "If you so much as breathe wrong near one of the princess's plants, I'll rearrange your organs so that they spell 'idiot' in Zverti. No second chances."

Frankly, Vitaly deserved it for trying to kill her. Galina had no qualms about that.

Vitaly's face darkened with anger. "If you're starting to sympathize with the alurea, just come out and say it. I won't spend a night under the same roof as a loyalist."

Galina could feel the tension building, coiling like a snake ready to strike. She was prepared to defend herself if it came to it.

But then Sera spoke up, her voice a balm to their raw nerves. "Enough, Vitalik," she said. "Don't talk to my sister like that, or I might have to bite you."

Vitaly's lips curved into a slow, sly smile. "Is that a promise? Because you know me, *vorovka*. I'd insult someone endlessly for that kind of attention."

Sera chuckled, then studied the scattered vessels and bowls with the discerning eye of an operative. A maelstrom of emotions battered at Galina's control. She loved Sera, but her sister was raised to hate and overthrow the alurea. If Sera found out Vasilisa was vulnerable, what would she do?

Galina's nerves spiked as Vitaly approached the worktable. She held her breath as he inspected the blooms sprawled across the surface—Vasilisa's treatment for pain—hoping he wouldn't know what it was. But Sera was another matter. She'd been a village healer in Dolsk and trained under Irina. Her knowledge of plants was extensive.

Vitaly leaned in, regarding the flowers intently. "What is this?"

Exhaling slowly, Galina focused on her sister's face for any sign of recognition.

Sure enough, it came. Sera's eyes flared wide, and Galina felt a pit open up in her stomach. She had told her sister about the names crossed out in the alurean records, the children who had died under mysterious circumstances—victims of an illness the royals didn't want their enemies to discover.

Sera's gaze locked onto Galina's.

Don't tell him. Please, don't tell him.

This was Vasilisa's secret—the only place in the world where she was safe. And Galina had risked it all.

"Nothing." Sera's lips pressed together like she was holding back a flood of emotions. "Adds a bit of sweetness to tea, I hear."

Vitaly rolled his eyes, clearly uninterested in the whims of a royal princess. "Tell me what I'm looking for, *vorovka*."

Sera retrieved a crumpled scrap of paper from her pocket and unfurled it with a flourish. "I've made a list. Yours are the ones even a child could spot."

He snatched it from her hand and peered at it, his expression souring. "Only if they could decipher your atrocious handwriting."

"That's why I drew the pictures like you were five. Start at the back; Galina and I will meet you halfway." Sera waited until he vanished down the long path to speak. "All that equipment is used for making plant-based remedies," she said to Galina. "You owe me some explanations."

Galina had never held back the truth from Sera. Not once. And there was a good reason for that. Sera was the only person in this godsforsaken world who knew what Galina had been forced to do in Irina's scorched interrogation room. How many broken, ruined bodies had been sacrificed in that black hole? Their bones reduced to ash, their blood staining the stonework.

That room was a graveyard.

Galina had been raised to believe that her zmeya was a weapon—a creature of war. Irina had bonded her to a god of destruction, indoctrinating her into an ideology of brutality that left no place for compassion or mercy.

Vasilisa had shown Galina a path that went against all she had ever known—one that promised more than violence and subjugation.

The princess used her godpower to help people.

And Galina was risking everything. Her mission, her relationship with her sister, her very life. And for what? A chance at more.

Sera was far too observant. "Galya," she said with a heavy sigh. "You foolish, foolish girl."

Galina couldn't disagree. It was reckless to indulge in any emotions for the empress's daughter. She wagered it all, including countless lives. Her desires had clouded her judgment.

"I know." There was no point in trying to defend herself.

Sera began gathering her plants. "Honestly, I suspected something was up with you and the princess when you told me a godfrost-wielding royal wasn't a problem."

"I can't help it. I have feelings for her."

Sera gave her a sardonic look. "I could tell from the love bite on your neck when you stumbled in from the glasshouse yesterday that you caught some feelings. Moving up in the world, aren't we? From bored village wives to princesses."

Galina winced. "I may have gotten carried away."

"Oh, I know all about getting carried away," Sera muttered under her breath as they collected the plants in silence.

Galina tried to summon an excuse or justification for her foolishness—but nothing came to mind, only an endless void of quiet remorse. "Do you despise me?" she asked hesitantly, afraid of what her sister's answer might be.

Sera's head snapped up in disbelief. "*Despise* you? Of course not. What kind of question is that?"

Galina gently pulled the leaves from the *dem goc*, careful not to bruise them as she deposited them into a bowl she had pilfered from her bedchamber. The glasshouse was quiet, save for the soft rustle of the plants and the occasional creaking of floorboards as the sisters continued their task.

She took a deep breath, bracing herself for what she was about to say. "But I kept Vasilisa from you. After everything we went through, I feel things about her I've never felt about anyone—and I should have told you."

Her sibling stayed silent while picking flowers. "I'd be lying if I said I was thrilled," Sera finally said.

A howling emptiness echoed in Galina's chest. "I know."

Sera snorted, amusement warring with exasperation on her face. "Don't mistake my lack of enthusiasm for disapproval. I fell in love with a godsdamn fugitive assassin who's got a penchant for blowing shit up."

"Technically, so did he," Galina pointed out.

"My code of ethics is marginally superior," Sera grumbled. "But may I ask what the appeal is?"

Galina couldn't help but smile. "She's witty. I like her. Our dragons like each other. She's not like the empress or the other alurea. And she..." *She makes me feel like I can have a home again.*

Sera heaved a sigh of relief. "Thank the gods. I was worried you'd say, 'I was looking for some action and she was in the right place.'"

"*Sera!*" Galina laughed despite herself. "I love you."

Sera's expression softened. "I love you, too. And for what it's worth, I'm not judging. You did keep me in your life even after my husband tried killing you twice."

Emerging from the shadows with a bowl in his hand, Vitaly said, "I could have sworn I apologized for that."

Galina's eyes narrowed at him. "No, you didn't."

Vitaly shrugged nonchalantly. "Maybe not in so many words, but I felt a twinge of discomfort earlier that could've passed for regret, which is practically the same thing." He turned to his wife with a hint of amusement. "By the way, your plants? One of them smells like actual shit. Would've been nice if you warned me."

Sera's expression shifted, and she gave a sharp laugh that was half mockery and half menace. "You noticed."

"Of course I did. You think you're so clever, tormenting me at every turn," he said with a tsk. "What now?"

Sera wordlessly took the bowl from Vitaly and placed it on top of hers, careful not to damage the herbs inside. "I might be able to use godpower to speed up the plant synthesis, but I'll need a few days. The process is delicate, and the wrong quantities could ruin the panacea."

Vitaly's face darkened, his brow furrowing in disapproval. "You'll have to bleed for your zmeya again."

Sera hesitated for a moment before replying, "Yes."

"In that case, no."

"I don't like it any more than you do, but unless you have access to the equipment I need?" At his scowl, Sera said, "Didn't think so."

Vitaly's eyes fell on the worktable, taking in the tubes, vials, and apparatuses like a wolf sizing up its prey. Galina shivered. Sera was right; he was an assassin with questionable morals. To anyone other than her sister, that made him dangerous.

"Any of this useful?" he asked Sera.

Galina spoke up before she could stop herself. "That's—" *That's Vasilisa's,* Galina wanted to say, but the implications of her words kept her from speaking them. "Stealing those won't go unnoticed."

Vitaly's pale gray gaze shifted to Sera, an eyebrow raised in query. "*Vorovka*?"

Sera's lips pressed into a thin line, uncertainty warring in her features.

But before she could reply, footsteps whispered in the hallway. "Galyusha? What's going on?"

In a flash, Vitaly pounced. He seized Vasilisa roughly and held a blade at her throat, muffling her startled gasp beneath his iron grip. His weapon dug into her flesh ruthlessly as he wrenched her back against him.

Galina's heart lurched as Vasilisa's cane fell to the floor. The sound reverberated in the glasshouse like thunder.

"*Don't!*" The word left Galina in a hoarse croak.

But Vitaly remained unmoved. The weapon pressed deeper into Vasilisa's skin, drawing a crimson line. Vasilisa's eyes widened as she gasped for air.

"You need her equipment, Sera," Vitaly said. "And now she's seen us. Ask me, and I'll slit her throat."

Galina's breath heaved in her chest as that tiny trickle of blood descended, seeping through Vasilisa's nightdress. Her entire focus was on that mark, that indication of how close Vasilisa was to dying. With a single push, the slightest bit of pressure from Vitaly's knife, she'd be gone.

"Please, Sera," Galina's voice cracked with emotion. "Let me talk to her. Ask him to put the blade down."

Vitaly's gaze stayed on his wife, hard and cold as steel. Sera hesitated, caught between her loyalty to her sister and her distrust of the alurean princess. Galina was aware of the risks. Vasilisa could unleash the godfrost, a torrent of ice that could obliterate Sera and Vitaly in a heartbeat.

But Galina hoped Vasilisa would listen. Her countenance remained unreadable, but there was a glint of understanding there. She knew Galina was lying about her origins in Rontsy and had deceived the empress from the start. She had called Galina a spy right out of the gate.

"Please," Galina begged once more.

Don't let him do this. Trust me. Trust me.

Sera closed her eyes and spoke softly to Vitaly. "Let her go, Vitalik."

The moment stretched into eternity. Finally, he slowly withdrew the blade and stepped back. Galina rushed forward, her hands shaking as she tentatively touched Vasilisa's cheek. The princess flinched, but she didn't shy away.

"I'll explain everything, all right?" Galina promised fiercely. "I promise. I'll tell you about my past."

Vasilisa's gaze searched Galina's, her body taut as she said, "In my study."

The princess picked up her cane, and Galina followed her to await her judgment.

52

VASILISA

Vasilisa was still trembling when they entered her study.

She stared out the window, but the view beyond was just a blur of colors. She couldn't stop thinking of Galina's guilt-ridden face in the glasshouse. The woman's anguish had shredded Vasilisa's insides, leaving her heart and soul in tatters. Or maybe it was something deeper, more intangible. Something that couldn't be named or measured.

As the door clicked shut, Vasilisa jolted from her reverie. She felt Galina's presence behind her, heavy and oppressive, the silence between them nearly deafening. A thousand questions tumbled through her mind, but only three mattered. *Who are you? Do I even know you? Did I ever?*

"Are you in trouble?" Vasilisa asked instead, her voice edged with steel. The uninvited guests in her glasshouse were a dangerous liability, and she wanted answers before things got out of hand. "Tell me everything, and I'll get you out of this mess alive."

Galina let out a long sigh that Vasilisa felt in her bones. "They're not my trouble. I don't know where to start."

"At the beginning," Vasilisa snapped, her patience wearing thin. "Why do I have the two assholes who damn near killed us stashed in my private wing? They've had drawings of those two in my morning broadsheets for days."

"My foster sister, Serafima Mikhailovna, and her husband, Vitaly Sergeyevich," Galina replied in a low voice. "It was the only place I could think of that would keep them out of harm's way."

"*Out of harm's way?*" Vasilisa repeated with a dry, bitter laugh. "That's a joke, right? You're related to the people who just blew up a ballroom with us inside. You must have a hell of a tale if you're sheltering them now, Galina Feodorovna. If that's even your real name."

Galina flinched. "It's my name."

"At least we've got one truth out of you," Vasilisa said with a snarl. "But that's the bare minimum. Now start talking. I know you're not from Rontsy, and you may have lied about being from the north. So, where do you come from? Is it a village on Sopolese land that my family conquered? Is it worth joining forces with those who want us dead?"

Galina's eyes blazed like wildfire. "Oh, of course. *If only* I were your enemy. Maybe you wouldn't be here, wondering why I saved your life. Or why the mere mention of my home causes me so much pain." Galina took a step closer. "Did it ever occur to you why I brought up the Sgor invasion the other night? I lost everything in that conflict because your mother stole it from me."

Vasilisa went still at Galina's words. When she had revealed the constellations of gemstones on the glasshouse roof, Galina's anguished expression was etched into Vasilisa's memory—a cruel reminder of the home she'd lost, razed to ash by Vasilisa's mother.

"Where did it happen?" Vasilisa whispered, barely able to speak past her emotions.

Pain twisted Galina's face as she murmured, "Olensk. The empress unleashed her godfire, and the village was obliterated in minutes. I was the only survivor."

Vasilisa couldn't help but think of the scars crisscrossing the right side of Galina's body. She was supposed to be invulnerable to the empress's deadly godpower, yet she bore the mark of its wrath.

"But you have godfire," Vasilisa said, bewildered. "How could it leave a mark on you?"

Galina turned away sharply. "I wasn't bonded to a zmeya then. It was summoned into my body when I was a child. Same as my sister."

Vasilisa reared back in disbelief, her breath hitching in her throat. "How was that even possible?"

Galina reached out with a steadying hand, and Vasilisa was too dazed to shake her off. "My foster mother found the process for caging zmei in the alurean records."

Vasilisa had only seen some of the archives. During her grandfather's reign they had been available at the university, but after the faithless uprising among the students, the books were ripped from their shelves and scattered across the various royal estates of Tumanny like ashes in the wind. Vasilisa read that the alurea tried to eradicate the ingredients that allowed them to trap the zmei—and for the best. Those methods she learned about were barbaric, forcing excruciating physiological shifts on children to capture the gods. The death toll was staggering.

"How did you survive?" Vasilisa asked in a hushed tone.

Galina's countenance twisted, a dark veil shrouding her expression. "I had an incentive," Galina replied, her voice tinged with bitterness.

Vasilisa's gaze locked onto Galina, the woman who had shattered her world with ease and remade it in her image. She was a thief who had stolen a piece of Vasilisa's heart, and now she held it in her hand, and all she had to do was squeeze.

Vasilisa knew it was foolish to trust her, but she couldn't resist the pull of Galina's haunted eyes and secrets—a thousand mysteries waiting to be solved.

Anxiety welled inside her, a stormy sea crashing against the shoreline of her heart—the raging waves threatening to consume everything in their path.

Vasilisa gripped her cane hard, the polished alder wood groaning under the force. "So, you're here to kill my mother and me?" she asked. "Would that satisfy you? Retribution?"

The other woman hesitated before answering. It should have scared Vasilisa that she had let a potential assassin into her private quarters, but the tremble in Galina's hands gave her pause.

Galina spoke then, each word as sharp as broken glass. "I promised to tell you the truth. I considered it. There was no justice for Olensk or any of the villages before or after us. I still wonder how many other little girls were like me. Survivors of alurean wars left with nothing—no homes, no families. Every time I look at your mother, I imagine all the different ways I'd make her suffer."

Vasilisa turned away, looking out the window. The snow was coming down hard, blanketing the landscape in white. "And me? Did you think of any ways to kill me?"

Galina's features softened. "No."

She snorted. "No? Then what punishment have you decided for someone who profits from the suffering of others?" Vasilisa's voice was sharp. "Come on, Galusha. Don't let the black marks against my name in the ledger cloud your judgment. My ancestors built this palace on the backs of the oppressed and the corpses of kings. Every plant in my glasshouse was bought as a tribute for the daughter of the empress who killed your family. Aren't I guilty of the same sins that keep you awake at night?"

Galina stared at her, unblinking. "Do you want my forgiveness or my condemnation?"

Vasilisa eased into her chair, her body worn and heavy with exhaustion. "Honestly, I'm not sure," she said wearily. "I thought the woman who wanted me dead might have some insight."

Galina's gaze was steady and unflinching. "I'm not here to punish you, Vasya. Your glasshouse has the ingredients for Sera's panacea—enough to amplify my bond with the zmeya and activate its lustrate ability. It's—"

"I know what it is," Vasilisa interrupted, sitting back in her seat.

Typically, she would have scoffed at the notion of rousing a dormant godpower; once an alurea reached maturity, abilities didn't just come out of hibernation. But then again, a few moments ago, Vasilisa wouldn't have thought it was feasible to gather the required components to summon and cage a god in a commoner's body, so who was she to say what was impossible?

"The last person bonded to a zmeya with that godpower was over five thousand years ago. What makes you think a panacea will work?"

Galina's hand trembled against the window frame, her expression betraying a bone-deep exhaustion that Vasilisa knew all too well. The kind that followed her into her dreams and haunted her even in sleep.

"Because I'm bonded to that same god. And I have to believe it will," she said, her voice low and soft. "I have to believe that there's a future where rulers can't reduce entire villages to ashes in mere minutes. Where you don't have to hide your illness out of fear. Maybe it won't be perfect, Vasya. But we deserve better than this."

Vasilisa studied Galina's fragile form, lingering on the delicate line of her shoulders. Despite her appearance, this woman carried a burden far beyond what anyone should bear.

"The weight of countless lives is a crushing responsibility, Galyusha."

Galina raised her chin with determination. "Yes," she replied. "That's why I'm asking you to carry it with me."

Vasilisa fell silent. She thought of her bedchamber and the cloying scent of her drugs. Of the unbearable isolation of her palace wing, the only place she could find solace in the cage the alurea had built for her.

We deserve better than this.

"Say something," Galina finally whispered.

Vasilisa gripped her cane tightly. "What do you want me to say?"

Galina moved in, dropping to the floor and gripping the arms of Vasilisa's chair as she spoke softly. "I know what I'm asking, and I understand the price you'll pay. Tell me no, and I'll take Sera and Vitaly and leave. I'd never demand more than you're able to give."

Vasilisa weighed Galina's words against the life she had created for herself. The glasshouse she tended, the poisons she concocted in the dead of night—these were her weapons, her armor, her fortress. But even protection had its limits. One day, the empress would recall the dangers of a daughter who symbolized the decline of alurean power. And when that day came, Vasilisa's fate would be sealed.

Why couldn't she change it? Why couldn't she surrender herself to this woman whose touch was gentle, whose embrace was warm? Why not?

"Say the word, and I'll be gone," Galina murmured.

The thought of never seeing her again twisted Vasilisa's heart, squeezing like a fist. She leaned forward, set her cane aside, and buried her hands in Galina's hair. "Stay," she breathed, their lips touching. "Stay with me, Galyusha."

Galina's exhale was a whisper of need. "More?"

"All of it," Vasilisa growled, thick with longing.

The other woman wasted no time tearing at her own dress, fingers fumbling with buttons and laces until the fabric pooled on the floor. Galina stood before Vasilisa, exposed and vulnerable, yet exquisitely beautiful. Each scar and imperfection was a testament to her strength and resilience.

"Come here," Vasilisa said.

Galina's wicked grin was all the invitation she needed. Vasilisa surged forward, her lips meeting Galina's with an infinite hunger, a void waiting to be filled. Her desire grew more insatiable. A fierce growl ripped from her throat as she yanked Galina onto her lap and explored every delectable curve of her.

Their zmei rose and coiled in threads of power, caressing their skin with an almost tender touch—as if they were lovers long lost and reunited.

Their bond intensified, pleasure and pain melding into a single, unbearable sensation. Flames and frost clashed, humming in the air like an electric current. Vasilisa clung to Galina, fought for control, pushing her to the brink of ecstasy.

It should have been impossible for them to fit together. They were two halves born from distinct elements. Fire burned on one side, ice on the other, the world folding in on itself as their bodies collided—an alchemical storm created from the collision of opposites.

"I can't promise you a future with me," Vasilisa said, her breathing ragged. "But I can offer you this breath. And the next. And all those that follow, for as long as you'll take them."

"Then make me yours," Galina whispered.

Vasilisa answered with a groan as her fingertips mapped out the scars on Galina's skin—each one a memory etched in agony's ink.

Ignoring the jolt of pain up her legs, Vasilisa shifted their position, pushing Galina back onto the chair as she knelt before her. Tonight, she wanted to drown out her pain with pleasure.

"Vasya," Galina breathed out, her eyes glazed with desire. "You don't have to—"

"Quiet," Vasilisa said, gently nipping Galina's thigh in a reprimand. "Or do you want me to stop?"

A laugh left her as she sank her hand into Vasilisa's hair. "Don't you dare."

Vasilisa's lips curved into a smile. She lowered her head, pressing reverent kisses along Galina's skin, coaxing her thighs to part further. Her tongue flicked out, tasting the wet heat of the other woman's core.

Galina's back arched up from the chair, a gasp of pleasure ripping from her throat. "That. Right there."

Vasilisa obliged, savoring every taste, every sensation, as Galina's breathless moans filled the room, each one a desperate plea for more.

And Vasilisa answered each silent prayer.

Galina's hands twisted in Vasilisa's hair as if it were the only thing tethering her to reality. Vasilisa trailed the tips of her fingers across the contours of Galina's skin, scrawling delicate lines and constellations that promised to unravel her.

Come for me. Vasilisa followed that thought with a pulse of power, a command laced with pleasure.

Galina ignited.

She gasped in climax, and their two forces collided: the fierce blaze of Galina's godfire clashing against Vasilisa's godfrost.

They shared a bond so powerful it could burn the stars.

Galina exhaled Vasilisa's name in a whisper of surrender.

Vasilisa rose to her knees, steadying herself on the chair's armrests as she tenderly brushed her lips against Galina's cheek. "I've been in hiding for too long, Galyusha," Vasilisa breathed against her skin. "Too many years spent with a black mark on my name. So let's tear down the empire together."

53

KATYA

The alurean architects had outdone themselves with the prison hold beneath Zolotiye, a hellhole built to contain those who dared to commit treason against the crown.

Katya's shivers wracked her thin frame as she lay sprawled on the frigid stone floor of her pitch-black cell, clad in only her delicate handmaiden's attire. No overcoat to protect her from the dungeon's bitter chill. She drew herself into a tight ball and tried to suppress the coughing fit that threatened the stillness.

It was the scratching that turned her blood cold, the skittering of rats creeping closer to her. A while ago, she'd felt their razor-sharp claws scraping across her feet as they circled her, waiting for her to succumb to her injuries.

General Vasilchikov had been merciless and methodical in his torture—breaking each bone in her body with the precision of a master torturer. Her right arm had been shattered in three places, her left in two, and her fingers fractured and bent at grotesque angles.

Healers had been summoned to mend her broken body only so Vasilchikov could break it again.

Where are they? the general had snapped, tossing water into her face as she'd blacked out. *If you want this pain to end, tell me where they are.*

But Katya was ready. As the empress's former handmaiden, she'd honed resilience under alurean interrogation and knew how to keep secrets and play the game of power and deception. She had been burnt alive and brought back from the brink. She was no stranger to pain.

The reverberating clang of a steel door slammed shut, echoing through the winding halls of the subterranean hold.

The prison had been emptied of all its prisoners to prepare for Sera and Vitaly's capture; the empress was determined not to let them slip through her grasp again.

Katya was the exception, of course. A handmaiden who had dared to betray her mistress was a rare and valuable commodity. She would be executed in a manner befitting her treachery. Made an example of—dragged before a heaving mob of nobles and supplicants hungry for her blood.

The clamor of footsteps grew louder in the dismal dungeon, and the light of a single lantern brightened until it nearly blinded her. Katya squinted against the glare. The hours—or was it days?—spent in this wretched hole instilled in her a deep love of the dark. The lantern's rays were like a thousand needles in her eyes.

"Out," Empress Isidora commanded, her voice icier than the chamber. "I want to speak to Ekaterina Isidorakh alone."

The sentries left. When the key scraped in the lock, Katya held her breath, knowing whatever came next would not be pleasant.

The empress swept in, her heels clacking on the stone floor like the ticking of a clock counting down to Katya's doom. "Can't you rise and curtsy for your sovereign? Or do I need to bring in another healer?"

Katya shifted against the cold, rough ground, her aching limbs protesting with every movement. "I won't bow to you," she said, her voice low and hoarse.

In the dim light, she felt a slight sense of relief. In this dank and musty cell, she was stripped of her former life, her bells and overcoat taken away. For once, she was free from the constant performance she had been forced to endure, free from the endless dance of polite society. In the shadows and silence, she found a strange sort of liberation.

The empress was not so easily dissuaded. Katya heard the rustle of silk as Isidora approached, her delicate features etched with worry. "Katenka," she said softly, her voice bouncing off the stone walls. "I'm sorry it came to this. I didn't want you in this filthy place, questioned by General Vasilchikov."

Katya didn't reply—she just watched the empress warily.

"Please," Isidora said. "Tell me the truth. Did you betray me to the faithless?"

What was the point of lying now? Katya had nothing left to lose. No more duties to perform, no more roles to play. Every day in that cell was another step closer to the inevitable. Wasn't there a certain freedom in that? Her death watch had reached its final hour.

So she looked the empress in the eye and spoke her words with a crystalline clarity. "Yes. I betrayed you." *And what's more?* "I would do it again."

The empress's eyes turned to chips of jagged ice, as cold and pitiless as a tundra. Katya felt a slight sense of satisfaction as the stones of her cell warmed, radiating with the heat of Isidora's godpower.

"Was any of it real, Katenka?" she asked, her voice hollow and hurt. "Did you lie when you called me *suvya*? Did you work with my enemies while I treated you like a daughter?"

Katya rose to her feet, the pain in her limbs forgotten in her fury. "A daughter? I was your *servant*."

Empress Isidora grasped her by the throat, her grip unyielding. "I gave you everything."

Katya refused to back down, to cower before the woman who had taken so many lives. She had been silenced for too long, forced to endure the empress's whims and desires without a voice of her own.

"You gave me *nothing*," she hissed, her words coming out in a near-strangled whisper. "You took everything—my freedom, my dignity, my soul. Dug your heels into my back and made me attend to you day and night. You broke my bones and called it love."

Isidora's face twisted with rage, her eyes blazing with fury. "I brought you healers. I did whatever I could to care for you."

"To fix me so you could do it again," Katya said. "How were you any different from General Vasilchikov? What have I endured today at his hands that I didn't already endure at yours?"

Isidora flinched, pain contorting her features. "Have you hated me this entire time?" she whispered. "Did it mean nothing when I shared my pain with you during my husband's cruel reign? Didn't you feel anything?"

"Anger," Katya said, low and fierce. She gripped Isidora's wrist, enduring the heat of the empress's skin against her own. "Because you murdered my sister. And you killed countless other handmaidens and servants, leaving their corpses for the staff to clean up."

Isidora sucked in a jagged breath. "I apologized to you for Sofia," she said. "I promoted you from your maid duties and took you to Liesgau. I bought you silks and jewelry to adorn yourself."

Katya gave a brittle laugh, her eyes blazing with fury. "*Promoted* me from my maid duties? My duties have stayed with me for six years. I know what you did to every other handmaiden before me. You can wrap me in silks, call me *knesí*, and rest your head on my shoulder. But you can't erase the memory of everything you've done. A silk dress doesn't lessen the weight of your foot on my spine."

Beneath the ornate fabric of Isidora's bodice, her chest heaved, her barely contained rage filling the small prison with heat. Katya already accepted she might not meet her end on the stone platform but in her dark, filthy cell. Murdered by the empress in a fit of rage like every handmaiden before her.

Isidora averted her gaze, and for a split second Katya could have sworn she detected regret in her eyes. But then it was gone, a mirage born from lantern light and treacherous shadows. It was strange to witness the ordinarily unflappable monarch so vulnerable, to realize that Katya was the source of her pain.

"I came to offer you your position back." Isidora's voice was thick with emotion. "All you had to do was tell me where the fugitives are hiding. But I can see now it's not something you want."

"No," she said with finality. "Nothing you offer me could make me put those bells on again. I'd rather die."

Her words struck the empress like a blow. The other woman's lips flattened. "Then I'll leave you in General Vasilchikov's care. And I'll see you at your execution."

54

SERA

Sera stood at the table in the greenhouse, surrounded by piles of notes.

The sun filtered through the domed glass, casting a kaleidoscope of colors throughout the space. The natural ambiance provided a soothing background to her thoughts, a blessed respite from her mother's subterranean study. Even the tunnels had the clatter of Blackshore's bustling activity reverberating through its walls.

As she inhaled the sweet fragrance of the botanicals, Sera heard muffled footsteps behind her.

A strong arm wrapped around her waist. "*Ra spe*," Vitaly's velvet tenor whispered into her ear, still fragile with sleep. He dropped a tender kiss on her neck. "You left the bed too soon."

Sera bit back a smile and penned in an annotation. "If it were up to you, we would never leave it."

A long sigh. "Serafima, *vorovka*, you misunderstand." He pressed another kiss to her nape and murmured, "I had plans to slip under the blankets and make you come again."

Her body burned with the memory of the night before. After Galina's assurances of safety, Sera and Vitaly had retired to a bedroom in the Glasshouse Wing. But sleep was fleeting; she woke to find Vitaly's strong arms encircling her, and the familiarity of it was a bewildering jolt to her senses. She could have easily shed their clothing and taken him right then and there.

But Sera resisted—and she lay there, wanting and aching. As if sensing her turmoil, Vitaly's hand slid across the curve of her hip and then he drew up the covers. When his kiss grazed her stomach, she tensed and grabbed his hair. He paused, seeking her consent with only his scorching breath against her. Her response came swiftly as she pushed him between her thighs and arched into him as his tongue expertly brought her to ecstasy.

Afterward, he climbed beside her again, her scent clinging to his skin. Then he'd pulled her into his arms and went back to sleep. She was still left wanting—wanting all of him.

Sera snorted. "You were always insatiable."

"No more than yourself," Vitaly drawled, his words dripping with wickedness. "You've always been more than eager to join me."

She released a forlorn sigh. "And now I have work."

"Then I'll leave you to your notes," he said tenderly. "But when you need a distraction, come to bed."

Princess Vasilisa walked in, interrupting their moment. Vitaly's face twisted into a scowl at the sight of her. Sera placed a hand on his arm, silently warning him not to say anything stupid.

"Oh, I'm sorry," Vasilisa said. "I didn't mean to intrude."

"You're not," Sera assured her. "Vitalik was just on his way out."

"Maybe I've changed my mind, *vorovka*," he said softly, his gaze lingering on the other woman. "I'm happy to stay and help."

Princess Vasilisa's eyes were like a storm-tossed sea, filled with uncertainty and hidden currents. Sera knew better than to trust the empress's daughter, but Galina had gone and foolishly fallen in love with the woman. And Sera couldn't help but think that love was like a constant dagger pointed at your own heart.

Still, she needed to figure out this woman's intentions. Was she the kind to break Galina's heart into a million tiny pieces? Or would a friendly threat of face-breaking be enough to keep her in check?

The usual sisterly things.

What do you think about her? Sera asked her god. Maybe it had some instincts to share.

Her zmeya just gave a rumble that could have meant anything and settled back in its coiled position.

Sera rolled her eyes. *As always, thank you for that insightful contribution.*

She turned to her husband. "Don't worry about me," Sera told him in Zverti, knowing it wasn't a language the alurean nobles spoke. "My zmeya doesn't seem alarmed."

She decided not to mention the possibility that the god wanted her to die screaming.

Vitaly focused on Vasilisa as he lifted Sera's hand and grazed his lips across her wrist. "You're sure?" His response in Zverti was smooth; he hadn't hesitated. He switched between languages so easily.

"Yes."

"Fine." He pressed a last searing kiss to her knuckles. "But some advice: the knife you keep at your back is the sharpest, the easiest to throw, and even alurea die quickly when you stab them in the neck." With that, he dropped her hand and headed for the door.

Princess Vasilisa quietly stepped aside as he exited the glasshouse, relaxing only when his footsteps disappeared down the hall. "I really am sorry for interrupting."

Sera returned her attention to the papers scattered across the worktable. "Is Galya still sleeping?"

"Yes." Princess Vasilisa wandered closer, her slim and beautifully carved cane in a soft grip. "She told me about your mother's... experiments."

Sera penned another annotation in her notes. "Then you know I have a zmeya and can defend myself."

Princess Vasilisa's eyes met hers, keen and all too sharp. "And out of curiosity, how many knives do you carry on you for casual neck stabbing?"

Sera jolted with surprise. "You understand Zverti," she said flatly.

"*Sma, fast lo.*" But she didn't seem satisfied, only embarrassed. "Don't worry. I don't share the same beliefs as the other courtiers about the language."

Sera's fingers clenched the page as if trying to draw blood from it. "It wouldn't matter even if you did. It doesn't shock me that the empress's daughter would disregard the consequences of learning the same language that could get a supplicant locked up in prison."

The words hit Princess Vasilisa like a slap, her body flinching in response. "I'll leave you alone," she said quickly.

Godsblood. Galina would be furious with her if Sera didn't at least try. "No," Sera said, holding up a placating hand. "Please stay. I'm sorry for my outburst. I shouldn't have spoken to you like that after you offered to help us."

The princess studied the scattered pages littering the worktable. Irina's handwriting in Zverti was elegant and bold, the script of someone who had learned it without fear of reprisal—Zverti had still been legal in her youth. Sera's was unsteady and uncertain, scrawled across the page in a jagged mess of ink and desperation. She had rarely written in her mother tongue, so each letter was an agonizing trial.

"These are your mother's records?" Vasilisa asked.

"Yes. She inscribed them in a complex cryptogram that I had the torturous pleasure of decoding for six weeks," Sera replied, contemplating how much information she should divulge to an alurea who might turn on her. But Sera had promised Galina that she would try. "I've run a few tests with Galina's blood, but now I need to figure out how to make the same formula without all the fancy kit in my study."

Princess Vasilisa approached, her regard sharp as she perused the notes. "You're thinking godpower?"

Sera's fingers tapped an anxious beat on the table. "If I can. My god's not exactly the most cooperative partner. Galina's is better, but—"

"But she's never done this sort of minute work before," Princess Vasilisa finished. "She could with practice, but zmei with the godfire are blunter in their abilities. The godfrost requires more delicacy."

Sera's eyebrows shot up. "You've done this before?"

The princess's expression turned guarded. "To treat my illness."

It clicked then; Sera understood why Galina empathized with Vasilisa and her fragile glass world. The princess was vulnerable, her mobility restricted by her illness. It wouldn't take much for someone to exploit any perceived weakness—manipulate her access to the medicine she needed. And with the faithless running rampant in the city, that was a genuine danger.

Her mind made, Sera pushed the book closer to Princess Vasilisa. "Then let me tell you what I've found."

Princess Vasilisa smiled, and Sera knew why her sister had risked everything.

Sera staggered to her room, a dull ache throbbing in her skull. She had spent hours with Vasilisa, making plans to synthesize the panacea. And by the gods, they'd done it. Or, at least, they had something that might work.

And now, some well-earned respite.

As she heaved open the door, Sera steeled herself for reproach from her husband; after all, it was well past sunset and she had yet to take a break. But instead of a scolding, Sera found only an empty chamber and a hastily scrawled note on the pillow.

Typical.

Palace reconnaissance. Back soon. —V

"Shit," she snarled, tucking the paper away in her pocket.

Rest would have to wait—she needed to locate Vitaly before he got himself killed.

55

VITALY

Vitaly slipped through the palace halls like a ghost.

Espionage was an art form he relished—a game, a test of wit and cunning against his opponents. His childhood as a thief was a benefit; the gutters had been his training ground, where one misstep meant a quick and brutal end.

He found that the greatest weapons in his arsenal were his ability to blend in, to become invisible, to listen, and to learn. Absorb the servants' gossip—piece together the puzzle of imperial conflicts.

It was easy compared to the heists of his youth.

The knowledge Vitaly amassed as a faithless operative was a treasure trove of intel that could tip the scales of war. In Sundyr, he'd learned the routines of the alurean elite, the maneuvers of their armies, the plots for their conquests—all of it passed through his sharp ears and into the hands of the faithless.

The fate of kingdoms and empires hung on the information he gathered.

He couldn't squander the opportunity to use his time at Zolotiye to his benefit.

Vitaly melted into the shadows of a cramped alcove, watching two maids scurry past him with arms full of freshly laundered linens. The palace had been silent in the Glasshouse Wing, not a soul stirring except for the occasional dust mote.

But the main halls were different.

The palace was crawling with activity, with servants rushing in and out of rooms and sentries keeping a watchful eye on the comings and goings of the staff. Vitaly's ears pricked at every sound, his heart hammering in his chest as he carefully navigated the chaos.

Vitaly was never one to flinch at danger. He reveled in it, had sharpened his skills to a keen edge, poised to strike.

The alurean mavens had quickly restored the wreckage his explosives inflicted on the ballroom and its surroundings. Twenty minutes prior, he'd overheard a servant sigh in relief that the howling gales no longer blew snow through the blown-out windows—her relief to even still be alive.

Vitaly tried to ignore the reminder that if his bombs had inflicted worse damage—killed Sera's sister or Katya—his marriage would have been demolished with it. He had fate to thank for intervening.

Maybe his good fortune was undeserved. He didn't give a shit about anyone but Sera, after all. She sanded down his rough edges, the counterweight to his brutish instincts—his voice of reason. He was her weapon to wield, and he'd gladly stain his soul with blood for her so she'd never have to bear the burden of deciding who lived and died for revolution.

He'd take any unearned luck and hoard it if he had to. Thank the gods every day that his stupidity hadn't lost him his wife.

Vitaly strode purposefully down the grand hall, aiming to let himself into the sumptuous private chambers ahead. The palace was a grotesque display of opulence, but it only became more repugnant with each step he took—a giant *fuck you* to the impoverished city at the bottom of the hill, forced to stare at its gilded domes.

The golden light that filled the rotunda was sickeningly bright. It illuminated every detail of the palace's excess, a thin veneer attempting to conceal the rot beneath.

As he walked, each trinket, vase, bust, statue, and painting seemed to taunt him with their uselessness. It was disgusting how these rich bastards flaunted their wealth while so many others struggled to survive.

The memories of Vitaly's past hit him like a sack of bricks. He could feel the mud that clung to his hands and knees as he scraped for crumbs on the unforgiving streets. The cloying sweetness of the cake that churned in his empty stomach, mocking him for his hunger.

And then there was the sound of the alurean courtiers' laughter, the cackling guffaws that filled the air as they watched from their gilded carriages.

Their callous aristocratic brains undoubtedly found it hilarious to watch children scuffle over scraps like starving dogs in a pile of filth. Hunger had a way of stripping dignity and humanity away with ease. To them, Vitaly was an animal crawling for their amusement. They sauntered through the streets of the Blackshore like tourists gaping at a foreign country where starvation drove citizens to their knees.

It was all entertainment for these royal assholes.

No surprise when he saw how they lived; the glittering halls of Zolotiye, its opulent chambers, luxurious carpets, and shimmering gemstones that glittered like stars across their floors. Where they wanted for nothing and were waited on hand and foot by servants who had no choice but to do their bidding or die.

Vitaly's hands clenched tightly as he retreated to a small alcove to collect himself.

Stay calm, Vitalik.

Stay. Calm.

But his thoughts offered little solace. He shouldn't have left the Glasshouse Wing. There, at least, he could hold Sera close, breathe in her scent, kiss her, and feel her skin beneath his fingertips. If she were willing, he could ease himself inside her and fuck her until he forgot everything that plagued him. Until all he could focus on was her.

She was a gift he had no right to possess.

Vitaly was snapped from his stupor by the echoing boom of a door slamming shut. A maid barreled down the hall, nearly colliding with two other attendants. Her flushed face was tear-streaked, and her breath came in shallow gasps.

"Talya," one of the other maids said in concern. She wrapped an arm around the young girl's slim shoulders. "What happened?"

"I can't do this," Talya gasped. "I had to dress her this morning, but she was in a mood—"

"Hush now," the other maid said, trying to calm her down. "You're not making any sense. Katya dresses the empress."

"They've locked her up in the palace hold," Talya said, the words tumbling out like a landslide.

Vitaly felt his blood go cold. Katya was the only one outside the Glasshouse Wing who knew where he and Sera were.

"Shit," he breathed, straining to listen through the maids' immediate outburst of shocked chatter.

One of the women managed to sputter a question. "How? Why?"

Talya's response dropped to a whisper, making Vitaly lean in so far he almost overbalanced. "They're saying she's a faithless traitor."

"*Katya?*" Two choked gasps, as if the woman had been accused of sedition and something far worse, like cannibalism.

"*Shhh.*" Talya sounded urgent. "They say she got fed up with the empress's demands and betrayed her."

Silence hung like a shroud. Then a mournful murmur. "Poor Katya."

"*Hush, Agata,*" one of them snapped. "Before you get us all roasted alive."

"Sorry," Agata muttered. "But now Her Imperial Majesty will choose a new handmaiden, won't she? Talya, you dressed her this morning?"

"She's already on the hunt," Talya replied, trembling. "Do you remember how long anyone lasted before Sofia? Months. Poor Zina didn't even last a fortnight. And you know what happened to her—"

The maids' voices faded as they shuffled off in the opposite direction.

Vitaly had no time to worry; he needed to find out if Sera's spy was ready to betray them.

He stepped out of his hiding spot, but before he could take a single step, an iron grip seized his shoulder and yanked him into an empty parlor.

A voice he'd know anywhere hissed in his ear, "Vitaly Sergeyevich, you absolute *moron.*"

He exhaled a sigh of relief. Vitaly freed her hand from his coat and gently kissed her knuckles. "Serafima Mikhailovna, you always know how to sweet talk me."

When he turned to face her, Vitaly couldn't help but grin at the sight of her—skin flushed, all anger and indignation. *Beautiful.*

"You could have been caught and killed," she snarled, shutting the door behind them. "What was I supposed to do? Find a godsdamned note?"

If there was one thing Vitaly loved more than anything else in the world, it was when she got mad. She flared brighter than the stars.

He lifted his palm to cup her cheek, basking in the heat radiating from her. "So many words just to say you were worried about me."

"The gods only know why," she grumbled. "You've aged me a decade in one hour."

He let his eyes linger on every inch of her delectable body. "You're the most exquisite creature I've ever seen."

"Don't you dare flatter me right now. I'll punch you in the throat."

Gods, she was perfect—every jagged edge and every hidden softness. His ruthless girl. "You're fucking dazzling," he said, knowing full well it would set her off again.

And it did. "You're a *fucking* imbecile."

His smile only widened. "You're incredible."

"I *despise* you."

Vitaly moved until only a breath separated them. "I love you too, *vorovka*."

Sera leaned forward and nipped lightly at his lower lip in reprimand, before stepping back out of reach. "Tell me this absurd risk of yours was worth it, and I might forgive you. But no more kisses until then."

Vitaly's mirth faded. This woman always made him forget himself. For brief moments, she could shut out the world and fill every corner of his heart and mind.

But then reality would rudely interject itself.

"Your spy was caught," he said. "I'm sorry."

She recoiled, her hand covering her mouth. "Is she alive? Do you know?"

Vitaly shook his head. "Can't say for sure. The maid seemed to think so. She said Katya was in the palace hold."

The sudden calculating expression and stubborn set of her jaw was a bad sign. "Then I need to go get her—"

"No."

"Don't make decisions for me," she said in a low, threatening tone. "I told Katya I'd do everything possible to give her a future. I've lied enough. Don't ask me to break that promise."

Vitaly grabbed her shoulders, trying to reason with her. "If they've kept her alive, there's still time. But you can't go running through Zolotiye without a map. It's too dangerous. Finish your panacea, and we'll get Katya out."

Worry threatened her composure. "Right. I'm sorry. You're—"

Voices echoed from the hallway—approaching the parlor.

Quick as a viper, Vitaly pulled Sera to the ground and rolled them both behind a divan. The door flew open just a moment later, and he recognized the cutting voice of Empress Isidora.

"—trained in interrogation, General Vasilchikov. And yet you've worked on Ekaterina Isidorakh for hours and *still* have no fugitives to show for it. How often do my healers have to piece her back together because of your incompetence?"

"Your former handmaiden has proven to be more impervious to my methods than I expected, Your Imperial Majesty."

"I don't care," the empress shot back. "I'm disappointed in your performance, General."

"I apologize, Your Imperial Majesty," the general replied with a docility that spoke of fear. "I'll strive to improve my methods."

The sitting room was quiet, but it crackled with a strange tension. It was the calm before the storm, the stillness that came before a deadly predator pounced on its prey. Vitaly had never been within arm's reach of Isidora, but her presence from the royal balcony alone radiated power—a reminder of the speed with which she and her god could kill.

"What will you do to earn my mercy?" asked Isidora. "Beg for it? Kneel before your soldiers like a groveling dog? Should I have them bear witness to your humiliation?" The sound of her heels thumped against the carpet as she paced. "You promised me results, and all I have are empty cells and a handmaiden you can't break. How will you make amends?"

Sera pressed against Vitaly, her breathing shallow and quick. He comforted her with a gentle hand on her hair, but he knew she felt him move. His other palm hovered over the hilt of her knife, poised to draw it to protect her.

"Please," General Vasilchikov murmured, his voice barely audible.

The empress paused. "*Please?*"

Vitaly could almost hear the general's pulse quicken in his chest. "Please, Your Imperial Majesty."

"What was the name of your subordinate again?"

The sound of fabric rustling reached Vitaly's ears, and he wondered if the general was nervously adjusting his uniform. "Lieutenant Dukhonin, Your Imperial Majesty."

"And do you think Lieutenant Dukhonin would be more useful to me after your repeated failures?" The empress's words were like daggers, slicing through the air. "Maybe I should promote him."

"If that's your wish," General Vasilchikov replied, his voice shaking.

The empress's footsteps were almost inaudible as she moved around the chamber. "Tell me. Where do you believe Ekaterina Isidorakh could have hidden our fugitives?"

Silence filled the room, stretching into an uncomfortable stillness. Vitaly's heart raced in his chest, his mind screaming to get Sera out of there. He gently kissed her hair, hoping it wouldn't be their last moment together.

"I don't know." A mere whisper in the oppressive atmosphere.

A strangled gasp came from the other side of the divan. Vitaly peered out from behind the furniture and saw the empress had launched herself at the large man, nails raking deep furrows in the flesh of his neck.

"If you don't know," she snarled, "then what good are you to me?"

The general's response was choked off as Isidora tightened her grip on his throat. The air thickened with heat and power, making Vitaly's brow bead with sweat. His hand clenched tightly around Sera's knife, his knuckles turning white.

Sera clutched his coat.

They both knew what was coming.

Vitaly flinched as he watched General Vasilchikov's skin blister and blacken. The empress's palm clamped over the man's mouth, silencing his screams. All that escaped the general's lips was a pathetic, strangled rasp that sounded like a death rattle.

Godfire exploded across the general's uniform, orange and brilliant blue licking at the fabric, the very air around him. Vitaly's stomach lurched as he recalled another figure caught in a similar blaze, his brother Sergei turning to ash beneath a scorching firestorm. How his flesh had scorched black and became unrecognizable as human—his limbs twisted into a gnarled thing.

A deafening silence filled the room as the general's body crumbled into nothing but brittle bones and gray dust at the empress's feet. Vitaly still gripped Sera's blade, his heart thundering inside his chest.

The parlor door was yanked open, and Vitaly tensed, ready to defend himself and his wife from danger.

"Get me Lieutenant Dukhonin," the empress barked to someone. "Tell him he's been promoted."

The sound of the monarch's footsteps faded away as she exited the chamber, leaving Vitaly and Sera alone with the remains of General Vasilchikov.

Vitaly pressed his forehead against Sera's shoulder and slowly eased her knife back into its sheath.

56

SERA

Sera trembled with a volatile mix of emotions as she and Vitaly returned to the Glasshouse Wing.

When General Vasilchikov fell to the ground, murdered by the godfire, it was Vitaly who blazed through her thoughts. Vitaly, whose body she imagined reduced to ash by the empress's wrath—visions of losing him after all those wasted years apart.

Her fault.

Time was not in their favor—and today was a savage reminder.

She opened the door to their bedchamber and waited for her husband to follow before pushing him against the paneling.

Her lips met Vitaly's in a wild, frenzied kiss, her fingers fumbling and frantic as she tore at the buttons of his shirt.

Vitaly pushed back—a futile gesture. They were always destined to crash together, a force stronger than the pull of gravity. His pulse beat erratically at his throat. Every inch of him radiated with pent-up desire as their breathing collided, jagged and frenetic.

"Sera," he breathed, a plea and a prayer. His eyes were dark with a craving that matched hers.

"I need you." Her words came out in a demand, all emotion and desperation. She was an incendiary mess of conflicting feelings and wants, a chaos waiting to be disrupted or destroyed. "You promised me a distraction if I asked."

His gaze searched hers. "*Vorovka*," he murmured. "What happened back there—"

"No questions." Sera's voice was sharp. She didn't want to explain herself, not when the hunger inside her clawed and snarled and demanded release. Couldn't he feel it too? Didn't he sense the dark, spiked yearning in her heart? "I've told you what I need. Do you want me or not?"

But he did.

He always had and always would.

With a rough groan, Vitaly closed his eyes and changed their positions, pinning her against the door. His mouth crashed against hers with a ferocity that matched her own, his hands tracing patterns on her skin that made her nerves sing with pleasure.

He bent and twisted her desires to his will, shattered the walls she had built that kept him out. Sera's clothing was ripped away with a single tug, her defenses laid waste by his touch, her armor shredded. The blaze between them refused to be extinguished, no matter how long they spent apart.

Vitaly's lips drifted across Sera's bare shoulder, a gentle exploration to soothe the storm of emotions within her. Willing her into submission. But she was in no mood for softness.

Her zmeya rumbled restlessly—for once the human and the god agreed.

Sera's hand gripped his hair, a silent warning: *Don't give me soft. Not now. Give me what I want.*

Vitaly obliged, sinking his teeth into her flesh and branding her as his own. A sharp hiss left her lips as she clawed at his clothes. She needed to feel all of him, every inch of his skin. She stripped off his shirt with a demanding tug, and her fingers deftly unfastened his trousers.

The broken groan that escaped him was a declaration of war. Laid bare, hers to conquer—but she should have known better. Vitaly Sergeyevich Rysakov was her equal in every way. A partner in their clash of dominance and submission, where power was exchanged as often as breath. And if she thought she had him at her mercy, he would always claw his way back.

His voice brushed against her, a caress. "If you want me inside you, you have to say it."

"*Vitalik.*"

All she knew was his name and a plea that echoed in every touch: *Please. Please.*

Please.

"Don't you remember the rules? They never change." Vitaly's lips traced the shell of her ear, and when he spoke, the words seared into her. "Command me, Serafima."

Sera thought of victories and defeats, of words that carved divinity from the ether and pleasure as a blade to be wielded in dark places. Her body was a battleground of desire and pain, and it understood victory. She sank her teeth into his neck and scraped her nails across his back. Reveled in the harsh, desperate sound that ripped from his throat.

Her zmeya purred with approval, delighting in their shared power.

He's ours.

So she commanded: "Fuck me, Vitalik."

Vitaly hoisted Sera up and pinned her against the door as he thrust his cock deep inside her. Thoughts scattered beneath the onslaught of sensation: his scent, the fiery heat of his body, the hungry press of his lips on hers, the hard rhythm as he took her. This was all she ever wanted, to be lost in him, to forget the shattered pieces of their lives for one precious moment. And Vitaly was more than willing to give it all to her, responding to her every touch, every desire. They were two halves of the same weapon, forged by fire and pain. He was hers, and she was his, and they were as inseverable as flesh and bone.

"Serafima." Vitaly's voice was hoarse as he pounded into her. "*Fast na svo.*"

He drove her higher still until she shuddered against him and whispered those four words she hadn't spoken in years: "I love you too."

Afterward, Sera remained restless. Vitaly curled against her, but she lay awake, watching the snowflakes tumbling beyond the window. She thought he was asleep until his lips brushed against her neck.

"I saw you," she said, her voice rough with old wounds. "Two years ago."

Vitaly went rigid, his breath ghosting across her skin. "Where?"

"In Voroski. You were dressed as a trader in the market, and I was returning from the inner city, where I'd been tending to a sick girl." Her words betrayed none of the pain she kept locked inside. The same pain sliced open again by the empress's godfire. Too many years wasted, too many lies spoken. "I stood there, longing for the sound of your voice and the sight of you. When a merchant pointed you in my direction, I fled to Galina. Told her someone recognized me. We left immediately."

She felt him shift behind her, then gently prod her shoulder until she faced him. Vitaly stared at her, his beautiful features bathed in moonlight and shadows. "Why didn't you come to me?"

Sera sighed, her fingers tracing the curve of his cheekbone. She remembered that day in the market, the way the sun had caressed his skin—bronzed from the sweltering Liesgau summer. His gray eyes had been a wonder, reminiscent of the winter storm clouds in Tumanny. All that beauty stole her breath away until she'd whispered his name like a benediction.

But her god had stirred inside her, an unwelcome presence that filled her thoughts with doubts.

"I convinced myself that I was protecting Galina. I let her bear the blame instead of facing the truth—that I ran from you because I was a coward." Sera's hand cupped his cheek. "It was easier than telling you that you spent years married to a monster and never even knew."

She studied the lines etched into his forehead, evidence of worries. They weren't there when she had left him in Blackshore. Sera wondered what had caused them, whether it was her doing—yet one more thing to add to her burden.

"Is that what you believe?" Vitaly's voice carried a surprising gentleness. "That you're a monster?"

"I don't know," she confessed, dropping her hand from his face.

Vitaly made a low sound and shifted on top of her. "Listen to me, Serafima Mikhailovna," he said, bracing his arms on either side of her. "If you're a monster, then be a monster. Show the world your teeth. It makes no difference to me." He dipped his head and kissed her fiercely. "But don't ever use me as an excuse to make yourself smaller. That's something I won't stand for."

Her chest constricted. How had she survived all those years without him? She'd blamed it on her god, the endless wandering from one village to the next, searching for a scrap of sanctuary. But it was his absence. Always his absence. Leaving her stranded on the brink of oblivion. Every day, a fresh wound to her heart.

"I'm sorry I didn't come to you sooner," she said softly.

"Just don't run again, *vorovka*," he murmured, trailing kisses down her jawline. "I get bored when you're gone and end up doing stupid, reckless things."

"Looks like I'll have to keep you entertained," she replied, a playful grin spreading across her lips.

He chuckled, his mouth curving into a smile against her skin. "I was counting on it."

57

VASILISA

The note from Vasilisa's mother arrived while she was in the glasshouse preparing plants.

Galina shoved through the door and stopped short. "Where's Sera?"

Vasilisa wiped her hands and pushed her wheelchair away from the table. "Resting. She worked on the panacea with me this morning." She paused at the apprehension in Galina's features. "Is something wrong?"

Galina pressed a creased note into Vasilisa's hand. "A servant delivered this. It's from the empress."

Vasilisa unfolded the foolscap to find her mother's familiar elegant script: *Come directly to the temple with Galina Feodorovna. Be prepared to show yourself publicly on the balcony.*

She hurled the missive onto the table and cursed under her breath. Isidora demanded Vasilisa's presence with no time to prepare or brace herself for the inevitable price.

And did her mother care? No.

"If you can't go, I'll make an excuse," Galina offered.

"My mother doesn't tolerate excuses," she said grimly. "I'll go take my damn medicines."

Galina followed Vasilisa into her bedchamber and watched as she retrieved the small wooden case from her bedside that held her treatments.

She hesitated. This was a solitary task, one she had always performed alone. Even the empress thought it beneath her dignity to watch her daughter inject the treatments that kept her disease at bay. If she had, Isidora might have understood the steep cost of every public appearance.

But ignorance brought the monarch no pain; only Vasilisa carried that burden.

Despite the medicine that prolonged her life, her condition worsened each year. It was a slow wither, like petals plucked one by one until the flower had no bloom left. One day soon, she wouldn't be able to hide it any longer.

Galina lingered behind her—a welcome presence—but Vasilisa hesitated to open the case and reveal what she feared was too fragile for light or air.

What they had was so new and delicate, Vasilisa could hardly bear to intrude upon it with...

With me, she corrected the course of her thoughts. *With all of me. Every part of me exposed and vulnerable. What will she think?*

No one had ever been here with her, not like this. Vasilisa had only her zmeya for company, but even its voice was numbed by the drugs in her veins.

"You don't have to stay," she murmured, little more than a whisper over the drumming of her own heart.

"I'm aware of that." Galina's hand slipped into Vasilisa's hair, sweeping away the strands. She pressed her lips to the crook of Vasilisa's shoulder. "But are you saying it because you want to be alone? Or is it just for my benefit?"

The question hung heavy between them, a storm waiting to break. How long had it been since anyone truly saw her? Since anyone dared look beyond the lies her mother crafted? The princess everyone thought they knew was nothing but a fabrication of propaganda. She was a ghost, forgotten and hidden as if she'd never existed.

"I don't know," she finally said.

"Stop listening to the empress's voice in your head, Vasya," Galina said, dropping another kiss to Vasilisa's skin. "It's you and me in this room. No one else. So let me rephrase my question: do you want me to hold you while you do this?"

Tears pricked Vasilisa's eyes. Had it really been years since someone had touched her with kindness? Since she'd felt anything more than the fleeting bliss of momentary partners, lips that kissed her in the dark? Galina wanted to *hold* her.

"Yes," she whispered.

"Then come here."

Galina beckoned her to the armchair beside the fireplace. Vasilisa hoisted her kit, then rose from her wheelchair to settle between Galina's legs.

"Easy now," Galina said, her chin perched on Vasilisa's shoulder. She grasped the small wooden case of medicine bottles and held them out for Vasilisa.

Vasilisa relished the warmth and solace of Galina's arms. Then she withdrew her syringe from its container and plunged the needle into the first bottle to prepare the injection.

"What does this one do?" Galina's breath caressed Vasilisa's ear.

Vasilisa lifted her skirt to expose her thigh. "*Rars cuit,*" Vasilisa said as she pierced the meaty flesh of her leg. "Stabilizes my muscles for better movement."

She depressed the plunger and flinched at the sting of the medication as it infused into her veins. Her zmeya stirred at the intrusion, acutely aware of the foreign substance. It felt her pain and understood the toll of every public appearance.

Vasilisa proceeded with her next dose.

"And what about this one?" Galina inquired.

She positioned the syringe above her other thigh and

jabbed the needle in. "*Trib gleis.*" She drew a sharp breath as the remedy mingled with the previous injection. "Standard treatment. Slows the spread of the disease."

As she reached for another container, Vasilisa's pulse grew erratic. "*Vir tris,*" she said before Galina could ask. "Fights inflammation."

Galina's tender touch was like a thousand needles piercing Vasilisa's skin, but she couldn't push the other woman away. The feeling of Galina pressed against her was a comfort she never realized she needed during this agonizing process.

Vasilisa filled the syringe with the last vial, her hands trembling. "*Ciob hilne,*" she whispered, slowly pushing the needle in. The agony was excruciating, but it was a familiar pain she had grown used to.

As the drug took effect, the sensation drained away until all that remained was a lingering palpitation in her veins. She strained to hear her zmeya's voice, but it had fallen into a solemn stillness. Vasilisa longed for her dragon with a deep yearning, but when she tried to call to it, the god was distant. As if it was stranded in some far-off corner of her mind, as isolated as Vasilisa in her palace wing.

She leaned against Galina's chest, feeling the warmth radiating from her. Through a haze of numbness, Vasilisa gazed at the other woman with wonder. "I love you," she whispered.

Galina's fingers traced a gentle path along Vasilisa's cheek before she placed a tender kiss on her lips. "I love you too, Vasya."

As they marched down the corridor, Galina gripped Vasilisa's hand with fierce protectiveness. Guards had surrounded them the moment they stepped out of the Glasshouse Wing, and Vasilisa couldn't help but feel like a trapped animal.

Their leader, a smarmy bastard with a face that begged for a good beating, insisted that the dozen armed men trailing behind him were for her protection.

Galina's secret smile had sparked Vasilisa's dulled nerves back to life. *I love you,* she'd said.

And Vasilisa felt it with every cell of her being.

The alurean temple loomed ahead, its vaulted ceiling stretching high above them. It was the oldest part of the sprawling palace, built over a thousand years ago in tribute to the zmei of Smokova. A cruel joke of sorts, considering the dragons themselves were left to rot and die in alurean bodies while the temple walls boasted their image in glory. Winged beasts adorned every inch of stonework, symbols of freedom they would never know again.

The din echoed through the chamber, reverberating off the ancient stone walls. Vasilisa had heard this kind of noise before—worship ceremonies usually made for quite the spectacle—but this was different. These shouts were filled with an undeniable note of desperation.

Enough to make every hair on her arms stand on end.

Something was wrong.

Empress Isidora's gaze seared Galina and Vasilisa as they approached, her ire honing in on the interlaced fingers that betrayed their affection.

Isidora didn't concern herself with Vasilisa's love life; it was standard among the courtiers to engage in liaisons. But Vasilisa suspected her mother's animosity carried a calculation: how much did Galina know about Vasilisa's secret, and what did it mean for her already unstable empire?

"*Vuabo pue,*" Vasilisa said, dipping her head in greeting. "It's early for *obryad*, isn't it?"

The cacophony of the square swelled, but Vasilisa could only discern an indistinct mass past the gossamer veil. A frigid gust of wind tore through the temple hallway, bearing an acrid smell that constricted her throat. Smoke.

Dread descended on Vasilisa like a stone, pinning her to the ground.

"This isn't *obryad*." Isidora's tone was clipped. "You're to come out on the balcony with me. Show them your abilities. Remind them of the godfrost."

Galina and Vasilisa exchanged a worried glance. The only time her mother had ever summoned such a display of power was after Emperor Yuri's death. A warning to her enemies: *stand against us, and we'll tear you apart.*

Vasilisa leaned in, whispering, "Is everything all right, *vuabo pue*? Is it Sopol?"

Ignoring the question, the empress parted the curtains to reveal the harrowing sight below.

Vasilisa went motionless, unable to break her gaze away from the hordes outside Zolotiye. Not as many as during *obryad*, but enough—enough that their cries echoed through her mind like thunder. Enough that they crowded the road leading to the Blackshore.

What was left of it.

The city lay in ruins. Vasilisa surveyed the wreckage, the skeletal remains of buildings reaching toward the ashen sky like the fingers of the dead. The stench of smoke and death clung to the air, a grim reminder of what had been done here. From the Black to Khotchino, no area of the capital was unscathed by the fire that consumed it.

In the distance, flames still danced hungrily, devouring what little remained of the city. The wind carried the scent of burning rubble to the balcony, making Vasilisa's throat clench. She remembered the last time she had stood there, gazing out over the bustling streets and glittering spires. Now, there was only ruin.

Vasilisa's heart clenched as she surveyed the desperate, grieving crowd below. These were not joyful cries, but the wails of the broken and bereaved. Homes and livelihoods had been lost, families torn apart, lives destroyed.

Vasilisa rounded on her mother. "*What have you done?*"

A choked noise escaped Galina's lips. The sorrow and pain in her eyes spoke of a thousand tragedies, each a reminder of the empress's cruelty.

"I did what I had to do," Isidora declared, her chin high. "Our enemies have to be found, the faithless rooted out. War is coming, and I made my choice."

"But you didn't find your fugitives, did you?" Vasilisa spat. "If you had, we'd be watching their execution."

"I'll find them," Isidora promised, her voice chiseled from ice. "Even if I have to burn every building in the Blackshore to the ground."

Another broken sound left Galina, and Vasilisa wished she could take her away from Zolotiye and go somewhere safe. But there was no reprieve from Isidora—no refuge they could find.

Amidst the chaos and carnage, Vasilisa couldn't help but remember her mother so many years ago—the woman who had wept silently beside her bed and brought healers to save her only child. But had she been real? Or had Vasilisa's childhood adoration blinded her to the monster lurking beneath the surface?

"Don't do this," Vasilisa whispered, knowing Isidora could hear her over the crowd's clamor. "You have courtiers with enough power to rebuild the Blackshore. Send them out."

Isidora stood like a pillar of stone, her gaze unwavering. "When the faithless are all caught, I'll consider it. If the city shows me submission next *obryad.*"

The bile churned in Vasilisa's gut as her mother's words hit her like a punch to the stomach. "This isn't how you make them love you."

Isidora's gaze fixed on the frenzied mob below, a mass of bodies surging like the tides. "I don't want them to love me," she said, her voice low and dangerous. "I want them to fear me."

Isidora strode onto the balcony, her hand held high. The crowd's roar grew louder, and flames erupted around her, licking up her arm in a wild dance of godfire.

"Vasilochka." The empress gestured. "Come and let them see you." Galina's hand gripped Vasilisa's, but Isidora snapped, "Now, Vasilochka, or I'll have the guards remove her."

Galina's fingers slipped away, and Vasilisa stepped forward like a martyr to the lions.

Before she had fallen ill and withdrawn from the public—before her mother had shamed her into hiding like some disgraceful secret—Vasilisa's popularity had been unrivaled. She'd traveled the continent with an entourage of courtiers and diplomats, gracing every port, every town, and every city with her presence.

But that was a lifetime ago. Now Vasilisa was a ghost in her home, a shadow of the woman she'd once been.

The metropolis was a charred wasteland, the empire was on the brink of collapse, and where had she been all this time? Hidden away like a cursed princess in some tower, cultivating her plants like a godsdamn hermit. She had let her mother shame her into hiding from the world as if she were some scandalous secret.

No wonder the faithless movements were gaining traction, the uprisings were growing more common, and the Zverti publications proliferated like a rash. The people had no choice when one woman could set the city ablaze in minutes. Fire snaked down the empress's arm and moved with a will of its own, licking at her fingertips and growing ever brighter as her godpower surged. The flames seemed to curl around her limbs as if they were an extension of her. Vasilisa watched the fire shoot into the sky above the temple square, an inferno threatening to engulf the crowd below.

Galina knew that threat intimately, and Vasilisa had ignored it for too long.

She was complicit.

"Show your godfrost." The empress's voice reached Vasilisa as if from some great distance. "*Do it,* Vasilochka."

Vasilisa gritted her teeth and steeled herself for what was to come. The zmeya stirred sluggishly in her veins, its godpower a whisper of energy surrounding her in a frigid mist. Her arm rose, and frost erupted from her fingertips, crackling through the air like the chill of death itself. A show of strength that dispersed quickly.

Nothing like Isidora's godfire. Nothing like what the empress demanded from Vasilisa.

The crowd fell silent, either cowed or terrified by the reminder that Isidora and her daughter were not to be trifled with. With the spectacle complete, the empress grabbed Vasilisa and yanked her behind the curtains.

"You were holding back," Isidora snarled.

Heated anger rose within Vasilisa's veins, hotter than any godfire, born of all the years she'd quietly suffered and done this woman's bidding. For what?

For what?

"I won't perform for you, *vuabo pue,*" Vasilisa said, her voice a dangerous whisper. "Not anymore."

The empress bristled at the defiance, straightening up to address her sentries. "Take Vasilisa back to the Glasshouse Wing. Galina Feodorovna will remain with me."

Vasilisa's pulse sped up as she watched Galina's expression shift to one of worry. "Where are you taking Galina?"

Isidora scoffed at the question, gesturing impatiently to the sentries. "That's none of your concern. Take her."

As the guards moved in to escort Vasilisa away, Galina gave a slight nod of reassurance. But Vasilisa knew better than to take comfort in empty gestures. She had seen the darkness at the heart of this city, the twisted ambition that drove Isidora to do whatever it took to stay in power.

And she would not let her mother keep it.

58

SERA

Sera deposited the seedpods into her bowl with an audible exhale.

"That was quite the sigh," Vitaly remarked as he approached the worktable.

Being at ease with him was a curious comfort, a reprieve from the lies and half-truths that had shrouded their marriage. Fear of losing him was an iron anchor tethering her to the ground.

Vitaly's eyes met hers. "I can already tell you're overthinking whatever's going on inside that head of yours."

Sera ought to have been disconcerted by how effortlessly Vitaly could detect the slightest flicker of disquiet within her. But he'd been a fixture in her life for so long, he was like a sailor reading the sea's currents.

"How do you know what's going on in my head?" Sera asked, continuing to extract the small pods from the flower's innards.

"Impossible not to. You always drag twenty worries and fifty smaller nags behind you like a funeral procession," Vitaly said. "What is it?"

"Aside from the fact that Katya is still rotting in the hold while I sit here fumbling with these damn flowers? Tell me why we're not attempting a jailbreak."

"Because we can't risk it, and you're the only one who can finish this panacea. So what's making you doubt yourself?"

Sera squared her shoulders. "This is the *giche clinchan*," she murmured, holding the vibrant violet flower to the light. "Irina's panacea relies on a sap produced in its pods. The alurean archives listed ingredients needed for summoning and caging the gods, but not precise measurements. Irina died before she could figure out the right dosage of this."

Vitaly perused her notes, his brow furrowed in thought. "I'm guessing it's more complicated than adding more than your last attempt?"

"Damn right." Sera braced herself against the table and pointed at the bowl in front of her. "This is the only *giche clinchan* in the glasshouse, and I'm not sure it's enough. If I don't get this right, it could kill Galina. Or not work. Choose your disaster."

Vitaly hummed and stepped behind her. Before she could ask what he was doing, he placed his hands on her back, pressing his nimble fingers into her aching spine and kneading out every knot with expert skill. A sigh escaped her lips as warmth spread across her skin.

"Maybe the princess has other sources for the plant."

How was she supposed to concentrate when he touched her like this? Sera leaned forward with a soft moan.

"Even if she could," she eventually replied, "it takes years for these flowers to bloom; we don't have that kind of time." She paused. "Lower back, please."

Vitaly complied and chuckled low in his throat. "So, too much and she'll die; too little and it's useless. No wonder you're all tense."

"Maybe I'm tense because I've had no one to rub my aching back in years."

"My poor neglected wife."

Vitaly's fingers danced down Sera's spine, coaxing away the residual pain. And it wasn't just *her* that responded to Vitaly's touch. His hands softened the rough edges of the dragon's scales beneath Sera's vertebrae with deft movements. She felt her zmeya pulse with pleasure.

The god's reaction was clear: it liked Vitaly more than her.

"Anything else I can do for you, *vorovka*?" he murmured, his lips soft against her nape.

"A thousand things we don't have time for," Sera replied with a hint of regret.

"And no time to make, I suppose?" he asked in a whisper that made her skin flush.

Sera sighed, knowing they couldn't risk it. "Not today."

"I want a list of a thousand things, then. Later."

Let us have a later, she thought as she stared over the worktable.

Sera reached for the bowl of purple flowers when the glasshouse door burst open. Princess Vasilisa rushed inside, clutching a newspaper. She was light on her feet, with no sign of the cane she needed for support.

"How close are you to finishing the panacea?" Her voice was like sandpaper, all raw edges and agitation. Sweat glistened on her brow, and her chest heaved beneath the thick fabric of her coat.

Frankly, she looked like she might vomit on Sera's shoes at any moment—the princess must have taken a considerable dose of her treatments to walk without difficulty.

Vitaly instinctively put himself between Sera and the interloper. The princess was still an unknown quantity, and in their business, unknowns were bad news. Especially when they were alurea.

But Sera knew they couldn't afford to act on old instincts anymore, not if they wanted to survive this war. They needed allies, even if they came in unexpected packages.

"Close," Sera replied, setting a hand on Vitaly's shoulder in an unspoken directive to stand down. He promptly stepped aside. "What's wrong?"

The princess gripped the table's edge for balance. "My mother is burning the city down," she gasped out. "I saw it from the temple. The damage is… it's worse than anything I've seen before."

Sera felt her heart kick up a notch.

"How bad?" Vitaly asked, his voice low and dangerous.

"Bad enough that people are gathering at the gates, begging for mercy. But the empress won't listen. She's taking Galina out into the streets." Vasilisa held out a newspaper to Sera. "The names you asked me to find are in here. Finish the panacea, and I'll help you get to safety."

Sera snatched the broadsheet from Vasilisa's hands and scanned the obituaries for the three aliases she knew so well: Maria Pavlovna Filosofova, Matrena Nikolaeva Zhelyabova, and Evgenia Ivanovna Bochechkarova. It was a relief to see them there, coded in Anna's usual shorthand. It meant she was still alive.

"Anna says to meet her tomorrow at the abandoned mill on the north road, at the junction closest to Chembar," Sera said. "But what about Katya?" she asked, looking up at Vasilisa.

The princess flinched as if Sera had slapped her. "My mother has the palace heavily garrisoned. If I order them to free Katya, I won't be able to get Galina the panacea."

Sera threw the paper down in frustration, jaw hardening. "I can't just take off and leave them here."

"Sera," Vitaly said, his voice a warning.

She knew what that tone meant. He'd used it often enough in Sundyr when she'd gotten too close to danger for comfort—to remind her she was no good to anyone dead.

But this wasn't some covert operation or a stranger's life on the line. This was Katya—who had spent six years facing the empress's wrath and had yet to experience freedom—and Galina, whose bond with Sera went deeper than blood.

She'd made promises she intended to keep.

"I said I'm not leaving." She ignored the exasperated sound from her husband and turned to Vasilisa. "Is there any way to break Katya out of the hold without involving you?"

Vasilisa shook her head. "It was built to imprison high-risk traitors. The only way she's coming out of there is when it's time for her execution, and my mother won't do that until she has you both in custody."

Sera's mind raced, recklessly calculating the odds of success. Death seemed to be the common denominator in each plan, with the only difference being how quickly and painfully it would come for her. She could only choose the least shitty of her schemes and hope for the best.

Her husband studied her, all too aware of what imbecilic ideas filled her thoughts. "That particular look never seems to bode well."

"Wait, what does it mean?" Vasilisa asked him.

"That's her death-wish face. The last time she had it, I ended up with a knife in my shoulder. Just ignore it."

Sera rolled her eyes. "We got out alive last time, didn't we? And I patched you up real nice. You know full well our options right now are all stupid."

Vitaly shrugged nonchalantly. "There's always the option that serves ourselves."

"This would be much easier if you didn't subject every damn scheme to your twisted moral compass."

"Don't blame me for calling out your reckless plan." He ran his fingers through his hair. "Fine, let's hear it."

Sera straightened, steeling herself against any objections that may come her way. "We'll get ourselves arrested. Provide the empress with a compelling enough reason to order our immediate execution. That way, we'll all be together in the square."

Vitaly's expression darkened. "We'll be surrounded by courtiers and guards," he said, his voice raw with emotion. "If anything goes wrong, we won't stand a chance of escaping."

"He's right," Princess Vasilisa interjected, her tone calm and composed in contrast to Sera's agitated husband. "Not every courtier fled after the bombing. Many would love to watch the traitors responsible burn."

"That won't happen if you get the panacea to Galina," Sera argued.

"And if it doesn't work?" Vitaly asked her. "If your ingredients are wrong and there's nothing between us and the empress's godfire?"

Sera and Vitaly's gazes collided, the silence tense with unspoken words.

It was agonizing, the way he looked at her—as if he envisioned her already immolated, her ashes carried by the winter winds. But she had to stay and battle for the Blackshore. Sacrificing Tumanny citizens for more time with him wasn't an option.

That was a line she wouldn't cross.

"You knew there was always a possibility it would end like this," she said quietly. "We both did."

As Vitaly reached for Sera, Vasilisa wordlessly stepped into one of the glasshouse aisles to give them privacy.

He cradled her face, thumb tracing the angle of her cheekbone. "Look at me," he whispered in Zverti. His pale gray gaze searched hers desperately. "Tell me if this is what you want. If you're in, I'm in. I'll stand by your side and burn with you if it comes to that. But I'm a selfish bastard. And I've got four years to make up for. *Four years*, Sera. Let me take it. Let me steal it if I have to."

Sera sighed and took his hand, pressing her lips to his knuckles. "And yet you followed me into every operation in Sundyr. Strange, for a selfish bastard."

Vitaly offered a small smile. "Well, you know me, *vorovka*.

You keep playing the hero, and someone had to remind you martyrs make for more funerals than victories. Between the two of us, I was always the villain."

"You also said martyrs breed more revolutionaries than criminals."

"Fuck what I said," he growled.

She grinned, cupping his cheek. "That's more like it. Now come on. Us dying of old age was never the likely scenario. We always knew it'd be you and me fighting back. If not today, then tomorrow or a fortnight from now. But *today*, we might just live."

She thought he would argue, try to convince her to leave once more. But she should have known better. Vitaly Sergeyevich Rysakov didn't beg, and even though he possessed a ruthless heart, that ruthless heart was *hers*.

He pressed his lips against hers, hard and hungry. Warmth flooded her as she pulled him closer, desperate for more of him. His touch was electric, and she could feel the heat of his desire as she lifted his shirt, seeking the texture of his skin. Vitaly groaned as her nails dug into his back, and some wild passion took hold. He tugged on her hair, baring the line of her throat to him as if it were an offering. His breathing was ragged as his lips skimmed against her pulse.

But time was not on their side—and she couldn't bargain for more.

Sera held him close before finally pulling away. Vitaly gazed at her with lust-filled eyes, panting. Sera wished they could have stayed that way forever.

"So, is that a yes?"

He chuckled, the sound hoarse. "That wasn't a yes. *That* was an incentive. We live through this, and I'll make good on that promise."

59

GALINA

The view from the empress's carriage was devastating.

The wheels clacked and rattled as they struggled to progress down the once immaculate cobblestone street, now reduced to a battlefield. The wind mavens tried to sweep the debris aside, but it was futile. Piles of rubble littered the road, with crowds of angry citizens gathering around them, shouting dissent.

Sentries fought to keep the enraged commoners at bay, but their godpower was no match for the collective fury of the people. Shouts and jeers rose above the din of horse hooves and carriage wheels, each word carrying an unmistakable message of grief and rage.

Watching from the safety of the imperial coach, Galina saw the despair etched on the faces of her fellow citizens. Their hands reached out in desperation, begging for recognition or justice. The soldiers, dressed in gleaming armor, used godpower to push back the crowd, but it only fueled their anger. Galina couldn't make out the words they were shouting, but she could feel the intensity of their emotion.

The stench of smoke, ash, and death filled the air. The cries of those who had lost everything in the empress's search reverberated around Galina like a physical force, crashing over her in a staggering wave.

It was like she was eight years old again, huddled in her parents' cottage cellar, trying to protect herself from the flames that raged above. The odor, then as now, threatened to overwhelm her; the screams of the dying nearly carried her away.

Galina couldn't save Olensk. But she could help the Blackshore.

"Look at them," Empress Isidora murmured, cutting through the chaos. "Remember what I told you about how fickle supplicants are? Today they'll worship you, and tomorrow they'll betray you."

Galina's fingernails bit into her palms as she faced the empress. "Is that why you've razed half the city, Your Imperial Majesty?" she asked, maintaining a mask of composure. "To remind the people of the consequences of betrayal?"

The urge to lunge across the carriage and choke the life from the empress was almost irresistible. She could feel her zmeya thrumming, begging for release. It longed to reduce the sneering visage before her to smoldering ash.

But Isidora couldn't be burned while she was bonded to a dragon with the godfire—and Galina couldn't help anyone from the palace hold.

Soon, she'd do more than sit by and watch this woman destroy lives.

"Maybe." Her eyes narrowed as she peered out over the ashen remains of the Tumanny capital. "Or maybe it's to remind these ungrateful wretches of what we are." Isidora trailed her fingers along the window frame of her carriage. "My guards have uncovered a mountain of seditious paraphernalia in this city. These people see us on the royal balcony and forget we're vessels for creatures of destruction.

Disloyalty can't be tolerated." A ferocity crept into the empress's voice. "But what about your god? What does it tell you?"

Galina's zmeya coiled tightly within her, restless and dangerous. But it was hers, and she refused to let it control her. She had no intention of becoming a person who sacrificed an entire village for the sake of war.

"I don't have the same connection to mine, Your Imperial Majesty," Galina replied.

But her wrath would have its uses later.

The empress regarded her with a mixture of disappointment and contempt. "What a shame," she said as the carriage stopped. "If you bonded deeper with your zmeya, you'd understand why the faithless should be punished. We're the ones who caged the gods, and the zmei were born to destroy. We should welcome that instinct. It's our birthright."

It was time to disembark. The carriage door opened into the haze-filled streets—a thick stench of smoke wafting through the air. As they stepped from the conveyance, an eruption of noise slammed into them—screams so loud they shook the remaining buildings and rattled windows. Guards shouted over the din while godpower crackled in the atmosphere, shoving commoners to the ground with enough force to break bones.

But the alurea could not muffle their words: *Vmonkt pror va! Vmonkt pror va!*

The empress stood beside Galina, her expression cold. "Listen to them. Half their city is ash, and they spit in the face of their monarch by defying my laws and speaking their language. Their insubordination flourished under my husband's rule. That's why he's rotting in his grave."

The empress couldn't fathom the turmoil in Galina's soul; this woman didn't speak Zverti. Banning it had only stoked resentment—what kind of leaders couldn't understand the language of their subjects? Who employed their ignorance as another weapon of oppression? The empress didn't know that the people in that mob weren't using Zverti to defy *her* but to implore Galina.

Begging her to save them.

Galina wasn't like their monarch. Her zmeya wasn't a deity to be worshipped—it was a captive. Her body was a cage for a being forcibly extracted from its realm and thrust into a foreign host.

Her zmeya writhed against her bones, an imprisoned animal clawing for freedom with every breath. Freedom she'd never be able to give it, even if she wanted. She couldn't break her own bond with the lustrate.

"Why did you bring me here, Your Imperial Majesty?" Galina spoke softly.

"So they witnessed you standing beside me after all they've lost," Empress Isidora replied. "And so they know you're mine."

Galina fought to maintain her composure as power tingled at her fingertips. Her dragon roared like the colossal beast it was, stretching within its enclosure with an unwavering thirst for destruction.

Not yet, she murmured to it. *Not yet. Your blaze couldn't harm the empress.*

Not. Yet.

A soldier abruptly diverged from the others, bolting over to where a man adorned in a general's uniform stood, awaiting the empress's acknowledgment. The soldier whispered anxiously in the man's ear.

Satisfaction flickered across the general's face as he muttered something to the soldier in a low voice, then dispatched him back into formation. The general strode forward and bowed before the empress. "Your Imperial Majesty," he intoned.

The empress regarded him coolly, gesturing for him to rise. "General Dukhonin," she responded. "I trust you'll perform better than your predecessor—General Vasilchikov turned out to be... lacking."

"You'll be pleased to know my officers have located and captured the criminals you wanted," the general reported triumphantly.

Galina felt like a million knives had pierced her heart. Sera? Captured? That couldn't be true.

Empress Isidora's expression was a fortress. The kind of look that could make even the bravest soldiers tremble. "Choose your next words carefully. If you tell me you've caught my fugitives, they'd better be the ones I want. Otherwise, I'll have to find another general to finish the job."

General Dukhonin looked about to swallow his tongue, but he managed to nod. "You have my word. They were trying to breach Zolotiye's walls with explosives."

Galina's heart clenched in an iron grip as fear and worry threatened to consume her.

The thought of losing Sera was too much to bear. How could she be so foolish? What had Sera been *thinking*? Why would her sister risk herself like this?

Damn it, Sera.

She tamped down her emotions before the empress noticed her panic.

"Take them to the temple square," Isidora said, her voice dripping with satisfaction. "And send one of your men to fetch Ekaterina Isidorakh from the hold. Summon the courtiers. I won't let these terrorists live another day." She turned to Galina. "You'll sit by my side."

Galina forced herself to maintain a calm façade as they climbed back into the conveyance. Her hands wouldn't stop trembling. She knew she had to control her emotions; any sign of weakness could be fatal.

She had to trust that Sera was too clever to be caught doing something as reckless as this. Sera always had a plan.

She *had* to have a plan.

The carriage wound up the steep, narrow route to Zolotiye's temple, but Galina hardly noticed the city's devastation as they passed. The news of the execution had spread among the gathered crowds, and the commoners bustled up the road toward the public square, where the killing platform stood as a permanent fixture outside the temple. It was a stark reminder that every supplicant put to death was a betrayer of their gods, a traitor to their country.

Galina was numb as the conveyance rolled to a stop. She and the empress stepped onto the glittering marble square where the royals murdered so many. As they made their way to the dais, Isidora signaled the guards to bring the prisoners.

And Galina watched as Sera, Vitaly, and Katya emerged, flanked by sentries.

60

SERA

Sera's nostrils flared at the reek of smoke and ruin.

The vile scent cut through the air that hung like a shroud over the Blackshore. The once-proud metropolis was now reduced to a war zone.

But there was no enemy army here. No distant invaders sought to conquer and plunder. No, just an empress who had turned against her people.

Vitaly tugged hard at his restraints. Sera could feel the same ferocity building inside of her. The weight of the alurean atrocities threatened to drive the last breath from her lungs.

The guards shoved Sera and Vitaly forward. Ahead of them, a group of soldiers marched in formation, escorting Katya. The former handmaiden had an air of resignation, as if she had already accepted her fate. Sera noticed what could only be evidence of torture: a gash crossing her cheekbone, purpling bruises marring her jawline, and a split lip.

When Katya had seen Sera and Vitaly being arrested earlier, she'd paled with alarm. But a meaningful glance from Sera had silenced her, communicating that their capture was no mistake.

Sera's plan was risky.

She was putting her trust in an alurean princess.

Shouts echoed as the sentries dragged Sera and Vitaly past the temple gates and into the square beyond. This hastily arranged execution lacked the pomp and circumstance of previous high-profile killings—the kind that Sera and Vitaly might have been subjected to in normal circumstances.

The *Tumanny Courier* had advertised Irina's execution as a macabre show, luring people from all corners of the land to witness that grisly scene. But this time, the sentries kept the commoners locked outside the square, fearing their wrath if things turned ugly. Guards lined the gilded portcullis, ready to unleash godpower against any who threatened to upset the monarchy's tyrannical display.

The angry chorus of curses and insults from beyond those gates echoed louder. Was it directed at Sera? Executions always seemed to attract the most motley assortment of onlookers, from faithless to loyalists alike, yet never before had the Blackshore seen its monarch turn on her people so viciously.

The square was a morbid carnival, complete with the royal boxes flanking the platform. Courtiers sat like a bunch of stuffed peacocks in their fancy silks and fur-lined coats. They were arranged according to rank, with the most powerful given prime spots to gawk at the prisoners.

There were fewer of those pompous assholes, thanks to Vitaly's bombing. The blast didn't just take out lives—it sent many nobles running to their country estates or wherever the hell they could hide. If Sera's panacea didn't work, the courtiers outside of Blackshore would learn of her demise over morning tea.

They'd celebrate her murder.

The crowd parted as two women approached the dais near the killing platform: Empress Isidora and Galina. Sera barely recognized her sister, all finely coiffed in an elegant dress. Galina's expression was tight, and when she met Sera's eyes, something shifted in her countenance.

Sera knew Galina was worried, and she couldn't do anything to let her know about the plan. Sera and Vitaly would be ash in minutes if the empress had the slightest inkling.

Galina stood next to the empress, who eyed the captives with the same disdain one would reserve for vermin.

Sera stumbled forward as the guard shoved her, causing her to bump into Vitaly and Katya as they climbed the stairs to the platform. Fury pulsed through her, an emotion her zmeya comprehended. She and the bastard dragon were in angry agreement.

The empress's gaze shifted from Sera to Vitaly, her pleasure unmistakable and cruel. "You haven't lied to me, General Dukhonin," she said, turning to the uniformed man behind her. "These are the ones. You'll be rewarded handsomely for your work."

"Thank you, Your Imperial Majesty," he murmured.

"And their names?"

"Vitaly Sergeyevich Rysakov and Serafima Mikhailovna Rysakova, Your Imperial Majesty. You'll be pleased to know they were already wanted on charges of sedition."

The empress's lips curved into a smile as sharp as a knife's edge. "Married? How fortunate they get to die together. Not everyone is so lucky."

A cacophony of noise rose from the courtier boxes. The empress turned to observe her closest alurea, who stood to gawk at the prisoners and hurl insults.

Sera could hear the cries for her death, for Vitaly's, and for Katya's. Beyond the boxes, the crowd outside the gates was an incomprehensible jumble of sound. From Sera's position, she could hardly make out their faces or separate their screams.

The empress raised a slender hand, and silence descended like a deathly pall across the congregation. Her voice was crystalline sharp above the clamor: "Loyal courtiers and faithful supplicants of the Blackshore, my heart bleeds for the anguish we've all suffered together—"

Vitaly snorted and muttered a low insult that would have made Sera grin if not for the fact that they were about to die.

"—I understand these past few days have not been easy. But once I purge the faithless from our city, we'll rebuild it stronger. A shining beacon to withstand rebels and invading armies. We'll defeat them all." She gestured to Sera, Vitaly, and Katya. "These prisoners betrayed me, they betrayed you, and they betrayed Tumanny. When you watch them burn today, remember that."

Raucous, irreverent cries erupted from the courtier boxes. Clashing yells came from the throng of citizens. Vitaly edged closer to Sera, their limbs colliding. It was a small gesture, but one she clung to as if it could offer her deliverance.

The empress strode amongst her captives again, her heels clicking a menacing rhythm on the marble dais. "I'll be merciful and grant a swift end to those who plead. Will my prisoners use the opportunity to ask my forgiveness?"

"Eat shit," Vitaly snarled.

A guard turned and punched Vitaly in the gut, sinking him to the ground. Empress Isidora's smile didn't waver as she leaned down and gripped Vitaly's chin tightly. "As for you, Vitaly Sergeyevich, I'll be creative. I'll torture and toy with you until you grovel at my feet and beg me to end you."

He spat in the empress's face.

The empress's eyes blazed. The guard made to pounce, but she halted him with a mere gesture, then signaled to an attendant stationed near the dais. The servant dutifully produced a handkerchief. "For that, your wife goes before you. A slow death while you watch," she hissed, dabbing at herself with the cloth. "Your husband sealed your fate, Serafima Mikhailovna."

"If you had grabbed me first," Sera said, "you'd be wearing my spit instead of his."

Empress Isidora's lips drew taut. Rather than scolding Sera, the empress approached her final captive. "And what about you, Ekaterina Isidorakh?" she said, her voice thick with some emotion that surprised Sera. "Will you spit in my face or plead for forgiveness?"

Katya's lifted her chin, exposing her battered and bloodied visage to the light. Her quiet resistance was a thing of beauty. "How many times have I begged for mercy throughout the years, *suvya*?"

Isidora sighed and brushed her fingers over the handmaiden's cheek. "I've never spared traitors, *knesi*," she murmured. "But if you kiss my ring and pledge your loyalty, I'll provide you with a chamber as grand as mine."

"A prison," Katya said flatly.

"Call it a prison or call it home. You'll be safe there."

"I won't kiss your ring, *suvya*. I won't give you another day of my life."

Isidora's hand dropped, and her countenance hardened. "Then prepare for a slow death, like the others."

She took a step back and scrutinized her prisoners once more. Sera's heart pounded against her ribcage as the empress prepared her godpower. Where was Vasilisa?

Behind the empress, Galina's self-control began to crumble. Her shoulders straightened as she braced for a fight. Sera imperceptibly shook her head: *hold on*.

Wait.

But Isidora readied a blast, and the heat of her godfire rippled through the surrounding air. Flames danced along her fingertips. She parted her lips to speak—

"*Mother!*"

Isidora turned sharply to where Vasilisa emerged from the palace, steering her wheelchair through the archway. Sera grinned.

The princess had finally come to their rescue.

61

VASILISA

Vasilisa's shoulders heaved with labored exhales, her lungs burning from exertion as she emerged from the palace.

After completing the panacea with Sera, she'd injected herself with a reversal agent to neutralize the effects of her treatments. A risky move, but it was the only way to communicate with her zmeya without succumbing to the drug's influence. As much as Vasilisa would've preferred to use her energy to create a door from the Glasshouse Wing to the square, that would have taken more godpower than she could spare. Leaving Galina unprotected was not an option.

Vasilisa wouldn't take chances. Not today.

Both decisions came with the detriment of pain. Crossing the palace's immense corridors—for the second time that day—was a dizzying journey that left Vasilisa short of breath. Sweat had dripped from her temples, and cold shivers had run through her body. The palace was never designed with mobility aids in mind, and Vasilisa had to use godpower more than once to lift her chair and descend a series of stairs.

The godpower left her dizzy and disoriented. But she clenched her jaw and forced herself onward, paying no mind to the gawking onlookers. Her thoughts were razors honed to a deadly edge: *get to Galina; protect the city.*

Winter winds whipped through the square as Vasilisa urged her chair forward. Thank the gods, the mavens had cleared the snow. But even then, every jolt of movement sent fresh waves of pain through her chest. She took a deep breath and another, steeling herself for what was to come.

Heads swiveled toward Vasilisa. Hundreds of eyes locked onto her as she came into the light, unashamed and undaunted. A sense of calm descended over her as she held her ground, staring back at them all.

Let them see her. Let them know.

The pain had always been there, a constant thrum of discomfort she had long grown accustomed to. But this strange buoyancy in her weary bones was new, almost... pleasant. The loneliness had dug so deep that she never realized it had weight to it. Was this what it felt like to stop hiding?

The courtiers murmured in disbelief. The crowd outside the gates gasped. It was unheard of for an alurea to present themselves in public with anything less than perfect health and vitality. Even those injured in the recent bombing wouldn't dare show themselves with such blatant evidence of their wounds. Vasilisa's appearance was bold, laying her physical vulnerabilities bare for potential enemies to exploit.

Vasilisa didn't give a damn. She could not get from the Glasshouse Wing to the temple without the aid of her chair, and Galina needed her help.

And there was one person she wanted to witness her like this: fierce and brave—no longer isolated in that remote palace wing.

No more hiding in shadows.

"Mother," she said again, lower this time. The acoustics of the square carried her voice.

Isidora blanched at the sight of her. Vasilisa was aware of the sweat dripping down her forehead, the trembling in her limbs. To her mother, these were signs of weakness; to Vasilisa, they were symbols of rebellion.

Go ahead, look at me, she thought, gripping the armrests of her chair. *Take a good long look and know you won't control me anymore. I refuse to be a prisoner in the Glasshouse Wing, waiting for you to decide what to do with me. Want to kill me? Now's your chance.*

Look. At. Me.

Vasilisa ground her teeth and readied herself. She braced her muscles, hardening them like tempered steel, turning her determination into a suit of armor.

"Vasilochka," her mother hissed. "What are you doing?" Empress Isidora marched down the steps of the platform and seized Vasilisa's arm. "Stand up and come with me. We'll pretend this is all the whims of a spoiled princess."

From the corner of her eye, Vasilisa saw Sera preparing to use the godpower that would free her, Vitaly, and Katya from their shackles. All she needed was one more moment of distraction.

Vasilisa stayed seated in her chair as if it was her godsdamned throne. No empress, army, or god could move her from that seat. She had a thick cloth in her dress folds, concealing a syringe and some weapons.

"No, *vuabo pue*. I won't do that for you. Not anymore."

Empress Isidora's eyes darted from Vasilisa to her stunned courtiers and then to the throngs of people gathered outside the gate. Straightening her spine, she assumed the stance of a battle-hardened commander.

That was the crux of it, wasn't it? Isidora had fought Vasilisa's sickness like an invading army, hoping to cover up her weaknesses. And when that didn't work, she treated it like a gaping hole in her defenses. Isidora was so consumed by appearances that she'd rather bury her daughter beneath six feet of dirt than let the world see her.

Empress Isidora swung her focus back to Vasilisa. "Don't push me, Vasilochka," she said through her teeth as heat spread from her touch. "I said *stand.*"

"And I said *no.*"

Isidora's grip tightened, sending waves of pain through Vasilisa's arm. The prickling sensations mixed with her mother's godpower, creating a searing agony that threatened to overwhelm her. Vasilisa's zmeya hissed and coiled with a strength equal to her mother's god.

Isidora's eyes narrowed, and the air crackled with energy. "You're making me regret not choosing the poison, *fle cui,*" she growled. "I may not put you on that platform with our traitors, but I'll fix the mistake one way or another."

Mistake?

Vasilisa's eyes flicked past her mother to Galina. She saw the love there, the resilience and support, filling her with a renewed sense of purpose. She wasn't a mistake, wasn't weak or shameful.

She had her own power, her own courage.

And she knew how to use it.

"You can try," she said in a low voice. "But I don't think you have what it takes to break me."

Her godpower surged, a rush that coursed through her veins. Her zmeya roared, finally free to unleash the godfrost it had been forbidden to wield for years. For three decades, her zmeya had been a caged beast. A dragon turned house pet. But it was still a predator above all else, driven by a primal desire for destruction.

And destruction it would have.

Later, Vasilisa would pay the price for channeling her god.

Empress Isidora recoiled as Vasilisa's chill reached her skin. Her face twisted with comprehension as she realized Vasilisa was no longer her obedient daughter.

Never again.

"*Vasilisa!*"

Sera's urgent shout rang across the square, a call that Vasilisa answered without hesitation. With a flick of her wrist, she tossed the cloth-bound package to Sera's feet and unleashed the full might of her godpower in a deafening battle cry.

The godfrost exploded from her fingers, hurtling toward the empress with a thousand razor-sharp shards of ice. But Isidora countered with a scorching blast of godfire.

The godpower met in a show of force that shook the stones beneath them. Fire clashed with frost, and Vasilisa gritted her teeth against the agonizing impact of her mother's godfire. Her ability had laid entire armies to waste and ruined whole kingdoms, and Vasilisa knew she couldn't withstand her mother's assault forever.

She just needed to hold on long enough for Galina to make her move.

62

GALINA

Galina watched with grim determination as a guard lunged toward Sera. His godpower was poised to strike, but Galina unleashed a blast of fire so fierce that it instantly engulfed the sentry.

The other guards responded quickly, unleashing a barrage of godpower that would have made even the most seasoned warrior tremble. But Galina was ready for them. She channeled her zmeya and summoned a wall of flame surrounding her and her allies, shielding them from harm.

The godpower bounced harmlessly off the fiery barrier, leaving the courtiers and guards circling on the outside. Galina smiled smugly; they were no match for her god. Only the empress could challenge her—and right now, she was preoccupied with Vasilisa.

But that wouldn't last forever.

Sera hurried over, plucking at the strings on a thick parcel of cloth. "That was quick thinking," she told Galina as she kneeled to set the bundle on the ground.

Vitaly snorted. "Can't believe that fucking princess

pulled through," he said, watching his wife. "Thought for sure she'd let us burn."

"I'm half tempted to finish the job," Galina snapped, crouching beside Sera. "You had me worried out of my damn mind. I would have liked some warning. Katya, were you in on this madness?"

The handmaiden shook her head, her bruised jawline catching the flickering light of the blaze. "I was just as shocked as you were."

"Stop bitching, *vitsvi*," Sera said to Galina. "I made a call, took a shitty plan. Vitalik gave me an earful about it."

"Should've given you more than that," Vitaly grumbled.

Galina's grip on her godpower tightened as the platform temperature rose. She could handle it—she had always withstood the flames—but the others were already sweating.

Sera unrolled the bundle and revealed a syringe and four throwing knives. Galina felt a surge of relief mixed with unease as Sera started prepping the injection.

A crack of thunder shattered the uneasy silence, drawing everyone's attention. The clouds blackened with foreboding—the weather mavens were about to unleash a raging storm to extinguish the godfire. Holding on to her fiery barricade during the deluge would take every ounce of strength Galina had.

"Hurry up, Sera," Vitaly said.

"Not helping," Sera replied sharply. She passed him a bundle of weapons. "Here. These are for you. Make yourself useful and go throw knives at some mavens."

"Sharp toys *and* your permission to slaughter alurea?" Vitaly grinned with delight. "Ah, *vorovka*, my beautiful orchestrator of mayhem, you always know the way to my heart."

The rain soaked the platform in a matter of seconds. Galina was drenched through, her clothes clinging to her skin.

"Arm," Sera commanded her brusquely.

Galina shook off the waterlogged coat and held out her arm. "How long will this take?"

"Not a damn clue," Sera said. Rivulets of rainwater and sweat ran down her face, but she wiped it away without pause. "Hopefully, fast enough that we won't die. How's our defense looking?"

"It's holding." Galina glanced at Vasilisa, still locked in combat with Isidora.

It was difficult to make out anything through the flames of her godfire—but even from here, Vasilisa's posture was unmistakably weary. Galina's composure wavered at the sight, her flame wall sputtering and thinning. Vasilisa had already endured several treatments and made the arduous trek to the temple. Gods alone knew how long she could maintain the godfrost.

"Don't watch her right now," Sera warned as she jabbed the needle into Galina's arm. "Be ready. This is going to hurt, and you'll lose control of the godfire."

"And what about—" Galina swallowed. *You*. "What about you?"

Sera managed a faint smile on her lips. "I'm a survivor, remember? But I want you to know that it's been an honor having you as my sister. You were the one thing my mother got right."

She depressed the plunger and forced the panacea into Galina's veins. And Galina's entire body erupted in pain.

63

SERA

Sera stepped back as Galina's mouth opened in a soundless scream. The godfire that surrounded them blazed brighter as her body shuddered and twisted. Worry clawed at Sera's heart, but she had no time to dwell on it now.

The rain drummed against the flaming barrier that held like a bulwark against the sentries, close to snuffing out their sanctuary at any second. Courtiers and guards lurked in the gap between the inferno, ready for a war that could end with spilled blood. The mavens' tempest strangled Galina's defenses, made vulnerable by the pain of the panacea.

It was only a matter of time before it would give out.

Katya stood beside Sera, determination etched into her features. She looked as if she was prepared to face death itself.

"Katya," Sera said, drawing the other woman's attention. "Watch over Galya. Stay by her side; guide her through this."

Katya nodded, her eyes resolute and focused. "And you?" she asked.

Sera's smile was brittle. "I'll keep you both safe for as long as I can."

Without wasting a moment, Katya kneeled next to Galina, who had curled up on the marble platform. Sera stared into the waning fire and refused to surrender to fear. She couldn't afford to slip into that dark abyss; if she did, she'd be right back where she started, a scared little girl forced to watch her sister suffer under Irina's cruel treatments.

But Sera was not her mother.

A warm, calloused hand grasped hers, and Sera lifted her eyes to see Vitaly standing beside her, his gaze steady—her anchor in the storm.

Give me your godpower for him, she begged her zmeya. *Not for me. For him.*

The bastard dragon stretched and yawned. Sera had pleaded with the god too many times, and its rejection had become routine. She had ignored its language again, stubbornly trying to bargain with anything other than the blood price it always wanted.

But then, with a suddenness that caught her off guard, the zmeya pressed its limb against her palm—gripping Vitaly's hand with her. He jerked in surprise, but didn't pull away. The dragon's soft purr of satisfaction rumbled through her.

Sera saw her opportunity for victory and seized it. "Kiss me," she whispered to Vitaly.

He obeyed without hesitation. No questions asked, no answers demanded. His lips were soft as they met hers—a kiss with the intensity of a last breath.

A last touch.

Gods, she hoped not. She wanted another chance to make things right—to have that life together that had always felt out of reach.

Her god reveled in their kiss. After so many years of demanding sacrifice, here was something it craved more than blood: adoration. For once, her dragon understood reverence—and love.

Sera pressed her forehead to Vitaly's as her protective god-power roared to life. The dragon spoke in the Exalted Tongue, and Sera's shield expanded around them. Safeguarding the only one who had ever shown it affection.

The one who'd claimed Sera's heart.

Her shining barrier slammed into place just as the wall of godfire guttered out. It resonated with the energy of a satisfied god—that was a first for Sera.

Vitaly's gaze drifted over the luminescent shield. "No blood price?"

"My zmeya likes you."

Vitaly grinned. "Little dragon, I might just have to return the favor."

Such a damn charmer.

Her zmeya thrummed with contentment.

Then Sera's shield shook as a sudden wave of godpower struck. Vitaly moved in a flash, his blade slicing through her barrier with deadly precision.

Vitaly flashed a feral grin. "Weather maven in the neck," he announced.

No wonder her god favored him; he was fluent in the language of chaos.

She shook her head, laughing despite herself. "You're all kinds of messed up, you know that?"

"You wouldn't have me any other way," Vitaly said, putting his arms around her. "I let you boss me."

"And I love bossing you." She stepped closer and nipped at his jaw, whispering, "Now shut up and kiss me again."

He needed no further encouragement.

And Sera's dragon held the shield, stronger and steadier than ever.

64

VASILISA

Vasilisa swayed in her chair, her body trembling with the effort of controlling the godfrost.

It had been years since she'd channeled godpower for longer than a few minutes, let alone wielded the godfrost as a weapon. The strain was almost too much to bear, her fingers numb and unresponsive as she struggled to maintain control.

Across the square, Isidora glared at her with a look of grim determination, a fierce fire burning in her eyes. She was not playing games. Vasilisa could see it, feel it in the scorching heat of the godfire that threatened to consume her.

But she wasn't about to back down.

She knew she'd given her mother ample reason to put her down; Isidora's options were limited now. In their court, poison or a blade would have been seen as acts of mercy—a way to spare a broken child from a life of suffering. Choices long gone. All that was left was this vicious, merciless battle, a fight to the death between a mother and her daughter.

They were enemies now.

But Vasilisa refused to go quietly. Icy blue flames danced at her fingertips and through the air between them, rising to meet a swirling shroud of mist. She channeled all her energy and willpower into keeping it from sputtering out.

Godfire pushed against her, but Vasilisa was ready. She surrendered to the strength of the zmeya's embrace. Its scales flexed and moved beneath her skin like armor—an additional layer of defense against the onslaught of fire.

She might not survive this battle, but she was determined to go down fighting.

The intensity was almost unbearable as the two forces clashed. The air distorted under the pressure of their struggle while sparks of flame and ice flew in all directions. Heat and electricity crackled as they fought, godfire and godfrost weaving around each other like beasts. Sweat beaded Vasilisa's forehead as she stood firm against her mother's attack.

"Drop the godpower, Vasilochka," the empress yelled over the storm. "You can't beat me."

Beat?

The word tumbled around in Vasilisa's mind. She remembered her mother's soothing and encouraging voice as she lay sick in bed.

We'll beat this, Vasilochka.

The empress regarded Vasilisa's affliction as a horde of invading forces amassing at Tumanny's borders, threatening her hard-won dominions. The empress triumphed in every battle she had ever waged.

But something changed the moment the healer pressed the poison into her hand. The empress had come to terms with her inevitable defeat in this struggle, but instead of accepting it gracefully, she had transformed it into a new war, a personal vendetta against the daughter who had put everything she had built in jeopardy.

All enemies died by violence.

Vasilisa felt the godpower of the sentries and courtiers like a thunderclap at her back as they rallied to defend their empress. A thrashing tempest roiled around her, lightning striking the palace again and again. Wind so fierce it almost tipped her chair and snuffed out the spark of her own power. Stonework shattered in every direction.

The godfire gained ground, licking at Vasilisa's fingers in a vengeful flame.

Hurry, Galina. Hurry.

In her periphery, Vasilisa saw Galina on her knees on the platform—agony etched into every line of her body. An ache pounded through Vasilisa's chest. She wished she had the time and ability to heal her lover and hold her until the pain was over. But all Vasilisa could do was follow Sera's lead and keep Galina safe until the panacea took effect.

Shield her with all she had and pray their reckless plan worked.

The mavens joined forces against Galina, attacking Sera's shield and using their combined power to throw Vasilisa off-kilter. She couldn't afford to waste more seconds, not with the empress's godfire poised to burn through the last remaining inches of ice.

And Vasilisa couldn't risk losing more.

She drove the mavens back with a bitter bombardment, then constructed a wall of ice between them so solid they couldn't get through it—a momentary respite before she felt the heat of Isidora's godfire lapping at her fingertips, burning away yet another inch of her defenses.

She only had moments left before the wall came down completely.

Only a little longer, she told herself. *Hold it for just a little longer.*

"Hurry, Galina," she whispered.

65

GALINA

Galina's fingernails scraped against the marble platform as her veins lit up with agony.

Memories flashed—the underground annex, Irina's cruel experiments, her screams ringing off the cold stone walls.

Irina's voice echoed in her mind. *It will only hurt a little, Galechka—only a little.*

That scared girl from Olensk was gone. In her place stood a weapon tempered by years of suffering.

A chance for retribution burned in her heart like molten iron.

"Galya," someone called to her from the shadows—someone who had once consoled her and cooled her burning flesh with ice.

But where was that ice now?

"Katya?" Galina croaked, hope and desperation battling within her.

Pain seared through her body, a punishing sensation that stretched her skin taut over her bones. Her zmeya clawed and writhed, threatening to shatter the fragile layers of her ribcage beneath its relentless force. She forced air into her lungs, shuddering as she fell to the ground.

"Galya," Katya said more urgently, barely audible above the chaos of Galina's thoughts. "I cast off the bells." Her god stilled, listening to Katya. "If I make it to tomorrow, I'll throw them into the sea and watch them sink."

Hope flickered in Galina like a single star in the night sky.

Katya's words reached deep within her, cooling the raging inferno of the panacea that coursed through her veins. She imagined the bells sinking beneath the waves, exactly where she had longed to scatter her family's ashes.

More. Keep talking. Talk to me.

Her zmeya had fallen silent, stretching its wings as if testing the cage rebuilding around it.

Galina heard Katya's voice, gentle but firm, rising above the chaos in her mind.

"There's still so much to do, Galya," the other woman murmured, her soothing tones banishing every doubt from Galina's thoughts.

Calming others was Katya's gift, honed to perfection over years of hardship and suffering. And now, she used it to quiet the great beast that raged within Galina as the panacea worked its magic, mending broken bones and repairing torn muscles and tissue.

"We have an entire life ahead of us," Katya continued, her words brimming with hope and promise. "I've lived with a deathwatch ticking in my head for too long. But I'm ready to find out what it's like to live without it. So please, get up, Galya. Get up, and let's live."

Galina's eyes fluttered open to see Katya sitting beside her.

Behind Katya, Sera swayed with exhaustion—each protective layer of godpower taking more of her strength. And Vasilisa? She slouched in her chair, her godfrost slowly slipping away. They were all counting on Galina, depending on her to fight for them. All those people outside the gates, whose lives had been shattered like hers? They needed her. If she died today, Isidora would go to war with Sopol.

And she would show the Blackshore no mercy.

She thought of those words written in Irina's tunnels, carved into the stonework by those who had rebelled before her.

Na itsi pris om vmonkt stvu zde mazvo fsta mazvo.

You can only bend the alder tree little by little.

Now, she held the power to uproot it.

Galina surged to her feet, her eyes meeting Katya's in a moment of shared understanding. The zmeya inside her stirred, its wings unfolding. They were intertwined, flesh and scale and spirit, a creature born of the bond between sisters.

She stepped forward, her voice a whisper in the air. "Let the shield go, Sera."

The command carried the weight of a promise.

Sera released her barrier with a shuddering breath, and Vitaly caught her as she staggered.

Galina's zmeya roared through her bones, a breathtaking rush of magic that hummed beneath her skin. It was a storm, a tempest that shook the very foundations of the palace, tearing through the square with explosive force. Galina stood at the center of it all, eyes aglow with a queen's fury and a destroyer's zeal.

Her zmeya coiled tightly around her frame, snarling fiercely in defense of those Galina loved most. It was a beast that answered only to her commands.

She descended the platform's stairs, each step cracking underfoot like thunder. Isidora watched as she approached, no doubt expecting her savior. But Galina ignored her, focusing on Vasilisa.

With a gentle touch, Galina smoothed a hand down Vasilisa's shoulder. "I've got you," she whispered tenderly before kissing the other woman's cheek. "Stop fighting, Vasya. Let me finish it."

The godfrost fell around them, ice glittering like diamonds in the palace square. Galina held Vasilisa tight against her body, shielding her from the chaos.

The princess trembled against Galina with exhaustion—a weariness she'd pay for later.

This ends now.

Galina's god rose and spoke through her in the Exalted Tongue. With a snarl, she slammed her godpower into the surrounding mavens, shoving them all to the ground. Now it was just the empress and her—a battle she'd craved since she rose from the ashes of Olensk.

"What are you doing?" Isidora hissed.

"I'm seeking justice for my family," Galina replied through gritted teeth, her voice imbued with power that burned. A hatred she'd kept bottled up for so many years.

It was time.

Galina's godpower surged again, thrumming with an intensity that threatened to rip her apart at the seams. She welcomed the pain and craved it.

With pain came victory.

The empress's power collided with Galina's, the force shaking the palace's foundations. But Isidora was no match for Galina—no match for the years of suffering that had honed her into a weapon. No match for the bond with her dragon forged through agony and wrath.

Like a blade's edge hardened in the heart of a dying star, Galina's will was unyielding—unbending. As obstinate as all the gods in Smokova.

Her god yearned for more—a reckoning. To liberate its kind from thousands of years of shackles and servitude, to grant them freedom again. This was not a quiet rumble of discontent. Its power surged through Galina until she burned with godpower. Until her body sang with its strength.

Her skin tingled and hummed as her zmeya flexed inside her skeleton, rippling with anticipation.

And then—destruction. A cataclysm unfurling in an instant. It shattered the bone prison that contained Isidora's god, ripping apart the bond between the empress and her dragon. Violently and savagely.

The zmeya burst free from Isidora's body—a glistening flurry of scales and wings that shot into the sky. Gasps echoed at the sight of it, a behemoth long trapped in a bone cage finally liberated to soar the skies. The beast glowed golden in the fading light, wings stretching majestically across the horizon. An impressive silhouette against the skyline. It cut through the clouds like a dagger, its roar echoing through the city, rattling windowpanes and shuddering walls.

Was it a cry of agony? Or joy? Or was it the bellow of anger? Damned if Galina could tell.

With another fierce howl, the zmeya looped again, and her god acted swiftly. It tore open the door between worlds—a deep, vicious slash of black against the firmament. A void that swallowed all light, yawning wide, as her godpower shoved the empress's dragon into Smokova where it belonged.

The zmeya vanished into its realm like a fading dream.

Galina staggered, knees threatening to buckle as her god yanked its power back. The portal faded as abruptly as it had come, leaving nothing behind but the scent of ozone.

She fixed her gaze on the empress, triumphant.

Isidora trembled and gasped—a small and pitiful thing. "What have you done?" she hissed.

Galina regarded her with a cold detachment. "What was necessary," she said. "What any of us would do to protect those we love." Galina released Vasilisa and slowly approached the monarch. "I broke your bond with your god, Isidora Leopoldovna."

Isidora's features shifted from shock to fury. She lunged forward with a desperate cry.

"*Kneel*," Galina snarled. Her voice was threaded with her zmeya's power—an undeniable command.

The former empress crashed to her knees like a supplicant.

At that moment, Isidora looked pitiful and powerless, a far cry from the indomitable figure she had been only minutes before. Her breathing was frantic, her hair wild, and the silk clothes she'd donned like armor were tattered and stained. But it was the look on Isidora's face that told Galina she had finally broken her—the panic, the helplessness.

Without her dragon, Isidora was nothing.

On her knees, she was less than nothing.

Galina glanced up at the platform to see Vitaly, Sera, and Katya watching her—and beyond them, a sea of astonished faces: courtiers, guards, commoners by the gate.

Then the gathered throng sank to the ground in submission.

But Galina raised a hand and let her zmeya amplify her voice. "I won't have you bow," she said, her words ringing across the square. "Not to anyone. For too long, the alurea forced our people to kneel in the dirt while they razed our homes. That ends now." She lowered her head and looked directly at Isidora. "I've fantasized about having you at my mercy for years, the way you left me after destroying Olensk. But I'm better than you. The Blackshore will decide your fate. And they'll finally be able to determine their own."

66

KATYA

A fortnight later

Katya shivered against the relentless chill of the ocean. The sand seeped through her toes and into her bones, but the sea was a newfound pleasure she could never enjoy before. The briny scent in the air, the cold northern breeze, the waves that swirled at her feet—all of it new to her.

She was alive, and she wanted to experience *everything*.

The bells in her hand jingled as she stared down at the chains that had hung like a noose around her neck for so long.

"For you, Sofia," she whispered, imagining her sister beside her. "And for all the handmaidens who came before."

She reared back and hurled those wretched chains into the sea, watching them sink into a watery grave.

And the oppressive weight on her chest finally lifted.

"You'll catch your death in that water." Anna's voice came from behind her.

Weeks before, Sera had brought Katya to the rendezvous point, where Anna had taken her to a small cottage in Kiyskoye, a village in the Tumanny north. Within its humble walls, Katya had found sanctuary, away from the demands of the palace and the ever-present threat of death.

Katya smiled down at her numb toes. "I like it," she said to Anna.

Anna had been busy over the last few weeks, shuttling back and forth from the Blackshore to help other commoners impacted by Empress Isidora's destruction. Meanwhile, Galina used her zmeya to rebuild the city and provide shelter for the displaced.

"Mm. Still too damn cold for me." Anna came forward and handed her a letter. "This is from Sera."

Fear immediately knotted in Katya's stomach. "Is everything all right?"

Anna snorted and kicked at the sand beneath her feet. "Alurea fleeing Tumanny, joining with Sopol's army, and preparing to make war? I'm sure everything's fine."

Katya grimaced. "I meant about the empress. Has her fate been decided?"

A heavy sigh escaped Anna's lips as she spoke. "I voted for execution, but the others chose exile. Maybe, for her, that's worse."

Katya nodded, understanding the gravity of the punishment. For a woman who had been so consumed with maintaining her power and authority, being banished to the most remote and isolated regions of Tumanny was a fate worse than death. There, she would have no one to fawn over her, no one to control.

And no one she could hurt.

Katya opened the letter, scanning its contents. It was brief, but its implications made her go still. "She's asking me to consider a position on the provisional council," she said, her voice barely above a whisper. "She wants someone knowledgeable about alurean politics there while they plan for an invasion."

"Interested?" Anna asked with a smile.

Katya had never been offered a place of authority. For so long, she'd been a mere object, existing only to serve and please others to survive. But now, she had the chance to use all her knowledge and carve out a new path. To make a difference and create something better with all she had learned.

"Yes," she said, stronger this time. "I think I am."

EPILOGUE

Sera tracked Vitaly to a cramped study deep within the corridors of Zolotiye. The chamber was a confusion of parchment and furniture, and her husband sat at the cluttered desk, lost in thought.

Sera smiled. She loved seeing him like this—tangled and scowling.

Her mess.

"How long have you been at this?" she asked, leaning into the door frame.

Vitaly grunted, running a hand through his already-disheveled hair, eyes bleary as he glanced up at her. "Too damn long."

No surprise there. Setting up a provisional government with an army breathing down their necks? Enough to drive any sane individual screaming into madness. He'd been poring over reports from across Sundyr—sifting through intel gathered by his network of spies and informants.

"Anything good?" Sera asked.

"Depends on your definition," Vitaly muttered, shuffling through the papers on his desk. "If you're asking whether we're all going to die, the answer's still a solid maybe."

"Better than a solid 'we're screwed.' I'll take it," she said with a shrug.

Some alurea had fled Tumanny and sought refuge among former adversaries and allies in Sundyr, while Galina concentrated on disabling the court's most powerful mavens. She severed the bonds that kept their zmei captive and sent them into exile with the empress. It was hardly an ideal resolution, but the council had no other option. Their foremost concern? Protecting the Tumanny people at any cost.

To fill the power void, they formed a temporary cabinet of community members—with Galina and Vasilisa taking the reins as co-rulers in name only to aid the transition until a more stable governing body could be established. Even then, laws would restrict their authority to nothing more than figureheads who resided in the palace; Vasilisa needed access to the glasshouse for her medicine.

Sera hoped the alurea would die out with them. They would be the last monarchs Tumanny ever had to endure.

She sauntered over to Vitaly's desk and gave him a nudge. "Take a few hours," she said, flashing him a grin. "Those missives will still be sitting here, mocking you, when you return."

Vitaly leaned back in his chair and regarded his wife. "Since when do you put off work, Serafima?"

"Since I've spent two weeks healing from overusing my godpower, and you have yet to touch me. You made me some promises for surviving that, and I intend to collect my due."

A spark of lust flared in his eyes before he quickly shuttered it. "We have an army to prepare for—"

"Shut up, Vitalik," Sera interrupted, straddling his lap. She buried her hands in his hair and leaned in close. "You know the rules—when I command, you obey. And right now, I see fit to remind you of your promises. All of them."

Vitaly met her gaze, and their heated connection burned bright between them. Sera's zmeya stretched in pleasure at his fixed attention, her bastard dragon utterly smitten.

That made the both of them.

"Command?" he asked with a lazy smile.

She trailed her mouth over his jawline, barely brushing her lips against him as she spoke. "That's right. My zmeya agrees that you've been neglecting your duty. And your duty is my pleasure."

"Poor little dragon," he murmured, nuzzling Sera's cheek. "Poor, poor *vorovka*. How do you want me to atone for my neglect?"

Sera laughed. "I have four years' worth of ideas and you asked me to make a list of a thousand things. Let's not waste another minute."

A flush of delight washed over Galina as she observed Vasilisa making her medicines. Watching the other woman use her godpower was a breathtaking spectacle. Her hands moved quickly and gracefully as she synthesized her treatments.

For more than a sennight, Vasilisa battled to recover from the chaos in the square. The fever scorched through her veins for four long days, but Galina was there, tending to her every need. Night after night, she kept vigil by Vasilisa's side while Sera took over during the day.

Between sleep, Galina worked tirelessly with her zmeya to break the bonds between alurea and their gods, banishing courtiers up north with Isidora. And only after everything was taken care of would Galina collapse from sheer exhaustion, often dozing off at Vasilisa's bedside.

Finally, Vasilisa opened her eyes one morning, reached for Galina's hand, and gently kissed her palm.

And Galina had finally let herself breathe.

Vasilisa was still on the mend. Whenever she visited the

glasshouse, she relied on her chair, and Galina was there to help. Nothing brought her more joy than watching Vasilisa make her remedies and potions—well, except kissing her.

"You're staring," Vasilisa said with a slow grin. "You're about to make me blush."

"I can't help it," Galina confessed, a smile tugging at her lips. "You're just so beautiful when you work."

Vasilisa's gaze returned to her task, but not before a hint of pink illuminated her cheeks. "Oh, so you're *determined* to make me blush today. I see how it is."

"That's right." Galina leaned in, bracing herself against the table. "Marry me, Vasya."

The other woman went still. "I—"

"You're on the brink of fretting, so let me have another minute. I can anticipate all your arguments before you even utter them." Galina scooted closer and rested her palm on Vasilisa's cheek. "You're sick. But I don't care. I may need to look after you one day when you can no longer create your medicines, and I'll do it gladly. Is there anything else?"

Vasilisa gazed at her, transfixed. "What about when the alurea strike again?"

"I'm ready for them. I'll stand by your side, along with Sera, Vitaly, and Katya. Just like before. Will you marry me?"

"And if I die?" she whispered.

"Vasya," Galina said, her voice softening, "I'll cherish every moment we have together. Will you marry me?"

Vasilisa seized Galina's shirt, pulling her in for a fierce kiss. "Yes," she exhaled. "I'll marry you."

Let the armies come, Galina thought as she kissed Vasilisa back.

She had everything to fight for.

Sera and Galina stood at the edge of the Dark Sea, bracing themselves for the impending army on the other side. Their hands entwined. They'd survived impossible odds before, come face-to-face with death.

They'd do it again.

As they gazed out at the horizon, storm clouds gathered in the distance, a harbinger of the onslaught that awaited them.

"Ready?" Galina asked Sera.

Sera nodded, a fierce light burning in her gaze. "My zmeya and I have an understanding. We both have a weakness for criminals with sharp cheekbones and pretty voices."

Galina found herself smiling back, even as she braced herself for the fight to come. Yet for the first time, victory seemed like a real possibility, not just survival. Despite the looming darkness, a glimmer of hope shone through. Sera's bond with her dragon would be shattered one day, and her mind and body would be her own again.

One day, maybe they could rest.

But now, they had a battle to wage, an army to fend off. They had to protect everything they had worked so hard for—everything they had gained.

After all, they finally had a place to call home.

LANGUAGE KEY

THE GODS

Zmei (/zmʲej/): The plural and masculine (singular) form of the dragons bonded to the alurea

Zmeya (/zmʲeja/): The feminine (singular) form of the dragons bonded to the alurea

ZVERTI

Dushegreya (/duʂɪˈgrʲejə/): A fitted jacket worn over a sarafan

Fast na fpraokhi (/fʲasʲtʲ na fpraˈoxi/): I missed you

Fast na fsi smovishchar (/fʲasʲtʲ na fsʲi smoˈviɕːar/): I won't hurt you

Fast na svo (/fʲasʲtʲ na svʲo/): I love you

Fednezno it (/fedʲˈnʲezno it/): Fucking fool

Fednezno zdro (/fedʲˈnʲezno zdro/): Fucking hell

Lifche (/lʲifˈtɕe/): Sorry

Na itsi pris om vmonkt stvu zde mazvo fsta mazvo (/na iˈtsi pris om vmʲonkt gdʲu zde mazˈvo fsta mazˈvo/): You can only bend the alder tree little by little

Ra (/ra/): Good

Ra dri khork (/ra drʲi xork/): Good afternoon

Ra spe (/ra spe/): Good morning

Ra vzda (/ra vzda/): Good evening

Rubakha (/ruˈbaxə/): Shirt worn beneath the sarafan

Sa zlu (/sa zlu/): Go away
Sarafan (/ˈsærəfæn/): Traditional dress worn by commoners
Sen za? (/sen za/): Comprehend me?
Sma, fast lo. (/smʲa, fʲasʲtʲ lʲo/): Yes, I do
Stsot (/st͡sotʲ/): Friend
Sva non vmonkt blu! (/sva nʲonʲ vmʲonkt blʲu/): Run for the stairs!
Vdre dilp (/vdre dilp/): Wake up
Vitsvi (/vitsˈvi/: Sister
Vmekhva (/vmekhˈva/): Sweetheart
Vmonkt pror va (/vmʲonkt prʲor va/): The common god
Vmonkt smospongro stre lo (/vmʲonkt smosˈpʲongro͵gro strʲe lʲo/): The fuck she did
Vorovka (/vɐˈrovkə/): Thief
Vorovka pro fse ku (/vɐˈrovkə pro fsʲe ku): Thief of my heart
Zdo vitsvi to (/zdo vitsˈvi to/): Beautiful sister mine

GRAND IMPERIAL

Fle cui (/flɛ kɥi/): Daughter
Knesi (/niˈsiː/): Term of endearment for someone younger
Obryad (/ɔˈbrʲæd/): A monthly ritual for alurean worship
Suvya (/suvˈya/) : Term of endearment for an elder
Vuabo pue (/ˈvwabɔ pwe/): Mother (mother mine)

BOTANICS

Ab scienvio (/aːb ˈskienwio̯/): A perfume-emitting flower in Vasilisa's glasshouse
Bei io (/bei̯ io̯/): Lunar night, a sleep aid that Vasilisa gives Galina
Cegre pleddaus (/ˈkegre ˈpleddau̯s/): The flower in Vasilisa's garden that blooms under the moonlight
Ciob hilne (/kio̯b ˈhilne/): Vasilisa's pain treatment

Coe pau (/koe̯ pau̯/): An ink-like metal etched into Sera and Galina's bones to summon forth the desired god

Dem goc (/deːm gok/): A plant included in Sera's panacea

Dem gre (/deːm gre/): A plant that took Vasilisa five years to germinate

Io scíspol (/io̯ skisˈpol/): A night blooming flower in Vasilisa's glasshouse

Pana ae (/ˈpana ae̯/): A native plant that grows wild near the Dark Sea, traditionally embroidered onto the sarafan

Praepeurbu scilot (/ˈprae̯ peu̯rbu ˈskilot/): An ingredient Irina used to ready human vessels to hold a deity

Rars cuit (/rars kui̯t/): Stabilises Vasilisa's muscles for mobility

Spunc peurbu (/spunk ˈpeu̯rbu/): An ingredient Irina used to shatter human bones to prepare them for a deity

Tríb gleis (/trib glei̯s/): Slows Vasilisa's disease progression

Vír tris (/wir tris/): Inflammation aid in Vasilisa's treatments

ACKNOWLEDGMENTS

At a time of career frustration, I asked my husband to pick a project for me just to get me out of a bout of writer's block. Of all the ideas on my list he could have chosen, he went with the most difficult one. Many drafts later, after I tore out plots and characters, he would apologize for this.

But that difficult idea became this book. I'm so grateful to Mr. May for having the audacity to test me. No apologies necessary.

A big thanks to my agents—Russell Galen, a saint of patience, for sticking with me during the long submission process of this book, and Danny Baror, who went above and beyond during the whirlwind summer when this sold.

To the phenomenal Daphne Tonge at Daphne Press. From my debut until now, she's given me such unwavering support. I'm thrilled to have worked with her on this project. And to my editor, Davi Lancett, who helped shape this book and find its voice. I can't express how lucky I am and how much I've learned from him. Thank you to the incredible Daphne Press/Illumicrate team, especially Caitlin Lomas. Your dedication, hard work, and infectious enthusiasm—I owe you more than words can say.

And the wonderful team at DAW Books in the US, especially Katie Hoffman, Joshua Starr, and Sarah Christensen Fu, for everything they've done for this book.

Tess Sharpe, my sister of the soul. I couldn't survive publishing without you.

Last, but never least, my readers. Thank you for embarking on this new journey with me.

ABOUT THE AUTHOR

ELIZABETH MAY is the #1 *Sunday Times* bestselling author of *To Cage a God*, the Seven Devils duology (co-written with L.R. Lam), The Falconer series, and romance novels under the pseudonym Katrina Kendrick. She is Californian by birth and Scottish by choice, and holds a Ph.D. from the University of St Andrews. She currently resides on an 18th-century farm in the Scottish countryside with her husband, three cats, and a lively hive of honeybees that live inside the wall of her old farmhouse.

For more information, follow her on Instagram @_elizabethmay or visit her website www.elizabethmaywrites.com.

A Dark and Drowning Tide

Allison Saft

A sharp-tongued folklorist and her academic rival must solve their mentor's murder in this lush sapphic fantasy romance from the *New York Times* bestselling author of *A Far Wilder Magic.*

Lorelei Kaskel, a folklorist with a quick temper and an even quicker wit, is on an expedition with six eccentric nobles in search of a mythical spring of untold power. The king wants to harness the fabled water source from which magic flows to secure his reign, and Lorelei is determined to prove herself. It's a small cost to make her dream come true: to become a naturalist, able to travel freely to faraway lands.

The expedition gets off to a harrowing start when its leader, Lorelei's beloved mentor, is murdered in her quarters aboard their ship. The suspects are her five remaining expedition mates. The only person Lorelei knows must be innocent is her longtime academic rival, the insufferably gallant and maddeningly beautiful Sylvia von Wolff. Now in charge of the expedition, Lorelei must find the spring before the murderer strikes again, and a coup begins in earnest.

But other dangers lurk in the dark: forests that rearrange themselves at night, rivers with slumbering dragons hiding beneath the water, and shapeshifting beasts out for blood. As Lorelei and Sylvia grudgingly work together to uncover the truth and resist their growing feelings for each other, they discover that their leader had secrets of her own. Secrets that make Lorelei question whether justice is worth pursuing, and if this kingdom is worth saving at all.

Daphne Press

Bride of the Shadow King

Sylvia Mercedes

For fans of *The Bridge Kingdom* and *A Deal with the Elf King*, this sweeping tale of love and betrayal blends sweet and spice.

A SHUNNED PRINCESS.

A RELUCTANT KING.

A MARRIAGE THAT COULD SAVE BOTH THEIR KINGDOMS . . .

BUT DESTROY THEIR HEARTS.

Though she is the eldest daughter, Princess Faraine lives in the background, shunned from court and kept out of sight. Her chronic illness makes her a liability to the crown, and she has learned to give place to her beautiful, favored younger sister in all things.

When the handsome and enigmatic Shadow King comes seeking a bride, Faraine is not surprised that her sister is his choice.

Though not eager to take a human bride, King Vor is willing to do what is necessary for the sake of his people. When he meets the lively Princess Ilsevel, he quickly agrees to a marriage arrangement.

So why can't he get the haunting eyes of her older sister out of his head?

"Utterly swoon worthy!"
ELISE KOVA
Bestselling author of *A Deal with the Elf King*